Soul
Hunters

By the same author

THE COOLER
THE MAN FROM YESTERDAY
CHANCE AWAKENING
TARA KANE
THE GOERING TESTAMENT
TRAITOR FOR A CAUSE
ULTIMATE ISSUE
FERRET

Soul Hunters

GEORGE MARKSTEIN

FRANKLIN WATTS
NEW YORK
1987

540 2029

Library of Congress Catalog Card Number: 86-50611
ISBN: 0-531-15033-X
Copyright © 1986 by George Markstein
First printed in 1986 by Hodder and Stoughton, Great Britain.
First printed in the United States in 1987 by Franklin Watts, New York.
All rights reserved.
5 4 3 2

"Soul Hunters"
Yuri Andropov's definition of spies in his speech to commemorate the foundation of the Komitet Gosudarstvennoy Bezopasnosti – the KGB

"It's a great huge game of chess that's being played – all over the world – if this is the world at all, you know."
Lewis Carroll: Through the Looking Glass

Prologue

He looked very ordinary. In his late twenties, thin, a shock of hair, studious, not very well dressed. They had booked him on an Intourist package tour, and his passport described him as a research assistant.

Today was the reason they had sent him. He was due to meet his contact, briefly, at ten minutes to noon at the corner of Nevsky Prospekt and Gogol Street.

There was really no reason why he should be uneasy, Gregson told himself. Nothing suspicious had happened. Not as far as he could tell. Nothing unusual. It was probably nerves now that the moment had come.

"Stop at the first lamp post past the traffic lights, by the colonnade, and look at the street map, like a tourist who is trying to find his bearings."

The contact would approach him, a helpful stranger offering to put a visitor in the right direction. It would only last a few moments. Then the stranger would disappear, and Gregson would have the roll of film.

That was all. He would become an ordinary tourist again. Then a week later he would deliver the roll of film to them in London.

It was so simple. Nothing to worry about. "Just don't draw attention to yourself," they had said. "Be part of the group."

Now it was time. He had spent the morning looking at some of the landmarks of Leningrad, like the tourist he was, then he had strolled to the meeting place.

Gregson had bought a small street guide, and he stood

by the fifth archway of the colonnade, next to the lamp standard nearest to the traffic signals. He had timed it pretty well. His watch said 11:49. He began to play the pantomime, examining the guide book, turning to the index, finding the street map he wanted, looking at it with a furrowed brow. He was the picture of the puzzled tourist looking for a destination.

A few people were passing, but nobody seemed to notice him. He kept turning the pages, then looking at the map again. He was beginning to feel foolish, standing there, giving his performance to the empty air. He'd been doing it for a couple of minutes, which seemed like an eternity. He wondered how long he should wait.

There was a contingency arrangement, of course. If the meeting at the lamp post aborted, the instructions were to sit, at four o'clock, on the left hand bench outside the railings at the entrance to the Lutheran church of St Peter, near Zhelyabov Street. His contact would appear then.

It was now just after 11:51. He knew it was unwise to loiter too long. Of course, things could always go wrong with a split second arrangement, but they had taught him that punctuality was part of the system, part of the security. Being late was like fumbling with the password.

No, he had waited long enough, decided Gregson. The best thing was to go back to the hotel, and then try at the church in the afternoon.

Then the contact came. She was a rather stout middle aged woman with a shopping basket, and startled Gregson. He had expected a man. No reason, they hadn't told him who it would be, but he had simply assumed it. He had of course wondered who the contact would turn out to be. He had even had a romantic vision that it might be a beautiful girl, but he had quickly dismissed that as nonsense. No, the contact would definitely be a man, he had convinced himself of that. Maybe a dissident.

"I see that you are looking at the map," said the woman in Russian. "Are you a stranger?"

8

"I am looking for the Hermitage," replied Gregson, as arranged. "Ya zabludilsya. I have lost my way."

"Here, I will show you." She took the guide book from his hand, and looked at the street map. "There it is." She indicated the spot, and passed the book back to him, and as he took it, she slipped a small container into his hand. It was done swiftly, unobtrusively. The film has been delivered.

"Do svidaniya," said the woman. And she walked off rapidly.

He slipped the spool into his pocket with a sense of enormous relief. The foreboding had vanished. The link up had been made, from now on he didn't have to take any more real risks. He wasn't too worried about getting the roll of film out of the country. It would be easy to hide among his things. No reason why they should search his belongings anyway. No, from now on it was plain sailing.

That was when the car pulled up at the pavement, alongside him. It was a black Chaika, the official car of many Soviet government departments. The door opened and two men got out. They were hatless, and their hair was cut short.

"Excuse me," said one of them in English, and stood in front of Gregson. His companion was behind Gregson.

"Kay Gay Bay," said the man, pronouncing it the Russian way, and he flashed an identity card with his photograph. "You are under arrest."

Gregson felt the blood draining from his face. "This is . . . this is ridiculous," he stammered. "I am an English tourist. I am staying at the Moskva Hotel with the Intourist party. You can check."

"You are Stephen Gregson, and you have been engaged in espionage," said the man who spoke English.

The one behind Gregson put his hand in Gregson's pocket and pulled out the container.

"You see, the evidence," said the other triumphantly. "Proof."

Then Gregson knew it was a set up. They had laid a trap for him. It all figured. They knew he was keeping the appointment. They saw the woman make contact, but they did not arrest her. She was one of them. They knew what she had passed to him, and they knew where he had it, because they had been watching him the whole time.

"You are making a mistake," argued Gregson. "I don't know what you are talking about."

They took him by the arms, and pushed him into the car.

"Where are you taking me?" cried Gregson.

The car door slammed, and shot off along Nevsky Prospekt. There were two men in front, but they had not said a word, and didn't even bother to look at him.

Gregson sat squashed in the back seat, jammed between the two KGB men. Their elbows dug into his ribs. But worse than the discomfort was the fear he felt.

"I want to see the British consul," said Gregson.

They laughed, and Gregson suddenly wondered how expendable he really was to London.

1

He stuck on the moustache and regarded himself critically in the mirror. Yes, he looked the part of the investigator, unscrupulous, ambitious, a stalwart of the state's security machine.

Evgeny Alekseivitch Borisov, People's Artist of the Soviet Union, studied his reflection. He saw a face which served its master well, and was adept at concealing his real thoughts. He leant forward and smoothed down one side of the false moustache.

They had given him the star dressing room, as befitted his status, but the Maxim Gorky State Russian Dramatic Theatre in Minsk was the city's oldest, and its facilities did not measure up to what Borisov was used to in Moscow. There was no TV, no refrigerator, and the sofa needed re-covering.

Not that he could complain about conditions on this provincial tour. He had been given a double room on the eighth floor of the Yubelinaya Hotel. The hotel resembled a concrete box on stilts, but, unlike the theatre, it was modern, comfortable in an impersonal way. A chauffeur-driven car had also been provided, to take him to and from the theatre.

Borisov wondered if the double room was the idea of Lev Kopkin, the stage manager. He didn't trust Kopkin. Kopkin had another role on the tour – he was the eyes and ears of the Ministry. He watched all of them. And he knew of course about Maya.

Typical of the little arse licker to ensure that Borisov had a double room to team up with Maya if he felt so inclined. It gave him something to put in his report.

Borisov extricated a cigarette from his packet of *Javas*. It would be his last smoke until after the performance. He lit it, and grimaced. The carton of American cigarettes he had been given had spoiled him. Pity they were all gone.

Never mind. He could tell he would be good on stage tonight. *Autumn of the Investigator* was a play he enjoyed.

There was a tap on the door, and without waiting to be asked, Maya came in. She was already made-up for the stage, and it enhanced her good looks. As always, she wafted perfume.

She rushed over to Borisov, and hugged him. "No," she warned, "don't kiss me. You'll smudge my make-up."

He had had no intention of kissing her. In fact, she was beginning to take things for granted just a little too much. This bursting into his dressing room, for instance, when he was getting ready to go on.

"I've got to finish off, Maya Aleksandrovna Petrova," he said, mock severely. "I'll see you later."

She pouted, and gave a good rendition of tossing her head. "How do you know I'll be available?"

"You'll be available," said Borisov, turning his back and reaching for some powder.

But she didn't move. "Listen," she trilled. "I've got some fantastic news. They've asked me to do *Alya* at the Sovremennik. Can you imagine?"

He had heard about the play. It was all the trendy rage in Moscow. It was set in a gymnasium, and the characters were a women's handball team. He winced.

"I'm sure you'll bounce about very prettily," he remarked.

"Pig!" cried Maya, and slammed the door of the dressing room.

Do I really need her, wondered Borisov, as he finished off his make-up. Was it vanity that required her in his bed? Because she was half his age, and reminded him of his days as a young actor? She often bored him, with her continuous back stage gossip, and her not very subtle efforts to use their

12

relationship to promote her own career. Yes, she was very good looking, she had a desirable body, and she made love the way she acted, enthusiastically. Trouble was she was starting to get on his nerves.

Ah, well, reflected Borisov, all that will soon be resolved.

Exactly thirty minutes before curtain up, and right on cue, Kopkin banged on the door for the half hour.

"I know," called out Borisov. To his surprise, Kopkin entered. He carried a bouquet of roses.

"From the Union of Byelorussian Writers," he announced. "I'll put them in a vase. Or do you want them sent to the hotel?" The little eyes behind the gold rimmed glasses gleamed with pleasure. "You have no concept, Evgeny Alekseivitch, what a success this tour has been. The people of Minsk are overwhelmed. I can tell you everybody is absolutely delighted."

Clearly, thought Borisov, you've had a pat from the Ministry.

"Just put the flowers anywhere, will you?"

"By the way," announced Kopkin. "We have our return flight. We leave Minsk at eleven in the morning on Saturday. We'll have a week in Moscow before we depart for London."

Borisov's face betrayed nothing. He had talked very little about the forthcoming tour of London. A season of modern Russian plays. Volodin. Dudarev. Fedotov. A cultural exchange on which the Ministry set considerable importance.

"I shall be glad when all this travelling is finished," continued Kopkin. "It is very upsetting to one's domestic arrangements, is it not?"

Was the little rat mocking him, wondered Borisov. But Kopkin looked quite earnest.

"Well, Evgeny Alekseivitch, I mustn't keep you. See you after the show." And he made his exit, still carrying the bunch of roses.

As curtain time approached, Borisov tried to shut everything else from his mind, and concentrate entirely on the role he was about to play, go over his lines, and think about his performance. But tonight, his thoughts were on other things. It came as a shock to suddenly realise that he had been staring at the wall, unseeing, unmoving, his mind far away from the dressing room in Minsk.

Borisov, a disciplined man, seldom drank before facing an audience. But tonight he walked to the cupboard and got out the bottle of vodka. He poured himself a good measure, and tossed it back.

He sat down on the only armchair in the dressing room, and closed his eyes. He must have dozed for a good quarter of an hour, but it only seemed to have been a few minutes before again there was a knock on the door, and the call boy's voice announced:

"Beginners on stage."

Borisov opened his eyes, and awareness of what was going to happen flooded his mind. He went over to the dressing table, and gave himself another inspection in the mirror.

"It's up to you, tovarishch," he said aloud to himself, and smiled. It was a sardonic smile.

He buttoned his jacket, straightened his collar, and left the dressing room.

The curtain was about to go up.

2

The transmission came on the air about 20:45 and could be heard on the short wave band, reasonably clearly, over a considerable area of the Soviet Union, including Byelorussia and the Ukraine.

It came on unannounced, and did not identify its origin. The broadcast lasted roughly half an hour, and part of it was taken up by the playing of Russian folk songs. The rest of the time the announcer thanked the listeners for tuning in, and promised future transmissions.

"Keep listening for us around this time on the 48 metre band, comrades. You'll hear some interesting things."

Then the broadcast went off the air, as abruptly as it had come on. The transmission caught the Fifth Department, charged with radio surveillance, completely by surprise. The jamming service, whose job it was to blot out undesirable broadcasts, was caught wrong footed.

Soviet monitors taped it, but the analysis of its contents baffled them. Nothing political had been said, and unless the folk songs were part of some complicated code, there appeared to be no point to the transmission. The only significant thing was the promise, such as it might be, that the audience would hear "those interesting things" in future broadcasts.

A full report went to Sergein Lapin, the Minister of Radio and Television, and the Fifth Department asked the Directorate Technical Facilities Group to try and trace the origin of the transmission.

The thing that worried Lapin was that, without saying so in actual words, the announcer had given the impression that the broadcast came from inside the Soviet Union.

3

He was sure Freudenhof had never changed, not since the Kaiser, not since Hitler, not since Adenauer. The allied bombers hadn't bothered with it. Jack-booted Nazis and American battle tanks had come and gone, but Freudenhof remained untouched.

Garner was wrong, of course. The sleepy Bavarian town,

15

nestling among forests of fir trees, had its secrets, but they weren't obvious to someone being driven through it in a staff car.

"It's Hansel and Gretel country," Rathbone had said, rather sourly, when he'd briefed Garner in room 8011 in Horse Guards Avenue. "But then, I always thought Hansel and Gretel was a pretty nasty story."

Now, looking out of the car, Garner did see some modern touches among the mediaeval ginger bread houses. There were TV aerials on the old roofs, American Express logos outside the gasthaus, and in the arcaded market square stood the granite statue of a Wehrmacht soldier, symbolising both Freudenhof's war dead, and Hitlerian art. But those were just passing glimpses.

The staff car turned along a country road lined by the ever present fir trees, until it rounded a bend, where its progress was barred by a red and white striped barrier. An American soldier stepped forward.

He was an interesting soldier. His trousers were tucked into his combat boots, laced high. The boots shone like a mirror. Round his neck he had a camouflage mottled silk scarf, and he wore a dark green beret with an embroidered coat of arms on the left side. He was armed with a pistol, and carried a clip board.

The soldier didn't say anything. He just bent down and looked at Garner in the back of the car, then at his driver.

"Captain Garner," said the driver.

The soldier checked his clip board and nodded. Almost simultaneously the red and white pole was raised.

"Welcome," said the soldier in Russian, and saluted.

The car accelerated along the country road. Garner was looking for sign posts, fences, buildings, anything, but there was nothing except fir trees.

Then they came to what looked like the entrance of a country estate. At the end of a long, beautifully kept drive stood a large country mansion. A couple of US Army jeeps were parked in front of it.

As Garner got out of the staff car, an officer came down the steps of the entrance. Dressed exactly like the guard at the barrier, beret, silk scarf, jump boots, but with a first lieutenant's silver bars pinned to the collar of the open necked shirt.

Garner looked more closely. The officer was a woman, tall, slim, with short blonde hair. She had just a hint of make-up, almost unnoticeable, but the uniform suited her lithe, athletic figure. She was armed, like the guard, with a pistol.

Yes, of course, thought Garner, women are fighting soldiers in the American Army. They do battle training, they use guns, they are given bayonet drill, and throw hand grenades. This one also had paratroop wings pinned on her uniform.

Garner was wearing civilian clothes, as he had been instructed, and when the woman lieutenant saluted him, very precisely and correctly, he was momentarily stumped on protocol. Did they expect him to salute back an officer in uniform dressed in civvies?

In this unit, anything goes, he decided, and gave a salute.

"Captain Garner?" she said, holding out her right hand. "May I have your orders, sir?"

Garner gave her the manilla envelope. She opened it, and glanced at the sheet she pulled out.

"Your ID please, sir," she said.

He produced his identity card, and she compared him with the photograph on it. Her face, cold, attractive, was quite expressionless. She might have been examining a piece of furniture. She gave him back the identity card.

"The colonel's expecting you, sir," she announced. "This way, please."

It was a palatial house, the ancestral home of some old aristocratic family. Garner and his escort walked on thick luxurious carpets, and along corridors the walls of which were hung with oil paintings and trophies. There were also many mediaeval weapons, swords, halberds, crossbows. They passed some ornate hangings depicting hunting scenes, and stopped outside a door guarded by another soldier in a beret. He snapped to attention, and the lieutenant knocked.

"Enter," commanded a voice, and Garner was led into the presence of Colonel Jerome B. Blau.

"Only the American Army seems to produce that sort of officer," Rathbone had said at the briefing. "It's a certain breed. Patton was one. MacArthur. You know the kind. Larger than life. One-man Wagnerian operas."

"Captain Garner, sir," said the woman lieutenant and stood ramrod straight.

"Thank you, Jones," acknowledged the colonel. She turned smartly, and left the room.

As an office, it revealed little. No tell-tale maps on the walls, no pictures, no filing cabinets. There were french windows, looking out on the grounds.

Blau stood behind his desk, an imposing, massive man with the silver eagles of a full colonel. His head was bald, the proverbial bull head, he had the nose of a boxer, broad shoulders, and the appearance of enormous physical strength. His eyes were very blue, and stared at Garner unwavering, unblinking. His mouth was ugly, the lips turned downwards, and yet he had laugh lines. It must be a fearful laugh, thought Garner. He hoped he wouldn't hear it. Garner read some of his military record from his uniform. He wore four rows of medals and campaign ribbons. The Silver Star. The Bronze Star. The Purple Heart. A command parachutist's insignia. The combat infantryman's badge. And on his right breast a presidential citation with two stars.

The extraordinary thing about Colonel Blau was his hands. They were sensitive, cultured, with long tapering fingers. It was as if the hands of a concert pianist had been grafted on to the wrists of an all-in wrestler.

"Sit down, Captain Garner," ordered the colonel, with a curt nod of his head.

Garner perched on a chair opposite the massive bare desk. All it had on it was a plain, buff folder. Blau tapped it.

18

"I have your record here," he said. "Interesting. I respect the SAS. They're real soldiers. But I didn't really want you here. Nothing personal, you understand."

"Yes, sir." What else could he say?

"To tell you the truth, we're too busy to look after visiting tourists."

The blue eyes fixed on Garner to see how he would react.

"I'm not exactly a tourist, colonel," pointed out Garner, "and training exchanges are long established. Your Special Forces have been to Hereford. Our people have trained at Bad Tolz . . ."

The ugly mouth scowled.

"Nothing is established in this outfit, captain. And this is not Bad Tolz. What we do is special in every sense of the word. You have been imposed on me by higher authority. I want that understood."

"Exactly, colonel," agreed Garner. "We're all obeying orders."

He thought back to room 8011. If Colonel Blau knew what his real orders were . . .

"You've seen action, I take it?" said Blau.

"Yes, sir."

"A couple of shoot-outs, huh? Some scared terrorists shitting themselves in an attic? Irish kids? Half frozen Argentinians in the Falklands?" He waited, but Garner said nothing. "Chicken shit, captain. That's not what it's about. With all due respect."

"Maybe that's why I'm here," suggested Garner. "To find out what it's all about. With all due respect, sir."

His eyes had been taking in the surroundings, including the plaque on the wall. Two crossed arrows and a dagger. With the motto underneath:

"De oppresso liber."

To free the oppressed.

Blau followed his glance. "Yeah," he nodded, "there you have it. That's what it's all about, captain. That's our mission. Now you got the point."

19

It had come sooner than he expected. Garner took the plunge.

"Is that why your sentry greets one in Russian?"

The ugly mouth twisted into a smile. He indicated the folder. "You speak Russian well?"

"I know it, sir."

Blau drew himself up. "Everybody in this outfit speaks it, captain." He said it proudly. "We wouldn't give you house room if you didn't." Then he glowered at Garner. "So how long do you think you're going to hang around with us?"

It could not have been more unfriendly. Its tone was clear. When do we get rid of you?

"As long as it takes. I think sixty days, the orders specify . . ."

"Sixty days! Jesus! That's an eternity, captain. A lot can happen in sixty days . . ."

Don't read a threat into it, thought Garner. Don't get jumpy.

"Anyway," went on the colonel, "here's how it works. You're here to study our methods. My methods. OK. I didn't ask for you. I don't think it's any of your people's goddam business what we do here or how we do it. We don't need this kind of hands across the sea exchange garbage, if you'll forgive me. However, Heidelberg said yes, so you're here." He snorted.

"I'll try not to get in your way, sir."

Blau's lips curled. "Oh, we'll take care of that, mister, don't worry." He opened the folder in front of him, and scanned it briefly, as if to check something. Then he looked up. "I'll assign you to Major Skinner's group. He's good at sorting out the men from the boys."

"Thank you, sir."

Blau gave him a sharp look, but Garner's face was blank.

"One other thing, captain. I don't know what they told you about us, but forget it. You get me?"

For a moment Garner felt uneasy. It was almost as if Blau was aware what Rathbone had told him in London. As if he was warning him . . . Then he decided he was reading the wrong meaning into it.

The colonel flicked the intercom by the side of his desk. Her voice answered immediately.

"Yes, sir?"

"Come in, Jones."

The intercom clicked off and a moment later there was a tap on the door, and the blonde lieutenant entered.

"Show our guest to his quarters, Jones," ordered Blau.

"Yes, sir." She was quite impassive.

"Major Skinner is going to be looking after him," added the colonel.

She had ignored Garner since coming into the room, but now, briefly, her eyes flicked over him.

"Waldheim, sir?" she asked the colonel.

"First thing in the morning," said Blau. He turned to Garner. "Waldheim's our little playground, captain. I hope you enjoy it."

And, abruptly, his hand waved dismissal.

"This way, captain," said the blonde.

As he turned, Garner saw the colonel put his folder in a drawer in his desk. He closed the drawer with a finality that wasn't reassuring.

4

The room was spartan, with an iron bed, a thin mattress, Army blankets, a wash basin, an old fashioned armchair and a utilitarian wardrobe.

"I hope you will be comfortable," said Lieutenant Jones, and he wasn't quite sure if she meant it to be supreme irony.

"I'm sure I'll be all right."

They had brought his case from the staff car to the room, and deposited it on the floor.

"Let me know if there's anything you need," she added, and turned to go.

"Can I ask a personal question?" said Garner.

She looked at him coldly. "Such as?"

"How did you get into this outfit?" He was genuinely curious.

"I volunteered, captain. Like everybody here."

"And this?" He nodded at her silver parachutist's badge.

"I qualified. Satisfied?"

"I'm sorry if I sound stupid, but I didn't expect to meet somebody like – you. In this outfit."

"A woman, you mean?"

"Well, yes."

"Don't they have women in your SAS, captain?"

"No. Not yet anyway . . ."

"What's the matter?" she asked, "don't you people think women can kill efficiently?" The sneer was blatant.

"I suppose we've still got to come to terms with it. It takes some getting used to . . ."

She regarded him thoughtfully. "You know, you could have fooled me, sir."

"I beg your pardon?"

"You being SF," she said.

"SF?" Garner was puzzled.

"SF. Special Forces. I can usually tell right away. As soon as a man comes into a room. There's something – well, special about them. I guess it's a way of life . . ."

He sensed a trap. "You mean, I'm not your idea of one?"

She became very correct. "I'm sorry, sir. I'm out of line."

He wanted to draw her out. "No, go ahead. Speak your mind."

"No, sir, it's nothing. I guess I haven't met SAS before . . ."

He wondered what she looked like without the beret, without that uniform which was so unfeminine, the lace up jump boots, no pistol holster belted round her waist . . .

"Well, since we're being personal, lieutenant, what can I call you, other than lieutenant?" he smiled at her.

22

"My name is Jones, sir."

"What comes before the Jones?"

She looked at him unblinking. "My initials are K.D."

He wasn't going to be put off. "K.D. stands for what?"

"That's what I'm called, sir," she replied stiffly. "K.D. Jones. My friends . . ."

"Yes?" He wondered about the friends of this cold, deadly blonde.

"My friends call me K.D."

"OK," said Garner. "I'll call you K.D."

She was icy. "I'm sorry, sir, you are not a friend. You are a fellow officer, and I think it appropriate if we stick to the military courtesies, sir." She saluted, mockingly he thought, and left the room.

The briefing in room 8011 may have been thorough, he mused, sitting down on the hard bed, but she was something Rathbone hadn't warned him about.

None the less, he seemed to have pulled it off. He had been watching for the signals, but so far they didn't seem to have suspected that there was no Captain Garner of the SAS.

"You can carry it off," Rathbone had assured him complacently. "You're good at that sort of thing."

Of course, it was easy for Rathbone, sitting behind his desk in Whitehall.

"Why do I have to be SAS?" Garner had asked him.

"It's the only way we can get an exchange visit set up," explained Rathbone. "They and the SAS are the only ones who have the arrangement."

Now, all that seemed so long ago, and so far away.

Garner stood up, and walked round the small room. It was cell-like, bare, cold. They certainly didn't believe in comfort for visitors.

In the toilet next door hung a calendar. Garner stared at it. It was a Russian calendar, and the eight Soviet national holidays were clearly marked.

5

Simonov, the theatre company's producer, had suggested a little dinner after the show. Borisov expected to find the rest of the cast there too, but when he arrived at the restaurant in the Ulitsa Yanki Kupala, Simonov was sitting at a table laid for two.

"I hear this is quite a good place," he greeted Borisov. "We must try the stuffed liver. And their potato pancakes are said to be as good as one's mother makes."

His treble chin, the round fat face, and the bonhomie disguised Simonov's cunning. He was the great survivor, who managed to convey the impression that he challenged the system, yet was highly acceptable to authority. A man apparently eager to question the establishment who was also one of its most reliable propagandists.

"We never seem to have a chance to talk quietly on our own, my dear friend," he said earnestly. "Here's to friendship." He raised his mug of kvass, and they both drank.

Borisov watched him curiously. Simonov always had a purpose.

Whoever had told him about the Zhuravinka was right; the cuisine was excellent, and the service refreshingly efficient. The stuffed liver came with potatoes and mushrooms in sour cream, and was delicious.

"I am looking forward to London," confessed Simonov. "I think we all are, don't you?"

Borisov carefully wiped his mouth. "It should be very interesting."

"I know the company will enjoy itself," went on Simonov enthusiastically. "And what a great opportunity, Evgeny

Alekseivitch, to give people over there an insight into our souls. To demonstrate that we, as artists, question and challenge preconceptions as much as anyone on the other side."

Careful, thought Borisov. This is the kind of conversation that could be misconstrued.

"Yes," he agreed, choosing his words with caution. "I am sure they will be interested to see examples of modern Soviet drama."

A bit of sour cream was dribbling down one of Simonov's chins, but Borisov decided against telling him.

The fat man looked around, then leaned forward. "Of course, I need not tell you that in our capacity as cultural ambassadors we will be observed every second of the day. They will judge our country by us individually. Everyone must be on their best behaviour. I will look to you, dear comrade, to help me . . ."

Borisov gave him a stony look. "How?" he asked.

Simonov spread his pudgy hands. "You know so well what actors get up to on tour . . . and in a foreign country, with so many temptations . . ."

"I think that by the time we have given seven performances a week, got used to the food, and tried to make ourselves understood, we'll be too tired to be tempted by anything except bed."

Simonov gurgled with appreciative laughter, his stomach shaking slightly. "Yes, but who else will be in the bed, I ask myself?" He thought this so amusing that he laughed again aloud. Then his face clouded over. "The Lyubimov affair must be a warning to all of us," he muttered.

Of course, thought Borisov, Yuri Lyubimov, director of the Taganka, rankled. He never came back from his stint in London at the Lyric Theatre, Hammersmith.

Then Simonov changed the subject. "I wanted to take *And the Silver Cord will Snap* to London, but the minister thought it wasn't quite the right play," he confided. "I don't see why. Maybe Kazantsev is out of favour at the moment, but he is a marvellous writer and it's a very good piece, don't you agree?"

25

Ah, said Borisov to himself, he has changed roles. He is now the establishment critic. The acceptable rebel.

He smiled at the producer. "I hear that the theatre won't have simultaneous translation, so unless the audience understands Russian, they won't know what we're saying, will they?"

Simonov frowned. "That is not a positive statement, dear colleague. We must assume that they will understand every word, and we must perform as if the Central Committee was in the front row. As I am sure you will. You who are a professional to your finger tips." He signalled to the waiter and demanded a piece of "your famous honey cake". "Another of their specialities," he informed Borisov. Clearly he had been briefed in great detail. "Of course I shouldn't eat such sweet things, but one can't go through life only doing the right things, can one?" And he patted his stomach affectionately.

At the right moment, Borisov excused himself. "I must get back to the hotel. I promised Polina I would phone her tonight."

"Of course," nodded Simonov, "and how is your dear wife?"

"Quite well," replied Borisov curtly.

"She must find it a little boring, stuck in Moscow all on her own," said Simonov. "You must bring her back a nice present from London. Something woollen, perhaps. Scottish wool is very good." He signalled for the bill. "I would like to take my little woman with me, but you know the Ministry's attitude. We must not be distracted on such important trips." He sighed. "Sometimes I wonder if they understand that we artistes are human beings, and have sensitive feelings."

"Oh I'm sure they do," said Borisov, and Simonov shot him a doubtful glance.

After they had put on their coats, they embraced.

"Thank you for an excellent dinner," said Borisov.

"You see," smiled Simonov, rather smugly, "my spies were correct. It is a good restaurant."

Absolutely, thought Borisov as he waved goodbye. Your spies, dear friend, are always correct.

He got back to the Yubelinaya and took the lift to the eighth floor. When he opened the door, the light was on.

"You've been a long time," said Maya peevishly. She was in the bed, undressed. "I thought you were never coming."

"I've been with Simonov." As he said it he resented giving her an explanation. What the devil did it have to do with her? And who gave her the right to make free and easy with his room?

"How did you get in here?" he asked.

She smiled knowingly. "How do you think? I asked them to let me in. After all, it is no secret about us."

"It *is* my room."

She laughed. "Well, we can go to mine, if you prefer. But your bed is bigger."

He threw his coat on a chair. "I have to make a phone call," he announced.

The bed sheet had slipped, and she made no effort to cover her breasts.

"That's all right," she said coolly, "go ahead. I won't eavesdrop." She stretched herself languidly.

He sat down on the bed. "Maya, listen . . ."

"Yes?"

But he knew if he spoke his mind it might be the end of their affair, and as he looked at her, he desired her body, and her nakedness called to him. So he said nothing.

"Come to bed," she said. "I'm cold."

She received him, as always, with passion, and later they lay in the dark, silent.

"You still want to make that phone call?" she asked, suddenly.

"It's too late now," answered Borisov.

"I'm sure your wife wouldn't mind." She was being patronising to Polina. She could afford to be; after all, Polina's man had just made love to her.

"No," said Borisov. "I won't call tonight."

In the darkness, Maya smiled. But she was wrong if she believed that her lover was thinking about the women in his life. Borisov's mind was occupied with something quite different.

He was thinking about London. What the woman who lay next to him didn't know was that in London he was going to seek asylum in the West.

6

It took Andreyan twenty minutes to walk from his flat in Holland Park to the embassy of the USSR in Kensington Palace Gardens. He could do it in twelve minutes, at a brisk pace, but he liked to stroll rather more slowly.

He always found it a useful walk. It gave him a window on the world when he went to work every morning. Short as it was, it gave him an opportunity to look at England through a microscope. He always took in the familiar landmarks – the old house, for instance, of Tony Benn, where the park bench used to be stuck in the front garden. Moscow thought Benn was quite an important figure, but Andreyan sometimes referred to him rather unkindly in his reports to the Ministry, calling him a tea room Marxist.

He liked looking at the posters and graffiti on various walls and hoardings along the way, announcements of forthcoming demonstrations, marches, meetings, pickets, assemblies. The English protest industry always amused him. It was so predictable.

He enjoyed the cross section of people he would come across. You could see them all in Notting Hill Gate, unshaven anarchists, pretty models, staid businessmen, bohemians, drug addicts, politicians, immigrants, the rich, the poor, and just the ordinary Londoners. Rather different to most of the people he saw in his working day behind the walls of the embassy.

Andreyan had long given up checking whether anyone was trailing him on his walk. He knew the British were watching him. His phone at home was certainly tapped. He smiled at the thought; as if he would discuss state secrets over British Telecom! He had a suspicion that they vetted his mail. Good luck to them.

But he also knew they were good. If they had anyone following him, they would be hard to spot. It could of course be that young man with the Imperial College scarf, or the thin man with the brief case, the woman in the raincoat, anyone. It didn't matter. If they thought he was using the Gate Cinema as a dead letter drop, or picking up micro film from the magazine shelves of W. H. Smith they were going to be disappointed.

Officially, Sergei Mikhailovitch Andreyan was an information counsellor at the embassy. Unofficially he had other jobs . . .

He enjoyed the London posting. His English was fluent, but that wasn't the main reason Moscow had given him this assignment. He was considered a man with a future, and the service looked on London as a necessary step up the ladder, so the Department allowed him considerable freedom. Leonov, his boss at the embassy, kept a fatherly eye on him, but that was all.

He stepped off the pavement to cross the road and accidentally bumped into a rather pretty girl dressed in red.

"Sorry," apologised Andreyan.

She smiled at him, and rushed on. Just for a moment he wondered whether it really had been an accident. Had she brushed against him deliberately? He felt for his wallet and his address book. They were safe. Really, he thought, he should stop being so suspicious, but that was the way he had been trained, and he knew he would never change.

· He glanced round to see if he could still spot the girl, but she had jumped into a cab. Andreyan liked good looking women, and he had, momentarily, despite his wariness, been attracted to the girl in red. Not of course that he would have followed it up. He just would have enjoyed having another look at her.

Then his mind switched to his work load. He had a lot to do. He wanted to make sure that all the necessary arrangements had been made for the Soviet theatre season in London. Simonov was bringing the company over to present plays in Russian. Quite a distinguished cast. The *Guardian* had already asked for an interview with Borisov, the leading man.

They were all reliable people, of course. Simonov was a party man, and Borisov a People's Artist. But the Department wanted to keep an eye on things. Andreyan knew what was expected of him.

And there was the report on Rathbone. The Ministry was being a nuisance about that. He had already sent an informative file about Rathbone to Moscow, but the First Chief Directorate wanted to know more. Andreyan could just visualise them, on the fifth floor of that half-moon shaped building on the Moscow Ring Road, poring over the dossier, then saying, "Get Andreyan to dig deeper; after all, he's in London, right on the spot."

"What do they expect me to do, take a cab to Whitehall, walk into his office, and interrogate Rathbone about his department?" he had asked Leonov.

The grey haired colonel had smiled at him. "Why not, Sergei Mikhailovitch?"

Leonov's sense of humour was notorious, and there were those who worried about his jokes deep into the night.

Andreyan had finished drafting the report, but he wanted to read it just once more before he passed it over for encyphering. He hadn't been able to add much to the file. Rathbone spoke Russian fluently, that certainly made him different from most of the paper shufflers. His section was apparently cover named Special Liaison, whatever that meant. He had spent some time in Washington. He rarely drank alcohol. That rather worried Andreyan; he didn't trust people who didn't drink. But the most curious thing about Rathbone was that he kept submerging. There were gaps that the Directorate hadn't been able to fill. Rathbone seemed to have disappeared from view for periods in his career, and nobody knew where he had been or what he had been doing.

A Japanese man in a Burberry stopped Andreyan.

"Please," he said with a toothy smile, "where is . . ." He looked at a piece of paper in his hand. "Where is Bark Place?"

"You're almost on top of it," said Andreyan in his accentless English. "Take the second left . . ."

The Japanese bowed slightly. "Thank you."

Andreyan enjoyed giving people street directions. He knew London well, and being able to show off his geographical know-all was a favourite indulgence. He had once completely baffled a *Tass* correspondent by confiding that what he really wanted to do, his great ambition, was to pass a London taxi driver's police test of the city's localities.

He looked at his watch. The walk had taken eighteen minutes. He crossed Bayswater Road and passed the Diplomatic Protection Group officer who was patrolling up and down. In two minutes Andreyan would be in No 18 Kensington Palace Gardens.

Then he would start being a spy.

7

The secret report from the Fifth Directorate was the last thing Lapin wanted to see on his desk at the Ministry of Radio and Television. He was due to attend a meeting of the

Central Committee in the afternoon, and he would hate to see this little problem on the agenda at the last minute.

The Directorate informed him that during the night the mysterious pirate station had unexpectedly come on the air again. And it was beginning to show its teeth. It identified itself as "Russkaya Volya", Russian Freedom. It also had a news item.

"Citizens of Moscow, there is no reason to panic. The crack in the Tokamak nuclear reactor at the Institute of Atomic Energy does not threaten the safety of the city. The radiation is not strong enough to imperil your health or injure your children. It is a serious incident, and the reason the authorities have not announced it is purely to avoid causing you worry. To be absolutely safe, simply avoid the neighbourhood of the Institute."

Of course it was obvious what these bastards were trying to do, cursed the minister. The oldest trick in the world, disinformation. Deny a rumour to give it credence. There had been no incident at the Institute. No nuclear reactor had developed a crack. But if this story got around . . .

Lapin re-read the report carefully. *Russkaya Volya*. That was interesting. It was the name of the newspaper Lenin had closed down in 1917. It printed stories about the Bolsheviks that could not be allowed, and there were those who said that October 24, the night the paper died, was the execution of independent journalism. Most Russians had never heard of *Russkaya Volya*. Now, suddenly, it was reborn in the ether. Russian Freedom, indeed.

The minister chewed his lip. The Fifth Directorate's report was remarkable for the things it didn't say. That would never do. He picked up the phone and called Colonel General Arkady Zotov, head of GRU information services.

"This pirate station," he growled. "What have you found out about it?"

Zotov cleared his throat at the other end.

"We're still making inquiries, comrade minister," he said carefully.

32

"Oh really?" Lapin did not disguise his sarcasm. "How much longer will it take?"

"What precisely do you want to know?" asked Zotov. Time. That was all he wanted to gain. Time to think.

"Well, I should have thought the questions are obvious. Who is doing this broadcast? Where is it coming from? That's for a start."

There was a pause at the other end of the phone.

"Comrade minister, they're trying to give the impression that they are operating inside our borders. Our technical experts seem inclined to the view that that is incorrect."

Lapin tried to control himself. "Damn it, what kind of answer is that? Surely you've got the technological means to track the origin of these transmissions . . ."

"Very difficult, minister," said Zotov hurriedly.

"So where do your 'technical experts' think it originates?"

Zotov hated committing himself. "I should say . . . abroad."

"And who is doing it?"

"Comrade minister, who can say?" Zotov squirmed in his chair. He also knew about the Central Committee meeting in a few hours. He knew that if this business came up, Lapin would not hesitate to drop him in the proverbial mire. "I suspect a CIA operation. Or maybe émigrés? Enemies of our country, of course."

Lapin was silent for so long that Zotov thought he had gone off the line. But he was still there.

"General," he said. "What are you going to do about intercepting these transmissions? I don't want these rumours flying round the ether. I demand that this rubbish be jammed, every syllable of it, you understand?"

"Yes, of course." Zotov swore under his breath. "There are technical difficulties, though. You see, the times of these transmissions seem to vary. I mean, 20:45 last time. 23:30 this time. It is very complicated to have counter measures available round the clock. Our resources . . ."

"I will report to the Central Committee," snarled Lapin

33

and put down the phone. At least, he thought with satisfaction, he had ruined Zotov's day.

But the satisfaction did not last long. He had a feeling he would hear a lot more of the pirate station that called itself Russian Freedom.

8

To Colonel Blau it was the jewel box. Others knew it as Site 11, and didn't talk about it, because its very existence was unmentionable. It was enclosed by three electrified wire fences, and watched every minute of the day by the glass eyes of closed circuit surveillance lenses. It lay hidden away, deep in the forest, its location carefully picked for its remoteness and inaccessibility.

Long ago, in the '50s, it had been constructed as part of a super secret NATO project for the provision of covert, concealed storage dumps where, unknown to the world, and invisible to prying eyes, unmentionable things could be housed in total secrecy.

Most of it was underground behind ten inch thick steel doors embedded in concrete, beyond which ran an underground passage which opened into the subterranean vault that housed the jewels. The store inside was air conditioned, with carefully regulated temperature levels, and constantly illuminated. The place was automated, and access could only be gained by those who were privy to a complicated and foolproof system of electronic devices, time locks, and secret number codes.

Site 11's location was known to very few people. These secret dumps, dotted in obscure, often disguised hideaways, were not listed on official schedules of military installations, and only a handful of USAREUR's top planning officials at headquarters in Heidelberg knew of their existence.

Site 11 was small, and superficially insignificant. The hyper classification of the few documents that listed it, plus the critical secrecy grading of its purpose, helped those who thought it best to keep the world uninformed about its presence.

So, when in 1983 a little known NATO accord was issued, ordering the withdrawal of 1,400 obsolete nuclear war heads from Europe, the secrecy surrounding the US Army's tactical nuclear stock pile in Europe meant that only a very few men were aware of what was going on.

There were, at that time, 6,000 tactical nuclear weapons in the Army's battlefield arsenal. Colonel Blau, newly arrived in Germany, was assigned to the small, select team supervising the dispersal of out-dated nuclear infantry and artillery weapons.

That was when he came across the jewels – 300 W-54s. Nuclear land mines. Infantry, for the use of. Small, compact, easily carried by one man. Fitting snugly into a sleeping bag. And each with an explosive nuclear force of up to ten kilotons – 10,000 lb of high explosive. Half a dozen of these land mines, planted in the ground, could devastate a city . . .

Colonel Blau was one of the team privy to the list of obsolete Army weapons being withdrawn from Europe, including outmoded 9-megaton artillery war heads, MK 36s nukes, certain nuclear shells – and all the land mines.

They were all being replaced with 9,000 new war heads, including enhanced-radiation atomic missiles for the artillery, new W-80 rockets, and other tactical weapons. It was all part of the overall scheme to equip the military with 15,000 nuclear war heads by the end of the decade, and a possible peak of 32,000 weapons by 1990.

Compared with that arsenal, the 300 ten kiloton land mines were small fry indeed. And yet . . .

They were small, compact, unobtrusive. They didn't weigh that much. They took up little space. Blau's brainchild was that, with the curtain of secrecy that surrounded the movement of nuclear munitions, and the shifting of arsenals, it might not be too difficult to do some interesting paper shuffling . . .

Three hundred atomic land mines were finally shipped out of Germany. On paper.

Actually, there were only 200. The other 100 remained behind. Hidden in the depths of the secret vault of Site 11. Jewels secure in his own treasure house.

The Pentagon was crazy to get rid of them, felt Blau. These little babies, so trim, so neat, so mobile, easy to carry, simple to handle, they brought a new refinement to special warfare. They turned a small troop of men into a devastating force with the explosive power of a mass invasion. Half a dozen volunteers planting nuclear land mines in cities, on motorways, at airfields . . .

That indeed was special warfare.

When Colonel Blau took over the Freudenhof command, and was given his own project, he had some anxious moments about Site 11. He kept worrying if somewhere, in an arsenal in New Mexico, or at a staff meeting at the Pentagon, the inventory of obsolete weapons would be checked and audited. If somebody started counting war heads, if suddenly two and two didn't make four, and a doctored computer print out was analysed in detail, then . . .

But it had never happened. Anything to do with the weapons had the Atomic Q classification, was graded higher even than top secret, and nobody asked too many questions. In fact, they didn't know enough to ask.

There were, of course, awkward moments. An Inspector General's team visited to check on war contingency plans, and wanted to know more about special weapons storage. They had a list of installations they asked to inspect. They even asked to see a typical Omega dump – the code word for the secret sites – and Blau took them to a vacant one near Baden Baden. But they never asked to see Site 11.

Some not so dumb German politician stood up in the

Bundestag defence committee and asked the State Secretary in the Defence Ministry, Herr Kurt Wuerzbach, what had happened to the American Army's obsolete Atomic Demolition Mines, reportedly stored in military arsenals in the US zone since 1964. Luckily Herr Wuerzbach assured him that the removal of obsolete nukes from Germany had been proceeding as planned.

The nosey politician had persisted, expressing concern about mines, each with the power of an atom bomb, which could be carried around by one man, but Herr Wuerzbach had calmed his fears.

"There are many things one can carry which are not really designed for carrying," he had wittily told the Bundestag.

It had all passed, and nobody had taken any notice. Blau relaxed again.

He kept a close eye on Site 11, of course. Major Skinner knew what was kept there, but he could be trusted. Skinner was an officer of like mind. As for the men who guarded the forest dump, they knew it was something to do with "special weapons", but that covered a multitude of possibilities. Anyway, they were Blau's men. They were Green Berets.

As a man who knew he had been born with the stamp of destiny on him, Blau looked on his jewels as the key to his plans. If properly enriched a couple of W-54s had the explosive power of the bombs which pulverised Hiroshima and Nagasaki, yet they were only a foot in diameter, 15 inches long, weighing approximately 150 lb.

When the day came, they could indeed liberate the oppressed. Green Beret teams, each about twelve men strong, operating inside Eastern Europe, working as self-contained groups, raising the flag of revolt among the local population, arming and leading them. Each team mobilising, say, 500 guerillas, destroying communications, blowing up trains and bridges . . .

And, with one land mine, capable of wiping out an entire Soviet armoured division . . .

Yes, the mines were the crux. He thanked God he had them.

37

Because Blau knew the day would come. Sometimes he even indulged in the dream that instead of waiting for it to come, and going into action when the summons came, he would actually bring it about. There were moments when he felt that those in power in Washington didn't understand the inevitable. Instead of taking the initiative, they were too weak, too nervous to make the necessary decisions . . .

That's when Blau would close his eyes, lean back and visualise sending his team into the East, dropping them deep in enemy territory, unleashing his Russian speaking elite spearheads, and using them to light the fire that would consume the tyranny that enslaved Eastern Europe. For he was convinced it only needed a fuse to burn for the whole empire to explode.

No, he was not mad. He was a realist. Another great soldier had had the same vision – Major General Walker, commander of the 24th Infantry Division at Augsburg. He had been ready to take his crack troops into action against the common enemy with nuclear artillery. Only he had been brought down by the prevaricators in Washington. He had been too trusting. Colonel Blau was not about to make the same mistake.

Naturally, he had his suspicions that people were watching him. The generals in Heidelberg had their reservations, he knew that. There were those in Brussels, on the NATO staff, who were wary of him. But to none of them had he given the opportunity of baulking him. He was too smart for that.

And least of all did they know his biggest secret, that he had managed to acquire his own private arsenal of nuclear weapons.

But recently a nagging thought had been bothering him. This British officer. Captain Garner. Something about him didn't fit. Sure, his Green Berets had had periodic exchanges with the SAS troopers. Certainly it was all within the framework of NATO co-operative training. Colonel Blau prided himself on his instincts, however. They never let him down. Now his instincts told him that Captain Garner had been sent to snoop. To find out things.

38

Well, decided the colonel, let him. It didn't matter at all.
It didn't matter because Captain Garner was bound to have
a fatal accident quite soon.

9

The last night in Moscow was difficult for Borisov. He was
playing a part, and for him, of all people, it shouldn't have
been much of an ordeal. But he felt awkward, like an actor
performing a role which he knew didn't suit him. Though
word perfect, the emotion was lacking.

"You'll be back in a fortnight," Polina consoled him, as if
he had to be encouraged to make the trip to London. "It will
go very quickly, you'll see."

"Yes," he agreed, "it'll be over in no time."

She was wearing her navy blue dress with the smart white
collar, which she knew he liked. She wanted to please him.

"Maybe when you get back, we can have a little holiday,"
she suggested hopefully. "It would be nice to get away to
Miskhor for a few days."

They had a small dacha there, amid the poplars by the
seashore. A holiday cottage in the Crimea was one of the
privileges Borisov had earned as a People's Artist.

He nodded. "That's a good idea."

"It will do you good," said Polina. "All this touring is very
tiring. You look a bit strained."

"Nonsense," he growled. Her solicitude was the last thing
he needed.

"I worry about you sometimes," she said a little sadly.
"They overwork you."

"The price of success," he smiled drily.

He felt like a spectator watching a stage play. He could

predict the action that was unfolding. He even knew how the evening would end. Polina would be amorous, and they'd make love. She expected him on his last night to feel romantic. His last night . . .

"What would you like me to bring you back from London?" he asked, and immediately hated himself for his hypocrisy. He wasn't coming back, and he wouldn't be bringing her back anything. Perhaps, came a quick thought, he could send it to her, and keep his promise to her that way.

"Only you," said Polina, and that didn't make it any easier.

"Oh, you have to have something from London," insisted Borisov. He thought of Simonov's suggestion. "What about a nice woollen sweater?"

"Whatever," shrugged Polina. "I don't mind." She had packed for him, and now busied herself with one of the two cases. "Is the whole company going?" she asked.

"Yes."

"Maya Petrova too?" She tried hard to make it sound casual.

"Yes. Why do you ask?"

"I know how keen she is to see the West," said Polina. "Do you know, it wouldn't surprise me if she has ideas about trying to become a film star over there. Emigrating to Hollywood."

Borisov glanced across at his wife. It was a tricky statement. If she made it within hearing of the Ministry, Maya's exit visa would be stopped. He wondered if Polina was hinting at something. It was one way she could get back at the little bitch.

"Oh, that's rubbish," said Borisov. "She'd be like a fish out of water."

"It hasn't stopped some of the others," sniffed Polina. "They always seem to open their arms to deserters."

Is that what she's going to call me when it happens, he wondered.

She came up to him and put her arms round him.

"Anyway," she said, hugging him, "let's not spend our last evening talking about Maya Petrova. Let's forget about the tour. Take the phone off the hook. Lock the door." She pressed her body close to his.

"What would you like to do?" he asked.

"Can't you guess?" she smiled, and kissed him.

Later, in bed, Borisov lay with his eyes open and thought about what was ahead. For a mad, crazy moment, he considered telling Polina all about it.

Sitting up in bed and saying, "Listen, I'm not coming back. I'm staying over there." And Polina staring at him, aghast, then whispering:

"Why?"

And Borisov answering: "Because I have to."

But that was play acting too. He couldn't tell her, of course. The truth was much too dangerous. And the irony was that he had to conceal it not only to safeguard himself, but to protect her too.

"Darling," came Polina's voice from next to him.

"Yes?"

"Do you know something?"

"What?"

"I love you very much."

He turned to her in bed, and held her close.

A lot of people were going to get hurt, he realised, and he was one of them.

10

The regime at Waldheim was a backbreaker, and there were times when Garner doubted if his body could cope. He had undergone special training at Hereford in preparation for the assignment, and he had managed to finish a combat course. But the eight week syllabus at Waldheim was something he had never experienced.

From the moment he was awoken at 5:30 a.m. to lights out at 10 p.m. he was a machine. The routine began with thirty push ups, which had to be completed within 120 seconds. Then, prior to breakfast, six pull ups and a one mile run, to be finished inside eight minutes, after which the real day began. A continuing time-table of field tests, stalking exercises, mock ambushes, observations exercises, close combat, tactical manoeuvres, concealment tests. Darkness brought no relief, with a succession of night firing, covert patrols, booby trapping, and mock reconnaissance raids.

He learnt a lot about the kind of outfit Colonel Blau had created. The most revealing part was the lectures. There was one on Terror, Implicit and Explicit.

"Let's not kid ourselves," said a gaunt wiry master sergeant addressing his class, "terror can be mighty useful. If they're not for us, they're agin us, check?"

He stared at the group and seemed satisfied that they had grasped the point.

"The fact is, gentlemen, that if they're agin us, we have to scare the shit out of them. Ambush them. Kidnap them. Shame, ridicule and humiliate the bad guys. Got the message?"

He walked up and down among them, thwacking a thin cane against his thigh. He seemed to like the sharp sound it made.

"When you're behind the lines, deep in hostile territory, the fear you create is your ally. You got to tune your violence like a goddam fiddle. You got to know the degree of violence necessary to make them co-operate, how far you can go before it starts getting counter productive. I mean, don't shoot the fucking kids. You alienate the mothers."

He waited for the laugh, but the Green Berets took him very seriously.

The sergeant stopped in front of Garner.

42

"Now you, sir, knowing the British, I guess you don't approve?"

"I'm just here to learn," replied Garner.

"Sure. And with respect, captain, your army has a lot to learn."

"I think you're right, sergeant," murmured Garner. For a moment the sergeant narrowed his eyes. Then he strolled on.

Colonel Blau, thought Garner, has re-written the Guerilla War Manual. He had read FM 95-1A before he came over, and it didn't say any of this. The colonel was training his troops his way. He decided to keep very quiet.

"Now just remember one thing," the sergeant was saying. "We are coming to liberate. There are millions of people over there just waiting for the chance to rise up and kick out the commies. We're coming and we're going to show them how to do it. We're going to organise them and arm them and lead them. You're on a crusade, fellows, and let me tell you something, the way we're going to do it, nobody can stop us."

Garner took in every word, and thought, Christ, they were right in room 8011. These people really meant it. Colonel Blau had created himself a private army. And he's got plans. Plans like re-drawing the map of Europe.

There was a great deal Garner had to find out, but he had to move carefully. The training routine and the exercises left little spare time, and he was constantly under the eyes of Major Skinner, or one of the unsmiling, ever watchful NCOs. The other men had little time for him; he was an outsider, an alien. That was the strangest thing about this outfit, they seemed to be bound together by a secret allegiance, a common bond.

Stuck out here, in a small corner of Bavaria, secluded in forest land, shrouded in operational secrecy, far from headquarters in Heidelberg, Colonel Blau ruled supreme. Special Forces were traditionally a law unto themselves, and he had taken it one degree further.

Be very careful, be very cautious, Garner told himself.

43

Then came Exercise Salvo, a field test for Garner's company. He found himself in a camouflage suit, concealed deep in the undergrowth, face blackened, and his sole link with the rest of the unit a walkie-talkie radio. He was armed with a 7.62 mm sniper rifle, loaded with five rounds of blank ammunition. He was the key lookout, hidden from the enemy, charged with watching out for the hostile forces.

He had been there for about two hours when the radio message came: "Proceed to Orange Ten Five."

Garner got out his map, and looked for the reference point. It was a cluster of trees at the end of a narrow forest path. Only 400 yards away.

Warily he emerged from his cover, and started to make his way up the path. The reason for the message wasn't clear. Perhaps they wished to re-draw the sniper line. Cautiously he made his progress along the path, watching the trees in case hostile scouts were concealed in the branches.

It was by sheer chance that, at that precise moment, he glanced down, and saw the trip wire. It was half hidden by leaves and grass, right in his path. One more step would have brought his foot in contact with it.

Inch by inch, Garner followed the trip wire, then he saw the device it was set to trigger. All units were using blank ammunition in Exercise Salvo, but this was no dummy trap. It was the real thing. If he had pulled the wire by stepping on it, it would have exploded the booby trap. And he would have been blown apart.

Garner stood very still for a moment. Some perspiration slowly trickled down his face, and mixed with his black camouflage paint. His mouth felt dry.

Very gingerly he bent down, and cut the trip wire. Then he straightened up. They had tried to kill him. They had sent a radio message to make sure that he would have to pass this spot and, hopefully, set off the booby trap. Somebody had rigged it specially for him.

They wanted him out of the way. But Garner had other plans. He still hadn't got to see what Rathbone wanted to

44

know about. He still hadn't had a chance to locate it. But he was going to. Oh yes, he was going to.

He was damned if he was going to let them kill him before he had found what he had come for.

11

The door to the entrance in Monmouth Street could have done with a coat of paint, and the small brass name plate had not been polished in a long while. "Europa League. 2nd floor" was all it said.

The two flights of stairs were equally dingy, and there was a faintly musty smell. The first floor had been occupied by the offices of a correspondence school in transcendental mysticism, which had tried to teach Yoga by mail. Unfortunately it did not enrol enough students to pay the rent.

The Europa League was something different. It had no financial problems. In fact, despite its unprepossessing premises, its account at an American Bank in Mayfair was always kept in a very healthy state. The origin of those funds, which were replenished at regular intervals, was lost in a complicated maze which led from Texas to Switzerland, and to London via Luxembourg through Liechtenstein.

Not that the offices of the League ever suggested wealth. They were as dowdy as the rest of the building, and even the secretary's electric typewriter had seen better days. Miss Hurst, the secretary, was, nevertheless, a remarkably efficient woman; so efficient, in fact, that outsiders might have wondered why she wasted her time in such a backwater. The phones did not ring very often, correspondence was desultory, and few people stopped by. Had they probed deeper, however, they would have been surprised to discover how highly paid Miss Hurst was, her linguistic capabilities, and various other talents one hardly expected to be buried in back stairs in a side street.

Apart from a tiny waiting room, there was only one other office. It was used by Dr Jury.

According to the Europa League's letter-head, Dr Leonard Jury was the Chief Executive. Just what the League did was not clearly defined to the outside world, although there were those who knew only too well.

On the wall facing Dr Jury's desk was a big map of Europe, and behind his swivel chair stood a bookcase containing volumes like "Forgery, Disinformation and Political Operations" (Special Report No 88, US State Department), the Diary of Major General Petr Grigorevich Grigorenko, "Demographic Trends in USSR 1950–2000", Handbook of Intelligence and Guerilla Warfare, Prominent Personalities in the USSR, bound reports by the Foreign Broadcast Information Service, and a file of BBC Monitoring Service digests. There was also a copy of *Alice in Wonderland*. Dr Jury liked Alice, and always kept a volume of her adventures close at hand.

The precise activities of the Europa League were undefined. So was Dr Jury. Just exactly what he was a doctor in or of was not revealed to the world. He made no claims to have a medical background, though he hinted at academic connections. There was an undefined suggestion of government service. He could be beautifully vague. He travelled on a United States passport, but his accent was English, he spoke Russian fluently, and read German for pleasure.

As for the League, when pressed he referred to it as "a clearing house".

"We collect information," he would explain, which was true enough, in a way. The information was chiefly about Eastern Europe, the Warsaw Pact powers.

He was very interested in their personalities. Miss Hurst kept thick files of cuttings about people in the news in

46

Eastern countries, politicians, athletes, actors, writers. All the Russian newspapers came to the second floor in Monmouth Street, *Pravda*, *Trud*, *Izvestia*, the *Literary Gazette*. So did Polish and Czech papers.

And Dr Jury had connections. He had friends in Bush House, and Fleet Street's professional Kremlin watchers knew his value; he could always be relied on for background information about some obscure member of the Supreme Soviet, or a suddenly promoted Red Army general. He was recognised at the Institute for the Study of Conflict, and he had given some lectures. He visited the United States frequently, and often made trips to Germany. He also had close contacts among the exiles. He kept in touch with them, helped them, advised them, spoke to them in their own language, and thought their thoughts.

As a man, he was unimpressive. He wore glasses, and tended to blink nervously. He was mild in manner, and appeared rather shy. His memory was prodigious; he had instant recall, seldom forgot a name, rattled off dates and places, and always remembered faces.

There were those who didn't trust him. He'd been fired by Radio Free Europe, it was said, because of the way he edited certain broadcasts. He believed in propaganda, not news, and would slant certain texts accordingly.

Moscow was well aware of his existence, and Colonel Leonov, at the embassy in London, kept an eye on his activities. The First Chief Directorate had a file on Dr Jury.

Within the Directorate, there was considerable disagreement about him and his activities in Monmouth Street. There were those who looked on Jury as an opportunist, a professional cold war warrior who had succeeded in obtaining the backing of private individuals in the United States and was making a good living out of his role as an "expert" on Communism.

Others regarded him with much greater suspicion. They considered him to be "official", working for Washington, backed by funds from Langley, charged with covert sub-version, spreading disinformation against the East.

Either way, it had been decided Jury was a man who needed watching and whose activities might have to be curtailed one day.

Which was one reason why certain precautions were taken at Monmouth Street. To enter, a buzzer had to be pressed. The door would not open until the visitor identified himself. On the stairs was a closed circuit camera, and Miss Hurst scrutinised any visitor on her monitor screen before she would let them enter the outer office, and all phone calls were automatically taped. At night, various alarms and electronic devices were switched on, and anyone breaking in had little chance of success. There was also a direct alarm line to Bow Street police station.

One of Andreyan's first assignments when he was posted to London was to photograph the building. He also managed to get a couple of pictures of Dr Jury, one of him walking along the street, the other getting out of a cab, and one of Miss Hurst when she went to have a sandwich lunch in Shaftesbury Avenue. The pictures were passed on to Moscow in the diplomatic bag.

Moscow also wanted a picture of Dr Jury's wife, which proved rather harder to get because Mrs Jury never visited Monmouth Street. The Jurys lived in Fulham, and Andreyan spent two days trying to get a photo of her without being spotted. She was rather a surprise. She was attractive, even glamorous, not at all the sort of wife Andreyan had expected the unprepossessing Dr Jury to have. She was well dressed, and drove a rather flashy sports car.

"Isn't she good looking?" he commented to Leonov when he handed over the pictures. "I wonder what she sees in him?"

In answer the colonel gave him a bleak look.

"You think they'll want to know more about her?" asked Andreyan, hopefully. Mrs Jury intrigued him.

"If they do, they will inform us," replied the colonel dourly.

On the second floor of Monmouth Street, the only sign of Mrs Jury was her photograph. Her husband had it on his desk.

Jury arrived at Monmouth Street shortly before three o'clock, and called Miss Hurst into his office.

"I have to go to Munich," he announced. "Book me on a morning flight, will you?"

"Certainly, doctor," said Miss Hurst. There were only the two of them in the office, but relations were formal. "When will you be coming back?"

"Oh, probably the next day. But you'd better leave it open."

"Very good." Then she thought again. "What about hotel reservations?"

"That's being taken care of," said Dr Jury.

She left the room. He made a couple of phone calls and looked through some papers he had taken from his brief case. There was also the new copy of *Pravda*, which he spread out on his desk and pored over.

Ten minutes later Miss Hurst knocked on the door and came in.

"Mr Rathbone is here."

Jury folded *Pravda*.

"Good," he said. "I've been expecting him."

12

Suddenly a floodlight switched on, bathing Garner in a brilliant white glare which made him screw up his eyes. He was still within a couple of feet of the outer ring of the three barbed wire fences, and had been careful where he stepped.

But somebody, somewhere must have been watching him, and turned on the light.

Garner stood motionless. The light seemed to be aimed at his face, blinding him. The sudden shock was paralysing. Part of his mind was urging him to turn and run, but the other half kept signalling caution. You're trapped, it told him.

"Stand still," ordered a metallic voice. "Don't move."

Garner's eyes were beginning to adjust to the bright light, and he turned his head in the direction of the voice.

"Stand still," repeated the loudspeaker.

Out of the surrounding darkness a jeep emerged and pulled up beside him, its long thin aerial trembling like an insect's tendril as it braked. There was only one man in it, a lanky figure in combat gear.

The figure got out, and came towards him. The light was still on Garner's face, and he couldn't recognise the man.

"Put your hands on your head, mister," ordered the figure.

"I'm Captain Garner . . ."

"Shut up."

Garner heard a shouted command somewhere behind him, then more shadowy figures appeared. Two, or three men, all vague shadows beyond the glare of the floodlight. Unexpectedly, a dog growled.

"Search him," commanded the figure. One of the shadows ran his hands over Garner's body. His face was expressionless.

"He's clean," the shadow reported. He gave Garner a slight push. "Stand still."

Garner heard a radio crackling, and he thought the man from the jeep was speaking softly into a walkie-talkie. He wished he could make out what he was saying.

Suddenly, as unexpectedly as it had come on, the floodlight was switched off. The sudden darkness, after the blinding brilliance in his eyes, confused Garner's vision once more. Most of what he saw was shadowy, indistinct. He screwed up his eyes to make out the faces of the men. Their features were difficult to define, but they were all in uniform, they all wore berets.

"Where's your green pass?" asked the man from the jeep.

Green pass? Garner didn't know what he was talking about.

"I'm Captain Garner," he repeated. "I have my ID. In my top pocket . . ."

He began to reach for it, but somebody grabbed his arm and held it.

"No green pass?"

"I don't know what you mean . . ."

The man snapped his fingers, and the troopers reacted immediately. Two of them took hold of Garner and a third man tied a blindfold round his eyes.

"Hey . . ." yelled Garner, struggling. They held him more firmly, and he lashed out with one foot.

That was the last thing he knew. They hit him very efficiently, the kind of blow that needs expertise. It struck the right spot, and the world blacked out.

13

How many days had it been? How many weeks? Gregson had lost count. He no longer knew which day of the week it was, or even the time of the day. All that he saw, twenty-four hours out of twenty-four hours, were the brick walls all around him and the electric light bulb which shone down on his head. He did not know daylight any more, or darkness. His watch had been taken from him, so he could not tell the time.

He slept in a cell which was perpetually illuminated. There was no window, nor were there any in the corridor along which he occasionally shuffled.

He was unshaven, because they wouldn't let him have a razor. He had nothing to read and nothing with which to write.

He didn't even know where he was. They had kept him in Leningrad for the first couple of days, but then he'd been given an injection and had blacked out. When he did finally wake up, he had been moved. He suspected he was in Moscow, but he wasn't sure.

The guards were not unkind. They didn't hit him or abuse him. They brought him food and escorted him to the toilet, but they didn't talk to him, and that was the worst part. If this went on, this shapeless existence, he knew that he would eventually go stark raving crazy.

The interrogations were the only thing that kept him sane. They were a contact with other faces, which actually made them almost a high point. He never thought the day would come when he'd actually look forward to being questioned by the KGB.

Today a new man came to his cell. He had a sympathetic, cultured manner and he introduced himself as Major Anastas.

"You know they've used you as a pawn, don't you," he said.

"Who are you talking about?"

"The people who recruited you. Who have used you. Look," and Major Anastas held up the spool that the woman had given him.

"This was a diversion, Paul. They couldn't care less about it. They set it all up to distract us. The spool was blank."

Anastas waited for a reaction, but Gregson just looked at him dumbly.

"The sad truth is that you're unimportant, and they decided to make us waste our time with you. Unfortunately, you will have to pay the price," the Major sighed. "I'm sorry for you, I really am. Don't you think it's rather foolish to sacrifice yourself for people who couldn't care less about you, and send you on a decoy mission to distract our attention?"

"Is it raining?" asked Gregson.

Anastas blinked. "What was that?"

"What's the weather like? I haven't seen it for so long, I keep dreaming of rain."

"I am sorry. You could make things easier for yourself, if you co-operated. I hate to see an intelligent person locked up in such conditions." The major sat down on the edge of Gregson's bunk. "I would be very pleased to report that you wished to be of assistance, because then everything would change. I guarantee you would get better food, blankets, and an hour's exercise in the fresh air every day. Every day, even when it rains," he added with a wry smile.

Gregson scratched himself. He badly needed a bath. He itched.

"When am I going to be tried?" he asked.

Anastas looked pained. "Please, don't make life even more difficult for yourself. If you face the military tribunal on a charge of espionage, I am afraid the prosecutor might ask for . . . for an exemplary sentence. So, let us not talk about trials."

"What else is there?"

The major glanced away. "Oh, there are all sorts of possibilities."

"Such as?"

Anastas stood up. "We have lots of questions to ask you, Paul. Answer them fully and honestly, tell us what we want to know, and all this may have a happy ending."

Gregson laughed.

"Think about it," said Anastas, and he banged on the cell door for the guard to unlock it.

"Tell me," said Gregson. "Is today Wednesday or Thursday?"

The major looked at him. He was no longer sympathetic.

"For you, my friend, it doesn't matter. From now on, it won't even matter what year it is."

The door banged shut, and Gregson was left sitting in the glare of the electric light bulb.

14

He groaned and turned over, then, like a switch being flicked, consciousness was back, and he opened his eyes. He was staring at a wall with a damp patch.

Garner's neck hurt, and his head throbbed as he took it all in. He was alone in bed, naked, covered by a pink duvet, and his uniform hung over the back of a chair. The cramped room was empty and he had never seen it before in his life. It was sleazy and shabby with an oppressively low ceiling. The floor boards were bare, except for a worn mat in front of the bed, and a chamber pot. By the dirty window with its finger-marked panes stood an armchair and a wooden table, with an ashtray. A single cigarette stub still smouldered in it.

He tried to recall what had happened. He remembered being caught at the enclosure, the men who surrounded him, he remembered being blindfolded, but after that nothing.

What was he doing here? He tried to get up, and groaned. He felt dizzy, but he had to find out where he was. He had to get to the window. He had to get to the door.

Then the door opened, and a woman in a threadbare dressing gown came in, carrying a bottle of brandy and two glasses. She put them on the table, then poured a generous measure into each glass.

She looked across at him, and saw that he was staring at her.

"Ach, so you are awake," she said in English with an excruciating German accent. She came towards him, the glasses in her hands. She was big, blowzy, and her dressing gown did little to conceal her balloon-like breasts. Black roots showed through her peroxided blonde hair, and she wore a lipstick that made her lips appear greasy.

She came over to the bed and bent over Garner.

"So, you have slept well, liebling," she said, sitting down on the bed. She placed the two glasses on the floor, and then put her arms round him, and pressed him to her massive bosom. "And now we have fun, yes?"

"Who are you?" he croaked, trying to fight her off and come to terms with reality. He tried again. "Where am I?"

"Bitte?"

"I have to get up," he said, shoving her aside. But she pushed him back on to the mattress.

"No. We are not finished. We have much time. Have a drink."

She bent down, gave one of the glasses to Garner and raised the other.

"We celebrate," she said. "Prosit."

She took a hard, long gulp of the brandy, then frowned.

"Liebling, you are not drinking, that is not nice. Hedwig will be sad."

She took the glass from his hand and held it to his mouth. He tried not to swallow, and some of the brandy dribbled down his chin. The blowzy blonde looked annoyed.

"Dummkopf!" she muttered.

He heard the sound of footsteps outside. Somebody was coming up the stairs. Then another woman burst in. She wore a laced up corset, and stockings held up by garters. Incongruously, she had her hair in pigtails. When she saw Garner in bed and the blonde, she paused.

"Geh weg," cried the blonde, angrily. "Kanst du nicht sehen ich mache Geschaeft?"

"Entschuldigen," replied the woman in pigtails, and

hurriedly shut the door. The blonde went over, and locked it from the inside.

"Now we do not get disturbed," she beamed.

Garner was beginning to think more clearly. His German did not let him down. "Go away," the blonde had said, "can't you see I'm doing business?" And she had used the familiar "du" with the other woman.

Though he still didn't understand how he got here, he now knew where he was, and what the blonde did for a living.

"Listen," he said, "this is a mistake. I have no money. I cannot pay. I must go."

She burst out laughing.

"Liebling, you are so sweet. Everything has been paid. All is OK." She bent forward and hugged him and through her dressing gown he could feel her flabby nipples against his chest. "And you are so nice, Hedwig would do it for nothing. You are Hedwig's boy friend." She kissed him again, wetly. "We only have Amis here. GIs. You are the first Englishman."

"Hedwig," he began matter of factly. She smiled coyly at him. "I need to get back. Where am I? Where is this?"

She seemed a little surprised. "Don't you know? You are in Freudenhof. The best house in Freudenhof. The best girls. And I am the best girl . . ."

"I have to get back to Waldheim," insisted Garner. "I am stationed there. With an American unit. Now let me get up."

"Ahh," cooed Hedwig, "but first we enjoy ourselves."

She undid the rest of her dressing gown, then stood up and stepped out of it. Naked she was big, and her large breasts were in scale with the rest of her. She was a Brunhilde, with an ample stomach and hips. She was gross.

"You like?" asked Hedwig.

Garner was sickened. She pulled back the duvet and wormed herself next to him in bed. She enfolded him in her arms, and entwined her legs round his.

"Now you only think of Hedwig," she crooned.

That was how he lay when the door crashed in.

There stood three soldiers in dark green berets, one of them a sergeant. The sergeant had a drawn .45 and he did not disguise his contempt when he saw Garner in bed with the blonde. But he stuck to protocol.

"Captain Garner?"

Garner sat up, very aware of his nakedness and how it all appeared. Hedwig, suddenly modest, grabbed the duvet and covered her breasts.

"Yes, sergeant."

"You're under arrest. Please get dressed."

The please sounded like a sneer.

"Now just a moment, sergeant . . ."

"Get dressed, sir," commanded the sergeant, "or we'll drag you back the way you are. You please yourself, sir."

The two soldiers with him were not smiling.

Hedwig started crying. "He has not paid me, the pig."

"Tough, sister," retorted the sergeant.

After Garner had dressed, several girls watched as he was led down the staircase in handcuffs.

"Don't come back," shouted one mockingly, "don't ever come back."

In the staff car, he asked the sergeant: "What's the charge anyway?"

The sergeant regarded him morosely. "I wouldn't know, sir. I only carry out orders."

"So, what are your orders?"

"To bring you in. And . . ."

He hesitated.

"Well?"

"If you try to escape, to shoot you. Sir."

"I think there's been a mistake," said Garner.

"Yes, sir." The sergeant allowed himself a chilly smile. "You made it."

57

15

The company emerged from the Aeroflot jet led by Simonov, who wore an overcoat with a sable fur collar. They were all smartly dressed, and smiled broadly. The last man off the plane was Lev Kopkin, the stage manager.

The embassy had laid on a suitable welcome at Heathrow, including two children who rushed forward and presented the leading players with bouquets of flowers.

Immigration formalities went smoothly and customs only cursorily inspected their luggage.

Andreyan felt superfluous. Leonov had insisted that he should be at Heathrow when the actors arrived, and had even provided an embassy car with chauffeur for him.

"I thought I'd meet them at the hotel," Andreyan suggested, but Leonov had already made up his mind.

"We should be seen to be there," he explained. He meant the KGB, but there was no need to be specific. Andreyan knew who "we" were.

Before the company arrived in London, the Directorate had already supplied the embassy with a file on each of the actors, giving their personal details, photographs, and useful background information. The file indicated that Kopkin acted as contact man, and could be called on, if necessary. It also advised that Kopkin would provide confidential reports during the London season, and that his contact would be Andreyan.

"Make yourself known to him, if you get the chance," Leonov had advised Andreyan.

He recognised Kopkin as the group filed out of the customs

hall. He looked like his file photo peering short sightedly through his gold rimmed spectacles. He was keeping well back, letting the actors take the limelight.

Then came the little reception in the Press Lounge. Simonov made a short speech, which was duly translated by a girl from the embassy.

"We are so happy to have come to the land of Shakespeare," Simonov declaimed in Russian, while the embassy girl rushed to keep up with him. "We are here, dear comrades, to strengthen our mutual cultural ties, and to cultivate the friendship and understanding of our two countries. The theatre brings truth and peace to our nations . . ."

It was a copy book speech, and it would do Simonov no harm at all with the Ministry. He was still in full flow, as the company lined up to have their pictures taken. Maya Petrova hastily linked arms with Borisov so that they would be photographed together. They had fixed smiles, and looked very happy.

Andreyan studied the people crowding round the group. He recognised some of them. As an information counsellor he had made occasional contact with them. He knew the man with the bow tie from the *Guardian*, and the BBC woman. And of course he knew the eager beaver from *Tass* who was flourishing the microphone of his tape recorder into everybody's face.

Andreyan's eyes kept returning to the actress beside the famous Borisov. She had a marvellous figure, and a dazzling smile. She knew how to dress, and he had a great desire to get to know her. He looked down at the list of names he had with him. Ah yes. That must be Maya Petrova. He promised himself that as soon as he got back to his office he would read her file. He wanted to know more about her.

She was certainly nestling close to Evgeny Borisov. He noticed how she had linked arms with him, and how, so it seemed to him, they exchanged a quite intimate look. Andreyan decided he must find out from the useful Kopkin if

59

they were lovers. He did not pursue whether that was official interest on behalf of the Directorate, or private curiosity. All he knew was that he found Maya Petrova unusually attractive.

As he was staring at her, she turned and caught his eyes. Their looks met, and for a moment they held. That was when Andreyan decided to introduce himself.

The BBC woman had cornered Simonov and the interpreter, and more pictures were being taken. Kopkin was standing rather forlornly by an airline counter.

"Comrade Kopkin?" enquired Andreyan courteously.

The little man looked at him nervously.

"It's all right, comrade," said Andreyan, "I'm from the embassy. Perhaps the Ministry gave you my name? Sergei Mikhailovitch Andreyan? I'm with the Directorate . . ."

Kopkin swallowed hard. "Oh yes. Of course. They told me . . . At your service, Comrade Andreyan . . ."

"We will be in contact," said Andreyan. "Just carry on."

"Where can I reach you?" asked Kopkin eagerly. "If necessary . . ." He was anxious to please. He wanted the Ministry to know that he was keen to do his job.

"You don't," replied Andreyan. "*I* get in touch with you. You understand?"

"I understand."

Andreyan nodded and moved off. He didn't like informers.

As he walked away, a man in a blue blazer watched him.

There's no doubt, thought John Alcott, men like Andreyan are a new model in the Directorate. They look like public school boys or Madison Avenue advertising men, they dress well, they have a ready smile, they speak English fluently, they like good living and have an eye for attractive women, and they are very dangerous.

He had never spoken to Andreyan, but he felt he knew him well. They had built up quite a dossier on him. They even knew the name of the milkman who delivered a pint a day to the Holland Park doorstep. They tapped his phone, which was a waste of time, and they knew he liked jazz, and sometimes went by himself to Ronnie Scott's club in Soho.

On the concourse, the party from Moscow gathered itself together. A coach was waiting for them outside the arrival building.

"So this is London," said Maya Petrova happily.

"What have you seen?" asked Borisov sourly. "An airport, that's all. All airports are alike. Sheremetievo, Heathrow, Kennedy. How is this different?"

"Oh, I'm so excited," cried Maya. "This is what I've been looking forward to." She glanced at him. "Haven't you?"

He hesitated.

"I'm not sure," he said finally.

"Come along, my children, we mustn't keep people waiting," boomed Simonov.

They boarded the coach. Andreyan watched it drive off, then got into the embassy car.

"Back to town," he ordered the driver.

John Alcott went into a phone box and dialled a London number. It was a direct line that went straight through and was known to very few individuals.

"Mr Rathbone?" said Alcott. "They're on their way."

16

They had been driving through the Bavarian countryside for more than an hour, and Garner had lost his sense of direction. Once they passed through a small village, but this wasn't the way back to Waldheim that he knew.

Then along the country road they came to a wayside shrine, the old weather-beaten statue of the Virgin regarding them

61

with an enigmatic smile. Some bunches of faded flowers lay at her feet.

The one thing Garner didn't expect happened. The car slowed down and stopped beside the Madonna.

"Let's get out," said the sergeant.

"What, here?"

"Right here, sir." He was very disciplined, and couldn't help observing protocol.

The other two soldiers remained in the drab olive military car.

"What's going on, sergeant?" asked Garner.

The sergeant produced a packet of cigarettes. "Smoke, sir?"

For a moment, Garner felt panic. This was like the ritual of an execution. The condemned man being offered his final cigarette.

No one else was around. There was nobody to witness anything.

The sergeant glanced at his manacled wrists. "Oh, I guess you don't need those any more, do you, sir?" he said, and unlocked the handcuffs.

Garner rubbed his wrists, and looked at him, puzzled.

"What exactly is happening, sergeant?" he demanded.

The sergeant offered his pack of cigarettes. Garner shook his head.

"Why have we stopped?"

"Orders, sir." His tone implied that that explained everything.

Damn it, thought Garner. I've had enough of their games.

"Well, I'm not going to stand around here . . ." he began, then stopped. The sergeant put his hand on his pistol holster.

"I wouldn't try anything, sir," he said pleasantly.

The other two Green Berets were staring at him from the car.

The sergeant was looking up the road, and Garner saw what he had spotted; a blue Volkswagen approaching.

The sergeant waved, and the Volkswagen pulled up beside the staff car, alongside the shrine.

Major Skinner got out, and returned the sergeant's salute. "Well done," he grunted. He glanced at Garner. "Anything to report, sergeant?" he asked.

"Nothing at all, sir."

Skinner nodded. He had a leathery, weather-beaten face, and beneath his beret his head was almost shaven. He had a deep scar under his left eye. He had won the Silver Star at the last defence of Tan Son Nhut. He was a man who had suffered, and would one day have his revenge.

"Major Skinner, what exactly are we doing here?" asked Garner.

For the first time Skinner acknowledged Garner's presence.

"Ah," he said coldly, "our British ally. What's your problem, captain?"

"Your men have dragged me here . . ."

"Now listen, and listen good," said Skinner very quietly, butting in. His rage was barely repressed. "You're lucky you're not one of us. If you were a Yank, I'd throw the fucking book at you. You know what I'd like to do with a son of a bitch like you?" He controlled himself with difficulty. "Some fucking officer you are, going over the hill, shacking up in a lousy cat house, and having to be dragged back to your outfit."

"You know that's not what happened," said Garner, but he understood.

Skinner walked round him slowly in a circle, as if he was inspecting some strange object. "You've had a nervous breakdown, haven't you? You're a psycho." He took a deep breath. "I can't have you court martialled, but I'm not having you set foot in our barracks again. You're through. I'm going to do Uncle Sam a big favour. Here." He held out a bunch of keys. "Take them."

Garner stared at him.

"They're the keys to that Volkswagen. Get into it, and start driving. Shove off, mister. Now." He grabbed Garner's hand, and pressed the bunch of keys into it.

"Your things are already in the car. It's all fixed. You

63

ought to thank me, mister." Skinner bared his teeth. "And the colonel."

They were all looking at him, the sergeant, the two men in the car, Skinner.

"Don't worry about the paper work," smiled Skinner. "We'll take care of that. It'll all be done by the book. Strictly regulation . . ."

Garner felt very cold suddenly. "You know you can't do this . . ."

"Try us," said Skinner. He took Garner by the arm. "Let's go. Take off."

"Where?"

"What do I care? Go to hell. Back where you came from. You could even be across the Czech border in a couple of hours. Right, sergeant?"

"Right, sir," nodded the sergeant, poker faced.

"The tank's full," said Skinner. "Just keep driving."

Garner got into the car, and started the engine. Major Skinner tapped on the window. Garner rolled it down.

"You never did tell me," leered Skinner, his face pressed close. "In that cat house. Was she a good fuck?" And he slammed his fist against the car door like a starter's signal.

Garner put his foot down hard on the accelerator. He wanted to get away from them as fast as he could. In the rear-view mirror he could see them standing round the staff car, all watching him. He was hunched forward over the wheel, tense, half expecting a bullet to hit him at any moment.

But the bullet never came.

He drove along the country road looking for a sign-post, a marker, anything to establish his exact location. His first priority was to find a telephone and call the consulate in Munich. That was where he had his contact.

He had to get a message to Rathbone as quickly as possible.

17

As a public relations exercise, the embassy reception for the Moscow theatre company was a glittering success, and that's the way the ambassador duly reported it to the Foreign Ministry.

The actors played their roles to perfection, with Simonov basking in the limelight, and showing his cast how to do it. He sat happily on a sofa in the ornate room, giving an interview to an enthusiastic man with a bow tie who was recording him and the interpreter for a *Kaleidoscope* programme.

Drinks circulated on trays carried by smiling embassy secretaries, and above it all rose the chatter of conversation and occasional outbursts of laughter.

But the star of the evening was Maya Petrova. She had taken great care to appear at her most dazzling. After a lengthy session at a hairdresser, she had spent hours on her make-up. She wore a simple black dress which contrasted magnificently with her pale complexion and bright red lips, and gave a delicious hint of the figure it covered. Maya's smile was warm, inviting and she readily turned to whoever approached her, and made them feel welcome. She had a knack of listening to what strangers were saying as if she was really interested, which flattered any man's ego. She was determined to be noticed.

Andreyan stood quietly on the sidelines, watching her with some amusement. She was on the make, that was clear. At Heathrow she had made a spectacular entry: now she was following it up in style. And he noticed something else; her eyes were roaming, taking in all the people around her, assessing them, grading them. She would study someone for a moment, then turn her attention to someone else. She wanted to impress, and she was anxious to find the right people to pick on.

Occasionally, she gave a fleeting smile to Evgeny Borisov, then she'd turn elsewhere. Borisov, as befitted a performer of his status, a People's Artist, was chatting with the ambassador, and an English impresario who specialised in bringing Soviet artists over to Britain. He had been instrumental in arranging this tour, and was a welcome visitor at the embassy.

Andreyan went over to one of the secretaries and took two glasses of champagne off her tray. Then he moved across to Maya.

"I thought you might like a drink," he smiled.

"I've already had one," she said and smiled back. He knew she was trying to place him. "I mustn't drink too much, must I?"

"Why not, Maya Aleksandrovna?"

She arched an eyebrow. "You know who I am?"

"Of course," said Andreyan. Who she was, her lover, her antecedents, everything. The dossier was detailed. "I am a devoted admirer."

"And who are you?"

"Sergei Mikhailovitch Andreyan. A diplomat." He raised his glass. "To you."

As they clinked glasses, his eyes appraised her quite openly. Her face, her neck, the curves of her breasts under the dress.

She looked straight at him. "A diplomat? Here at the embassy?"

He nodded.

"How fascinating. You must be very important."

"Not at all," said Andreyan. "But I am very lucky."

"Oh?"

"To have met you. If I was not here at the embassy I would never have had the opportunity, would I?"

She smiled again. "Oh, I don't know, Sergei Mikhailovitch. The opportunity might well have offered itself."

He noticed that Colonel Leonov was watching them from across the room. Not that there was any reason why Andreyan shouldn't chat up the delicious Maya Petrova. Still . . .

"I am very excited about being in London," she said.

Andreyan took the plunge. "Perhaps I will be able to show you one or two things, while you're over here."

The way she widened her eyes pleased him.

"That sounds intriguing . . ."

"So," said a voice. "I see you have found company."

They turned to find Borisov with a fixed smile on his face.

"Introduce me, Maya," he instructed.

She flashed him a cold look. There were times when three were definitely not company.

"Sergei Mikhailovitch, this is People's Artist Evgeny Alekseivitch Borisov."

"Your reputation has preceded you," said Andreyan, and Borisov stiffened for a fleeting moment. "Everybody at the embassy has been looking forward to seeing you perform in London."

"I hope I will not be a disappointment," murmured Borisov. He turned to Maya. "Will you be long, my dear?"

"I think the ambassador is looking for you," she said coolly. "Over there, with our producer." It was almost as if she was passing on a command. Borisov's smile was taut, but he played it out with aplomb.

"I will see you later," he said. He knew Maya. He could see she was interested in the diplomat. So often he had found her a nuisance, and wished he was rid of her. Now, seeing her chatting to this suave man, he wanted to take her with him.

Borisov walked off, and she flashed a quick smile at Andreyan. You understand, it said, he means nothing. Just a colleague. A friend. But nothing serious.

67

"Your champagne is getting warm," pointed out Andreyan.

"I think you want to get me drunk," she reprimanded mischievously.

"And why should I want that?"

"I could think of something."

For a moment their eyes met.

"I would like to see you again," said Andreyan.

"To show me London?"

"Who knows?" said Andreyan carefully.

"I'm going to be very busy, Sergei Mikhailovitch. Simonov, that man there, is a slave driver. We have seven performances a week, and rehearsals, and costume fittings, and I don't know if there will be time . . ."

"There will be time," said Andreyan firmly.

"The discipline is very strict . . ."

"We will get together," promised Andreyan.

She surprised herself by her reply.

"I'd like that," she said.

It could do no harm, she rationalised. He is obviously a high flyer. Moscow wouldn't have sent him to London, wouldn't have assigned him to the embassy if he wasn't. He is confident, sure of himself, even in this room, with the ambassador a few feet away, and all the other senior people. Perhaps he is KGB . . . No, it wouldn't do any harm at all to get a little involved.

She smiled at him and joined a group of actors by the buffet, where the canapés of caviare, smoked salmon and herring were being decimated.

Borisov saw it all. His annoyance with Maya had subsided. After all, their relationship would soon be terminated by events. Sipping a glass of mineral water, he concentrated on Colonel Leonov. They had been briefly introduced, and what was said was enough to tell Borisov that this was the man from the Directorate.

So, he knew instinctively, was the fellow who had been making a play for Maya.

Borisov was not a man who prayed, but at this point he wouldn't have minded the assurance of some higher power that nothing was going to go wrong.

18

The activities of the pirate station calling itself Russkaya Volya were beginning to be a gadfly to the Committee of State Security. It wasn't so much that the broadcasts were important, it was the impotence of the state machine to counter them which enraged Marshal Viktor Pavlov, the new chairman of the Committee.

For Sergein Lapin, the Minister for Radio and Television, Russkaya Volya was like a bad ulcer which played up at awkward times. The illicit broadcasts, irregular and haphazard, baffled the state monitoring service.

To start with, they were not what would be expected from a foreign propaganda station. Analysis of the transmissions showed that they were hostile to the United States and to NATO. This made them very dangerous, because it meant that a Russian listening to them might be misled into thinking they were of local origin. The theme often seemed to be that inefficiency and corruption were harming the efforts of the socialist countries, and that communists deserved something better than the leadership they were getting from the Kremlin.

Also, the strange station spent a lot of time trying to make it appear as if it was broadcasting illicitly from inside the Soviet Union.

"Comrades," the announcer would say, "we don't know how long we can stay on the air tonight, the locator vans are out trying to find us, we may have to break off transmission at any time."

On two occasions the broadcasts came to a sudden, dramatic end.

"They're here," shouted a voice, against a background of hammering on doors and glass breaking, then dead silence. It gave a very faithful impression of an underground radio station being raided. The theatricals were realistically done, and those who picked up the broadcasts must have been glued to their sets with excitement.

The KGB and the GRU went to great lengths each time to check if, anywhere in the country, there had been such an incident the night before – and of course they always drew a blank.

And because the station claimed to be Russian, broadcasting to Russians, the Central Committee was increasingly concerned about it. Dissatisfied communists would spread discontent.

Russkaya Volya cunningly supplied a steady ration of rumours to its listeners which, if spread around, could make millions insecure.

For example, one broadcast alleged that "unpatriotic hooligans" had sabotaged cars on the assembly line at the Volzhsky automobile works, and that as a result hundreds of the Zhiguli model, the most popular car in the USSR, modelled on the Fiat saloon, were unsafe to drive. The station claimed that the faults had not been spotted before the cars were released, and that anyone driving such a Zhiguli was in great danger.

Another broadcast claimed that doctors at the Institute of Transplants and Artificial Body Organs in Moscow were experimenting with real organs taken from prisoners in the Gulag. It was sheer nonsense, but echoed and re-echoed by gossips, spread around by ignorant people who didn't even know where the story had originated, it might cause consternation.

Allegations of profiteering, neglect and official inefficiency

70

were all neatly inserted, almost obliquely, into so-called news stories.

Jamming Russkaya Volya wasn't easy. The Central Committee had 3,000 powerful transmitters at its disposal which could superimpose a chorus of whining static and domestic broadcasts over Western stations, but they had to cover the enormous output of all transmissions from Western Germany and British soil – 1,000 hours a week of propaganda from Voice of America, Radio Free Europe, and Radio Liberty, from Bonn, more from the BBC, the French and others.

Also, it was very difficult to blot out a station which came on at irregular times, on different days, and followed an erratic pattern.

The tracing of Russkaya Volya had now been given highest priority. Of course, even if they located it, there was still the problem of dealing with it, if it was based within foreign jurisdiction.

However, Marshal Pavlov was a man of great imagination, and as soon as he took over his job, he had decided to tackle this problem like a chess game. He was an excellent player, and when he was still at the Frunze Academy, it had been noted that he was both a ruthless and a humorous player.

The experts of Radio Technical Intelligence Group were cautious people, and Lapin had, in the meantime, received a report from them in which, without committing themselves, they hinted that they believed the transmissions came from north-west Europe.

"It would seem possible, though not certain, that the broadcasts originate from somewhere in, near or around the British Isles," said the report warily.

Sergein Lapin got very excited about this.

"We must ask our Resident in London to investigate," he pressed. "I suggest we sent an urgent signal to our people there."

Marshal Pavlov beamed at him. He always enjoyed being a few moves ahead of his opponent.

71

"That's already been taken care of, comrade minister," he announced. "The wheels were set in motion some time ago."

Lapin did not hide his surprise.

"I only got the report this morning," he said. "How on earth did you know?"

The marshal smiled.

"Dear friend, that is my job."

19

As a step on the career ladder, Her Britannic Majesty's Consulate in Munich does not rate very high. The daily agenda of lost passports, visas for Middle East travel documents, financial assistance for destitute British tourists, and cultural relations does not produce an atmosphere of feverish excitement.

But, from time to time, more interesting things occupy certain members of the staff. Creighton, for instance, had his own safe in his office, of which only he knew the combination. He occasionally received coded signals which only he could decipher, and, now and then, he would make trips. To the Czech border. To Austria.

Creighton did not only owe his allegiance to the Foreign and Commonwealth Office. His interests were rather more far reaching, and his talents deceptive. He talked cricket a lot, and liked playing bridge. He spoke reasonable German, but never let on that he also spoke Hungarian.

Peggy, who doubled as secretary for Creighton and the Vice Consul, quite fancied him, and was rather disappointed when he took her to the Oktoberfest and stayed respectfully sober.

She knew something hush hush was going on when Creighton told her that a Captain Garner was coming, and could she let him know the moment he turned up.

There had been a call from Garner earlier in the day, and afterwards Creighton had secluded himself in his office and encyphered a lengthy signal which he asked to be sent to London, priority.

Peggy was cleared for secret information, but Creighton kept it all to himself. He also made a call to London, and soon afterwards a coded telex came for Creighton signed "Rathbone".

"Something up, James?" she asked.

He shook his head. "Heavens no. Just bumf."

She didn't believe a word of it.

Garner was due at the consulate about 3 p.m. and when he hadn't arrived an hour later, Creighton came into her room.

"Any word from Garner?"

"No. I would have told you," she said reproachfully. She prided herself on her efficiency.

"Well, let me know the moment he gets here," he instructed.

"Is he something important?"

"Not really," he said. "I'll be in my office."

He was sitting there, doing the crossword in a two day old edition of *The Times*, when she came in.

"James," she said.

He looked up. "Yes? He's here?"

"I've just had the police on the phone."

"The police?"

"I'm afraid there's been an accident. They say a British officer's been killed. Captain Garner."

He stared at her and slowly, very slowly, said: "Garner's *dead*?"

"I'm so sorry," said Peggy.

"Tell me exactly what they said." He was very tense, very quiet.

73

"It's a bit confusing. It's the state police. They say he was driving on the Autobahn and a lorry crashed into him. They're still trying to find the lorry."

"What do you mean?"

She looked at the pad in her hand, on which she had made notes.

"They said the lorry did not stop. And Captain Garner's car caught fire and exploded."

"Good god!" He looked like a man in shock.

"They're trying to sort it out. They say the car he was driving was stolen. A blue Volkswagen. Reported stolen from Waldheim. I don't know where that is . . ."

"I see," said Creighton, matter of factly. He was thinking, rapidly.

"I don't understand what he was doing in a stolen car," Peggy was saying, but he cut her short.

"Thank you," he said. She stood, surprised.

"I have to send a flash signal to London," added Creighton. "If you'll excuse me . . ."

He started to go over to his private safe.

The message he encyphered for Rathbone was short and to the point.

Things had gone wrong. Badly wrong.

20

Standing guard outside Colonel Blau's office door was a tricky assignment. Like a lightning conductor, the man on the post was the first to detect the colonel's mood each day. The troopers snapped to attention, never knowing how the colonel would react. Sometimes he just nodded curtly, and marched straight on. But there were days when he stopped, and coldly scrutinised the soldier. Then anything could happen.

He might grunt, and say nothing more. Or he would frown, and suddenly find fault.

"Straighten that, soldier."

"Yessir."

"Don't let me see you like that again."

"Nossir."

If that was all, the guard mouthed a silent prayer of thanks that the saints had preserved him against further divine rage. But there were occasions when the colonel suddenly jabbed the startled guard with his finger.

"You're a disgrace, soldier. Brace up."

Such a reprimand was usually followed by thirty days' latrine duty, or restriction to barracks, supervised by Major Skinner, which was an experience to be avoided.

The colonel's door was always guarded, day and night. It was symbolic duty, typical of the way he ran his unit. A private tradition of a private army.

Most men who got the assignment outside the door hoped fervently that they would stay invisible, and be ignored until their relief came. Yet, like all the Green Berets, they were devoted to Blau, and despite their fears, it was a post of honour to stand guard for him. Any of them would have given their life for him.

Blau cared for his men. There were stories of the colonel cutting red tape to facilitate compassionate leave home in cases of personal emergency. He once stayed up half the night consoling an NCO whose wife was suing for divorce. It was said that in another case he personally paid the air fare of a trooper whose father had been taken ill, and who couldn't get a military flight for a week. He listened to his men's problems, knew about their families, remembered their first names, and their home towns.

On this morning, he came to the office at 7:10 a.m. It wasn't unusual for Blau to be so early; he didn't stick to

75

official hours, and he liked to be around when he wasn't expected.

The guard outside the door stiffened, and saluted him. As was procedure, he stared straight ahead, trying not to attract the colonel's eyes, yet attempting to gauge his mood. He had a surprise.

"Nice day, soldier," beamed the colonel.

The trooper swallowed. "Yessir."

Blau nodded amiably, and entered his office. The soldier held his breath. Would he reappear? Was this some kind of sucker trap? Was the colonel trying on something?

But the door remained shut, and the trooper relaxed. Soon after, Lieutenant Jones was summoned.

"Good morning, K.D.," said the colonel.

She looked at him, surprised. Such familiarity first thing was rare.

"Sit down," ordered the colonel. "Grab a notebook."

He was definitely in a good mood, she decided. She waited dutifully.

Blau looked at her approvingly. She was sharp. He approved of sharp people. She didn't say an unnecessary word, she was efficient, she handled herself well, and she had changed his mind about women in the Army. At one time, Blau would never have tolerated a woman officer in his outfit, and when the Pentagon had decided that females could be assigned to combat units in the field in support roles, he had sworn to ensure it would never happen to his command.

The orders assigning her referred to "Jones, K.D.", so how the hell was he expected to know she would turn out to be a woman. But she had convinced him. Hell, she could be a man, she was so intelligent. Except she sure didn't look like a man.

That was the enigma about Jones. What the hell was she doing in the military? She wasn't a dyke, but she had never got involved with any of the men in the unit. Or any other man, as far as he knew, since she had arrived in Germany.

76

As for the officers, they seemed a little wary of her. They'd seen her on the assault course, they had watched her in combat games; she was a crack shot; and she had become the colonel's aide. All in all, they kept their distance.

"I want you to type this yourself," said the colonel. "Only one copy, for me personally. I don't want any of this to go through channels. Is that clear?"

"Yes, sir. It's classified, I take it?"

She said it without interest, coolly, as if it was a perfectly normal procedure.

Blau cleared his throat. "It's – sensitive. Very sensitive. It's to General Norland. Major General Cyrus Norland."

She made a note and looked up. "The deputy commander, USAREUR. At Heidelberg?"

Her face betrayed nothing.

"That's right," said Blau. "It's for him only. No other eyes to see."

"Yes, sir. Subject?"

"Captain Garner."

Her pencil smoothly recorded his instructions.

"One. Captain Garner," began the Colonel, pacing up and down as he dictated, "on TDY this command as exchange officer under the NATO Special Forces training programme, absented himself from his duty station without authority at approximately 1800 hours on Tuesday."

Her shorthand was immaculate. She waited for him to continue, her face expressionless.

"Two. At 1130 hours on Thursday, Captain Garner was found in an off limits establishment in company with a known prostitute." The colonel broke off to see if she reacted. Her face remained blank. "As he was AWOL, he was placed under arrest, and arrangements were made for an escort from this command to return him to this unit.

"Three. At approximately 1500 hours, Captain Garner escaped from custody. He appears to have stolen a civilian Volkswagen.

"Four. The Bavarian State Police informed this command

77

on Friday that at about 1700 hours Captain Garner had been involved in an automobile accident on the Munich autobahn. He was at the time driving the stolen Volkswagen. Regretfully, the vehicle involved in the accident did not stop.

"Five. The British Consulate in Munich has been informed of the facts.

"Six. The disposal of this case is no longer of concern to this command since Captain Garner, a British citizen, was a member of a foreign service, and not subject to US military laws and regulations." Colonel Blau stopped dictating and looked at her. "Well, how's that?" he asked.

"I'll type it right away, with one copy for you," she replied. But she spoke with a slight hesitation. Blau did not miss that.

"Something bothering you, lieutenant?"

She paused. Then she said slowly: "If this is going all the way to Heidelberg, to the general . . . well, sir, I was wondering. It doesn't mention anything about Site 11 . . ."

He sat down.

"What about Site 11?" he asked silkily.

"Well, sir . . . I heard something about . . . him snooping around Site 11. He had a run in with the security guard or something . . ."

"Lieutenant Jones," said Blau. "Let's just forget about Site 11, shall we? We don't discuss Site 11."

Her eyes looked at him challengingly. "But supposing there's a board of inquiry . . ."

Blau smiled. "K.D., I don't have to spell anything out to you. There won't be a board of inquiry, I promise you. Tubby and I were classmates at the Point."

"Tubby?"

"General Norland. He takes care of things. He'll take care of this."

"Yes, sir," she nodded. "But what about the British? Garner was SAS. Won't they want to know what happened? I mean, will they believe their man got killed going over the hill to fuck a whore?"

78

If a man had said it, Blau wouldn't have blinked an eyelid. Coming from this attractive blonde, the language jolted.

"SAS officers don't go AWOL and steal cars, do they?" she continued.

He recovered himself. "K.D.," he said slowly, "I'll tell you something for your ears only, understand?" He paused. "I wouldn't worry about the SAS. I don't think they're worried about him. And I wouldn't worry about the British Army. Relax. Like I say, it'll all be taken care of . . ."

"You mean, he wasn't SAS at all?" she asked.

He admired her at that point. Christ, she was on the ball. With a woman like that one could go far.

"Now," he said, "when you've typed that document, I want you to do a nice little courier job. I want you to take it to Heidelberg yourself, and hand it to General Norland personally. Only to him. No one else."

"Of course, not through channels," she smiled, echoing him.

"Smart girl," said the colonel. And he meant it.

21

Discretion played a big part in Andreyan's life, but bringing Maya to his flat in Holland Park was a reasonable risk. Leonov might raise an eyebrow, but he would disapprove much more if Andreyan had booked into a hotel. That might have involved an assumed name, and could have led to complications.

Andreyan had the first floor flat of a Victorian house rented by the embassy. The ground floor was occupied by Kutuzov, the assistant naval attaché, and his fat wife. The

Kutuzovs were boring people, but good neighbours because they spent most of their weekends at Hawkhurst, the embassy's country club in Kent. They treated Andreyan with caution; they knew what he represented, and to whom he reported.

Naturally, they were all aware that the house in the quiet side street behind Holland Park Avenue was under surveillance. Sometimes Andreyan would look at the curtained windows of the houses across the road and wonder behind which one the camera was positioned. Kutuzov didn't think the British went to that length, they probably merely carried out spot checks. Andreyan suspected they were rather more thorough.

There was no doubt, however, that their phones were constantly monitored, and the post was tactfully scrutinised, even the circulars and free offers which, unwanted though they were, came to Soviet diplomats by second class mail.

Maya did not play hard to get when Andreyan came back stage after the second evening's performance at the theatre in Hammersmith. The first night had been a big hit, with a party afterwards to celebrate the London opening. Andreyan waited for the following night to pick her up after the show.

"I really shouldn't be gadding about, Sergei Mikhailovitch," she said, holding on to his arm. "There is an extra rehearsal in the morning . . ."

"The morning is a long way off. You need to relax."

"Where are we going?" she asked. She noticed that Borisov was watching them.

"A little restaurant," said Andreyan.

It was behind Kensington High Street, and dimly lit. The menu was in French, and there were only a few tables. One of its attractions was that one could see who came in. A shadow would not remain unnoticed.

Maya looked across at Andreyan, and liked what she saw. He was quite handsome, she thought, and he had interesting eyes. Pity that they were never still, always roaming, but they were shrewd, intelligent. He was cultured too. He could provide an entertaining interlude.

"I want to ask you something, Maya Aleksandrovna," he said gently.

"Oh?"

"If it embarrasses you, I will understand, but I think I should know."

She laughed a little nervously. "What is it that the embassy wants to know?"

"Not the embassy," he said. "I need to know. It is your relationship with Evgeny Alekseivitch. How serious is it? How permanent?"

Her eyes opened wide. "Why do you ask?"

"I do not want to complicate matters."

She had to stop herself bursting out laughing. She never would have believed he was so old fashioned, so formal. "Relationship? My dear, he is a colleague. A fellow artiste. I respect him, of course . . ."

He regarded her stonily. "My information is . . ." He corrected himself. "I believe that perhaps you both have a . . . an understanding? You see, I do not want to cause complications. I would like to see a lot of you while you are in London, Maya Aleksandrovna, but I do not want to do anything incorrect."

My God, she thought, he talks as if we are negotiating a twenty year treaty.

"I saw him looking at you when we left the theatre," added Andreyan. "If it's in any way awkward . . ."

She reached out and took his hand. "Sergei Mikhailovitch, there is nothing between him and me, I assure you. He is a married man, very happily married. I think you have misunderstood . . ."

That's not what the Ministry's reports say, he thought. Or your file.

She smiled at him, and in the candlelight she looked bewitching. "Why so serious anyway? We are not arranging a marriage, are we?"

In the taxi afterwards, she nestled against him. She had an expensive French perfume, and he wondered where she had got it from – it would hardly be on sale in Moscow. Not that that should be a problem for her. Maya, he was beginning to find out, was a woman who took her opportunities where she found them.

Once he glanced out of the back window of the cab.

"What are you looking for?" she asked innocently.

"Nothing," he said.

"To see if we're being followed?"

He gave her a quick look. He was surprised that she should be aware of such things.

"Does it matter?" she said, without waiting for his answer. "Or are you ashamed of being seen with an actress, Mr Diplomat?"

That was when he leant over and kissed her.

When they arrived at his house, she made no attempt to get out of the cab.

"You know what the time is?" she said.

"After midnight."

"I will be in trouble if I don't get back to the hotel. We are not supposed to stay out . . ."

He knew the instructions. A coach took the performers to and from their hotel in Bloomsbury to the theatre in Hammersmith and returned them after the show. He had a vision of Lev Kopkin, keen to prove how well he did his job, eagerly reporting to him that Maya Aleksandrovna Petrova had not been on the coach after the performance, and had stayed out all night. A gross breach of discipline. A matter for the Ministry.

It would be amusing.

"Don't worry," Andreyan assured her. "I'll take care of it."

Yes, she thought at that moment, I *was* right. He is KGB.

She got out of the cab. "Just one drink," she said.

The lights were out in the Kutuzovs' ground floor flat.

82

They always went to bed by eleven. Andreyan led the way upstairs.

"Make yourself at home," said Andreyan. "The bathroom is along the corridor."

He went over to the big front windows to draw the curtains. He looked down the street. It was empty. The house opposite was dark. No one was watching him as far as he knew, not that he cared a damn. They could make a film and a sound recording of everything that was going to happen from now on.

Maya came into the room.

"You've got a nice place here," she commented. By Moscow standards, it was high luxury.

"It's an embassy flat," said Andreyan. "It comes with the job."

She regarded him challengingly across the glass of Scotch she had requested ("I am in England, I would like Scotch").

"Tell me," she asked, "do you always bring your women here?"

He hesitated. "You're asking me to betray diplomatic secrets."

"I wouldn't dream of asking you to betray anything," she smiled. She nodded at a framed photograph of an officer in Soviet Army uniform and a dark haired woman, standing by a bookcase. "Who are they?"

"My parents."

Maya went over, picked up the picture and studied it more closely.

"Your father, he's a general?"

"Yes."

She put the frame down. "Are you the only son?"

"No," said Andreyan curtly.

"Oh? How many brothers?"

"Just one."

"I have a sister," said Maya. "She is very dull. She is a paediatrician."

"If she's like you, I'm sure she isn't dull."

83

Maya smiled. "How is it that you are not married, Sergei Mikhailovitch? I thought they liked our people in foreign countries to be married?"

"They also like people who are mobile. Specialists. Always available."

"Like you?"

He shrugged.

She drained her whisky, then looked at the slim gold watch on her wrist. "It is very late. I must go."

She was sitting on the sofa and he went over, took her hands, and slowly pulled her to her feet.

"Oh no," he said. "You still haven't seen the bedroom."

22

Scattered round Central London are buildings which, on the whole, have singularly uninspiring façades, and are never listed in the phone book. Some disguise their identity with misleading name plates describing them as offices of the Inland Revenue, the Department of Health and Social Security, the Ministry of Transport, and, in one case, the Inner London Probation Service. Others remain completely anonymous.

Within these buildings are housed the branches, sections, divisions, departments, and the off-shoots, of the British Intelligence apparatus. To most people, who pass them daily, they are invisible.

Few pedestrians entering Euston Square underground station at the corner of Gower Street take much notice of the six storied office block access. People who shop at Liberty's department store hardly ever give a second look at the curtained windows of the bland, square block in Great Marlborough Street. The squat building in Ebury Bridge Road does not attract attention. Nor does the block of offices in Northumberland Avenue. As for the red brick and stone neo-Georgian building in Curzon Street, it is faceless to the point of absurdity. Horseferry Road, South Audley Street, Regent Street, all have their invisible offices.

Rathbone had an anonymous office in Great Peter Street. SL3 – Special Liaison, Rathbone's department – kept to itself. It reported to IS35 – Intelligence Secretariat 35. Its premises, equally featureless, were in Marsham Street.

There were those, in the inner circle of the Intelligence Directorate, who viewed Rathbone's section with a certain misgiving. To start with, the designation itself was deceptive. Rathbone didn't really liaise with anybody. He did his own thing. His section worked to his orders. There was no SL1 or SL2. SL3 was the only department.

Once, at a rather heated meeting of the Joint Intelligence Committee, somebody had directly challenged Rathbone.

"Who do you liaise with anyway, specially or otherwise?" the representative from MI6 had asked.

"Special Projects," replied Rathbone, poker faced. "Special Liaison liaises with Special Projects. I can't say anything beyond that."

He could get away with that sort of thing with almost anybody – except Cheyne.

Cheyne, as head of Intelligence Secretariat 35, was the line to the top. He had the entry, and the clout. He played golf with the Director, and watched polo at Windsor with the Minister. Cheyne could not be crossed.

And he had summoned Rathbone. Rather formally.

"You know I don't ask questions, Colin," began Cheyne. "That's not how you and I work."

Rathbone knew immediately that questions were about to be asked.

"It's the Garner business. Untidy. Very untidy," went on Cheyne, playing with an engraved paper knife. He had

85

acquired it in Cairo, and twice, over the years, he had accidentally cut himself with its vicious, razor sharp blade. But he still liked playing with the knife. "I'm getting tremors. Ministry of Defence. Foreign Office. Quite a few tremors. Five on the Richter scale." He looked expectantly at Rathbone. "What's it all about, Colin?"

Rathbone took a deep breath. "You know we picked up these rumours? About this American unit in Bavaria. Undergoing special training. And the possibility that they'd got some obsolete nuclear weapons."

Cheyne pursed his lips. "Colin," he said, and he sounded a little disapproving. "The Americans are on to that. The Pentagon is investigating."

"Well, maybe. I thought it prudent for us to do some investigating of our own." He sat back and waited for the storm.

But Cheyne spoke quite mildly. "I see. So you sent Garner. Posing as an Army officer. On a training exchange?"

"As my report explained."

Cheyne twirled the paper knife on the desk. It came to rest with the point towards Rathbone. "Sorry about that," he said. "You'd be guilty, you know, if this was a naval court martial."

Rathbone said nothing.

Cheyne frowned. "Where were we? Ah yes. It's their problem, isn't it?"

"If some nutcase sets off a nuclear landmine under a Russian installation, it'll be our problem too, won't it?"

Cheyne stared hard at the knife blade. "Did Garner find out anything?" he asked after a pause.

Rathbone picked his words carefully. "I think he found what he was looking for. The last message I got was that he was returning urgently. He was making for the consulate in Munich."

Cheyne reached across languidly and drew a thin file towards him. He opened it and read the top page briefly, to refresh his memory. Then he closed the file.

"That's when he was killed on the autobahn. Driving a *stolen* car? After he'd been placed under arrest by the Yanks. What the hell was going on?"

"I think he found out too much," said Rathbone, looking straight at Cheyne. "He didn't steal a car, and it wasn't an accident. I think the whole thing was rigged. By this Colonel Blau."

Cheyne's eyebrows shot up a shade. "Tell me, did the Americans know that you were operating in their territory?"

"Not in so many words."

Cheyne smiled coldly. "You're too damn independent, Colin."

"But they know now," said Rathbone.

"And?"

"They promised they'd take care of it."

"And if they don't?"

"I will," replied Rathbone quietly.

Cheyne leant back in his chair, feeling the tip of the paper knife's blade, as if to reassure himself of its sharpness.

Rathbone waited.

Finally Cheyne said: "You've seen the central file."

Rathbone nodded.

"This Colonel Blau. He has connections. Interesting connections." Cheyne paused. "You're on to it?"

"Of course."

"All right." Cheyne stood up. "Be careful, Colin. I don't want an earthquake. If you do anything drastic, cover your tracks. Our tracks. Understand?"

"Of course," agreed Rathbone. Whoever went down, Cheyne was going to survive.

"If people start asking questions, I'll fudge the answers. But you take care."

"Understood," said Rathbone.

Cheyne still had the knife in his hand. He now laid it on the desk. "Keep me posted, Colin."

Rathbone gave him a nod.

"Oh, and Colin . . ."

87

Rathbone had reached the door. Now he stopped and waited.

"Pity about Garner," said Cheyne.

23

They all avoided his eyes when he got to the Ministry. Lapin was not a sensitive man, but even he sensed that something was wrong before he even took off his overcoat. The guard downstairs had been respectful enough, but as soon as he arrived on the second floor he felt the atmosphere. The smile his secretary gave him was definitely strained. Vorsov, his chief clerk, looked distinctly nervous.

It was explained when he read the transcript of Russkaya Volya's overnight transmission. The pirate station, diligently monitored and recorded, had excelled itself.

"Is it not time, comrades, that something was done about Sergein Lapin, the so-called Minister of Radio and Television," the illicit broadcast had declaimed. "This incompetent does not serve the party well, and should be relieved of his post. How on earth does he survive as a member of the Central Committee?

"He uses others as a scapegoat for his own inefficiency and inability. It was to cover up his own mistakes that he dismissed Viktor Lyuboutsev, the chief executive of Soviet television news. He was responsible for the scandal of Vladimir Danchev, the newscaster who denounced the glorious heroism of our sons and brothers in Afghanistan. Comrades, we deserve a minister who can do his job, not a time server who sits behind a desk to feather his own nest . . ."

Lapin's hand shook slightly. He stared at the typewritten

lines in disbelief. He was an expert in disinformation but this was a new dimension. These bastards were setting him up personally. This poison was being dripped at him.

He summoned Vorsov.

"This . . . this stuff," and he tossed the transcript aside with what he hoped would appear to be a haughty gesture of utter contempt, "this rubbish . . . has it been, er, disseminated yet?"

Vorsov was pale. "It has routine circulation, comrade minister. All monitoring transcripts are distributed to the concerned sections within the Directorate, and such additional recipients as . . ."

"Yes, yes," interrupted Lapin curtly. "I know the system. But has this gone to the Central Committee?"

"I imagine . . ." began Vorsov, but Lapin snarled at him "You are not here to imagine. I want information, and I don't expect to be given guesses, I want facts. I can make guesses myself, without your help, thank you."

"Will that be all, comrade minister?" asked Vorsov. He was a little shaken. Lapin had always kept his relationships with his subordinates on a correct, if distant level. Certainly he was always polite. Clearly the idea that he was a target of these pirates of the ether unsettled him.

Lapin was already regretting having snarled at Vorsov. As a former ambassador – he had very skilfully negotiated the thin ice of being Soviet envoy to Peking – he had enough experience of diplomacy. It was unwise to let his underlings think that he was worried.

"You hear a lot, don't you?" he said silkily. "Here and there?"

"I beg the minister's pardon," Vorsov said cautiously. "I'm not sure I understand . . ."

"This radio station. Are people listening to it? Is it building up an audience?"

Vorsov drew himself straight. "I am sure that no patriotic citizen would defile his ears with such poison, comrade minister."

The sigh that Lapin gave was quite audible. It was inevitable, he thought. How could he have expected any other kind of answer? If Vorsov admitted that he knew people were listening to the pirate station, that they picked up hostile propaganda, it would be tantamount to confessing anti-Soviet behaviour.

"Of course," Lapin nodded. "You are absolutely right."

"Will that be all then?" repeated Vorsov.

Lapin gave him a nod and watched him leave the office. Not for the first time he wondered about Vorsov. He was a Georgian, and had been transferred to Lapin's staff after the Danchev fiasco. Danchev was now in Tashkent, exiled for telling the world on a short wave broadcast that the Soviet Army in Afghanistan were invaders, not saviours. Lapin survived that disaster, but forty-eight hours afterwards the taciturn Vorsov was assigned to him as chief clerk. He tried to find out his background, but the personnel file remained unavailable.

Yes, he thought once again, it was distinctly unwise to reveal too much of one's thoughts in front of Vorsov.

He took stock. He tried to reassure himself that the fact he had been targeted by the underground station meant very little. It was a cunning ploy, in line with their attempt to portray the broadcasters as loyal Russians, transmitting from inside the Soviet Union, and only concerned with the well being of the people. Disinformation knew no rules. It could not reflect on him.

They might pick on anyone next. It didn't prove a thing.

The call on the secure line came from Pavlov. The marshal was in good humour.

"Have you been reading about yourself, comrade?" he roared with laughter over the phone. "We are all agog for the next instalment. Do you think they will have some juicy bits?"

Lapin clenched his left hand, but he controlled his voice. He was glad Pavlov could not see him. "It is not a humorous experience," he said reproachfully. "What I would like to

90

know is what is being done about it by the responsible organs of the state?"

It was as near as he could get to saying that the Directorate was failing in its job.

"Rest easy, my friend. We're doing more than you think. And we're making progress."

"I don't see any signs," said Lapin coldly. "I just keep reading this rubbish that they invade our air waves with."

"Put your faith in us," Pavlov assured him. "It's a neat little game, but we have all the cards."

He was still thinking about that when, at the end of the day, his chauffeur-driven Zil collected him at the entrance to the Ministry, and drove him to the Leninsky Prospekt. Lapin got out and told the driver that if he wasn't there in two hours' time to take the rest of the night off.

After all, he had great hopes that the ballerina he was about to visit would be quite happy to let him stay on at her flat . . .

It was only afterwards that he remembered what Pavlov had said and he suddenly wondered, uneasily, who it was who held the cards.

24

The summons from General Norland gave the colonel no hint of what was in store for him. As he jumped from the helicopter that had brought him to the landing strip at Heidelberg he felt quite benevolent towards desk soldiers. He had little time for paper shufflers who got in the way of real fighting men, but he accepted that somebody had to keep the bureaucrats happy. As long as they didn't get on his butt.

Tubby, of course, was going places. Blau knew that. He already had his two stars, and you didn't get the deputy's job at USAREUR unless somebody had your card marked. He had never made a secret of his ambition. Glory in the field was for others; Norland was after power at the Pentagon.

Norland had sent his driver to pick up Blau, and the colonel enjoyed riding in the general's car, even if the red two star insignia was tactfully sheathed while he was in it. They passed through a military housing area, and Blau, looking out, thought how soft they all looked. He didn't approve of soldiers overseas being encumbered with dependants; what the hell were the men doing over here, loaded down with women and kids and cooking pans. It took the edge off them. Christ, the Soviet Army didn't move around with domestic caravans.

The general, as always, made him feel welcome.

"Good to see you, Jerry," he smiled, and slapped the colonel on the back.

"Glad to be here, sir," said Blau. They may have been class mates at West Point, but those two stars made a difference. The "sir" was requisite, at least on first entry. It confirmed, for the record, that he recognised and acknowledged each other's status.

To his surprise, there was a civilian in the room. A man in a grey suit, with a pink shirt that had a button down collar. He had rather thin lips, and sharp eyes.

"Oh, you two don't know each other, do you?" said the general, as if he had only just realised it. "Jerry, this is Mr Dupree. Hal is on special assignment over here, aren't you, Hal?"

"That's it, general," nodded Dupree, and the thin lips curled into what passed for a smile.

Chickenshit civilians don't play games with me, thought Blau.

"So what's the assignment?" he asked.

"Colonel Blau is very direct," explained the general to

Dupree, almost apologetically. He turned to the colonel. "Hal works with the spooks." And he winked.

Momentarily, Blau had the uneasy feeling that Dupree was studying him, watching his reactions, assessing, filing.

"I guess I'll excuse myself, general," said Dupree. "I'll keep you posted on those other things . . ."

"Fine," said Norland.

"Glad to have met you, colonel," murmured the man, and left.

Curious, thought Blau. Why was I shown in while the general was still with Dupree? It's almost as if they wanted me to meet him.

Or maybe, him to meet me.

"What's he doing over here?" asked Blau after Dupree had closed the door.

"You know spooks," said the general vaguely. "They never tell one a darn thing."

OK, said Blau to himself, you want to play it close to the chest. That's fine by me.

"Sit down, Jerry," beamed the general. He stretched over, helped himself to a cigar, bit off the end, and spat it, accurately, into a small waste paper basket. Blau waited patiently while he lit the cigar, and puffed it contentedly.

"Tell me, how long have you been in the Army now?" asked Norland, studying him across the desk.

Blau was startled. "Thirty years next September."

"Something to be proud of," remarked the general thoughtfully. "Real proud."

Blau frowned. What was the point of this?

"I'd hate to see a record like that screwed up," sighed Norland abstractedly.

"I beg your pardon, sir?"

The general sat forward.

"I think you ought to get out, Jerry," he said gently. "Now. Quit while you're ahead."

Blau gaped at him.

93

"Put in your papers, old buddy, and enjoy life," the general went on relentlessly. "Nobody will get hurt."

For Blau it was like some bad dream. He sat, silent, disbelieving what he had heard. This could not be real. He stared at the general across the desk. At the two flags in the stand in the corner. Old Glory, and the red banner of a general officer. At the USAREUR coat of arms on the wall. The framed photo of the president. They weren't a mirage, none of them. This was really happening.

"I don't understand," croaked Blau.

Norland blew a cloud of cigar smoke. "You can't beat a Havana," he observed. "I hate the fucking son of a bitch, but his tobacco is ace." He settled back in his chair, and stared thoughtfully at Blau through the haze of his cigar's smoke. "Look at it this way. You got a good pension. Everybody respects you. You'll have a ball. As a matter of fact . . ."

"No," insisted Blau. "I'm not hanging up my hat. You've got to be kidding. Sir."

But the general didn't appear to have heard him.

"Sometimes I wonder why we don't all just quit and let them get on with it," he reflected. "Who needs the hassle? The civilians think they're so damn smart. OK. They'll soon be screaming for us to get 'em out of the shit." He bit on his cigar. "You've done nothing wrong in my book, Jerry, but I've learned one thing about this man's Army. There comes a time when discretion is the better part of valour. And you'd better show some discretion." He smiled encouragingly. "So it's all set, right? You quit, and go back home, and go fishing," he said exhaling a huge cloud of cigar smoke. "Christ, I'm not sure I don't envy you, you lucky bastard."

Blau drew himself upright. "I'm sorry, sir. I have no intention of leaving the service. My place is with my men."

The general nodded, as if he had been expecting it. He carefully balanced the cigar on the edge of an ashtray. When he spoke, his manner had changed. He was cold.

"I don't want to spell it out, colonel. You're through with

the Army. It is in everybody's interest that you get out. Understood?"

Blau's mouth was dry.

"You've become a liability to my command, Jerry. One I can no longer afford."

"Why?" cried Blau. "What the hell's wrong?"

The general slammed down his fist on his desk. "You know damn well. I'm being asked questions. People want to know things. They're starting to dig around. This British officer who got killed. They want to know more. It's getting messy. I don't need it, I don't want it. You got that clear?"

"I'm not quitting," Blau stated quietly. He was calmer now. "My report explained everything . . ."

"Your report is bullshit," snapped Norland. "You think I'm a moron, or something?" He took a deep breath. "I'm trying to save your neck, don't you see? There could be charges. A court martial. You know what that means."

He reached for his cigar and stuck it in his mouth again.

"Who's asking questions?" said Blau.

"What do you think Dupree is here for?" replied the general. "You're in trouble. Christ, you've tangled with NATO intelligence."

"Maybe I can get reassigned," suggested Blau after a pause. "Fort Bragg. Fort Lewis maybe. Stateside, with the Special Forces. They need instructors at Fort Bragg. Counter insurgency instructors. I'm good, you know I'm good. Get me a new posting."

He was playing with the West Point ring on his hand. It did not escape the general. He wore the same ring. He knew the class bond.

But he shook his head, a little sadly. "Sorry, Jerry. I'd like to, but it's gone too far. Of course, once you're a civilian . . ."

The bald headed man stared at him.

"I'm sure there'll be opportunities," the general reassured him. "Maybe I can drop a hint. Friends in the right quarters . . ."

He smiled benignly.

"What about my outfit?" asked Blau. "What happens to my programme? The special training? Our mission . . ."

"Don't worry," said the general. "I'll see to it myself. You're unique, Jerry, I can't hope for somebody like you, but I'll see to it that the command goes to the right kind of guy."

Blau thought for a moment. "Supposing I refuse? I just stay put. I say sorry, I'm not quitting for anybody."

There was silence. Then the general's face became a hard mask.

"I haven't heard you say that, colonel. For your sake." He glowered at Blau. "Listen, Jerry, I haven't sweated and worked for these," and he pointed to the two silver stars on his shoulder, "to have my career fucked up right now. You've gone over the line, Jerry, and it could drag me down. That won't happen, I promise you. Not you or anyone else will screw things up for me. You clear?"

Then Blau knew it was over. "All right, sir," he said. He swallowed. "If that's it then . . ."

Norland said nothing.

"I got some clearing up to do," added the colonel.

"Sure. That'll be no problem."

The general stood up.

"I'm sorry, buddy, it has to be this way. But it's not the end of things. I got a feeling you'll be around, fighting the same good fight. You can't keep a good guy down. You'll take off your soldier suit and carry on the war."

Blau straightened up. "I hope so," he said.

Norland held out his hand.

"Proud to have had you under me, Jerry. I know one thing too. When the balloon goes up, I want you in there, right alongside me. Good luck."

"Thank you, sir," said Blau. They clasped hands, very firmly. Then Blau stepped back, came to attention, and saluted the general.

As he walked from the general's office, he didn't feel like a man whose career had suddenly come to an end. He walked jauntily. A battle might have been lost, but the war was going on.

25

Dupree sat in the grill room on the 35th floor of the Holiday Inn in Augsburg, and decided that a mediaeval town like this was not the right place for Holiday Inns.

He'd travelled widely in the line of duty, and had become increasingly conscious of how alike it was all beginning to look. The same airports, the same luncheon counters, the same cheeseburgers, the same gong on the tannoy. It was very boring.

"You want to order now?" the waiter asked in English. They were so used to Americans that it had become a second language. They could tell them at a glance.

"I'm waiting for somebody," replied Dupree. "You can bring me a screwdriver."

He had just taken his first sip when she appeared from the lift, looked round for him, and smiled when she spotted him at the table. She came over, and sat down opposite him.

"Hi," he said.

"Sorry I'm late," apologised K.D. Jones. She looked, as always, cool, unruffled. She was in civilian clothes, a smart, elegant trouser suit.

He signalled the waiter, who brought the menu. She ordered a drink, and they decided what to eat.

Then she looked at him across the table enquiringly. "Well?" she asked.

"You've done a good job," he said and raised his glass. "They're pleased. Well done."

"What's happening, Hal?"

"We're wrapping it up. Blau's got his marching orders. The Army's going to do some house cleaning."

"You mean, there's going to be a whitewash job." She said it tersely, but without heat, like somebody stating a plain fact. "All this," she went on, "that poor bastard dead, and they're wrapping it up, just like that?"

"We investigated," he told her, after a pause. "The disposition of the case rests with higher authority."

"Don't talk like the bloody manual," she snapped.

The waiter brought their food and they were silent while he served them.

Then he said: "OK. But don't forget what this is all about. It's political. It's got implications . . . If it got out, it would do a lot of harm. It'd be a gift to the other side. It's got to be buried. Deep."

They ate in silence.

"Is that official?" she asked at last.

"Straight from the top."

"And Blau?"

He shrugged.

"Shit!" she swore.

"You're being reassigned, honey," he said.

"Oh?"

"They got something else for you."

Her reaction was chilly.

"Where?"

"You'll get your orders," he said.

She pushed her plate aside. "Hal. You know there's more to it. We haven't uncovered it all."

He wiped his mouth with the napkin. "We got enough, one way and the other, K.D. Leave it alone."

"Did you ever meet Garner?"

He shook his head. "No. I know his boss of course. Rathbone. In London. Pretty shrewd fellow."

"Garner walked right into it," she said. "He didn't really have a chance. Not in that set up."

Dupree shrugged. "That's the way it goes. I know a guy who caught the clap in Beirut in the line of duty."

Her eyes were daggers. "You're a son of a bitch, Hal, you know that?"

He grinned. "We're all lovely people, K.D. That's why we do the job we do." He looked at her plate. "You haven't eaten much."

"I'm not hungry," she said.

"Ace girl sleuth of the Defense Intelligence Agency's special division is letting the job get on top of her," he mocked her.

"You know what you can do," the blonde said evenly.

"Tell me," he grinned.

"I leave it to your imagination, but you'd probably get AIDS from yourself."

He pulled a face. "Jesus, you've been round the barracks too long. Soldiers are a bad influence on you."

They separated in the Maximilianstrasse.

He hugged the blonde.

"Keep your nose clean. And take care." Then he kissed her on the cheek. "You look great," he said appreciatively.

"Have a good day," said K.D. Jones and walked off.

26

Maya arranged to have the morning off from the company so that Andreyan could take her to see the sights of London, which turned out to be a shopping expedition. He had to smile at her wide-eyed, excited reaction. The boutiques particularly delighted her: she insisted on walking the length of Bond Street, down to Piccadilly, stopping every few yards to gaze at yet another window display. She gasped at some of the fashions, giggled at others. The shoe shops were her special delight.

Finally she could resist it no longer. She went into one. Surrounded by such variety, she was like a child in a sweet shop. She tried on a pair of stylish high-heeled court shoes.

"Aren't these beautiful?" she exclaimed, bright-eyed. "So elegant. So . . . so glamorous." They showed off her slim, shapely legs to perfection, even though the stiletto heels would be utterly impractical in the streets of Moscow. "They fit perfectly," she breathed.

"Would you like to have them?" asked Andreyan. But when he signalled to the shop assistant that they were taking the shoes, and brought out his wallet, Maya intervened.

"No, no," she said, "I am buying them. I have money. They gave us travellers cheques." She reached for her purse. "Here."

"A present," insisted Andreyan. "A present from London. To remember our morning together."

"No, Sergei Mikhailovitch, it is not right. You must not buy me gifts."

"Why not?" asked Andreyan. The shop girl could not follow their conversation in Russian and stood undecided.

"It is not proper," declared Maya.

Andreyan thought of their nights together, the intimacy they had shared in his bed, the warm closeness of their entwined bodies. How they had made love, and enjoyed one another.

"Nothing can be improper between us, my dear," he assured her.

She hesitated for a moment, then gave him a wonderful smile, and happily took the bag containing the shoes.

"I love them. I shall wear them everywhere."

"Not in the snow, I hope," grinned Andreyan.

Then they strolled through Burlington Arcade, and she

laughed aloud when he pointed out the top hatted beadle and translated the notice prohibiting running or whistling in the hallowed precincts.

"And I must not carry a parcel here," he announced solemnly. "Gentlemen are not allowed to have packages or bags. It is nekulturno."

"What about a lady?"

"The English are very practical," said Andreyan. "Somebody has to carry burdens, so ladies are exempt."

"It is time they had a revolution here," Maya argued with conviction. "Here." She gave him the bag with the shoes. "You take them. You are a diplomat. You have immunity. Let us see if he dares to arrest you." And she glared at the beadle, but he didn't even notice them, so Maya pursed her full, generous scarlet lips and tried to whistle.

"You will get us all put in the Tower," joked Andreyan. She was so carefree like somebody on holiday, free from discipline.

"I'll start running in a minute, if you're not careful," she teased. Then her attention was distracted by another shop window and she paused to admire a display of handbags.

A few feet away the man from D5 also stopped. He was faceless, inconspicuous as befitted his assignment. D5 were the watchers. It was the section that provided covert surveillance for the security services. Following the attaché from the Soviet embassy and his actress girl friend round the West End was not an onerous job, but it was easy to get careless. It would never do to be spotted.

"We should see some culture," suggested Andreyan. "There is the Royal Academy just around the corner. They have an interesting exhibition you should visit. Or we can go to a museum. They have some very famous ones . . ."

"Another time," said Maya. "Please. I am so enjoying myself."

What she really meant, he knew, was that she wanted to see more fashions, more clothes, more shoes, more beautiful things. Moscow was never like this. As an actress she had a good life. She had a nice wardrobe, some magnificent furs, but the wares displayed in these shops were beyond her dreams. How easy it was for a woman to be beautiful here.

"Do you think America is like this?" asked Maya suddenly, stopping outside Fortnum and Mason's.

He gave her a sharp sideways glance. "America is vulgar," said Andreyan, discouragingly. "It is loud, brash. It is not Europe."

"The shops on Fifth Avenue? They must be even better?"

He shrugged.

She looked with interest into the windows of Pan American, and studied the airline's tourist posters. "I would like to see America," she said with feeling.

He frowned. "Why?"

"I'm an actress," she said lightly. "Is there any actress who would not like to go to Hollywood and become famous?"

"Your English is not good enough, Maya Aleksandrovna," he retorted, a little coldly. "In that shop, you could not even buy a pair of shoes without help. You wouldn't know how to take a taxi."

She gave a tinkling laugh. "I can learn. I am very good at learning. You speak good English. You can teach me."

"So that you can get to Hollywood?"

She looked straight into his eyes. "Why not?" Then she added, as an afterthought, "I am only joking, of course."

"Of course."

The man from D5 bought an evening paper and observed them with some interest as they stood in front of the Pan Am ticket office. He wondered if they were going to go inside. That would make a very interesting item to report.

"Do you like being in London?" asked Maya, tucking a wisp of auburn hair away.

"Yes. It is very interesting."

"And you meet many people?"

"That's part of the job," said Andreyan. "Meeting people."

102

"Where else have you been?"

He hesitated. Not because he didn't want to tell her, but because there was an inbuilt caution about revealing details. One's background. One's training. One's mission. All these things were sensitive. But Maya . . . well, she was different.

"Oh, I've been in a few places," said Andreyan. "Prague. Berlin. Paris. London, of course."

"You're very lucky," Maya sighed. The man from D5 noticed that she was holding on to Andreyan's arm.

They walked to Piccadilly Circus, then Andreyan waved down a cab. He and the actress jumped inside. The watcher was lucky. He managed to get a cab behind them.

"Follow that taxi," he ordered. He had said it so often in the course of his duties that it no longer struck him as funny. He ignored the cab driver's look too.

They got out in Oxford Street, and the man from D5 followed them into Marks and Spencer's.

"Why have we come here?" asked Maya.

"One day," said Andreyan with conviction, "we will have stores like this. For everybody."

"They haven't asked us for any identification," she whispered to Andreyan.

"Why should they?"

"But this is a privilege store, isn't it? For important people. You can buy here because you are a diplomat?"

"No," said Andreyan. He realised how much he took things for granted.

Maya gave a squeal of delight when she saw the woollen goods and made for the counter displaying jumpers, sweaters, cardigans. "The rich buy here?" she asked, feeling a woollen jumper with relish.

Andreyan could not resist it. "I will tell you a state secret. Duchesses purchase their underwear here."

"The Queen?"

"Not the Queen."

He held up a navy blue cardigan against her.

"Now what is your size? Let us get a few things . . ."

103

She began to protest, delighted.

"You'll bless these in cold weather. And you'll be the belle of apartment 219B in Kutuzovsky Prospekt."

She had not told him the address of her flat in Moscow. But he was telling her that she had no secrets from him. It was like revealing his job, confirming what she suspected, admitting that he had read her records.

While he was talking he was piling up a stack of woollen things in her size and passing them over to the assistant.

"With the compliments of the embassy," he said as he paid.

"You are lying, Sergei Mikhailovitch."

"Of course," he smiled.

She pouted, but the hug she gave him said much more. It wasn't missed by the watcher. He was quite glad of the detour; he managed, while keeping his eye on them, to buy himself two pairs of socks.

They came out into Orchard Street, she happily clutching a big shopping bag.

"I'll take you back to the hotel," offered Andreyan. "Unless . . ." He paused hopefully. "Unless you want to have lunch first?"

"Don't you have to be back at the embassy?" she asked.

"You forget, my dear, I am on duty. This is official business." He gave her a wink.

"Right then," said Maya. "Lunch. Somewhere luxurious. Somewhere extravagant and outrageous. Please."

You'd really do well in Hollywood, thought Andreyan. Her cheeks were glowing, her eyes sparkling. Capitalism became her. She had enjoyed every minute touring pluto-cratic London. And, he had to admit, he had loved being with her. She amused him. She excited him. Though he knew her body now, she still had mysteries for him. She was intoxicating, like good brandy, and he had got a taste for her.

"Don't they wonder where you are?" he asked her in the cab. "What have you told Simonov?"

"Nothing," she replied.

"Is that wise?"

She smiled at him, a little arrogantly. "What can they do to me? When I am with you?"

At that moment he wondered if she was going to be dangerous. The thought crossed his mind that he was entangling himself in something that should be cut loose. It suddenly struck him that she might be using him. He hoped that wasn't so. Andreyan could be ruthless, and he hated the thought of Maya finding out just how ruthless.

He took her to the Mirabelle in Curzon Street. It pleased his sense of irony to squire her to a restaurant across the street from the headquarters of their MI5.

The D5 watcher would have liked to follow. It would be enjoyable to have a luxurious lunch on the taxpayer. But he knew the department would never wear the bill.

For him, lunch was a toasted cheese sandwich and a cup of tea, hastily consumed in a café round the corner in Shepherds Market, before he rushed back to his post.

27

Borisov had been sitting in the armchair in his hotel room for a long time, staring into space. The breakfast tray was largely untouched. This morning he had little appetite.

There was a faint tap on the door, but Borisov did not react immediately. He sat, unmoving, waiting perhaps to see if whoever it was would go away. He was in no mood to see people. He wanted to think.

The second knock on the door was a little louder, a little

sharper. Borisov frowned irritably. Slowly he got out of the armchair, walked over to the door, and unlocked it. Cautiously he half opened it, and peered through the gap. Simonov, huge, expansive, beamed at him.

"Dear colleague, I hope I am not intruding," he greeted Borisov. "I didn't know if you were already up."

It was ten minutes after eight, and few of the company emerged from their rooms much before nine in the morning. Like all actors, they were late starters.

"No," said Borisov, "it's all right. I've had breakfast."

"May I come in?" asked Simonov.

Borisov opened the door wider, and the producer entered the room. He looks more and more oily, thought Borisov, with his double chin, and greasy nose. He was tired of Simonov.

"I'm not interrupting anything, am I?" asked the fat man, his eyes darting around, as if he expected to spot something compromising. If you think Maya spent the night here, you're so wrong, Borisov felt like saying.

He sat on the unmade bed, and offered Simonov the armchair. The Bloomsbury hotel's rooms were sparsely furnished, and only provided one armchair to each bedroom.

"Quite a good house, last night," Simonov remarked conversationally. "Didn't you think?"

"They seemed to enjoy it," replied Borisov non-committally. He wasn't at all sure about the London audiences they were getting; sometimes he wondered if the applause really meant anything. How many of these people understood a Russian play anyway?

"So, tell me, how are *you* enjoying it all?" enquired Simonov. The eyes had stopped roaming and were fixed on him, sharp, alert.

Borisov felt uneasy. This was not like Simonov. He was a past master of bonhomie, he liked to pose as father confessor to all his company, but he didn't visit their rooms early in the morning to ask them how they were enjoying their job.

"It's tiring," Borisov said. "We've been pushing it,

haven't we? All these tours, all this travelling. I'm looking forward to a holiday."

"Ah." Simonov held up a pudgy hand. "But isn't it thrilling? New faces, new localities? Doesn't it make your adrenalin rise, Evgeny Alekseivitch? Think of the wonderful reception we've been getting. The goodwill we're creating?"

Borisov winced. Spare me the propaganda speeches, please. You sound more like a political commissar than a theatrical producer. You don't have to impress me, old man. I don't hand out the decorations.

"You look a little tired," he agreed, helping himself to a piece of cold toast from the breakfast tray. He began nibbling it. "There's nothing worrying you, is there?"

It was like an alarm signal. Suddenly Borisov was very alert.

"How is your dear wife? Have you been in touch? I'm sure Polina would love to get a phone call from you – put it on your bill, we will pay, don't worry."

"I'm sure she's all right," said Borisov curtly.

"I'm only concerned because I thought last night, on stage, you were a little . . . a little down." Simonov smiled at him. "It was nothing, but I know you so well, dear friend, I see these little things. I can tell when there are . . . pressures."

Borisov regarded him haughtily. "I wasn't aware that there was anything wrong with my performance?"

"Nothing is wrong," cried Simonov. "It was perfection. You are such a consummate professional you would never let your colleagues down. I simply felt that there have been moments when . . . when your mind has perhaps been on other things. You know how I care, and if there's anything that's bothering you . . ." He nibbled the piece of toast earnestly. "You don't mind, do you, my enquiring?"

"Not at all," said Borisov. "I appreciate it."

Simonov wiped some crumbs from his jacket.

"You'll soon be able to relax, dear comrade. In a couple of weeks we'll be back home, and you can take Polina to your

dacha and relax. Enjoy the fruits of your excellent labours."
He leant forward, and lowered his voice as if there was
somebody else in the room. "I can tell you, in great
confidence, that the Ministry is delighted with our tour, and
the reception we've received. They feel we are making an
important contribution to international relations. It wouldn't
surprise me if perhaps . . . a recognition . . ."

For a moment Borisov wondered if Simonov's eyes were
actually moist with emotion.

"That's good to know," said Borisov drily.

"How are things with Maya?" asked Simonov carefully.

"I haven't seen much of Maya Aleksandrovna lately."

"She's an independent little minx, isn't she?" nodded
Simonov. "Kopkin tells me she's been going around with
one of the people from the embassy."

"Oh?" Borisov's indifference was studied.

"What better way to see London, eh? Diplomatic privileges and all?" Simonov winked.

"Maya Aleksandrovna is her own mistress," said Borisov,
and rather liked the way he had put it.

"Of course, of course. I think your attitude is very
generous."

Bastard, thought Borisov.

Simonov lumbered to his feet. "Anyway, it is reassuring to
know that you have nothing on your mind. Nothing that is a
worry. I don't mind telling you that I'm looking forward too
to being home again. It is exciting to go abroad, but there is
no place like the motherland, is there?" He slapped Borisov
on the back. "Think of it, in a fortnight you'll be back in
Moscow."

"I can't wait," declared Borisov. He was a very good actor
at that moment, giving a splendid performance.

"See you in the coach later," smiled Simonov closing the
door softly. Borisov locked it behind him.

He went into the adjoining bathroom and splashed his
face with cold water. Then he lit a cigarette. Since coming to

108

London he had started smoking English cigarettes. He was getting himself used to the different taste.

After all, he would be smoking a lot of English cigarettes from now on.

28

The latest broadcast of the pirate station contained an item of little significance to most listeners, but which attracted considerable attention in certain quarters.

"Our great country is being ill served by some of the people who are sent abroad as diplomats. Surely, comrades, we deserve better than to be represented by the kind of opportunists we have in some of our embassies in capitalist countries. Take our embassy in London.

"Sergei Mikhailovitch Andreyan is one of our diplomats in that very cushy post. He lives well at our expense, and enjoys the fleshpots of London. Recently, dear listeners, he has been enjoying himself in the company of a Soviet actress who should know better. Shame on you, Maya Alexandra Petrova.

"Isn't it outrageous, friends, that so-called servants of the state spend their time on government service abusing their privileged position chasing actresses . . ."

The voice of the announcer, whoever he was, quivered with righteous indignation.

As a piece of propaganda, it was in line with the pirate station's policy of undermining authority and convincing loyal Russians that corruption, inefficiency and idle privilege were indeed rife in official circles. It was put over, as usual, from the point of view of disgruntled Communists, determined to expose those who were undermining the system.

The item about Andreyan was picked up with alacrity by the monitors, and it set secure telephones ringing on several desks.

Colonel General Arkady Zotov, head of the GRU information services, put it bluntly at a meeting of his security staff.

"They are playing a game," he growled, "and I am not amused. The broadcast is not important. They are doing it to tweak our nose. But I am interested in this. How do they know about this Sergei Mikhailovitch Andreyan? And this actress?"

He stopped when one of the staff officers raised his hand. "Yes, colonel?"

"This Maya Aleksandrovna Petrova. We have checked. She is in London now with Simonov's company. They are playing at the Lyric Theatre in Hammersmith. She is staying with the company at a hotel in Bloomsbury."

"Well done, colonel," said Zotov. He liked his staff to be one step ahead. "And Andreyan?"

The colonel pushed a folder across to the general. Zotov opened it, and read briefly. Then he looked up. "This is very useful. Thank you." And he closed the file.

Two hours later a coded high priority signal was sent to the embassy in Kensington Palace Gardens. It was also intercepted by a receiving station and immediately passed to GCHQ at Cheltenham. They unfortunately were having problems breaking this particular code.

In London, Colonel Leonov read the decyphered signal, and gave a mild curse. He hated this kind of query from Moscow. They should leave him to run this station, and not poke their noses into things that didn't concern them. Nevertheless, he pressed a button and summoned Andreyan.

"Sit down," said Leonov, passing over the decypher. "This came half a hour ago."

Andreyan read the message, and handed the yellow sheet of paper back to the colonel.

"Any comment?" asked Leonov.

"They should mind their own business."

"Exactly my thoughts," concurred the colonel. "However, we have to be diplomatic. What do you suggest?"

Andreyan thought for a moment. "I will compose a suitable signal in reply, if you like. You know the kind of thing I mean."

Leonov nodded. He liked Andreyan. One day he will be sitting at this desk, he thought. Or perhaps at an even more important one. "Good. Show me the draft when you are ready."

Andreyan started to leave.

"She is very good looking, Sergei Mikhailovitch," remarked the colonel. "I went to the theatre the other night, and I was quite taken with her." He smiled. "Make sure you don't do anything too indiscreet."

"I'll try not to, sir." Andreyan returned the smile.

"And be careful where you go. You see how you're being watched."

"Of course." He hesitated. "Do you think they are watching her too? There was a man following us the other morning, when I took her shopping . . ."

"I would have been surprised," said the colonel, "if there hadn't been."

Andreyan left and went to the embassy's referentura, where, behind steel doors, the most sensitive paper work is done. He composed a coded dispatch for the eyes of Colonel General Zotov.

Downstairs, Colonel Leonov had another caller. He came in nervously, blinking through his spectacles.

"Ah, comrade," said Leonov to Lev Kopkin, stage manager. "What have you come to tell me that is so urgent?"

29

Colonel Blau studied the rigid ranks of his troopers with pride. Yes, they stand tall, these men of mine. They stared back at him, unblinking, heads high, and he knew that, to them, he was the only man that mattered. After this parade, they would have a new commander. It was his farewell to this crack unit that he had licked into shape, this special little army that could run rings round the others. Each man was worth half a dozen ordinary GIs. They were more than tough, they were deadly. They spoke Russian fluently, they knew how to live off the land behind enemy lines, they could kill without weapons. They could see in the dark, and become invisible. They were cunning, and ruthless. He had taught them well.

It was not the normal change of command ceremony. Blau had decided to have his own final parade. He wasn't going to share it with the incoming colonel. The hand over would be a routine affair, but this was his personal goodbye. He felt sad, but he was damned if he was going to show it. Green Berets didn't give in to sentiment. However Blau felt inwardly, the squashed boxer's nose made him look pugnacious. His broad shoulders were squared. He didn't look like a man about to quit.

The silence was impressive. There were a few barked commands. Old Glory rustled on the tall flag pole. Somewhere in the distance was the drone of an aircraft. That was all. But every man's eye was on the colonel.

"Men," began the colonel, standing on the dais, his words echoing across the parade ground from the tannoy system, "you know the saying about old soldiers. Well, I'm about to fade away. We've made a good team, a great team. I know I'm leaving behind me the damnedest fighting outfit in Uncle Sam's army. I'm proud of you fellows and I know one thing, when the day comes and the whistle goes, you'll be in there and the sons of bitches won't know what's hit 'em."

He paused.

"We're special. We're the spearhead. The others talk. We do. We know that we're only marking time before the balloon goes up, and when that happens, while the others are trying to pick up the pieces, we'll be in there, ahead of any of them, hitting the enemy where he doesn't expect it, kicking him in the balls, doing it our way. We've only got one rule, and that's to win. You men know that nothing else counts."

He hesitated for a moment. Then he pointed dramatically eastwards.

"Out there, across the border, in Eastern Europe, and beyond, there are millions of slaves, just waiting for somebody to come and knock on the door and give them a gun and say 'right, fellows, this is it.' The goddam politicians haven't got the guts, otherwise we'd be in there already, freeing the poor bastards . . ."

Major Skinner and the small group of officers looked sideways at Blau. They hoped he'd take it easy. It was all off the record, of course, but this kind of talk, if it got known, could make things awkward.

But the colonel was in his stride. "We're ready, day and night. We've trained for it. We're prepared for it. We've got the know how, and we've got the weapons." He smiled grimly. "Yeah, we got the weapons. And I tell you this, we're not going to win by sitting doing nothing. The world belongs to those who do, not those who wait. We were defeated in Korea. We were licked in 'Nam. We got our teeth kicked in in the Lebanon. We're pussyfooting in Latin America. We've been blown up, and taken hostage, and held to ransom, and mocked, but it's going to stop. *We're* going to stop it. It only needs a little push, and the whole goddam mountain will fall

113

down. Give me 500 Green Berets, and I'll raise the flag of revolt and liberation all over Eastern Europe."

Blau stopped suddenly. He had been speaking rapidly, almost without thought. He had been speaking from the heart. Then he remembered where he was.

"The brass has decided that it's time I was put out to grass," he said, more slowly. "They've got an outfit here that's second to none. You guys are the best in the world. But they think you need a new commander. That's their privilege." He swallowed. Discipline was too inbred to criticise his superiors in front of the men. There was a lot he felt like saying, but this was not the place. He drew himself upright. "Men, I'm handing over command, but I'll be with you always in spirit, you know that. I'm never far away. I will think of you and our holy mission day and night, and maybe they'll find out there's some fight left in this old soldier. It's been a great privilege to command this outfit, and I'll tell you now, no commanding officer has ever had a finer bunch of dedicated men under him."

There were those who swore, afterwards, that they actually saw a tear in Blau's eyes.

He got down from the dias, then he slowly walked along the ranks of the assembled troopers, looking each one in the face. He nodded to some, had a quick smile for others. There were those in front of whom he stopped, and said a few words. In the past, an inspection by Colonel Blau had been a terrifying ordeal, feared by every man in the outfit, but today it was like a father with his children. He didn't hide his affection for his men, and they returned his warmth.

Two days later, Colonel Blau departed. There was a farewell party, but the colonel excused himself early and went to bed. And when he finally left the unit, no one saw him go. At dawn a staff car departed with the colonel. It was like Blau not to prolong farewells. Being a bachelor, he did not have that many household goods, and they were all dispatched ahead of him to a storage depot.

Twenty-four hours later, a Special Weapons Inspection

114

Team unexpectedly arrived at Waldheim. They produced orders, signed by Major General Norland, authorising them to enter Site 11.

It was an operation carried out in strict secrecy, and only Major Skinner was aware that the silent, taciturn specialists who composed the team found what they were looking for, a stock of 10-kiloton W-54 nuclear land mines, all listed obsolete. The team, although they did not say so to anyone at Waldheim, were acting on certain information supplied from intelligence sources. They worked silently, and quickly, and emptied the arsenal of its contents. Then they disappeared again, with their finds, as quietly as they came.

What they didn't know was that, stored at Site 11, had been a hundred of the man-sized nuclear land mines. They only found ninety.

The other ten weapons, each one capable of blowing a small town apart, had been removed some time before in wooden crates labelled as Colonel Blau's personal household goods.

By the time General Norland's men entered Site 11, the ten nuclear weapons were already stored in a warehouse across the river Main, in the Sachsenhausen district of Frankfurt.

The caretaker understood that the crates held furniture belonging to an American gentleman who would collect them when he needed them.

30

The intruder was fully briefed about the office in Monmouth Street.

"There is a direct alarm to the police, and if you set it off, you won't hear it. But we'll be aware if the police are coming, and we'll telephone you if it's time to get out. As soon as the phone rings, leave as quickly as you can."

"Anything else?" asked the intruder.

"Keep your eyes open for tell-tale lenses. Step cautiously. There may be infra-red alarms, so don't jump out of your skin if a bell suddenly goes off. Nobody takes much notice of burglar alarms in London anyway."

There weren't many people about when the intruder entered shortly after 1 a.m. A car was parked nearby with a driver, the engine running. His escape had been prepared.

Warily, he made his way up to the second floor in the dark, a torch lighting the steps. Above the door to the secretary's office, he saw the gadget and quickly, swiftly snipped the connection with small wire cutters. Then he used the unusual keys on the locks. He pushed open the door, and waited for a moment, but there was no sound.

Miss Hurst was a methodically neat woman and she had left the premises of the Europa League as usual, uncluttered, with no papers lying about. The intruder inspected her office, tried some drawers – then switched on the light. He produced a camera with a flash attachment, all very compact, and began taking a series of photographs of Miss Hurst's office. He took a lot of pictures, from various angles.

Then he turned the light off, and cautiously entered Dr Jury's office. Here he spent more time. He didn't attempt to break anything open. He left the filing cabinets untouched. But he was interested in the map on the wall, and the books on the shelves.

Here too he switched on the light, and took a large number of photographs of the office from all sides, and all views. He examined Dr Jury's desk minutely. He even looked at the pencils and the inkstand. There was an indexed phonebook lying beside the blotter, and, painstakingly, the intruder photographed every single page.

He picked up the framed photograph of Mrs Jury, studied it for a moment, then he laid it flat on the desk, and took a couple of pictures of it.

Suddenly the phone rang. The intruder switched off the light, and left the office, moving fast.

He ran down the two flights of stairs and when he got out into Monmouth Street the car was already in front of the entrance.

"Can't hear any sirens," said the intruder.

"You won't," grinned the driver. "They'll come silent, hoping to sneak up on you and catch you red-handed."

The car raced off towards St Martin's Lane. Soon afterwards a plain clothes police car stopped outside the building.

It didn't take the two CID men long to realise there had been a forcible entry into the premises of the Europa League. There were a couple of rather obvious clues – the cut wire outside the outer office, and the picture of Mrs Jury, lying face down on the desk.

There was no reason for the police to suspect that the object of the exercise was to make Dr Jury aware that his premises had been burgled.

31

Evgeny Alekseivitch Borisov walked out of his hotel in Bloomsbury and disappeared.

The rest of the cast wasn't due to set off for the theatre aboard its coach until 5 o'clock, three hours later, and it wasn't until then that people began to realise that Borisov wasn't around.

The discovery set off a chain reaction. Phones began ringing at the Soviet embassy, at Scotland Yard, in Fleet Street, and in Whitehall. The unhappiest man was Alcott, the D5 man who had been on duty in the hotel lobby, keeping an eye on the comings and goings of the Russians.

Ever since the company arrived at Heathrow Alcott had been assigned to them, and to say that he was bored with Russian actors was to put it mildly. As always, Rathbone did not give unnecessary explanations to his minions. He wanted observation kept, that was all. He wanted to know about any interesting or unusual or curious happenings. That was how he put it. "Interesting, unusual, or curious."

"Such as?" Alcott had asked.

"You'll know it when it happens," Rathbone had replied.

Alcott had mentally indexed the Russians into categories as he sat in an armchair near the reception desk doing the *Daily Telegraph* crossword and watching the traffic in the hotel lobby.

Some of the actors were down right dull. They were like commercial travellers. Others were never off stage. They played their roles all the time. The producer, Simonov, was one, expansive, loud, making each entry and exit at the hotel an event. However, the auburn-haired actress who always swept out of the lift as if she too was going on stage, she was something special. Alcott had her down on his list. Miss Petrova. She was the one who was having a thing with the embassy man, Andreyan. The surveillance team had followed them all over the place, and Alcott knew there was a standing instruction to watch Andreyan. The man was a fast worker, evidently. He had lost no time getting in with the Petrova girl.

Then there was Borisov. The leading man. One of their stars, apparently. A People's Artist. To Alcott he seemed to be nervous, restless. Borisov was constantly looking around, observing, peering at people. Alcott prided himself on being virtually invisible to those he watched, merging into the background like a piece of furniture, but he had the uneasy feeling that Borisov was aware of him. When he came into the lobby, his eyes seemed to search around until they found him. He put that in his report later, and Rathbone

118

commented rather sourly, after Borisov had vanished, "Didn't that tell you something? Didn't it make you think?"

Alcott kept a careful note. He made a list of visitors, journalists who came for interviews, theatre types, callers from the embassy. Kopkin was down on his list, a nosey little bugger, making himself important. On the whole, though, it was all terribly routine, and rather boring.

The one common feature was that they never went out on their own. It was the usual Russian system. Alcott and his colleagues in D5 had become familiar with it among Russian diplomats, visiting delegations, touring groups. Always stick together. Safety in numbers. It was double security: it ensured that no one did anything foolish on their own, and, equally, that no one could be approached individually. The visiting actors, apart from travelling to and from the theatre in Hammersmith in a coach, only went out of the hotel in groups of three or four, or even more.

All except the Petrova girl. She did her own thing. She even stayed out all night. Clearly, being the girl friend of Andreyan gave you special privileges, reflected Alcott. Lucky bastard. Alcott wouldn't have minded keeping the Petrova lass out all night. She could turn anyone's head.

When the post mortem came, Alcott tried to think back to when he had last seen Borisov. Although he had been on duty in the lobby, he couldn't remember seeing the actor. Perhaps the boredom of the assignment had got on top of him. It was a dull, drab hotel, aimed at package tours and second class tourists, just off Russell Square, and sitting in it day after day noting arrivals and departures would dull anyone's attention. Maybe he was just doing a crossword clue when Borisov saw his opportunity and sneaked out.

It was Kopkin who broke the news to Simonov and ruined the producer's day.

"I cannot find him anywhere," he announced breathlessly. "He is not in his room, nobody has seen him. There is no sign of him."

Simonov looked at his watch.

"Find him," he ordered. "We are late. We are due at the theatre."

"I tell you, he is not around," insisted Kopkin almost defiantly. It was as near as he dared to answer Simonov back.

This had never happened before, and Simonov began to feel a little sick.

"When did you last see him?"

"He had breakfast in his room this morning. After that, I don't remember . . ." In a perverse way, Kopkin was enjoying Simonov's discomfiture. If anything went wrong on this tour, the Ministry would make its displeasure more than felt. Serve the pompous frog right.

"All right," said Simonov. He was pale. "Go with the others in the bus. I'll join you at the theatre . . ."

"But, comrade . . ."

"Go," commanded Simonov.

They went off in the coach to Hammersmith and Simonov asked the reception desk for Borisov's key. He went upstairs and spent five minutes in the actor's room. When he came out, he was grim faced. From his own room, he called Andreyan at the embassy.

"Borisov has gone," he said, trying to sound calm.

Andreyan was very cool. "Gone?"

"He should be at the theatre. But he missed the coach and he's not in his room . . ."

"Did he go out?" Andreyan sounded quite impersonal.

"Yes," said Simonov in a low voice. He knew what was coming.

"Alone? You let him leave the hotel by himself?"

"We didn't know . . ."

"You're supposed to know," snapped Andreyan.

"He's taken . . . some of his things . . ."

"What!" He could hear Andreyan controlling himself. "What did he take?"

"I think . . . a suitcase . . . some personal things . . . clothes . . . and . . ."

"Listen," interrupted Andreyan tersely, "this is very serious. Do not tell anyone. I am coming right over." And he hung up.

It was when the theatre announced that an understudy would stand in for Evgeny Alekseivitch Borisov that the news of his disappearance began to become public. Half an hour after the curtain went up, the Press Association put out a flash:

"Soviet Actor Missing. E. A. Borisov, a leading member of the Moscow company appearing at the Lyric, Hammersmith, disappeared from his hotel today."

The performance went on as arranged, but during the interval, back stage, Maya went to her handbag and took out a snapshot of herself and Borisov.

They had their arms round each other, and it had been taken some time ago during a tour.

Maya struck a match, and burnt the photo. It might be incriminating, and Maya wasn't a woman who took chances.

Although *Tass* did not carry the story of Borisov's disappearance, and no Soviet news source referred to it, Russkaya Volya went on the air in the early hours of the morning and announced that the actor had vanished in London.

The pirate station was well informed. It said he had left his hotel after having breakfast in his room, and that an understudy had taken his part at the evening performance.

"A man of the stature of People's Artist Evgeny Alekseivitch Borisov does not just fade into thin air, comrades. He has a big following. He has given pleasure to thousands. Demand to know what has happened to him. Ask the authorities why they have kept the news of his disappearance from you. Ask what is behind it. What are they trying to hide?"

It was the classic ploy. The pirate transmitter was playing its usual game of planting doubt and rumour, hoping that its listeners would then do its work for it, and spread the story.

121

"You will hear more of the People's Artist Borisov," promised Russkaya Volya.

Marshal Pavlov listened to the tape of the broadcast impassively. He gave the clandestine operation full marks for efficiency, but looked forward to the time when he would destroy it.

His aide came in with a large manilla envelope. He was a smart young man, a captain, and the marshal approved of him.

"This has just come for you from London," said the aide. "In the diplomatic bag, sir, from the embassy."

Pavlov nodded. "They do have their uses," he said amiably.

The aide looked puzzled.

"Diplomatic bags," smiled the marshal. He was in a good mood.

After the aide had gone, the marshal opened the sealed envelope. He pulled out a sheaf of photographic prints. There were about thirty of them, 8" by 10", and they seemed to be photographs of the inside of some offices. The layout, the desks, the walls. There were also some photos of the pages of an address book, and the framed portrait of a woman. But most of the pictures were just general views of the rooms.

Pavlov rubbed his chin thoughtfully. He was a thorough man, and he liked to visualise his enemy. Not just the enemy, but his surroundings. He liked to see in his mind's eye the premises of the other side.

As for the photographed pages of the address book, the names and particulars would be listed separately and analysed with great care.

Finally he studied the photograph of the woman. She was good looking, no doubt of it, as she was in the other pictures they had of her.

He didn't quite know why, but it struck him that she might be the key. Mrs Jury could turn out to be a short cut to many things.

The marshal summoned his aide.

122

"Send a signal to London in our cypher," he ordered. "Addressed to Colonel Leonov. Thank him for the little intrusion into Monmouth Street, and for the photos. They're excellent. Andreyan is very handy with a camera."

32

The plant in the pot on the window-ledge of Cheyne's office was dying: the green leaves were turning brownish and it didn't look healthy. Rathbone wondered who was responsible for its care. Did his secretary look after it, or had Cheyne neglected its welfare?

"Are you with me, Colin?" cut in Cheyne's voice. The tone was reproachful.

"I'm sorry," apologised Rathbone. "I'm afraid my mind slipped . . ."

"I could see that," commented Cheyne icily. "I'll ask you again. What do we know about it?"

Rathbone stared at him. He hadn't had much sleep, and he was tired.

"What do we know about this Russian actor disappearing?" repeated Cheyne in the weary tones of an over patient teacher trying to make sense out of a rather dull pupil.

"Actually, nothing."

Cheyne sniffed with distaste. "Nothing? What do you mean?"

"We have no idea what's behind it, what happened, or where he is."

"But surely . . . I mean, you or Special Branch, or somebody . . ."

"Not a clue," said Rathbone.

"There are times, Colin, when experience tells me that I

would be foolish to believe you. I am sure you have a file this thick on it . . ."

"A thick file, with respect, doesn't mean we know anything."

Cheyne stood up. He began to walk up and down. He usually stood up, Rathbone knew, when he was conveying the views of his masters. Sometimes he wondered if this was a subconscious token of respect to their superiors. Cheyne probably stood up at home when BBC TV signed off and played "God Save the Queen".

"It's most inopportune, Colin. We do not want this kind of incident at the moment. It makes for headlines. It causes static. Are you sure you have nothing to do with it?"

Rathbone had plenty of patience. Today he needed it.

"Borisov has vanished, that we know. We don't know where he is. The Russians don't know where he is. Nobody knows why he's walked out. He's in their good books. He's a golden haired boy. So I don't think he's defected. He certainly hasn't approached us."

"Kidnapped?"

"By who? Very unlikely. Anyway, he packed some things. Took a suitcase."

"And just vanished?"

"Last seen in Russell Square."

Cheyne shook his head. "All very unlikely, Colin." He faced Rathbone. "Find him. Give him back. We don't need any unpleasantness over – over an actor."

Rathbone sighed. Cheyne was getting worse. The job was getting to him. He'd sell his grandmother down the proverbial river. No wonder he was so callous he let his plant die.

"Did this man Borisov make any sort of approaches to anybody?" asked Cheyne.

"No."

"Haven't you found out anything, Colin?" He was reproachful, hurt. "You're letting me down, Colin. I've always relied on you."

"Well . . ." said Rathbone.

Cheyne jumped on it. "Yes?" he cried, eagerly.

"It could be . . ." He hesitated. The less he told Cheyne the better.

"Go on."

"He's been having some sort of – relationship. With one of the actresses . . ."

"Well?"

"She's been seeing somebody from the embassy. Andreyan."

"Ah," said Cheyne. "Andreyan. How interesting. You intrigue me."

"It could be that Borisov is on the rebound," said Rathbone carefully. "Feels miffed."

"Jealousy is a wonderful reason for all kinds of behaviour," nodded Cheyne happily. "Treason, desertion, defection. Why not?"

If only it were that simple, thought Rathbone. Aloud he said: "Well, it's one possibility."

Cheyne came over and patted Rathbone on the shoulder.

"Well done, Colin. I feel much happier now. Something to go on. Follow it up. Use this girl. See where it leads you. But get him back to his people. We don't want him around. The text for the week is that we are friendly with Moscow, understand?"

Rathbone said nothing. It was wiser to stay silent. He was just sorry for the dying plant.

33

A black embassy car brought Simonov to Kensington Palace Gardens where Colonel Leonov personally interrogated him.

Simonov tried to look confident, but his face was pasty. Leonov welcomed him with a friendly smile that made Simonov even more nervous. Silently, he cursed Borisov. The damn fool was making life complicated for all of them.

There was a tape recorder on the desk between them, and as Simonov sat down, the colonel switched it on.

"You don't mind, do you?" he asked.

Simonov was familiar with their methods. The interview would have been taped anyway, he knew that. It would probably have been recorded by a secret microphone. The open display of the tape recorder was a warning. Don't make any mistake, it said, this is official, every word you say will be on the record. Simonov thought of the American films he had seen – "anything you say will be taken down and may be used against you."

"It saves someone having to take notes," went on the colonel reassuringly. "Would you like some tea?"

Simonov shook his head. He was thinking about the signed photograph of Gorbachev prominently displayed on the wall. Leonov had friends in high places. All the more reason to watch every word.

"Well," began the colonel. "This is all very unfortunate, isn't it?"

Simonov spread his hands. "Actors," he murmured, "you know what actors are like."

"I don't." It was rather less amiable.

"They are so temperamental, comrade colonel. Impulsive. Very moody creatures. They do unpredictable things." He spluttered to a halt. The colonel's steady stare was discouraging.

"So," said Leonov. "You say this was quite unpredictable?"

"Completely." Simonov's eagerness was pathetic, thought the colonel. "None of us had any idea this could happen. Of course not. If we had . . ."

"Yes?"

"We would have taken the appropriate steps."

"Such as?"

The room was warm, but that wasn't the reason Simonov was sweating. "We would have immediately informed the relevant authorities. Yourself, of course." He smiled nervously.

"He was a friend of yours?" enquired the colonel.

Simonov swallowed. "We are all friends. The whole company. We are comrades." He eyed the tape recorder uneasily. "But, of course one does not know everything . . ."

"Oh?" Leonov was interested. "What don't you know?"

A mistake, thought Simonov. That was a mistake.

"What I meant was that we don't necessarily discuss . . ." He petered out. He was doing himself no good.

"You don't necessarily discuss politics?" prompted the colonel.

"Oh no, I didn't mean that, after all, what is there to discuss about politics? No, I am trying to say that of course people have their own problems, which they keep to themselves. How can I be expected to know about them?" Beads of perspiration were visible along his upper lip.

"You are sure you wouldn't like some refreshment, my friend?" asked Leonov.

"No, thank you." The producer wanted to take out his handkerchief, and dab his face, but that, he felt, would have been a mistake. It would give the impression that he was nervous.

The colonel stared out of the window at the embassy garden. "It is such a pity this has happened," he mused, not looking at Simonov. "This was a very successful tour, a good contribution to cultural relations, and now it's all being spoiled. The ambassador is unhappy, the Ministry is unhappy, and when they're unhappy . . ." He sighed. "It is making headlines in the capitalist press. Look at this rubbish."

The colonel bent down and produced some newspapers which he threw on the desk. Simonov saw the headlines. "Actor Chooses Freedom." "Star Flees Reds." "Hunt for Missing Russian."

"Their press feeds on this kind of incident like maggots. It is sad that they have been given the opportunity to make a scandal." And his glance was very reproachful. "Now tell me, why do you think he did it?"

"Perhaps, a nervous breakdown," suggested Simonov hopefully. Surely nobody could blame him for that.

"Really?" The colonel didn't laugh aloud, but his tone implied utter disbelief.

"Evgeny Alekseivitch may have had problems . . . with his marriage, possibly . . ."

"Many people have problems with their marriage but they do not defect."

Simonov had a stricken expression. "Defect? Oh no. Who says he has defected? It could be amnesia. It could be . . ."

"Our job is to consider every possibility," pointed out Leonov grimly. "And I need not tell you, I am sure, that if it transpires he has deserted us there will be a full investigation. The authorities will go into all the circumstances, and the entire background . . ."

Simonov opened his mouth, and shut it again.

"You are the captain of the ship, and if you lose a member of the crew in a foreign port you must regard yourself as responsible, wouldn't you agree?" the colonel added.

Simonov could not take his eyes off the tape recorder and the slowly turning spool. He had an awful vision of a secretary typing the transcript of this meeting, and the typed pages being passed from hand to hand in the Ministry in Moscow, then landing in the in-tray of the disciplinary authorities . . .

"Of course," came the colonel's voice, "so far you have always been regarded as highly reliable, comrade Simonov. An admirable record, if I may say so."

"Thank you," mumbled Simonov.

"The authorities have had their reservations about some of your productions, though. You staged that Yuri Trifonov play, didn't you? About people denouncing each other?"

128

That's it, thought Simonov. They're preparing an indictment.

"But then," the colonel continued, "we are a free society and artists have every right of expression. Until now there has never been a serious shadow over you."

Simonov clutched the arms of the chair. "Comrade colonel," he croaked. "Is there anything – anything I can do? To help? To assist in resolving this problem?"

Leonov regarded him with a degree of contempt. "Yes," he nodded. "You can find Borisov for us."

"I? But how?"

The colonel shrugged. "We all have our problems. You asked me. I told you. Oh, and one other thing."

"Yes?" Simonov was all eagerness.

"The tour is almost over. You'll be returning to Moscow soon. Try to see to it that while you're over here, there aren't any further – embarrassments."

"Absolutely," promised Simonov. "You can rely on me. I will take every step. Absolute discipline will be maintained. I . . ."

"The car will take you back to your hotel," the colonel interrupted. He switched on his smile again. "Thank you for your co-operation."

He watched Simonov leave the room before he turned off the tape recorder. Then he pressed a button on his desk. Andreyan came in.

"Well?" asked the colonel.

"I told you," said Andreyan. "A bag of hot air."

"He reminded me of a wild boar," remarked Leonov. "Stupid but nasty. They can get vicious if they're frightened. I know, I used to hunt them."

Andreyan gave him a grin. "Don't let the academy hear you comparing a darling of the proletarian theatre to a boar . . ."

The colonel started taking the spool off the tape recorder.

"Sometimes, dear friend, I think you have been in London too long," he grinned back. He gave Andreyan the spool.

129

"Here. Mark it and make sure it's on its way to Moscow with the next courier. I think it'll make fascinating listening for them."

Just as he was leaving, Andreyan said: "By the way, thank you."

"For what?"

"For keeping her out of it," said Andreyan. "Not bringing Maya Aleksandrovna into it."

"Well," said the colonel. "You can do me a favour sometime."

34

Dr Jury knew who had broken into his office. He knew it as positively as if they had left a visiting card. The police told him it was obviously an amateur effort, nothing had been stolen, the intruders clearly couldn't find anything of value, and left again in disgust.

However, Dr Jury knew otherwise. They were giving him a warning. A shot across the bows. Next time they'd leave a booby trap. When the door opened, it would set off an explosion. Or they'd send him a parcel. A lethal parcel . . .

But instead of frightening Dr Jury, the intrusion gave him great personal satisfaction. It was confirmation that he was getting under somebody's skin. If they went to this trouble, he was beginning to annoy them. That was very reassuring.

He told Miss Hurst to check all the security arrangements, and to have the alarm system and the closed circuit cameras overhauled. If anything needs improving, have it done, no matter what it costs. Money was never a problem for the Europa League.

"The address book was lying on your desk," reported Miss Hurst. "They may have seen it . . ."

"Don't worry about it," Dr Jury assured her. "They probably even photographed it. It doesn't matter. They're unimportant names. That's why I left it out . . ."

He was a chess player, and he prided himself on his little gambits.

The day after the burglary a Special Branch man came to the second floor office in Monmouth Street.

"Detective Chief Inspector Binyon," he introduced himself, and Dr Jury raised his eyebrows, because that was quite a high rank for a man making routine inquiries. Also, Binyon was remarkably well dressed for a policeman, he thought. The shirt was Jermyn Street, the tasteful tie expensive silk, the suit well cut, the smart shoes top grade custom made.

"Yes, Inspector?" He signalled to Miss Hurst to make two cups of Nescafé.

"This little visit you had," said the inspector languidly, as if he was rather bored with the whole affair, "have you any thoughts about it?"

"Thoughts?"

"Who it might be? Why they bothered?"

"None at all. Have you?"

"I imagine there might be people who are quite interested in what you do," said the inspector.

"Research, you mean?"

"Yes. Research." He looked round at the map on the wall, the bookshelves. "I don't know much about the Europa League, actually . . ."

Miss Hurst brought in the two cups of coffee.

"There's milk in both," she said. "Do you take sugar?"

"I have my own." The inspector produced a flat tin and put a couple of sweeteners in his cup. "Thank you."

"We're privately funded," said Dr Jury when she had left. "Mostly from America. We are supported by donations."

131

"To do precisely what?"

Dr Jury blinked behind his glasses. He had been stirring his coffee. Now he put the spoon carefully in the saucer. He picked up the cup, took a sip, then put the cup down again.

"Tell me, Inspector . . ."

"Binyon."

"Tell me, Inspector Binyon, are we being investigated? I mean, are you on a formal inquiry?"

Binyon shook his head. "Not at all. I'm just following up this spot of bother you've had. It came across my desk . . ."

"You're Special Branch?"

"Does it show?" smiled Binyon. "Well, as a matter of fact, yes . . ."

"Why is Special Branch concerned? Just because some layabout made a botched effort at burglary?"

"Ah." Binyon nodded appreciatively. "Yes, I see your point. But you know how these things work . . . chain reaction, that sort of thing. The Europa League is – er – political. So we're concerned if there's a . . . well, we keep an eye on things. Reports are filed, carbon copies are passed across, and we get a routine check to do . . ."

It was a smooth bit of double talk, and they both knew it.

"Actually, the reason I'm here is something else," confided Binyon suddenly, as if he had decided to drop any pretence and own up with the truth. "We're trying to find somebody, and it struck us that you might possibly have a clue as to his whereabouts. Or at least a guess . . ."

"Who are we talking about?" asked Dr Jury.

"You may have read about him. It's been in the papers. He's a Russian actor, been appearing at the Lyric, the Moscow season. Have you been?"

Dr Jury shook his head.

"I thought you might have, seeing you're interested in Russian affairs," remarked Binyon smoothly. "Anyway, the man is missing. He disappeared from his hotel, and we're trying to find him. I wondered if possibly . . ."

Through the door, they could hear Miss Hurst typing. A fire engine came along Monmouth Street, and Dr Jury kept silent until the strident klaxon receded in the distance. Then he said gently: "You haven't even told me his name, Inspector."

"Of course, how stupid of me," said Binyon. He pulled out a little notebook, turned a page and read out:

"Evgeny Alexeivitch Borisov. That's the man."

"Have you asked the Russian embassy?" enquired Dr Jury.

"They are as anxious to find him as we are."

Dr Jury took off his spectacles and polished them with a tissue he had pulled from a box. While he was doing so, he peered short-sightedly at the inspector. "Tell me, why should I know anything about this man?"

I'd like to grab you, thought Binyon, and shake you, until your teeth rattle, I'd like to teach you not to fence with me, I'd like to . . .

But instead he said mildly: "You have contacts . . . with exiles. You keep in touch with émigrés from Eastern Europe, you have all kinds of useful connections. You're pretty well informed about defectors. You're a sort of clearing house, aren't you, you have your finger on the pulse . . ."

Dr Jury sat immovable.

"It seemed to me that if this man had decided to . . . shall we say, defect, you or your contacts would get to hear about it. Maybe he might even approach you . . ." The inspector stopped. He had gone as far as his brief allowed.

Dr Jury pushed the coffee cup aside and stood up. "I'm sorry," he said, "I wish I could help. I know nothing. Of course, if I pick up anything I'll be in touch, but I don't imagine I'll be that lucky." He looked at his watch. "The trouble is, I have another appointment so unfortunately . . ."

Binyon took his cue and rose. "Thank you for your time," he said formally. "I hope I haven't inconvenienced you. But if you do hear anything . . ."

"I'll be on to you first thing," smiled Dr Jury. He opened

133

the door. "Miss Hurst, would you show the inspector the way."

Alone in his office, he pulled the phone towards him and dialled a number not listed in the directory.

When Rathbone answered, Dr Jury was quite angry.

"I don't know whose idea it was, but I've had Special Branch round. Asking all sorts of questions. Snooping around. I don't like it. I don't need it. I thought you were looking after everything."

There was a pause at the other end of the line. Then Rathbone said: "Sometimes the right hand does not know what the left hand is doing. Who visited you?"

"He called himself Detective Chief Inspector Binyon."

"Interesting," murmured Rathbone. "And what did Chief Inspector Binyon want to know?"

"If I was involved in the disappearance of the actor Borisov."

"Binyon is a very sharp man," said Rathbone and chuckled.

That was when Dr Jury put the phone down rather abruptly.

Less than half an hour later Binyon entered the lobby of the Regent Palace Hotel. He stood looking around, like a man waiting to meet somebody. The lobby was crowded with a newly arrived coach party who were lining up to register. It was like a busy railway station. That was its attraction for some; one was easily lost in the throng, and anonymity was guaranteed.

Binyon did not have to wait too long before he spotted her. She came over, casually dressed, a big leather bag slung from one shoulder, the trouser suit an attractive green, her blonde hair short.

"Hi," she said.

"Let's go and have a cup of coffee, Miss Jones," said Binyon, leading the way.

Sitting across from her at a plastic table, he thought she was rather good looking.

"Well," he said, "where shall we start, Miss Jones?"

"Let's start," she smiled, "by you not calling me Miss Jones. Call me K.D."

35

Maya lay on her back, breathing gently, her naked body tingling after the love making. Andreyan rested his head against her breast, his eyes closed. He felt a supreme contentment, his desire appeased, his lust for her satiated.

It had been excessive, indulgent love making and after they had satisfied each other, they embraced again, and the passion surged just as strongly. There was something about her movements, the way she reacted, the very sound she made which Andreyan found irresistible.

The fingers of his right hand gently played with her left breast. She almost purred, then she stretched herself luxuriously.

"That was very beautiful," she sighed. "Thank you."

"I think . . ." began Andreyan and stopped.

She turned her head towards him. "You think . . . ?"

It wasn't wise, he knew, to say what he was about to tell her. A man in his situation shouldn't say it.

"I think I could be . . . in love with you," he admitted sombrely.

"But you're not sure?"

His training took over. "No," he said brutally. "I am not sure."

To his surprise, she reached over and planted her lips on his mouth and gave him a long, hard kiss.

"I'll wait till you are," she said. "But in the meantime we can have lots of fun."

Andreyan sat up abruptly. He reached over, and lit a cigarette.

"Put that out," she pleaded. "Come down here. We have plenty of time left . . ."

"We haven't," said Andreyan.

It was his tone that made her sit up on one elbow and look at him.

"What do you mean?" Her voice was low.

"You're going home," he said. "You're going home early. Everybody is. The whole company. They've cancelled the rest of the tour."

Her eyes widened. "Why?"

"Orders," said Andreyan. "From the Ministry. Straight from Moscow. It's the business with Borisov. They feel it is best that you are all recalled. They don't want any other complications."

"No," she said. "No. Not yet. Please."

Andreyan put his arm round her and drew her towards him. She gained some comfort from the warmth of his body.

"I'm sorry, my love. There is nothing I can do about it. We all have to obey orders. You know that. You have. I have. Simonov. No matter how high. The ambassador. When Moscow decides, we obey."

"But . . ." She was desperately trying to find a reason for a reprieve. "We're playing to good houses. They've sold tickets. For all the performances. We can't just leave . . ."

"They will return the money," he said gently. "They will explain that with the leading actor unavailable, it wouldn't be fair to perform with an understudy. They'll make it sound right, don't worry."

She pulled away from him, got out of bed, took a blanket from the bed and walked over to an armchair by the wardrobe. She wrapped the blanket round herself, and sat hunched in the armchair.

"Don't be silly," scolded Andreyan, "come back to bed. You'll get cold."

Maya knew how to be wilful. "I don't want to go back

home," she pouted. "You say you care for me, you have influence, you are at the embassy, and yet you're not prepared to lift a finger . . ."

"There is nothing I can do," reasoned Andreyan. "Don't you think . . ." He looked across at her. "Don't you think I hate the idea of you leaving?"

"So, do something," snapped Maya. Then she tried a new role. The hint of tears appeared in her eyes. She bit her lips, like a woman trying to stop herself breaking down in a torrent of sobbing. "I . . . I suppose it's all my fault," she cried.

"What do you mean?"

"If I hadn't been so . . . cold to Evgeny Alekseivitch. If I hadn't made him feel unloved . . ." A tear ran down her cheek.

"Are you saying . . ." began Andreyan, but she cut in.

"Yes, yes. I'm saying that I . . . turned my back on him, I probably made him run away . . ."

"You told me there was nothing between you and him," he challenged her. "I asked you. I took your word that it was all over between you. Now you tell me that's the reason he ran off – that you ditched him. Is that it?" This is ridiculous, he thought. Here he was sitting naked in bed, cross examining a witness like some investigator of the Directorate.

She was watching Andreyan warily. She didn't want to make him too angry. After all, he could make life very unpleasant for her . . .

"It's . . . it's possible," she sniffed. "Isn't it?"

"I think you make yourself too important," said Andreyan coldly. "You flatter your own ego."

She stared at him disbelieving. "What are you saying?"

"I'm saying that the fact we are sleeping together did not cause Evgeny Alekseivitch to defect, I assure you." He got out of bed. "Get dressed," he ordered.

This time she burst into tears.

"I'm sorry," she sobbed. "Forgive me. It's just that the idea of being sent back, leaving you, leaving . . ."

137

"Leaving the big stores," pointed out Andreyan unkindly. "The good life. That's what hurts, isn't it? Be honest."

She nodded, silently, her eyes never leaving his face.

"I had a dream," she said, the tears drying on her cheek. "Is that so terrible? I'm an actress. I live for the bright lights. Is it a crime to want beautiful clothes, luxuries, money?"

"Artists don't do so badly in our country, you know," said Andreyan. "You're not exactly under-privileged, with certificated roubles, and special stores." He paused. "You know, my beautiful, you must have great faith in me. What you have been saying in this room could have grave consequences for you."

She stood up, letting the blanket drop, and came over to him, beautiful in her nakedness.

"But you're not going to report me?" she pleaded, embracing him. "You're the one human being I can trust. What I tell you is locked up between us . . ." She pressed her body to him, and kissed him.

He pushed her away gently, then he asked her, very quietly: "What is it that you really want?"

"Don't laugh," she begged.

"I shan't."

"Promise?"

"Promise."

She took a deep breath. "I want to be a star in Hollywood. Not in Novgorod or Smolensk or Kiev. In Hollywood. I want to be famous in America."

He stared at her. "You're not serious. You can't be."

"I am," said Maya. "I want to get to Hollywood more than anything in the world."

She kissed him again. "And you, my lover, can get me there," she said. She looked him straight in the eye. "Can't you?"

36

Karl-Heinz Kleber – born in Ludwigshafen on 17 September, 1949, occupation, engineer – arrived at Gatwick on a charter flight from Brussels, and had no problems passing through immigration. He joined the EEC channel, and produced a West German passport. In spite of his appearance matching the photograph, none of the details was correct – though he was an engineer of no mean ability, having constructed at one time or another several ingenious explosive devices.

He boarded a London train, and looked out of the window at the pleasant English countryside for most of the short journey. Just occasionally he gave a cursory glance at the other passengers in the carriage, but they were scarcely aware of it. He had only one piece of luggage, a suitcase. Kleber always travelled light.

If somebody had opened the suitcase, or searched him, they would have found nothing out of the ordinary. He never transported explosives, and did not believe in carrrying guns on his person until he was actually going to use them. He would pick those things up from his suppliers whenever he needed them.

Kleber had not expected to come to England. The last few months had been rather busy, and he was looking forward to the prospect of some relaxation. To date, his schedule had left little time for rest. He had been responsible for the sudden demise of the *Newsweek* correspondent in Athens who was a CIA operative, and terminated an Israeli dentist in the Hague who worked for the Mossad. Then he had been rushed to Paris to eliminate a South African intelligence agent.

They never asked how he proposed to do a job, they knew Kleber would fulfil all their missions faultlessly. He had the sure touch that made him one of the highest paid operators in the business. His explosions always destroyed their targets, and when he used a gun, he needed only two shots. One did the actual killing, the second was a fail safe guarantee. His victims never lived even to reach a hospital. They were invariably dead by the time he had left the vicinity.

He was much appreciated by Viktor, the code name of the 13th Department, now known as V-section, which supervised "mokrye dela" – wet affairs – the spilling of blood. Kleber, they knew, could be relied upon, and he was, for somebody in his profession, a remarkably stable character. He drank very little, didn't use drugs, was cultured, and had been known to go to Mozart concerts alone.

Under various identities and guises, Kleber had, of course, come to the attention of the CIA and the British. The trouble was, no one knew for sure who he was. There were a few precious photographs, most of them blurred. In two he had moustaches, and different types of moustaches at that. In another, he wore a beard. There was one of him in dark glasses, and in yet another half his face was blotted out by shadow.

In his dossier there was no reference to involvement with women, and this gave Kleber the unmerited reputation in some circles of being gay. It was unfortunate, because it meant that those hunting him often frequented the wrong places in their search for him. The truth was that Kleber enjoyed women, and used women, but did not trust them. Women, in their turn, were attracted by his gentleness, his charm, but when they saw the coldness of his pale blue eyes some shuddered, while others were doubly attracted – and he knew it.

Before this assignment, he had been looking forward to a short holiday in the sun. He had been offered the use of a coastal villa in Libya by a colleague – if there were such people in his profession – who worked for Colonel Gadaffi.

140

Kleber had at times worked in tandem with Gadaffi's teams if their targets coincided. His loyalty, of course, belonged to Moscow, and their orders were paramount. Whatever the Department demanded, came first. But links with the Libyans had their uses . . .

What Kleber never told his Arab friends was that, as assassins, he had contempt for them. They were irrational, flamboyant, they boasted, they lacked patience.

Then he'd received his instructions and any visions of the hot sands and the blue ocean had immediately faded.

"Marshal Pavlov is personally interested in this," the courier had said knowingly. "It is delicate and very important. You understand?"

Kleber nodded.

"Because of the difficult nature of the assignment, there will be a bonus at the end of it," added the courier. Then he enquired if he needed any particular documentation.

"I'd like to use a West German passport, in the name of . . ." He paused. "Yes, Kleber."

"Kleber?"

"He was one of Napoleon's marshals," grinned the newly born Kleber. "The one who got assassinated . . ."

It seemed to amuse him, but the courier didn't smile – he hadn't been picked because of his sense of humour.

They discussed various other logistical matters including the question of passport photographs and made certain arrangements. Three days later the man with the pale blue eyes picked up his passport, and became Karl-Heinz Kleber.

Half an hour after he stepped on to it, the Gatwick train pulled into platform 17 at Victoria. Kleber collected his suitcase and got off.

As always, he paused for a moment before he went through the ticket barrier. It was second nature to check if anything was suspect; a couple of disinterested men hanging about beside the ticket collector, a sharp eyed observer scrutinising the exit, a face that didn't fit, a woman taking a picture. After a moment, Kleber was reassured. He walked confidently to get a taxi. Not from the queue in the station, but one plucked from the stream of traffic, which would be much more difficult to trace.

Before he'd left Brussels he'd been given the key and the address of the flat in London where he would be staying. It was in a mews, and had the advantage of being self-contained with its own front door, so he could come and go as he chose. The name "Kleber" was already over the bell when he arrived.

Although a modest apartment, it was nicely furnished. There were towels in the bathroom, and the bed was made. He tested it, and to his pleasure, the mattress wasn't too soft – Kleber disliked soft beds.

He went into the kitchen, there was food in the refrigerator, and he helped himself to some fresh orange juice they had thoughtfully provided in the ice box. He took the drink into the living room.

Kleber loved television, and there was a remote control set with a big screen. One solitary book lay on the round coffee table – a large scale street atlas of London, intricately indexed. He had to hand it to them, it was just the sort of reference book he would find useful. He eyed the phone. He had also been given some numbers to call if there was any trouble, but he was too well trained to trust that thing. He was never going to make an important call on this one, if he could avoid it, and he had a good idea that they would be wary of what they said on it. Or, at least, how they said it. As if to reassure himself, he went over and picked up the receiver. He heard the expected dialling tone. He smiled to himself. You idiot, what else did you expect? Clicking noises? He shook his head. Dummkopf!

He kicked off his shoes, and stretched out in the great big armchair. He loved these moments of relaxation, behind locked doors, safe within four walls, no strangers about, no unseen eyes prying, not having to talk or listen out. They made up for the constant watchfulness which was so much part of his life outside.

He wondered, quite dispassionately, what sort of man the actor called Borisov was. He was the reason for Kleber being in London. They rated him highly, apparently. People's Artist, no less. What the hell was an actor doing getting involved in this kind of business? The briefing had said he was married, but was on his own over here. It figured.

He had just taken a sip of the orange juice when the door buzzer went. Carefully he put the glass of orange juice down on the table, then he walked silently to the hall – his shoeless feet making no sound on the carpet. He peered through the curtain, trying to see into the mews and spot who was at the door. Then he saw her. A girl with dark hair, in a gaberdine raincoat, clutching a parcel, a bag dangling from her shoulder.

He cautiously opened the front door.

"Yes?"

She smiled through the gap. "I've come to welcome you to London. May I come in, Eclipse?"

He knew it was all right. "Eclipse" was his code word. Highly appropriate in a way, he thought, after all, he eclipsed people.

"Oh, this isn't bad at all, is it?" she said when she entered the living room. "Are you comfortable here?"

"It'll do fine." She was talking like a landlady.

"I won't stay," she said. "I just came by to bring you this." And she put the package on the coffee table.

"I'm Karl-Heinz Kleber," he introduced himself, rather hesitantly. If she knew his code name . . .

"I know," she smiled.

"And you are?"

"Why don't you call me Lesley," she said. "How's that?"

"I suppose it's all right, Lesley," he muttered.

"Is there anything you need?" she asked with a tone of finality.

"I don't think so. Anyway I know who to contact." He felt it was time to assert himself.

"Good," she said. "Today I am only the messenger."

She turned round at the front door.

"Good luck," she said, and was gone. He looked through the window, but there was no car, nothing.

He had expected to be contacted, and she knew his code name, so she came from them, he was sure. Nevertheless, he examined the parcel carefully, and made certain checks.

It was heavy, and when he finally opened the cardboard box, he found, wrapped in tissue paper, a Browning 9mm pistol. A good weapon, capable of firing 40 rounds at a target 50 yards away, and killing each time. There were also four spare magazines holding 13 rounds each, to be slid into the pistol grip of the gun.

Kleber weighed the gun lovingly. Fully loaded it was less than 3 lbs. A beautiful bit of design.

But there was more to the gun than that. It originally belonged to an American Marine who was blown to pieces in Beirut. It fell into the hands of a Shi'ite Muslim terrorist cell, and began its odyssey from Lebanon to Europe.

Its great virtue lay in the fact that if it ever came into the hands of Western security agencies, and they tried to track its origin, the trail would lead them right back to a dead leatherneck in Beirut.

A ballistics expert who dug its bullets out of its victim would get little joy.

Kleber was glad he had it at hand. The way things might go, it could be very useful.

37

When Borisov walked into Hampstead police station, a schoolgirl was talking to the sergeant behind the counter. She had been crying, and the sergeant was consoling her about the purse she had lost. Borisov looked at her sympathetically.

A policewoman at the back of the office saw Borisov standing unattended, and came over to the counter.

"And what can we do for you?" she asked pleasantly.

"I am a Soviet citizen," Borisov said in his accented English, as if that explained it all.

"Oh yes?" Her expression was blank.

"I wish to . . ." He stopped. This wasn't going the way it should.

The schoolgirl was just leaving, and the policewoman turned thankfully to the sergeant.

"Sarge, this gentleman is Russian," she said, "can I leave him with you?"

The sergeant finished jotting down some notes on his pad, then turned to Borisov. "How can I help you?"

"I wish to see someone," said Borisov.

"Change of address, is it?" nodded the sergeant. "You want the aliens' department."

"I'm asking for asylum," said Borisov.

The sergeant put down his pencil and straightened up. This could be the beginning of something complicated, he sensed. He tried to get his mind organised.

"You are a visitor to this country?" he asked carefully.

Borisov nodded. "Here," he said, "my passport," and he laid it on the counter.

The sergeant picked it up warily, and turned some of the pages. Then he made up his mind.

"Would you mind waiting a moment, sir?"

He disappeared into the charge office, and Borisov thought this could only happen in England. Imagine a foreigner walking into a police station in Moscow and asking for asylum; he certainly wouldn't be left standing staring at lost and wanted posters.

The sergeant returned with an inspector, who was holding the passport.

145

"You are Mr E. A. Borisov?" enquired the inspector, looking at the passport, then at Borisov.

"Yes."

"The sergeant said something about you wishing to . . . er . . . asking for asylum."

"Correct."

"I think you'd better come this way," suggested the inspector, and Borisov found himself ushered into a small interview room with a plain wooden table and two chairs.

Well, he thought, this is the first step.

"Would you like a cup of tea?" invited the inspector.

"Please."

"Two teas, Jenny," the inspector called over his shoulder, and the policewoman left her filing. "You take sugar?"

"It does not matter," said Borisov. "You are very kind."

The inspector waited.

"I do not wish to go back to Russia. I wish to stay here. I am asking to be here."

"Yes," said the inspector. "Well, you see, I think you'll find that's a matter for the Home Office. Nothing I can do about it. You must apply to them. We have no authority, you see . . ."

They are all alike, these underlings, thought Borisov. The militia. The frontier guards. The police. In every country.

There was a knock on the door and a man in plain clothes entered. He handed the inspector a sheet of paper and left again. The inspector read it, then looked up at Borisov.

"Ah," he said. "Everybody's been looking for you, Mr Borisov. You went missing, didn't you? From your hotel. In Bloomsbury? You're an actor, are you?"

After that, it changed. The inspector suddenly seemed to know what to do. The policewoman brought in the cups of tea, and he said:

"If you don't mind staying here, somebody will come to talk to you soon, and everything will be cleared up."

"Who will come?" asked Borisov.

146

"Somebody who can deal with your case." Then he added, "You'll be quite safe here, don't worry."

"Thank you," said Borisov, "I am sure of that."

He spent two hours waiting in that brown and cream painted room, but they looked after him. Twice the policewoman put her head in, and asked if he was all right, then a constable brought him lunch on a tray, salad, meat pie, prunes and custard and a big mug of hot milky tea. Borisov also noticed that, although the door was not locked, there was a uniformed policeman standing outside it. He wondered whether it was a guard to keep him in, or intruders out.

He surprised himself by being a little nervous. It was like standing in the wings, about to make the key entry. No need to be on edge, after all, he had been playing such roles all his acting life. He should take it in his stride, even if the stage was slightly unfamiliar.

The policewoman came in again. "Would you like something to read while you're waiting?" she asked. "You must be getting bored."

"Why not?" he smiled. She had taken off her tunic and now wore uniform shirt and skirt. It showed her figure to better advantage.

"I'll see what I can find," she promised.

But she didn't come back. Instead, a smartly dressed man with a sharp nose and rather high cheek bones entered.

"Mr Borisov?" he enquired politely, "my name is Detective Chief Inspector Binyon. Special Branch."

Ah, thought Borisov. Interesting.

"May I?" asked Binyon, sitting down on one of the chairs, as if this was a private home, and Borisov was the host. He pulled out a pack of cigarettes, and offered it to him.

"English, I'm afraid," he apologised, "*and* tipped. I hope you don't mind." Borisov took one, and Binyon lit it for him with a Ronson.

"You had us very worried, you know. After you disappeared from your hotel . . ."

"I'm sorry about that," said Borisov. "It was the best way."

He wondered why there was no one else present. Binyon didn't attempt to make any notes. And if he was wired . . .

As if to answer him, Binyon took off his jacket. "Bit close in here, don't you find it?" he said, and hung the jacket over the back of the chair. His shirt was crisp, immaculate. He had gold cuff links with some kind of crest.

"Anyway," said Binyon, "we have already informed the Soviet embassy that you are safe and well in Hampstead. I've got a car outside, and when you're ready I can take you straight there. You can be on a plane home tomorrow."

Borisov gaped at him. "What do you mean?"

"I'm sure they understand the strain you've been under. All those performances at the Lyric and the matinées, the travelling, the rushing about, good Lord, it's enough to give anybody a nervous breakdown, isn't it?"

"I've not had a nervous breakdown," cried Borisov, clenching his hands. "And I am not returning to Moscow, you understand . . ."

"Oh dear," said Binyon. "That is a bit awkward."

"I explained to that man out there that I wish to have asylum," said Borisov, breathing heavily. "I wish to stay in this country."

"I see." Binyon sounded as if this was the first he knew of it. "You mean, you wish to defect?" He gave Borisov a thin smile. "You understand, what I mean, defect? Come over? Desert your people?"

"I understand," agreed Borisov dully.

"You're sure?"

"I do not wish to defect. I want to have asylum."

Binyon shrugged. "I must say the difference escapes me, it's too subtle for me."

"Then," said Borisov coldly, "I would like to talk to somebody who understands it."

Binyon sniffed. "Quite so."

148

Borisov was watching him, closely. This was a very special kind of policeman.

"I must say, Mr Borisov, you speak excellent English. Much better than I imagined. Almost fluent. Except the accent, of course . . ."

In fact, he thought, you speak English better than your dossier indicated.

"So," said Borisov. "What happens to me now?"

"I have to report to – other people. They will make the decisions."

"Will that take long?"

"Oh I shouldn't think so." He stood up, and put on his silk lined jacket. "You've quite made up your mind, have you?" he asked. "About not going back to Moscow?"

"Yes," said Borisov.

"Pity," sighed Binyon. "That's a real pity."

He smiled politely at Borisov, but his eyes were hard. He gave a nod, and left.

Borisov sat and stared at the closed door for a long time.

38

The departure of Simonov's company from London was in marked contrast to its arrival: there were no bouquets, no flashlights, no press conferences. The bus picked them up from the gaunt hotel in Bloomsbury and whisked them to a service area at Heathrow where they remained out of sight.

Simonov had made a small curtain speech after the last performance, explaining that the season was curtailed for "technical reasons", and promising that they would all be back one day, but he said it like a man who knew it was a forlorn hope.

Andreyan saw them off at the airport.

"I am desolate that it should end like this," said Simonov. In the last few days he had lost weight, and there were shadows under his eyes.

"Do not blame yourself for anything," consoled Andreyan.

"How could there be such disloyalty," howled Simonov. "In Borisov we nursed a viper in our bosom. I never suspected . . ."

"Of course you didn't," assured Andreyan. He knew the speech was being made for the purposes of record, but he wished Simonov had waited until he landed in Moscow.

"Have you heard news of the reptile?" demanded the producer.

"I think the British are holding him."

"Well, I hope they lock him in their Tower and cut off his head. Damn the man. He is a saboteur." He drew himself upright. "I must thank you, dear comrade, for the great support you have given us poor artists in this trying situation."

Andreyan smiled. "Your visit was a great success. You read the critics. Especially the *Guardian*. A very worthy paper."

When Simonov wasn't in earshot, Lev Kopkin sidled up to Andreyan.

"I have made the fullest report," he whispered urgently. "Twenty-three pages. It is a very revealing document and I am sure that the Ministry will have to act accordingly. Would you like to endorse it?"

Andreyan regarded him with ill concealed contempt. "I don't think that's necessary," he said coldly. "I'm certain your word is good enough for the authorities. But tell me, what are the revelations?"

Kopkin lowered his voice and stepped nearer Andreyan, who tried to avoid getting a whiff of his breath. "Slackness," he reeled off, "ill discipline, lack of commitment, loose behaviour . . ."

"Oh yes, whose for instance?"

"All over the place," hissed Kopkin. "Simonov runs the company like a troupe of clowns, not a leading group of socialist artists. It was bound to happen, this Borisov business."

Poor Simonov, thought Andreyan. He's going to have a hard time in Moscow. Kopkin and his ilk will do all they can to stir it for him.

"I think it's a very talented group," he said. "You should all be proud of the high standard of performance. The ambassador was most impressed."

Kopkin blinked. "Oh, was he really?"

"Yes, comrade, and a report of that has gone to the Ministry too."

Kopkin looked bothered. "Well," he muttered, "perhaps in my enthusiasm I have expressed myself rather strongly. It could be advisable possibly to tone down a few of the remarks . . ."

"It could be advisable," said Andreyan unkindly.

The Aeroflot jet took off on time, and he stood and watched it fly into the distance. Then he went back to the embassy car.

Apart from Borisov, one other member of the group was missing on the return flight – but with official permission.

Maya, on the eve of the departure from London, had felt unwell. She was too ill to fly. The journey would kill her, she swore. She had to stay in bed. Once she was well again, she would fly on to Moscow by herself.

There were those who thought that Maya Petrova was giving one of her better performances, and that her illness, if it existed at all, was so mild that it would hardly affect her journey. However, as Maya herself said, there are always people jealous of one another.

The decision whether she should go or stay behind was placed on the shoulders of the embassy doctor. He went to her room, and examined her. His verdict was that it would be wiser if she stayed in bed and got rid of whatever bug it was that made her feel unwell before travelling anywhere.

151

So, under the circumstances, he advised the embassy that Simonov and company should leave without her, and that Maya stay behind in London until she was better.

What he did not state in his report was that he was a good friend of Andreyan's and that they'd had a long talk.

Maya showed a remarkable improvement hours after the plane had departed. In fact, she was sufficiently improved to visit Andreyan in his flat in Holland Park.

39

As soon as he accepted Cheyne's invitation to have lunch at his club, he realised he had fallen into a trap.

"Why don't you pick me up at the office," Cheyne suggested, "say 12:30."

It was in the car, on the way to Pall Mall, that Cheyne sprang the trap. The glass partition between them and the driver ensured that they had complete privacy.

"I have had it confirmed," said Cheyne, "we don't want to know about your Russian actor."

Where it was said was important. It wasn't an official meeting in the office. There was no record of it in the departmental diary. It was simply an idle conversation during a car ride. Rathbone noted the fact. How it was said was equally significant. The wording. The imperial "we". Don't challenge it, don't argue was the message. This is the word from on high. It comes from beyond me. It comes direct from *them*.

"What do you suggest we do with him?" asked Rathbone. "He's sitting in Hampstead police station, awaiting his fate."

Cheyne looked out of the car window at the statue of Abraham Lincoln in Parliament Square.

"What did you have in mind?" he murmured, not turning.

"I've got a lot of questions to ask," said Rathbone. "I'd like a chance to get the answers. I think a few days in a safe house . . ."

"No," snapped Cheyne. "No safe house. We don't want him detained by us. We want to wash our hands of him."

They gave you very precise instructions, didn't they, thought Rathbone.

"He is not worth the trouble, Colin. You know how delicate relations are. The talks in Geneva, and the New York meeting. They take offence so easily, and why should we give them any cause . . ."

As if you have ever cared before, said Rathbone to himself. It's never held you back previously.

"It's not as if he was anybody really important," added Cheyne. "I mean, a scientist, a military man, why yes, that's a catch, but an actor . . . I ask you!"

Tourist coaches were causing a hold up in Birdcage Walk, and the car came to a temporary halt, stuck in a stream of traffic.

"Has it ever struck you that Borisov might be more important than he seems?" said Rathbone.

"What do you mean?"

"I don't know. I'm just thinking aloud. And I think he needs debriefing."

Cheyne looked out of the window again.

"We have had our instructions," he said. "We'd like to be rid of him. He ought to go back to Moscow."

Rathbone felt growing anger. "What do you suggest? Deporting him? That would look great, wouldn't it? Russian seeks asylum and is kicked out. Handed back to the KGB . . ."

"Actually, it wouldn't be the first time, would it?" smiled Cheyne. Then he saw Rathbone's face. "I am not serious. I agree it would make unfortunate publicity. But I didn't mean anything like that . . ."

They sat in silence. Finally Rathbone broke it. "The position is this, then. Borisov has asked for asylum. He is waiting to hear our decision. HMG does not want to encourage him, but cannot be seen to kick him out. We'd like to be rid of him, but we don't know how. Correct?"

"An admirable summation, Colin," beamed Cheyne.

"So what does my section do?"

"Ah," said Cheyne. "I thought you'd ask that." He smiled cheerfully. "You must get together with the Russians and between you, you must see if you can't find a solution that avoids embarrassment all the way round." He sat back in the car, a look of contentment on his face.

"Hand him over, you mean?"

"I didn't say that, Colin. I said a solution that does not cause undue embarrassment. You're very adept at these things."

Rathbone said nothing.

"And Colin," continued Cheyne, "in a way you owe me a favour. You caused the whole department a great deal of problems. That business about poor Garner. I worked very hard to cover for you."

Bastard, thought Rathbone. You scheming double dealing bastard. But aloud, he was co-operative. "I'll see what can be done."

"First rate," said Cheyne, peering out of the window again. "Here we are. The club. I hope it's steak and kidney pudding today."

40

She had a terrible dream.

She was back in Moscow, she dreamt, and two men came to her flat.

"Come with us," they demanded, and Maya was driven in a car to the ochre coloured building in Dzerzhinsky Square. They escorted her down a long corridor to an office where a man with a scar on his lip started asking her questions. He didn't seem satisfied with her answers, and she was locked in a room.

Like all dreams, some of it was hazy but much of it seemed to be happening as she dreamt it. She was brought before a woman, middle aged, with a shiny face, who took over the interrogation. She told Maya that now the play acting would stop, it was no good being the helpless little actress, nobody was impressed. She would get the truth out of Maya, she promised, and she, for one, wasn't taken in by a pretty face and fluttering eyelashes.

The man with the scar came back, and showed Maya photographs taken in London. In a restaurant. In a store. In the street. With Andreyan. Arm in arm. Laughing. Getting out of a taxi. Kissing . . .

The dream got confused. From a great height she was looking down into a courtyard, as a figure was brought out, half carried, half dragged. She couldn't make out who the figure was, not even if it was a man or a woman, but she saw the firing squad, and she heard, quite clearly, the volley.

The woman inquisitor was laughing at her, but the man with the scar said it didn't have to be like that, not if she did her patriotic duty, and told them everything. Then Borisov entered the room, and sat down at the table and started playing chess with . . . again, she couldn't identify the person. Borisov never looked at her.

Then she was running down a corridor. At the far end was a door, and when she opened it, Simonov came towards her, smiling. But it was a different Simonov. He was wearing the uniform of a colonel, and as he approached everyone stood at attention. Then she was grabbed, and thrown into a cell.

The woman interrogator came in, and hit her across the face. Then the woman produced a thick file, and said the information was almost complete, they didn't have many

155

more inquiries to make, then they could close the case. Of course she could make it easier for herself by helping them ...

In her dream she screamed. She didn't know what they wanted from her, then the man with the scar handed her a bouquet of red roses. It was a token, he said, that they knew she was on their side. And he asked her, very gently, if it had never struck her that Andreyan might be working for the other side?

She stared at him, and the man nodded, rather sadly, and said that he was surprised she hadn't suspected it. Now that she knew, she must realise how dangerous it was to be involved with Andreyan.

Andreyan, lying in bed beside Maya, did not seem to be aware of anything.

"Good morning," he greeted her, when she opened her eyes. "Did you sleep well?"

She smiled at him. She was naked, and she reached for her wrap.

"No, don't," said Andreyan. "Show me how you make love first thing in the morning."

But, afterwards, she remembered the dream.

41

Andreyan arranged for an embassy car to take him to his appointment at the Dorchester. He could have taken a cab, but he wanted the meeting to be officially logged. This way everybody would record the journey, the policeman in Kensington Palace Gardens who notes these movements, and those whose eyes were always prying.

It was a delicate mission, a meeting in no man's land

under the flag of truce, an arrangement which suited both sides and could be denied by either. Rathbone was already sitting in the lounge, and Andreyan smiled and sat down in the chair next to him.

"I'm sorry to be late," he apologised, "the traffic . . ."

They looked at each other with undisguised interest, both thinking of the files they had on the other, the background dossiers they had assembled, the habits and inclinations and weaknesses each man hoped he knew about the other.

"My people felt there should be an informal contact . . ."

"And mine think that's a most constructive suggestion."

That's how it was set up. The Dorchester's lounge was considered suitably neutral, and eminently public. Nothing could be misunderstood. After all, Andreyan could hardly invite Rathbone to the embassy, and Soviet diplomats would be ill advised to visit the Special Section.

Rathbone looked just as Andreyan expected, exactly like his pictures, and he noticed that he wore an American shirt with a button down collar. Possibly a relic from his days in Washington.

Rathbone considered Andreyan lived up to the impression he had gained of him. Alert, intelligent, the hint of a sense of humour. Ready to smile, but very shrewd.

When they'd arranged the meeting, it was Rathbone who had suggested somewhere around Mayfair, and Andreyan who proposed the Dorchester as the venue. When he had told Leonov, the colonel grunted, "The drinks are expensive."

"Don't worry," Andreyan replied, "Rathbone doesn't touch alcohol."

True to form, he had a glass of orange juice on the table beside him.

"Can I get you something?" offered Rathbone.

"Perrier would be nice."

It registered with Rathbone. "You don't either?"

"Not today," said Andreyan.

The waiter brought the mineral water on a silver tray.

After he had gone, Rathbone turned to Andreyan.

"Men in our position should get to know one another, don't you think? I have felt for some time we should have periodic informal meetings. After all, our other colleagues do. The military attachés, for instance."

"Yes," agreed Andreyan. "As a matter of fact, we ought to take a leaf out of their book and have lunch now and then. They have a very good time, I'm told. The parties at the Gore Hotel were memorable . . ."

Including the time, he thought, when you people set up our naval man and took his picture after he'd celebrated too well. It was a lesson the embassy had not forgotten. They later retaliated with a snapshot of an American service attaché kissing a diplomatic wife rather too enthusiastically.

"Well now," said Rathbone. "I suppose we ought to get down to business."

Andreyan followed the brief he had been given carefully. "This meeting is of course quite unofficial, and as far as the record is concerned, it has never taken place," he began carefully. "You do understand, my friend?"

"Of course," said Rathbone.

"Our position is that we wish to have personal access to our citizen. We appreciate that you are being most helpful, and you are of course aware that we have a right in any case to see him. So I don't suppose there is any sort of problem, is there?"

"None at all," said Rathbone pleasantly. "You are at perfect liberty to talk to Mr Borisov."

"Good. Your attitude is appreciated, Mr Rathbone."

"Colin," said Rathbone. "Why don't you call me Colin?"

Andreyan blinked. Then he raised his glass of Perrier water and gave Rathbone a mock toast.

"Excellent, Colin. I am Sergei Mikhailovitch. Serge, if you like."

"Serge," said Rathbone and raised his glass too.

He wondered what Cheyne would make of it in his report. "We exchanged first names and introduced a note of informality." Then he wondered if he should put it in the report at all. He wanted to head off the inevitable "You're sure you're not getting too chummy," remark. He could write Cheyne's sermon:

"While of course we seek harmonious and cordial relations with them, we should not allow too close an association. You must remember at all times to keep it friendly but formal, and not to put yourself in a situation which could be misconstrued. A certain distance has to be kept."

"So, when can I see Borisov?" Andreyan broke into his thoughts.

"Any time," said Rathbone. "Tomorrow if you like. In the morning. I'll take you to him."

"You're holding him where?"

"He is still at Hampstead police station."

"Ah," said Andreyan. "Not at a safe house?"

"Oh no."

Interesting, reflected Andreyan. They don't seem in a hurry to whisk Borisov out of sight. In the past, they've hidden defectors within hours.

"He is well?"

"In excellent shape," replied Rathbone.

Andreyan nodded. "Good. His poor wife must be very worried. We shall inform her that he is all right."

"Are you married, Serge?" asked Rathbone almost casually.

Bastard, thought Andreyan. Playing games again. You know damn well what's going on. You know who I've been sleeping with. But he smiled. "I am that rare thing, Colin, a diplomat who is a desirable bachelor – so I like to think. Up to now, I am a free man."

Rathbone smiled back at him. "Enjoy it while you can."

"And you?" inquired Andreyan. Two can play at the game, you son of a bitch.

"It's a long story. One day we must both get drunk on mineral water and I will tell you."

159

"I'd like that." He hesitated. "Why don't we have dinner sometime?"

Rathbone gave him a curious look. "Why not?" he said at last. "It might be a very good idea."

"I am sure," continued Andreyan, "that we have lots to talk about. I enjoy being in England, and it always gives me pleasure to meet Englishmen."

Especially those in Special Liaison, but he didn't say it aloud.

"Have you had the chance to see much of the country?" asked Rathbone.

"My dear Colin, you forget, travel for us is very limited. Your Foreign Office regulations are very restrictive. Thirty miles does not give one much room to explore."

"Well," said Rathbone, "you can always ask for an exemption. The protocol people are very understanding. If there's anything special you have in mind . . ."

Andreyan nodded. "Yes, of course. Perhaps you can plead my case when the time comes . . ." And their eyes met, momentarily.

Rathbone looked at his watch. "Dear me, I'm afraid I'll have to leave. I've got a meeting."

They both stood up.

"It is arranged then. Hampstead police station. Tomorrow, at eleven? Good." Andreyan looked pleased. "I will try and persuade our missing comrade that there is no problem, and we will welcome him home with open arms. I am sure he will be delighted."

"I am sure," said Rathbone drily.

"Thank you, Colin, for your co-operation. I will report to my superiors how cordial my reception has been."

"But of course, this meeting has never taken place."

"Precisely," said Andreyan, then he held out his hand. "When all this is over, I look forward to our getting together, my friend."

His grip was very firm, and again, briefly, he looked Rathbone straight in the eye.

160

On the steps of the hotel he turned, and gave a wave. The black Soviet embassy car pulled up and Andreyan got in.

In the lobby, sitting over a pot of tea and buttered toast, Hal Dupree, of the Defense Intelligence Agency, watched with interest as Rathbone went to make a phone call.

He signalled the waiter to pay his bill. He wanted to get back to Grosvenor Square, and file a report about the fascinating meeting he had observed between the man from the Soviet embassy and the fellow from British Intelligence.

42

The pirate broadcasts of Russkaya Volya were increasing in frequency; they now came on the air, at irregular intervals, two or three times a night.

Their latest claim was that Simonov, the producer, had been arrested, and was being held responsible for the disastrous London tour of his company. This was a lie, but it sounded highly convincing to those who tuned their dial to seek out the illicit transmissions.

There were other lies too. Russkaya Volya announced air crashes that had never happened. Internal Aeroflot flights had a high accident rate, and several disasters had been kept from the Soviet public. The intention was clear – to undermine confidence in domestic air travel. Also, there were more allegations about growing corruption, and a story that a Soviet general had been executed by firing squad for "disloyalty".

Clearly those who operated the radio station believed in the shot gun system; they fired from all barrels, hoping that some of the pellets would hit home. If only a few of the lies were picked up, and spread by idle tongues, those behind the broadcasts would have achieved their object; to unsettle and confuse.

The Fifth Department, anxious to convince the Central Committee that it was actively investigating these activities, compiled a special report on the illicit stations that were poisoning the ether. There were actually quite a few. October Storm specialised in spreading rumours and false reports in Mongolia, of all places. Then there was Radio Iskra, named after the Bolshevik revolutionary underground paper. Iskra, meaning "Spark", poured out black propaganda in a steady stream, as well as Voice of the People, and another curious station calling itself Revolution. But Russkaya Volya was something special. By claiming to be an underground outfit run by true Communists and real Soviet patriots, intent only on exposing the failings of the present regime, it could fool those who would never bother to listen to anti-Russian propaganda.

Not only that, but Russkaya Volya cleverly mocked the West. It had little time for the Americans. It sneered at "the warmongers in the Pentagon". It lampooned the British. It expressed great hostility towards the Germans, reminding its listeners that it was Germany which invaded the motherland. All this larded with Soviet folk music, and slabs of patriotic fervour.

Of course, compared to the 2,000 hours a week in sixty-three foreign languages poured out by Moscow, and the avalanches of propaganda and news bulletins aimed at Eastern Europe by Radio Liberty, Radio Free Europe, Voice of America and all the other massive operators, the pinpricks of mavericks like Russkaya Volya were minute.

Nevertheless, as Marshal Pavlov had pointed out, a pinprick can infect the whole body. This little pirate station was dangerous. Even if only a few hundred listened to it each night, and only a handful repeated its lies, the germs were planted, and there was no telling where the infection might spread.

162

A special order went out to the 15,000 technicians manning the 3,000 powerful transmitters which the Soviet Union uses to jam foreign broadcasts to ensure that their nightly efforts intensified to blot out this pirate station.

The maximum effort will only have to be temporary, promised Marshal Pavlov. The cancer calling itself Russkaya Volya would soon be ruthlessly cut out.

43

"No," said Borisov. "I am not going back."

It was like a stage tableau. The British sitting on one side of the table, the Russians facing them. Sitting between them was Borisov.

"I am sorry," added Borisov. "I have made up my mind. It is finished."

The expression of the colourless gentleman from the Foreign Office, sitting beside Rathbone, was that of total distaste. His name was Harris, and he wore, unbelievably, an Eton school tie. He had a brief case with him which he never opened; Rathbone suspected he carried it as a symbol of office.

Andreyan said nothing, but Colonel Leonov glowered at Borisov.

"You have an obligation. You are a Soviet citizen. You have a Soviet decoration. You are married to a Soviet woman. Your duty is clear."

"It is not an easy decision," said Borisov. "But I have to live with it."

Leonov's face hardened. "I must warn you, comrade . . ."

"No threats, please, gentlemen," interrupted Harris languidly.

"Very well," growled Leonov. "I must simply remind you of the consequences of such an action."

Borisov said nothing.

"Do you not love your country?" asked Andreyan.

"Of course I do."

"But you wish to desert it?"

"It is not a political decision," said Borisov.

"No?"

Borisov suddenly laughed. A harsh, humourless laugh. They all looked at him.

"You are sick," declared Leonov, and nodded with conviction. "You have had a breakdown. I understand. You need to be in hospital. We shall take you home and arrange for you to receive psychiatric care so you will be well again." He beamed at them all, like a man who has come up with the ideal solution.

"I know all about psychiatric care," murmured Borisov.

Leonov avoided his look.

Harris cleared his throat. "I think I ought to say that as far as Her Majesty's government is concerned we are perfectly happy to see Mr Borisov return home. We will certainly not place any – er – impediment in his way."

"Ah," said Leonov. "The attitude of your authorities is appreciated. Is it not?" He glanced at Andreyan.

"It is what we expected," confirmed Andreyan. He saw Rathbone watching him.

"No," said Borisov. "I have told you. I do not wish to return."

They sat in rather embarrassed silence.

"Well, of course, we can't *force* anyone to go home," remarked Harris at last. He seemed to have swallowed something distasteful.

"Tell me," asked Rathbone, and it was the first time he had spoken, "why do you want to stay in this country?"

"It is a private matter," replied Borisov slowly. "I do not wish to discuss it in front of these . . . these . . ." He gestured

164

across at the two Russians. It was a contemptuous wave of his hand.

Leonov's face was slightly red. "Your attitude will be reported, I promise," he grated. "I will see to it myself . . ."

"Please," cautioned Harris painfully, his look of distaste even more pronounced.

"Please," echoed Andreyan, leaning closer to Borisov. "I must ask you again. Are you sure about this? You are an actor. Your profession is your life. How can you be an actor in the West? How could you do your work here?"

"I am not going back," repeated Borisov stubbornly. "You can keep me here till doomsday, you can keep badgering me, but I have decided. I wish to have asylum."

"Well, gentlemen," said Harris. "I think we seem to have reached stalemate. Mr Borisov has been given every opportunity to change his mind but since he persists." He shrugged. "I'm afraid that's the end of the matter."

Leonov's fist thudded on the table. "No!" he cried. "This man is our citizen. We demand that he be returned to us. We insist that he is placed in the hands of the embassy and . . ."

Harris stood up. "I'm sorry, but I think I said the matter is closed."

The two Russians left in an embassy Zil. It was a formal parting, but Andreyan whispered to Rathbone in the corridor: "We'll have dinner yet." Then he and Leonov walked out, and Borisov was taken back to a detention room.

"Messy business," sniffed Harris. "I don't like defectors, and I don't like Russian heavies."

And I don't like you, thought Rathbone, but he kept his own counsel.

"Well, it's over to you," said Harris. "You're stuck with chummy. I fear we have to give the blighter a visa. Pro tem anyway." Rathbone helped him on with his overcoat. It had a velvet collar. "I suppose it's really the end of the story for you," added Harris and picked up his brief case.

Oh no, thought Rathbone. Actually, it may only be the start.

Rathbone returned to his office, closed the door, and pulled the telephone towards him. For a moment or two he hesitated. Then he dialled a number. It was a long-distance number, and it took a little time for anyone to answer. Eventually, the phone was picked up at the other end, and Rathbone said: "May I speak to Father Stephen, please?"

44

Kleber's luck ran out at the corner of Regent Street and Maddox Street. As his car turned into the main traffic stream, a man on the pavement, waiting to cross the road, caught a brief glimpse of him behind the wheel. It was only for a second, but it was enough. It was Kleber's bad luck that the man was an El Al sky marshal, trained to memorise the faces of terrorists. He didn't know Kleber's name, but he remembered the face. It had been circulated to El Al and all Israeli missions after the dentist was murdered in the Hague, and there wasn't an Israeli security man in Europe who wasn't on alert for it.

Kleber's car shot on, and he never noticed the man who suddenly froze. He had no idea that he had been recognised, but as he drove on, the Israeli was writing the registration number of the Capri on a piece of paper.

As soon as he found a phone kiosk, he called a certain number and reported that he had spotted the Hague suspect. And he gave the car's registration.

Mossad is a small organisation, and has few personnel assigned to London, but their contacts are remarkable, and their lines of communication reach into many quarters.

So within ten minutes C13, the anti-terrorist squad at Scotland Yard, had been tipped off about Kleber's presence

166

in London. Around the same time the alert was circulated to the gentlemen who euphemistically call themselves "legal attachés" at the United States embassy.

This circulation of information works on a quid pro quo basis. Once a jig-saw is being built it is the form that anyone who finds a piece that fits informs the other interested parties.

The registration number of the Capri was quickly established as belonging to a hire car firm in Edgware Road. The detective who went there struck lucky. The licensee's name, he discovered, was Kleber. He had produced a West German passport, an international driver's licence, paid the deposit in cash and given the address of a small mews flat in Paddington.

It was typical of Kleber to use the name he had assumed and give his correct address. He was a great believer in not telling unnecessary lies. Once he assumed an identity, he stuck to it until it had to be discarded.

He had hired the car to be mobile. He probably wasn't going to use it a lot, taxis and the underground were more anonymous, but he wanted to have transport available at any time. The irony was that when he went for the drive in the West End he had no particular object in mind. He wanted to get used to the car, and become acclimatised to driving on the wrong side of the road. He was new to English traffic.

He stopped and bought a paper. He was toying with the idea of going to a concert that evening. Apart from the fact that he enjoyed good music, he found it gave him a marvellous opportunity to plan mentally. But perhaps it would be better to have an early night. On a mission, he was like an athlete in training. He inflicted a rigid regimen on himself.

Kleber switched on the car radio. The pop music was discordant and he pulled a face. He re-tuned the dial until he came across some Sibelius.

He was driving along the Embankment. He liked rivers running through cities. The Seine. The Neva. The Main. In the sunlight, the Thames and its river front looked attractive. He was enjoying himself, then he frowned. Was he getting over confident? Was he enjoying his mission too much? So far he had led a charmed life. But supposing . . .

His face for example. He was pretty sure they had no good picture of himself. And yet? Suppose they had got one? Then he reassured himself. Definitely not. The immigration officer at Gatwick hadn't even given him a second glance. If his face had been circulated . . .

And, of course, Viktor would never use him if he was compromised. They wouldn't have sent him over here.

He relaxed on the rest of the drive. Once this job was over, he would definitely take that vacation. He liked the thought of letting himself go, for once. He would relax, doze in the sun, stop looking over his shoulder. He'd find a woman and spoil her. Yes, he deserved a holiday.

Kleber whistled the Sibelius theme through his teeth as he approached the mews, then suddenly he stopped. It was nothing really, but he sensed danger. That, after all, was his insurance policy.

Parked at the top of the mews, quite innocuously, was a yellow British Telecom van. That was all. There were no men to be seen. Nobody was working in the mews. The van simply stood parked, two doors from his flat.

Kleber switched off the radio. He sat quietly, the car engine running.

He knew they had found him.

45

The head of C13 was the last arrival at the meeting and apologised for being late. How well dressed these spook coppers are, thought Rathbone, looking at him, and Binyon. There was nothing plain about their clothes.

168

The anti-terrorist branch was the host, and a Scotland Yard canteen lady brought in tea and biscuits, then left them to it. There was no formal agenda, but they were there to discuss one man: Kleber.

"There is no doubt in my mind that he has come to this country for a specific purpose," stated the head of C13 after they had gone over the preliminaries. "He only shows up when he's on assignment. He doesn't go for targets or opportunity. He is always after one particular person."

He said it with a certain amount of self satisfaction, like an oracle that has pronounced. Rathbone didn't take to him. Least of all he liked the oily hair, carefully plastered down.

"That's all very well," said Rathbone, and almost immediately regretted betraying his animosity, "but what would be more helpful is to know who you think he is targeting."

C13 glanced at him coldly. "I would have thought that's more in your line, Mr Rathbone," he retorted smoothly. "After all, you are Special Liaison. You have your fingers in all sorts of interesting pies. I was hoping you could tell us something."

The man from Special Branch cleared his throat. "My feeling is that he may be after an Israeli target," he said, rather diffidently. "One, the latest target he hit was an Israeli operative in Belgium."

"Holland," corrected Rathbone. "The Hague."

Special Branch inclined his head. "Absolutely correct. I am sorry. Anyway, that's point one. Point two, Kleber has been associating with Libyan elements. There seems to be a relationship of some kind between him and Tripoli. Three, Yoram is coming to London."

"Who is Yoram?" asked Rathbone, frowning. This was something he was not briefed on.

"Yoram," explained Special Branch, enjoying his knowledge, "is an Israeli go between. They send him around the place when they want to have unofficial negotiations with people who may not want to be seen talking to Israel. Moderates in the PLO, for example."

"So you think somebody like Gadaffi would be delighted to terminate him?"

"It's an educated guess," smiled Special Branch.

They're all so smug, thought Rathbone. Because they're on the inside track, because they are privy to so many covert happenings, they ooze an aura of being know-alls.

"Why come to London to kill Yoram?" asked Rathbone. "It's not the only place where they can get to him, is it?"

Special Branch shrugged.

C13 stirred his tea. "The question really is what we do about Kleber," he said.

"When we can get hold of him," added Special Branch.

"Precisely. As I see it, we have various options. We can, as soon as we have him in custody, deport him. No problem about that. Or we can try, once we have traced him, to keep tabs on him, stick with him wherever he goes, let him lead us to his contacts and, possibly, his target. Or . . ."

They all waited.

"We can ask one of Mr Rathbone's other sections to take over and deal with him."

"You mean, eliminate him?" asked Rathbone brutally.

C13 looked pained. "I'm sure you appreciate that, as a police officer, that thought could never enter my head."

It was at this point that Rathbone actually began to enjoy himself. "Perhaps I can help you gentlemen," he said, sounding rather smug. "You see we have a very good idea why Mr Kleber has come and who his target is."

All their heads swung round. The only man who hadn't said a word and looked faintly amused was Binyon. He sat beside his Special Branch colleague and there was a slight smile on his face as he waited for Rathbone to continue.

"We think his target is our Russian defector," announced Rathbone. "The actor Borisov."

C13 leant forward. He was frowning. He disliked surprises like that. "What do you base that on, Mr Rathbone?"

"We found a picture in his flat. With a couple of false passports and a supply of travellers cheques. Why should he have a photograph of Borisov – unless he had been given it when he got his orders?"

C13 pushed his tea cup to one side. It was a rather impatient gesture. "You found that in his *flat*?"

"Under the false bottom of his suitcase."

"You *entered* his flat?" C13's tone was hostile.

Rathbone nodded.

"With authority?"

Oh give over, thought Rathbone. Stop playing silly buggers. Did you really think we would apply for permission in triplicate, or go to Marylebone magistrates court and swear out a warrant? "As you said, we have our fingers in various pies," pointed out Rathbone maliciously.

"As soon as we located it, we watched his flat," said C13. "We had it staked out. We didn't notice anyone entering it."

I must commend Alcott, noted Rathbone mentally. He did a really professional job. The clowns weren't even aware that he was in the place under their noses.

"What have you done with the photo?"

"Taken possession of it."

C13 was outraged. "But that will tell him you've been through his things . . ."

Binyon smiled openly as Rathbone lashed out: "Oh come on, Kleber knows we've rumbled his hideout. He was probably watching you people when you were in the mews. Laughing at that British Telecom van of yours. You should really get a new vehicle. Try a Harrods delivery van."

C13's expression was sickly.

Binyon raised his hand. "Tell me, why do you think they've sent somebody to kill Borisov? What is so important about him? Why should they be so anxious to – er – execute Borisov? An actor?"

"That," nodded Rathbone, "is the really fascinating question. Why is Borisov a target?"

171

C13 was doodling on the pad lying in front of him. "What do you actually have on him? What's his profile?"

"He's an actor. Very well known in theatrical circles in Moscow. He's got quite a following, I gather. Until now, a pretty distinguished career, and obviously in the party's good books, that's why he's a People's Artist with all the perks."

"Doesn't sound like a man who defects," said C13 drily.

"Can you tell me who *is* the sort of man who defects?" asked Rathbone. His tone was silky. "I'd love to know the symptoms. They could be very useful to put in a guide book."

C13 doodled furiously. It was Binyon who chimed in: "What about his personal life? Married, isn't he?"

Rathbone nodded.

"Have they picked her up since he absconded? What's happened to her?" Binyon asked.

A signal to Moscow SIS station had already gone out, requesting them to covertly check on Mrs Borisov.

"So far, everything seems normal. She goes shopping, visits friends . . ."

"Everything is so bloody normal," grunted C13, "and yet they've sent a man like Kleber to eliminate him . . ."

"I heard," said Binyon almost diffidently, "that he had an affair with one of the actresses who came over, and that she's still over here."

C13 stopped doodling and looked up.

"Yes," said Rathbone, "indeed. But I'm afraid Miss Petrova has transferred her affections. She's having a, er, relationship with friend Andreyan." He smiled coldly. "It's quite an interesting situation," he added. "We're on to it."

They waited, but Rathbone said no more.

"It's not like people at their embassy, to get involved with visiting actresses," reflected C13. "Especially not people in Andreyan's job . . ."

"She's a very attractive lady," remarked Binyon. "I hear

the watchers are quite taken with her. Isn't that so, Colin?"
But Rathbone just nodded.

There was a tap on the door, and one of C13's men entered
with a piece of paper. He went over to his chief and gave it to
him. Then he left again, as quietly as he came. A man who
moves very silently, thought Rathbone.

C13 unfolded the paper and read it. Then he looked up at
them. "Gentlemen," he said, "we have some news of Kleber.
His Capri has been found abandoned, parked in Kentish
Town. There's no sign of Kleber himself."

"Well," said Binyon, "it's a hire car, and he knows we've
traced him, and his address. He's ditched the car, and I'd
say he's gone underground."

There was a moment's silence.

"Our Russian friend, the actor, you have him in safe
hands, do you?" asked C13 finally.

"In very safe hands," said Rathbone. He thought of
Father Stephen and, as always, he felt secure.

"May I ask where you are holding him?"

"Hopefully," said Rathbone, "in a place where Herr
Kleber won't find him."

46

Before they went to bed, Andreyan said nothing to her,
which was one of the things she resented most afterwards. It
was almost as if he wanted to ensure that she'd make love to
him before she knew, because later . . .

Andreyan, as she had found out, could be very gentle in
bed, but this time his passion was rough, almost violent. He
took her body, and while previously she had moaned and
sighed with pleasure at his love making, this time she cried

173

out with pain. It was almost as if he felt frustrated by her willingness to give herself to him, and wanted to force himself on her. She realised that there was another side to the Andreyan she knew, a violent, savage side.

Afterwards, he lay beside her, panting a little, his body damp with perspiration. She ached, and instead of the usual languid pleasure, she felt puzzled and a little angry. Why did he want to hurt her?

Then, in the dark, he said: "Tomorrow morning you must go to the consulate, and see Ostrov."

"Why? Who is Ostrov? Why do I have to see him?"

"To regularise things," replied Andreyan, and the way he said it he sounded like one of the party officials she was so used to. It was the way they all sounded when they said "It is required" or "Regulations demand" or "It is an order".

"I don't understand," whispered Maya.

"Ostrov will explain. It won't take long."

"Can you come with me?" she pleaded, in a little voice.

"No," said Andreyan. "It would not be proper. It is not my department."

She knew it was bad news. "But what . . . what does he want with me?"

"I told you," said Andreyan, and he sounded a little irritated. "It is an official requirement. To regularise your position."

They lay in the bed beside each other in silence after that, but they might each have been in different rooms. There was a wall between them.

Very quietly, because she didn't want him to hear her, she cried a little, her head buried in the pillow, and it was only then that, in the dark, he reached out for her.

"Listen, my love," he whispered, and he sounded amazingly tender after what had happened, "don't worry about anything. I will take care of you . . ."

He spoke almost as if he wanted to make sure that nobody could hear him, which was absurd of course. In the privacy of the bedroom, they were safe.

"I don't want to be separated from you," said Maya. "Please."

But the tenderness stopped. He turned his back to her, wished her good night, then all she heard was his steady breathing. No matter what was on his mind, Andreyan could go to sleep like an electric light that is switched off.

She arrived at the consulate in the Bayswater Road and was shown into Ostrov's office immediately. His window overlooked the traffic outside, and suddenly Maya felt a great longing to be out there, not within these walls, not on official soil . . .

"Ah, yes," said Ostrov, "I hope you brought your passport?"

She handed it to him. He looked at it, and wrote something in it. Then he unlocked a drawer and took out a rubber stamp and an ink pad. Carefully, meticulously, he stamped her passport. Then he gave it back to her.

"What is this?" she asked, her stomach tightening.

"It is a formality," said Ostrov. "Your exit visa from the Soviet Union. Allowing you to travel abroad. I have revoked it from midnight tomorrow."

Maya felt cold. "I . . . I don't understand . . ."

"It is quite simple. You must return to Moscow within twenty-four hours. If you are still abroad after midnight tomorrow, you will have violated your travel permission. Here." He opened another drawer, and handed her an airline ticket. "Your flight is tomorrow afternoon. Aeroflot. From Heathrow. Have a very pleasant journey." His smile was chilly, but that had no special meaning. It was simply Ostrov's manner.

"But . . . I . . . I don't want to leave London yet," stammered Maya. "I have made no plans to return so soon . . ."

"So soon?" Ostrov raised his eyebrows. "It was only for medical reasons that we agreed to you staying behind when your company returned home. You look very healthy to me now. Are you healthy? Well, are you?"

She nodded, dumbly.

"So, what is there to keep you here? Your place is in the homeland. You have no reason for not returning." His eyes were fixed on her, unrelenting, unblinking. The sun was shining through the window, but she thought of that awful dream. Of being interrogated, and held in that dark prison . . .

"But why . . . why now?" she asked desperately.

"Surely you know you cannot stay over here indefinitely," said Ostrov. "Why, even the British wouldn't allow it. They have only given you a limited entry visa. Soon you will be an illegal alien." He said the words with immense satisfaction. "I am sure," he added, "that you would not want to cause a diplomatic incident." He waited. "Would you?"

"No, of course not," she said in a low voice.

"You have twenty-four hours," said Ostrov, rising. "Do some shopping. I understand you like shopping in London. Get the things you need. Enjoy yourself, pack, and tomorrow you'll be back home. Isn't that a lovely thought?"

She came down the steps of the consulate, and walked past the policeman outside the entrance in a daze. He gave her a disinterested look.

She looked at the people in the street, the shops, the cars, and she felt rather like a condemned person whose execution was approaching. All her dreams of another life, of success in the dazzling world of London and Paris and New York, of stardom in Hollywood, acclaim on Broadway, sleek cars, luxurious penthouses, gorgeous clothes, they were all fading. Yes, she was like a moth round the naked flame of a candle, she knew what happened to moths, but if she was going to get burnt by the flames, she was going to enjoy it. She was going to live to the full, and to hell with you, comrades.

But that was all finished . . .

She went back to Holland Park, let herself into Andreyan's flat, and sat and sobbed.

He came back from the embassy early. He put his brief case down, and came over to her, putting his arms round her.

"What's the matter?" he said, looking at her tear-streaked face. For once she had allowed her make-up to go awry. The lipstick was smudged, and the mascara had run.

"I am leaving tomorrow," she said, flatly. "They have ordered me back."

"Ostrov?"

She glared at Andreyan. "Who else, damn it? You knew it, didn't you? You knew orders had come from Moscow, and you didn't do a thing about it. You didn't even warn me, you bastard."

"There was nothing I could do," he said a little sadly. "I cannot interfere."

"You cannot interfere!" she sneered. "You cannot do anything! No of course not. The KGB has no power. A KGB officer has no influence. You cannot lift a finger." She was crying again. "You know what a fool I am? I thought you loved me. I actually thought you cared for me."

Andreyan looked away. Then he faced her. "I do," he said very quietly. "I care for you more than you will ever know."

"Go to hell!" she shouted and dashed into the bathroom, slamming the door.

After she'd packed her things, they had something to eat. Andreyan said very little, and she did her best to ignore him. He had taken a folder out of his brief case and was sitting in the armchair studying it, and making notes on a pad. It became too much for her finally.

"Can't you say something?" she cried. "Do you have to read that thing the whole evening?"

"It's very important," said Andreyan. "I have to make an urgent report on it. I'm sorry but I have to work on it."

It was a terrible evening, and they said very little to one another. Then Andreyan announced that he was going to have a bath. She grunted something, and he left the room.

She sat there, glowering. The folder was lying on the armchair. She hated it. It was the damn thing that was more important than her. More important than her last day in

177

London. He buried himself in it and ignored her. She felt like tearing the bloody thing up.

Maya went over and picked it up. It was an official file from the embassy. It was yellow, and had a green ribbon round it and two red seals on the cover. "Most Secret" it said, "Not To Be Removed From The Referentura. Soviet Eyes Only. Officers Only. This is a State Document."

"What are you doing?" asked Andreyan from the doorway.

"Looking at your ever so important document," said Maya. "Do you mind?" Her voice was cold, sneering.

"You shouldn't even touch that," protested Andreyan, quite mildly.

"Oh really?" she taunted him. "Well, you shouldn't even have it here, should you? Isn't that what it says – 'Not to be removed from the referentura'? Isn't that a breach of security?"

He came over and took the file from her. "Don't be stupid," he snapped. "I have authority. This is an embassy apartment. It is Soviet soil. So, don't preach me sermons about security."

He put the file back in his brief case and locked it. "Leave it alone," he warned.

She changed her manner. "What's it about anyway?" she asked innocently.

"I can't tell you," he said, "you should know that. It is very important, that's all. Don't touch it. It's very secret."

They declared a truce after that, and in bed Andreyan was his old self. Kind, considerate, gentle.

"Don't worry, my love," he said, holding her, "you have a wonderful future ahead of you. A great career, great success . . ."

Suddenly all her hostility and resentment left her. "Without you . . ." she whispered. "I'm not sure if I want it like that . . ."

"Perhaps," said Andreyan, "it won't be quite like that. Perhaps we will meet again. It is after all a small world. Satellites orbit it in ninety minutes, what is distance?"

She snuggled up to him. "Do I really have to leave?" she asked.

"You know Moscow." He kissed her. "An order is an order."

They talked a lot more, then they embraced. Three times that night they made love: it was as if they both wanted to store up memories.

In the morning, they were very subdued.

"I will come with an embassy car to take you to Heathrow," said Andreyan.

Maya shook her head. "I'd rather you didn't. I'd rather we said goodbye now. I don't want to say farewell . . ." She swallowed.

"Nonsense," said Andreyan. "Of course I'll see you off. The embassy always shows courtesy to visiting guests. I will pick you up at noon." Then he kissed her, and held her, and for a moment she forgot all except his presence.

"See you later," called out Andreyan and waved to her from the door. And for one lasting moment looked her in the eyes, then he was gone.

She paced up and down, glancing at the time every few minutes. She had packed everything. Her luggage was piled up in the hall, ready. There was nothing else for her to do. She was helpless while her precious time was ticking away.

Then she saw the brief case. He hadn't taken it with him. Her first thought was to phone him at the embassy and let him know. Then another thought was born.

She hesitated, chewed her lip, and wandered around the flat. All the while a voice inside was asking, why not? Maya believed above all things that fate helps those who help themselves. After all, it wasn't her fault that he had left state secrets behind.

She tried to open the brief case but it was very difficult. She would obviously have to force it. She used a pair of kitchen scissors and a big sharp knife. It was hard work and she nearly sliced one of her fingers off. But finally she managed to get the yellow file out.

An hour later, she arrived at the American embassy in Grosvenor Square looking stunning, which was no accident. She had taken great pains with her appearance, put on an outfit that showed her and her excellent figure off to best advantage. She had taken equal care with her make-up.

The short cab ride to Mayfair was, in some ways, the longest journey Maya had ever made. After this, there would be no turning back. She had closed the door for ever. She saw nothing of the park they passed, or the traffic jam at Marble Arch. Even when the cab stopped at the embassy she had to remind herself that she had arrived, and from now on she could only continue with this journey. There was no return.

She walked into the embassy and to the man who received visitors and said the line she had been rehearsing since she'd first made her decision:

"I am a Soviet citizen and I have some important information."

He gave her a peculiar look, and turned to the Marine guard. She did not hear what he said, but the Marine started making phone calls, then another man appeared and escorted her to a waiting room.

She sat alone, shaking slightly. She wasn't sure if she wasn't feeling sick. The man who entered smiled warmly.

"Good morning," he said. "My name is Dupree. Can I help you?"

She was clutching the file. She had wrapped it in brown paper she had found in Andreyan's kitchen.

"I am Maya Aleksandrovna Petrova," she began falteringly. "I have brought a document . . ."

"It's all right," said Dupree, "you can speak Russian. I understand it quite well." He held out his hand for the parcel. "Is this it?" he asked.

But she made no move to give it to him.

"Please," she said, "this is very dangerous for me. I wish to have a promise."

"Oh yes?" Dupree eyed her warily. He hoped they had switched on the tape and were recording the interview.

180

"I must have your word. If I give you this, I want to go to America. I want to have a work permit. You have to take me to the United States. That is my condition."

"I see." Dupree perched on the corner of the table. "I must tell you that rather depends." And again he reached for the package.

"No!" said Maya. "You promise. Or I go."

"I was going to say," Dupree went on smoothly, "that rather depends on what you have got there."

He waited but she shook her head.

"It is very secret, it is very important, you will see."

What he next said surprised her.

"Do you have your passport, Miss Petrova?"

She gave it to him, and after he had looked at it he said: "I see they've cancelled your Soviet exit permit."

She nodded. "Of course. That is why I am here. I have no choice. I am not going back."

"And where have you been staying in London?" he asked.

"With a member of the Soviet embassy," said Maya. "Sergei Mikhailovitch Andreyan. You know of him?"

That was when Dupree became interested.

"He is KGB," added Maya. After all, what harm could that do now. She had plunged Andreyan into enough trouble, a little more couldn't make things worse for him.

"Indeed," said Dupree non-committally. Then he smiled at her. "I think you'd better show me this document. I promise you you'll be taken care of . . ."

There were those who might not have been reassured by Dupree's choice of phrase. Especially those who knew Dupree. Maya hesitated. But she had a good instinct. She knew the time had come to declare her hand.

"Here," she said, and gave him the package.

He unwrapped the yellow file, opened it, and started leafing through the pages. Then, very quietly, he stood up and said: "I won't be long, Miss Petrova."

He left the room. She glanced round her colourless surroundings and at a framed photograph of the Grand

181

Canyon on the wall. She looked at her watch, and realised Andreyan would soon be coming to fetch her from the flat in Holland Park. He would find her gone, the brief case ripped open, the yellow file missing. She shut her eyes. She didn't want to think about it.

Of course she regretted it. Andreyan would be in trouble. Terrible trouble. Losing a document like that . . . it could mean a trial, a labour camp, exile, maybe execution. She shuddered. No, not that. He wasn't a traitor, after all. Just careless. But was a KGB man allowed to be careless?

Then she thought, serve the bastard right. He didn't raise a finger to keep me with him. He made no effort to help me. Yes, he likes to fuck me, but when it came to using his influence for me, he did nothing. So I helped myself. I bought my own ticket. If the price is good enough. That was the question. Was the file important enough for the Americans?

She closed her eyes again. The waiting was nerve racking. How much longer would she be stuck in here? She went to the door and opened it. An armed American Marine was standing in the corridor.

"Yes, ma'am?" he said. His eyes were cold and he was unsmiling.

It was then that Maya realised she had not escaped at all.

47

The ornamental clock on the mantelpiece of Leonov's office chimed just as Andreyan tapped on his door.

The grey haired colonel covered up the foolscap pad of ruled paper on which he had been writing, and screwed the top on his fountain pen. Only then did he say "Enter".

Andreyan came in. He hadn't even taken off his raincoat. He was slightly breathless.

"Well?" said Leonov.

"She's taken it. She's gone off with it."

"Ah." He reached for a lacquered box on his desk and helped himself to a cigarette. He didn't offer one to Andreyan. He lit the cigarette, Andreyan watching him.

"So," said the colonel. "You were right." He waved a hand. "Do sit down."

Andreyan sat down in front of the desk.

"Where is she now?" asked Leonov.

"At the American embassy. I had the flat watched. She took a taxi and rushed straight there."

"With the document?"

"Of course."

The colonel smiled. "I must hand it to you, my friend. You know women."

"I know this woman," said Andreyan.

The colonel glanced across at the clock. "I think we had better tell Aeroflot that she will not be on the Moscow flight, don't you?"

"That," said Andreyan, "is a safe bet."

"Come, let us celebrate." The colonel stood up and went over to the cabinet under the red wall-hanging with the embroidered patriotic slogan. He took out a bottle of vodka and two crystal glasses. He poured them a drink each.

"To success," he toasted. They clinked glasses, and both drank the vodka in one gulp.

The colonel went back to sit in his leather chair.

"Do you think they will really bite?" he mused. "Will they not be sceptical?"

"Perhaps," said Andreyan. "But they'll be tempted. Terribly tempted. They know about her. Her relationship with me. She doesn't have to put on an act, does she? It's all true."

"And the file is a delicious morsel."

"Precisely. What a thing to get their hands on. They must think it's Christmas."

They looked at each other and laughed.

"You know," said Leonov slowly, "I have always admired your father. And I've been most impressed by your professionalism, dear Sergei Mikhailovitch. But I must honestly say your dedication is outstanding. Few men in our business would exploit an affair as skilfully as you have done. It has been a copy book exercise. I must commend you. I shall bring it to the notice of our superiors."

"Thank you," said Andreyan.

"The way the file was doctored was very ingenious too. I had to check it twice to convince myself it was a fake. At least, the parts that mattered."

"I had help," smiled Andreyan.

Then the colonel frowned. "Of course it is sad that she should be that sort of woman. With all the advantages she has in life. A career in the theatre. Certain privileges. Her country has treated her well, and this is how she repays it. It is very depressing. One doesn't expect this from a young Soviet woman."

He stubbed out his cigarette.

"Yes," agreed Andreyan. "But don't forget, it may yet turn out to be very useful to us. If they swallow this, we have confused them for months to come. The right hand won't know what the left is doing . . ."

"How often I have heard that in our work," sighed Leonov. "But you may be right."

Andreyan took a chance. "I am sure I am," he said.

He left the colonel, and went up to his own office. He hung up his raincoat, and sat down. He couldn't help smiling. It was so smooth, the whole thing and the beauty was that he had kept faith with Maya. She might not realise it, but he had handed her her wish on a plate; a one way ticket to her dream. With the American taxpayer picking up the tab. Andreyan chuckled because he had also done a perfect job for his masters. It was a classic misinformation operation, presenting them with a secret file which might seem too good to be true, yet was too juicy to ignore. And the best part was that the messenger was genuine and couldn't be cracked.

"Enjoy yourself, my love," Andreyan said aloud. "Lead them all a merry dance and have fun while you're doing it."

One day, perhaps, she would realise that by using her, he had kept his promise to her.

And Colonel Leonov could claim credit for a coup which, in the report he was already writing for Moscow, he would modestly say was all his own idea.

Andreyan was not at all a smug man, but at this moment he felt enormously satisfied. It was the satisfaction of a man who knew how to play the game.

48

The irony of it amused Dupree. His people informed the British about the Russian girl, and the man Whitehall sent round was the guy he'd seen having a cosy chat with her boy friend in the Dorchester.

Dupree wouldn't have told the British about her at all, if it had been left to him. The decision was made by Munro, the station chief. Munro was a stickler for protocol, and "mutual interest" understanding.

"It's all happening on British soil, Hal. You got to respect that. She walks in off the street, but it's within their jurisdiction."

"She's now on American territory," Dupree pointed out, but Munro was adamant.

"You let Cheyne know," he ordered.

"And the file? Do we tell them what she's brought us?"

Munro swallowed. His secretary walked in at that moment with a telex message, and he took advantage of the interruption.

"We'll talk later, OK? I've got to call Washington."

Of course Dupree would have played it differently. She would already have been on her way to Suffolk by car. Two hours later she would have arrived at Mildenhall air base. Then aboard a Military Air Transport Service jet. By tomorrow morning she'd have landed at Andrews air base, and this time tomorrow they'd be sweating the truth out of her in West Virginia, and the British wouldn't have known a thing. That's how he would have played it. But Munro was boss man. It was his local station, and he had a big pull at Langley.

Munro did his back slapping act when Rathbone arrived.

"Good to see you, Colin," he beamed, "how've you been keeping?"

"I need a holiday," complained Rathbone.

"Don't we all?" He took Rathbone by the arm, and led him into his office. Dupree had to admit that the way he briefed Rathbone was masterly. He told him the story of how Maya had come to the embassy and asked to be given an American visa. How she said that she was not going back to Moscow. He made it all sound important enough to justify them discussing it, but not so important that it should bother them a great deal. And he mentioned, almost as an afterthought, that she'd brought some document with her.

"Oh? What document?" Rathbone was interested.

"A folder with some papers," replied Munro dismissively. "Isn't that right, Hal?"

"That's it," agreed Dupree dutifully.

"You know who she's been sleeping with, don't you?" asked Rathbone. He was quite enjoying the game.

"Oh sure." Munro sounded almost disinterested. "One of their spooks. The number two spook. Andreyan."

"Sergei Mikhailovitch Andreyan is quite important," said Rathbone.

Buddy, you should know, thought Dupree.

"So I think the file might be interesting," added Rathbone.

"I'll let you have a photostat," promised Munro. "You can make up your own mind."

"Have you got it here?" enquired Rathbone. He glanced round, as if he expected it to be lying around.

"It's being processed," said Munro.

"Ah." Rathbone understood perfectly. They were being most co-operative. Up to a point. "Well, as soon as you can, send the material over, will you?"

"Rely on it," said Dupree. He picked his moment. "Say, what is your opinion of this Andreyan?" His eyes never left Rathbone's face.

"I'm sure it's the same as yours. Astute. Sharp. Very smooth. One of their best."

"And hardly, would you say, the kind of guy who leaves a top secret file lying around?" smiled Dupree coldly.

Munro was watching them like a spectator at Wimbledon, his eyes flicking from one to the other.

"Unless of course he wants us to get hold of it," added Dupree.

"And why should he want to do that?" said Rathbone quietly.

"Either to screw us up. Or . . ." He paused.

"Yes?"

"Maybe you know," suggested Dupree and looked at Rathbone challengingly.

After that it was small talk. Rathbone expressed appreciation on behalf of his section for their co-operation and the way they were keeping them in the picture. He said they naturally looked forward to receiving the material as soon as it was available.

Then he said: "What about Miss Petrova?"

There was a moment's silence.

"I guess all she wants is a one way ticket to God's country," shrugged Dupree.

"Are you giving her a visa?"

Munro and Dupree exchanged a glance. It was Munro who said: "Don't worry, we'll take care of Miss Petrova." He smiled. "As a matter of fact, she might be quite useful."

That was when Rathbone knew who they were really after. Andreyan.

49

Father Stephen's story was locked in a steel security cabinet in the depths of Central Registry marked "Secret". Only those with rather special classifications and clearance were allowed to look at it.

"Lachasse, John Edward. Born in Maidenhead, England, on July 30 1930. Only son of Professor and Mrs Henry Lachasse," it read. "Educated at Marylebone Grammar School. After matriculating (History, German, Russian and Physics), he attended, briefly, the London School of Economics.

"He joined the BBC monitoring service, and was based at Caversham, attached to the Russian unit. He was transferred to the Foreign Office and spent three years in Berlin with Section 14. During this time he became an interrogation specialist. He volunteered for covert duties and was arrested in Dresden, where he was detained for special questioning. The DDR handed him over to the Soviet authorities, and he was eventually exchanged by them in 1966 for Yaroslav Batov, who had been sentenced to fourteen years under Section 1 of the Official Secrets Act (see his file).

"Lachasse lost two fingers of his left hand during his detention in the East. He was subjected to severe treatment. On his return to the West he asked for special leave to go into retreat in a monastery. He subsequently decided to enter holy orders. Simple profession: August 27 1967. Solemn profession: September 1 1971. Ordination: November 13 1972. He was sent to Rome to study for a licentiate in philosophy for two years. He was made a novice master at Langford monastery in 1977, chaplain in 1980. He was appointed superior as natum at Mount Walton monastery in 1983.

"He was blessed as eleventh abbot of Mount Walton last year. He has added to his baptismal name that of St Stephen."

It was a discreet summary of Father Stephen's background. There was no mention of what he had actually done in Section 14, and the reason the other side was so anxious to get hold of him. They marked him down. They owed him, for he had done his job very well. And when they finally trapped him, they celebrated.

Nor was there much detail of how he came to be caught. It was a story of betrayal which had a file all to itself in another locked cabinet. There were those who said that if Lachasse hadn't decided to find his new vocation, it would have been understandable if he had devoted the rest of his life to settling a few scores.

Those who knew him found it hard at first to think of him as a man committed to charity, piety and devotion. In Section 14 he had built up a reputation of ruthlessness. His job was to break double agents and his reputation became quickly known in Potsdam and further east.

Cynics said that it was the treatment which he himself received which turned him to seek solace in religious retreat. He had suffered, after all. Losing two fingers during questioning was only part of it. Obviously he had had enough. He had been broken himself.

But Cheyne remembered him from the old days, and knew otherwise.

"Has he agreed?" he asked Rathbone.

"Yes."

"I'm surprised. I thought he'd want nothing to do with us."

"He doesn't," said Rathbone. "He's interested in Borisov."

"A soul to save?" There was the hint of a sneer in Cheyne's voice.

Rathbone shrugged.

"Ah well," said Cheyne, "at least it gets him off our hands."

"Father Stephen gave me a present." Rathbone didn't call him Lachasse anymore. He respected his new role.

"Oh yes?"

Rathbone showed him the little medal. "It commemorates the birth of St Benedict in 480," he explained.

"Really?" The sneer was still there. He turned the medal over. "What's all this Latin?"

"Non draco sit mihi dux," recited Rathbone. He had been a classics scholar at Westminster, and spoke Latin quite well.

Cheyne looked blank.

"It means 'Let not the Devil be my guide'," translated Rathbone.

"Does it now?" said Cheyne. "I wonder why on earth he gave you a thing like that?"

50

In diplomatic parlance, it was known as a démarche, a minuet to be danced in classical style. They would not, once the matter in hand was raised, be talking to each other, but rather at one another. What they said would be informal, and yet phrased in official style. The object of their meeting was to be able to report to their masters that it had taken place. It would neither change anyone's mind, nor alter events.

The participants were second league. The Soviet embassy, having requested the meeting, sent along the Chargé d'Affaires, instead of the ambassador. And the host was the Minister of State, not the Foreign Secretary. The two men greeted each other cordially in the big airy room overlooking the quadrangle of the Foreign Office. There were friendly smiles, and firm handshakes. Pleasantries were exchanged as they sat down.

Then, like a conductor calling a soloist to order, the Minister indicated that he was ready to stop the small talk, and begin the meeting. The Chargé acknowledged his courtesy, and began his rehearsed speech. Much of it was based on a briefing that had been radioed to the embassy in diplomatic cypher. GCHQ at Cheltenham was still transcribing it, but a rough version had already been decoded and laid before the Minister. So he had a good idea what was coming.

"I am instructed," intoned the Chargé, using the neutral voice which he reserved when he was speaking not as himself but as the mouthpiece of his state, "that my government is gravely concerned by the activities of certain radio stations operating within the jurisdiction of the United Kingdom and transmitting irresponsible and provocative broadcasts to the Soviet Union."

He paused. He had been word perfect.

"And what broadcasts are these?" asked the Minister, equally impassive.

"They originate from a station calling itself 'Russkaya Volya', which pretends to transmit from inside the Soviet Union. It spreads alarm, gross libels, false rumours, all part of a criminal attempt to mislead and confuse people in our country. I am instructed to point out that this is a violation of international law and in breach of all the universal broadcasting regulations."

The Minister's expression betrayed nothing. "You do not

191

suggest," he said, "that Her Majesty's Government is in any way responsible for these broadcasts, I take it?"

"Our technical experts assure us that the transmissions originate . . ." He paused momentarily, honing the words he was going to use; he wanted to be absolutely true to Moscow's instruction. ". . . that they originate from within the sphere of United Kingdom sovereignty."

"I must repeat," insisted the Minister stiffly. "It is not suggested that these are official broadcasts over which we have control?"

They were dancing gracefully, avoiding stepping on each other's toes.

"No," conceded the Chargé, "we are not saying they are BBC programmes. Though some of these, in the Russian services, have not been conducive to friendly relations between our two countries."

This bit was an unrehearsed addition, thrown in for effect. It would look good when he transmitted the verbatim account of this meeting to Moscow.

The Minister proceeded to do some elegant lying. "You will appreciate that all this comes as a complete surprise to me. It is the first time that I have heard of these broadcasts, but I can categorically assure you that they have nothing to do with Her Majesty's Government. I am sure you are aware of how we ourselves are plagued by pirate stations and such like . . ."

"My government," persisted the Chargé doggedly, "believe that the origin of these broadcasts is not unknown to your authorities."

All right my friend, thought the Minister. If you want to get a little rougher, I'm game. "Who *do* you suggest originates them?"

"Emigrés. Professional war mongers. Hirelings of fascist organisations. Provocateurs. I am sure you know the kind. There are plenty of them."

"And where is this so-called station located?" asked the Minister coldly. "From where does it broadcast?"

192

The Chargé, unlike the Minister, did not play poker, but he knew when the ante was being raised.

"Our specialists are actively pursuing this, and naturally, as soon as we have established the precise location we will of course inform you and, I might add, expect you to take the appropriate steps to eradicate this operation."

The Minister smiled. "In other words, you have no idea where the broadcasts come from."

The démarche had run its way, but the Chargé fired a parting broadside.

"Her Majesty's Government," he declaimed, and the Ministry of Foreign Affairs would have been proud of him, "is obliged to observe the conventions which prohibit this kind of pollution of the ether. To allow such activities is not compatible with the behaviour to be expected from a friendly nation. I am instructed to say that to tolerate these things is an indication of hostile intent, and cannot be accepted. We trust that Her Majesty's Government will therefore take the appropriate steps to rectify the situation." He stopped. They both knew he had done his job, and they both knew that nothing had been achieved.

"Thank you," said the Minister. "I will of course convey your government's views to the Foreign Secretary."

The Chargé visibly relaxed.

"Will I have the pleasure of seeing you and your lady wife at the garden party next week?" enquired the Minister.

"I do hope so," said the Chargé. "The French are such excellent hosts, aren't they?"

The Minister saw him to the door, where an aide was already waiting to escort the Soviet diplomat.

As soon as the door was shut, the Minister sat down in the armchair under the oil painting of Lord Palmerston, and closed his eyes. He often shut out the world after a trying meeting. It helped him to collect his thoughts.

He decided he liked the Russian. This new lot was so different from the old sour bunch, the crabby faces, the unsmiling expressions. The Chargé d'Affaires was a good example of the new school. Not, of course, that they were all like him.

He got up and settled himself behind his desk. After a moment he buzzed on his private phone.

"Jeffries," he said to his private secretary at the other end. "See if you can get me 35. Intelligence Secretariat 35." He sighed. One still had to spell things out for Jeffries. He was a replacement. "I want to talk to Mr Cheyne."

51

It was nothing new for Kleber to be in a city where they were hunting him, and London was no different to the others. The safest place to be was in the streets. There he could move about, a man like a million others. He liked crowds. Caught in the middle of them was like sheltering in a thick forest of trees. So he walked in the throngs, never rushing, never pushing. And, most important, he made sure he didn't draw attention to himself.

He never stared at policemen, that was rule number one. He walked past them as if they were street lamps, or looked through them. Never at their faces. Above all, he never caught their eyes. When he went into MacDonald's, he smiled politely, didn't mind if somebody jumped his place at the counter, took his cheeseburger and paper cup of coffee and sat quietly in the corner, reading the paper.

If he took a cab, he never told the driver the exact destination, even if it didn't matter. He made a point of getting out nearby, then walking a couple of blocks. Not that he was afraid the driver would remember him. It was simply second nature. That was why Kleber had survived so long.

He had received certain instructions, and these meant that he couldn't pull out, even if the authorities were aware that he was around. It was this reliability which had become his trade mark.

London offered many good bolt holes. The cinemas always provided darkness during the day. Or one could sit in the reference library off Leicester Square all day reading, and nobody bothered you. Then there was the Circle Line where one could ride round and round, and be out of sight, if that was what one wanted at that moment.

He had enough money on him, and the back up would provide more when he needed it. The dark-haired girl was a good quartermaster.

How they got to know he was in town he had no idea, but, curiously enough, it didn't worry him. He knew he hadn't been betrayed by his side. He trusted them. Something *had* gone wrong, but Kleber was a fatalist. He still had all the luck on his side, because otherwise he wouldn't have spotted the stake out. If the gods had turned against him, he would have walked straight into their arms. Or even had them bursting in on him in the middle of the night as he lay in bed.

This, of course, was the last time he would be Kleber. Karl-Heinz would cease to exist after this assignment. Next time he could be anything. A Swedish student. A Swiss doctor. He rather fancied his American accent; he might even become a tourist from across the Atlantic.

It was in Charing Cross Road that he first noticed he was being followed. In the beginning, he wasn't sure. But it seemed to him that he had noticed the man in the navy blazer earlier in Cambridge Circus. It was that curious sixth sense of his again. Seeing without looking. He *sensed* there was somebody behind him. He didn't look round. He just strolled on. He came to a bus stop and joined the three people standing there. Navy Blazer was lighting a cigarette in a doorway. The bus came, and Kleber used the people who got off it as a cover to move on. But outside Foyles

195

bookshop he did risk a quick look backwards, and saw the man behind him again.

Kleber went by the side of the bookshop through the alley into Greek Street. He saw a pornographic bookshop and entered.

Inside, he was confronted by rows of cellophane-wrapped magazines. He walked around, timing himself. He spent six minutes in the porn emporium, and finally walked out without buying anything, much to the disgust of the sallow-faced Mediterranean gentleman who presided over it. He turned up Greek Street, and began walking towards Soho Square. There he was again. Navy Blazer. Such an ordinary-looking fellow. He had thrown his cigarette away.

Kleber thought hard. He was sure now he had been found by one of their shadows. The man might have a two-way radio and summon assistance. But more likely, to judge by Kleber's knowledge, he would stick with him, in the hope that it would lead to accomplices, hide outs, connections.

That's what you think, my friend, said Kleber to himself.

Alcott, the shadow, was also trying to anticipate Kleber's actions. He didn't underestimate his quarry. He had no evidence that Kleber knew he was following him, but equally the man would take care not to let him know he was aware he had been targeted. He kept a safe distance behind Kleber, trying to ensure that there were enough people between them to shield him.

Kleber walked towards Tottenham Court Road. He wondered where the man in the blazer had first sighted him. He was sure it had been before he spotted him near the Palace Theatre, before Cambridge Circus. And he wondered how he came to have had his trail picked up. He walked purposefully, as if he was going to cross St Giles Circus, but then, suddenly, he swung round and dived into the Underground station. I'll give the bastard a run for his money, he thought.

He hastily bought a ticket from an automatic machine, and rode down the escalator. He made as if he was going for the Central line, then turned and raced down the steps to the Northern line. There wasn't a sign of the man in the blazer, yet Kleber wasn't convinced he'd shaken off the shadow. In situations like these, he liked to think it was he who was stalking his shadow. The man may have thought *he* was pursuing Kleber, but he didn't know his quarry.

Kleber joined about a dozen other people waiting for the next train. The electric indicator showed it would be the Barnet line. Already he could hear, at first faintly and then growing louder, the sound of the train in the tunnel as it approached the station.

It was at that moment that he saw the man in the blazer again. Standing further down the platform. In a curious way, Kleber felt reassured. The way his shadow vanished had worried him. It left questions unanswered.

The train pulled in, and the doors slid open. Kleber waited until the last moment, and so, further up the platform, did Alcott. Then Kleber got into his compartment, and saw his pursuer get into the next coach.

Kleber considered his options. As soon as he got off the train, the shadow would follow him. He knew that. He could perhaps hope to push his way through the passengers and escape to an exit, but he doubted if he could shake off this bloodhound. Or he could get off, and start leading the shadow a hell of a dance. Jump into a taxi. Go God knows where. Lead him round in circles. Of course he could, but to what point. He still wouldn't lose him.

Alcott, in the next compartment, was on edge. Following people like Andreyan and the actress had been easy, compared to this. Kleber, he knew, was wily, and an expert at this kind of thing. Every time the train stopped he rushed to the door, and stood poised to follow Kleber if he left his coach. But each time the man remained seated. Goodge Street, Euston, Camden Town. People got on and off, but Kleber stayed put.

Then, at Archway, everything happened very quickly. Kleber got off – and so did Alcott. But instead of changing

197

platforms to catch a different train, as Alcott half expected him to do, or rushing for the escalators to reach the exit, Kleber ran along the platform, and disappeared up the emergency staircase.

Alcott swore. He sprinted after Kleber, dropping all pretence at not following him. People got in his way, and he pushed an old lady who abused him as he ran to follow his man.

The staircase at Archway station winds in a spiral. It is long, and dark. Few people use it. It's a long haul to the top, and the climb is steep and exhausting.

Alcott began to ascend the stairs. Kleber had already disappeared, and would probably be near the top now. Yet he couldn't hear his footsteps, even though everything echoed in the stairwell. Alcott stood still for a moment, holding his breath. But there wasn't a sound. He resumed climbing up the spiral steps.

What he didn't expect happened. Kleber was standing on the staircase, about half way up, very still, a shadowy figure in the gloom. And as Alcott came up the stairs, Kleber fired. Just one shot. The 9 mm bullet struck Alcott in the middle of the forehead, shattered his skull and lodged in his brain. Alcott's face, in one split second, had become a bloody mess. His body slid down several steps.

Kleber ran up the rest of the stairs to the top, and walked through the ticket hall into Archway Road. He was humming the Sibelius theme that had been haunting him lately. Several buses were drawn up at the terminus, and he got on the upper deck of a No 27. By the time the bus left, no sign of commotion had come from the tube station. He heard no sirens, saw no crowd gathering. The staircase was a little-used exit from the station, very few people made the long climb.

Of course, when they found Alcott, they'd have a good idea who was responsible. It was like leaving his calling card. After all, they knew who Alcott had been tailing.

It was an hour before somebody else used the stairs at

Archway station and found the body. Alcott had a Ministry of Defence pass on him, and Scotland Yard called Rathbone's office and asked if somebody could identify the dead man.

Unfortunately most of Alcott's head had been blown away but his fingerprints checked.

"He must have got careless," commented Cheyne when he got the report.

He didn't look at the photographs taken in the mortuary. He hated gruesome pictures.

52

Maya woke up slowly. She was lying on a camp bed, fully clothed. There was a bitter, dry taste in her mouth and her eye lids felt heavy. She had some difficulty in focusing.

She couldn't make out her surroundings. The ceiling was curved, and the single window curtained. The door had a peep hole.

Maya was confused. She didn't understand how she came to be here. She tried to concentrate her mind. Yes. The American embassy. She was beginning to remember. She had sat in the interview room for a long time. She recalled that, and the Marine guarding the door.

The man who had interviewed her never came back. Now she had difficulty recalling his name.

Then there was the tall slim blonde who was very polite, but quite distant. She'd brought Maya a cup of coffee, and, after that, all that Maya could remember was getting drowsy and finally it all became nothing.

Her tongue felt thick, and everything around seemed slightly remote. She kept wondering about Andreyan. What had happened to him when he'd had to report her disappearance, and that of the file?

The door opened, and the blonde came in.

She gave Maya a cool smile. "Ah, good, you're awake. Did you have a good sleep?"

Maya felt the lack of warmth. The blonde was like a surgeon, impersonal, uninvolved.

Maya sat up on the bed. "Where am I?" she asked.

"You're perfectly safe, and I'm going to look after you," said the blonde. "Anything you need, just let me know."

"Who are you?" Maya licked her lips. "I don't understand . . ."

It was only then that she realised, with a shock, that they were speaking Russian, the blonde was word perfect.

"You're on a military installation," said the blonde. "It's the best place to protect you. Nobody can get to you here. Look." She went to the window and pulled the curtains open. Maya slowly got to her feet. She was still feeling a little groggy but she went over to the window and looked out. She saw some barbed wire fencing and beyond that, in the distance, a guard tower.

For a moment a terrible thought struck Maya. She had been kidnapped. They'd doped her, she'd passed out, and now they were playing some awful trick on her.

"What country is this?" she asked, almost terrified of the answer she'd get.

The blonde looked slightly startled. "Why, you're in England of course. Where did you think . . ."

Maya smiled weakly. She was a little giddy and she made her way back to the camp bed and sat on it. "I'm sorry," she said, "I'm so confused . . ."

"Well don't worry about a thing," said the blonde but there wasn't much sympathy in her tone.

"You still haven't told me . . . who you are." Maya was uneasy. "What is your name?"

"I work for the government," replied the blonde. "*Our* government. My name is Jones."

200

"I am Maya Aleksandrovna Petrova," said Maya, then realised how stupid that was. Of course the blonde knew. That was what it was all about. "Can you tell me what the embassy is doing about me? I have asked for a visa to the United States. Do you know what they have decided?"

"It's no longer with the embassy," answered the blonde. "Another agency has taken over."

Maya decided she didn't like the blonde. And she realised the feeling was mutual.

"I don't understand why I've been brought here," began Maya, but the blonde cut her short.

"I have already told you. It is for your own protection. It might not be healthy for you if . . . well, if they got hold of you. Now relax. You won't be here for ever. It's only while the necessary measures are taken."

Maya shivered a little. It might have been weakness. Or the cold eyes of the blonde. "How long?" asked Maya.

"Take it easy, Maya," said the blonde coolly. "We won't keep you here an hour longer than necessary."

Maybe if I tried being friendly it would help, thought Maya. So she asked:

"What is your name? Your first name?"

"K.D.," said the blonde. She saw Maya's puzzlement. "Some parents just give their children initials. K.D. is my first name. Maybe it's better if you call me Jones."

Maya took another chance. "What happened to the documents I gave your people? The referentura file."

The blonde shrugged. "I guess it's being processed."

"What does that mean, processed?"

There was a glint of malice in the blonde's eyes. "Maybe it means that they're checking on it. That wouldn't worry you, would it?"

"I don't understand," said Maya, and suddenly she was frightened. Perhaps it hadn't been so clever to use the file as a passport.

"Well, I wouldn't lose sleep about it," said the blonde.

She pulled the curtain shut again. "I'll bring some clothes, and some toilet things. Is there anything you don't eat?"

Maya shook her head.

"I'll be around," promised the blonde. "I won't be far from you. Not at any time. I'll be right there whenever you need me."

It didn't sound reassuring to Maya. It seemed, much more, to be a warning.

"Are we far from London?" asked Maya.

"Far enough." The blonde gave that cold smile again. "Miss anybody?"

Maya felt like hitting her, right across the face. But she didn't react, the blonde left. It was then that Maya spotted the microphone in the ceiling. They hadn't even bothered to make much effort to conceal it.

53

They had laid out a blotter, two pens, and a neat pile of ruled foolscap paper beside a reading lamp, and they hadn't forgotten an ink well. It bothered Borisov. What did they expect him to write? Letters? A confession? His last will and testament.

The crucifix bothered him too. It hung on the white-washed stone wall behind the bed. He wished it wasn't there. He actually tried to avoid looking at it. He didn't believe in it, of course, but he'd just as soon it wasn't staring down at him.

A printed notice was nailed to the inside of the door, like a tariff in a hotel. Only this didn't give the daily rates. "Rules for Guests" it was headed. Guests! Borisov smiled sarcastically. That's what they called it.

All meals, the notice decreed, were to be eaten in silence. Guests must take their recreation on their own, and only speak to the monks with the Abbot's permission. No noise was allowed in the sacred premises. No smoking was allowed in the cloisters. Periods of mandatory silence must be rigorously observed. And there was a timetable. The day began at 4 a.m. with Matins and Lauds. Then there were private masses, spiritual reading, and meditation. Breakfast at 8:15 a.m. Conventional High Mass at 10 a.m. Throughout the day there were Tierces and Sexts and Nones and Vespers. Lunch at 1 p.m., supper at 7:30 p.m. Compline. Bedtime at 9 p.m.

It's worse than a labour camp on strict regime, thought Borisov. Even in the Gulag they didn't have to get up at 4 a.m.

It was a thirteenth-century monastery, he'd learnt that much. Or at least, it had been built then. It was a castle originally, as the five foot thick walls testified. A moat surrounded the place. To cross, visitors had to go over a stone bridge to a gatehouse flanked by gaunt towers. Mount Walton was a forbidding place.

He'd been driven there from London by two of Rathbone's men. The journey took about an hour.

"We'd like you to stay there for a little bit," Rathbone said. "Just till things get straightened out. You'll be made very comfortable. The Abbot is a friend of ours."

It was not what Borisov expected. He had heard of the safe houses British Intelligence had. Little hideaways. Anonymous flats in London. Places in the country. But a mediaeval monastery!

He was taken to a guest room. There were two narrow slits instead of windows, openings for archers to pick off besieging soldiers long ago. But incongruously, the room had a shower and toilet attached. With soap, towels, and shaving things.

There was a plain wardrobe by the wall, and when Borisov opened it, he found clothes. New clothes on hangers, a sports jacket, flannels, and a raincoat. All in his size. And in the chest of drawers underwear and shirts were neatly laid out.

They had prepared for him, that was clear.

"Please," asked Borisov, "how long am I staying here?"

"Just a few days," said one of the men reassuringly. "Mr Rathbone will be in touch." Then they left him to himself.

Soon afterwards, there was a tap on the door and a monk entered. Over his habit he had an apron and he brought Borisov tea, two boiled eggs, bread and butter, and an apple. He put the tray down.

"I would like to see the . . . the Abbot," said Borisov.

The monk nodded, and smiled. But he did not say a word. Then, very quietly, he left, and gently closed the door behind him.

A bell started to toll, and Borisov thought he could hear, faintly, a low chant. He made up his mind.

He got up from the chair on which he had been sitting by the table, and went to the door.

But when he tried the handle it was locked.

Borisov said a very crude word in Russian. He banged on the door, but the bell continued tolling, and nobody came.

He hadn't touched the food, but now he decided he was hungry and might as well eat what the monk had brought. He began to pour himself a cup of tea, then froze. Slowly he put the tea pot down. He had just seen what lay on the tray, under the plate of bread and butter, flat and neatly folded.

It was a copy of *Pravda*, which at least helped to pass the time until the Abbot eventually visited him, some eighteen hours later.

"I hope I'm not disturbing you," he began, "and that you've been properly looked after."

Father Stephen was a tall, rather angular man with a high, domed forehead above an unlikely pair of horn rimmed spectacles. "May I sit down?"

Borisov was sitting at the table, and Stephen perched himself on the edge of the bed.

"There isn't much room, is there?" he smiled apologetically. His Russian was fluent, conversationally colloquial. "You must find this rather an odd place," he said quietly, almost diffidently.

Borisov couldn't take his eyes off Stephen's left hand. Where there should be a second and third fingers there were just stumps.

"I thought it best that nobody bothered you at first," the monk was saying. "That's why we left you alone, and let you sleep in this morning. We start our day rather early, but there was no reason to wake you." All the time he spoke, his eyes never left Borisov. "We tend to forget, living as we do, that outsiders need to get used to our way of life."

"Why am I being kept a prisoner like this?" asked Borisov.

Father Stephen looked surprised. "A prisoner? Who says that?"

"I am kept in here like a cage. The door is locked. I cannot go outside. Yes. A prisoner. Why?"

"Ah. The locked door." The monk nodded. "I do understand. Of course. Please forgive me. You see, my friend, it is not to keep you in. It is to keep others out."

Borisov frowned. "Others?"

"You are our guest and we are anxious to protect you. I think we may have been over zealous. From this moment the door will never be locked."

"And I am free to move about?"

"Free as the air," smiled the monk.

"And this," said Borisov. He picked up the copy of *Pravda* on the table. "Why this?"

"Something to read." He smiled again. "I thought it might pass the time. A touch of home . . ."

No, thought Borisov. You've got to do better than that. "I was surprised," he said. "One does not expect to find *Pravda* in a monastery in England."

"Oh, I read it to keep up with the language. I don't often

205

have the opportunity to speak it." And Stephen beamed at him. "I suppose you're wondering why they brought you here," he went on. "It's to help you adjust. Get accustomed to your new life. I'm told by the authorities that you've been through quite a lot. But let me assure you of one thing, here you are absolutely at liberty to come and go as you please. We want you to relax, to collect your thoughts, to feel free from pressure. We welcome guests like you. We don't seek to know their faith, their religion, we don't expect them to join in our activities. No one will try to convert you, no one will check on you. You are a free man."

"Remarkable," said Borisov. He kept staring at the left hand despite himself.

"I see you're curious about this," and Stephen raised the hand. "There is no mystery. It was the price of obstinacy. I was asked to answer some questions, and I was obstinate. I refused. So I was given a memento to remember the occasion."

"Where did that happen?"

"In Leningrad," replied the monk. "You ever met a Major Bulgakov?"

Borisov shook his head. The atmosphere had suddenly changed.

"No, I suppose you wouldn't have. An interesting man. Rather pitiless, I found. But very good at his job. KGB, you know." It was almost a throw away line. "Sometimes I wonder what he's done with my two fingers. An unworthy thought, I admit."

Borisov was staring at him, fascinated.

"I suppose in his own way, he was only doing it too," mused Stephen.

"Doing what?" asked Borisov in a low voice.

"Soul hunting. We're all soul hunters, aren't we?"

Borisov was very alert. "I've never heard that expression . . ."

The monk seemed surprised. "Haven't you, really? It was the fiftieth anniversary of the KGB. Back in '67. Andropov was the chairman of the Committee for State Security. He coined it in his anniversary speech. Soul hunters. Very apt. Don't you think it's a marvellous description?"

"It's quite effective," agreed Borisov.

"Oh, better than that, my friend. It sums up the essence of the business. Stealing blue prints, breaking codes, that sort of thing, it's all very routine, isn't it? But soul hunting, there is the real danger. Capture a man's soul, and you have the man."

I'll give you a run for your money, thought Borisov.

"In a way," he said, "I suppose you, as a priest, are just that. A soul hunter."

Stephen was delighted. "My dear man," he chuckled, "we shall get on famously. I shall learn a great deal from you. I am so delighted that you are our guest. Not that I will convert you – or you me."

"But I," said Borisov, "I am not a soul hunter."

"No," said the monk. "You are a very good actor."

And again he smiled.

54

"You seem preoccupied, Sergei Mikhailovitch," remarked Leonov, pushing aside the file of overnight signals from Moscow Centre. He had initialled each message to confirm he had read it.

"Not at all," said Andreyan.

"It's the actress, is it?" The colonel could be very perceptive.

Andreyan dropped all pretence. What was the point of

207

trying to fool wily Leonov? "I wonder how she's getting on," he admitted.

"Be reassured," said the colonel. "My guess is that she's enjoying every moment of her glory."

Andreyan felt relief that they didn't have to fence around any more.

"How do you think the Americans are treating her?"

Leonov wasn't sure, but he thought he detected a note of anxiety. He hoped he hadn't made an error of judgement. He had assured Moscow that Andreyan's personal involvement was superficial. He could surely be trusted to go to bed with a woman without it turning his head.

"Are you concerned?" he asked.

"I'd just like to know what's happening to her," shrugged Andreyan.

Time to soothe him, thought the colonel. "I'll tell you. By now they'll have spirited her out of London. To one of their installations, I'd say. Perhaps Chicksands. Or Lakenheath. They're keeping her in quarantine while they try to check on the material." He smiled. "Not that that will get them far. And they're busy seeing what they've got on her. Can't you hear the computers working overtime trying to crack her background? They won't find anything of course. It'll just confirm that she is what she says she is, an actress. That'll worry them a bit. So maybe they'll give her a grilling. What else can they do?"

Andreyan remained unconvinced.

"Quite soon, they'll fly her to the United States," went on Leonov. "She'll be on ice for a bit. They'll grill her about you. They'll show her photographs of you two together in London." Andreyan winced. "They'll try to get her to admit that you weren't just screwing," and he used an equally crude Russian word, "but that there was more in the relationship, that she was working for you, and acting on orders from Moscow. Then . . ."

"Yes," interrupted Andreyan, "what then?"

"They'll give up and try to get some propaganda value out

of it. 'Soviet Actress Chooses The West'. With her looks, she'll get her picture in every paper. Maybe you'll see her on the cover of *Time*." The colonel chuckled.

"And the file?" said Andreyan. "What will they do about the file?"

"I told you before. They'll mistrust it. They'll wonder if it is a set up. But you know this game, my friend. If an American in London walked into our embassy here with a secret document, we wouldn't trust him an inch, we'd suspect it's a plant – but Moscow could never be sure. Gift horses, you know. It's such a tempting dossier too, isn't it? Our alleged assessment of their agent structure in East Europe. The order of battle of what we believe are their spies. Fascinating. They'll dribble with delight, especially when they discover that we don't seem to know what *they* know." He was watching Andreyan, and decided the man wasn't really concerned about the dossier, it was the woman he was worried about. "As for Maya Aleksandrovna, don't worry about her. Either way she'll be all right. If they think she's brought them a basketful of goodies, they'll love her, and if they're not sure about it, they'll make her welcome, because it looks so good in the newspapers."

"I hope so," sighed Andreyan.

Leonov frowned. "You're not having regrets, are you? Second thoughts? That would be . . ."

He didn't finish, but Andreyan completed the sentence.

"That would be – unfortunate, would it?" he broke in.

"Well," said the colonel, "shall we say it might be better if you kept such thoughts to yourself." He came over and patted Andreyan on the shoulder. "Relax. She's in no danger."

"You know what we would do to a messenger who brought us fake secrets to mislead us?"

"Ah yes," nodded the colonel, "but you see, we're not them . . . and they certainly aren't us. So there is no problem."

He genuinely liked Andreyan, and he hoped the man wasn't going to be foolish about this female. Leonov was an old fashioned man, who looked on actresses as women destined to amuse and entertain men on and off stage. But that was all.

"You are sure, my dear friend, that she's really worth all this worry?" he enquired in his most avuncular manner. "I mean, I know she's very good looking, I have noticed this myself, but she is only an actress, isn't she? You saw her file. She gets around. Even Borisov . . ."

It was a mistake. Andreyan stood up. Suddenly he was cold, correct, formal. "Is there anything else, comrade colonel?" he asked.

"No," said Leonov mildly, "I think that's all for the moment." But as Andreyan turned to go, he called him back. "You've forgotten something," he said, tapping the file of decyphered radio messages. "These have to go back to the referentura."

Andreyan picked up the file.

"And don't mislay them," added the colonel somewhat unnecessarily. "They're secret. Don't forget that."

For a moment, Andreyan wondered if the grey haired man was, for the first time in their relationship, making a threat.

But then he dismissed the thought, and left.

In the referentura, he identified himself to the duty clerk who opened the heavy fireproof steel door that led to the restricted area in the embassy's basement. Then he logged the return of the batch of signals. He looked at them as he turned the lock of the message safe. There was one that caught his eyes.

"Most Secret. From Director to Igor."

Igor was Leonov's current code name.

"Approval given for Executive Action," said the message.

Suddenly Andreyan felt very insecure. He looked over at the clerk, but the man was busy writing in a record book. There was no reason why Andreyan should feel fear. But he wondered why Leonov had not mentioned it to him, though he hadn't hidden the message from him. Did the cunning old man want him to see it? Was he in fact trying to warn him?

Andreyan swallowed. Then he took the sheaf of messages and put them into the safe. He locked it again, and signed out.

He didn't know what Executive Action was in store. But from now on he wouldn't turn his back. On anyone.

55

The inquest on Alcott was well stage managed and lasted five minutes.

"I only propose to open this inquiry today, and the proceedings will then be adjourned to a date to be announced," said the coroner.

So all that was called, to the frustration of the two reporters, was brief medical testimony, and formal evidence of identification.

Then Detective Chief Inspector Binyon went into the witness box.

"There are further inquiries to be made, sir," he said smoothly, "and we would appreciate an adjournment."

The coroner peered at him across his half moon glasses. The one thing Binyon had not mentioned was that he was Special Branch, but the coroner was aware of it. There had been a brief session before the hearing in the privacy of his office. "When do you think you will be ready to proceed?" asked the coroner.

Binyon was word perfect. "We have certain leads, sir, but we do not know at this stage how long it will take to resolve all the matters."

Rathbone, sitting in the second row of the public seats, sighed. It was amazing, at times, how easy it was not to tell the truth without ever actually lying.

"Very well then," said the coroner, and started writing. "I will adjourn this inquest sine die."

"Thank you, sir," said Binyon, and the reporters cursed. The story had just gone down the drain.

In the car back to the office, Rathbone wondered what Alcott would have made of the profession he had acquired in death.

He had been listed on the coroner's list as "commercial traveller".

56

It was in the garden of the monastery, as they passed the fish pond, that Borisov said: "I am curious about one thing."

"And what is that?" inquired Stephen gently.

"You don't ask me any questions. Why is it you don't want to know more about me?"

"Because it's got nothing to do with me, my dear friend. You are not here to be . . ." he searched for the word, " . . . to be debriefed. You are our guest, and you do what you like. Of course, if you want to talk, I will always listen . . ."

Borisov said nothing.

"Is there something you have on your mind?" Stephen asked. Without waiting for a reply, he pointed at a tree by the ivy covered wall. "It's 400 years old, imagine that. Columbus hadn't even found America when it was planted."

Trees, thought Borisov. Damn trees. Devious bastards, these monks. They talk about one thing, and mean another.

"The reason I've . . . stayed over here, why I've . . ."

"Defected?" prompted Stephen smoothly.

"I don't like that word," said Borisov. "I'm not a deserter. I have not betrayed my country."

Stephen indicated a bench. "Why don't we sit down?"

"There comes a time when one makes a decision," Borisov wasn't looking at Stephen. He started to speak rapidly, like a man who has a lot to say and little time. "I thought about it long and hard. I knew I wouldn't have the opportunity again. It wasn't an easy decision, believe me. One does not cut oneself off from one's roots lightly. It's specially difficult for somebody like me, an actor."

"Of course," nodded Stephen sympathetically. Borisov expected him to say something else. To ask, perhaps, "So why did you do it?" But Stephen just waited.

"The system, you see . . ." Borisov went on, then stopped. Damn this monk. Why didn't he make it easier? He glanced at Stephen's left hand. "You got out too, didn't you? You must have decided to forget the past. After what you went through? You escaped, didn't you?"

The monk shook his head. "I'm afraid one never really escapes," he sighed. For a moment, they sat in silence.

Then Borisov asked: "What have they told you about me?"

" 'They'?"

"The British authorities. What do they say about Borisov?"

Stephen smiled. "They are a little puzzled. And they don't know what to do with you. I suspect you're a bit of an embarrassment. You see, you're not a real catch. You're not a nuclear scientist or a diplomat or somebody with a load of secrets. Out of ten, you probably only score two or three. Forgive me."

Borisov smiled back at him. "No, not at all. That's why they've brought me here. I can't do any harm in a monastery. For the time being, it's a solution. Later on . . ."

"They'll find something for you."

"I'm sure," said Borisov. "The question is, will I do it?"

Stephen gave him a quick glance, then stood up. "Come," he said, and he led Borisov through a door along a dark corridor, which was oppressive and gloomy after the sunshine in the garden. They went down some steps, and

213

through another door into a big cavernous room lined with bookshelves.

"This is the library," said Stephen. "Please treat it as your own."

There were, literally, thousands of books, from ceiling to floor, in dozens of languages.

"You'll find plenty of Russian books here," explained Stephen, walking with him past rows of shelves. "Poetry, drama, history."

There were others. Beautifully bound volumes with elaborate gold lettering on their spines, vellum bound folios, books in Hebrew and Arabic and Greek, tomes on canon law, theology and philosophy, books about mysticism and magic. Even a copy of Karl Marx's *Das Kapital*.

And in one corner, there was a big bookcase with the volumes securely locked behind glass.

"Yes," said Stephen, when Borisov stopped in front of it, "those are forbidden fruit. They're on the index. They offend . . . theological orthodoxy."

"As Stalin might have said," commented Borisov. It wasn't diplomatic, but he couldn't resist it. Stephen ignored the remark.

"They might disrupt the harmonious thoughts of our community."

"Exactly," said Borisov. Maybe the soul hunter had a chink in his armour. "That's one way he might have put it, too."

Stephen produced a key from his cassock, and handed it to him.

"You are at perfect liberty to read any of them. Nothing is forbidden to you." Again that cool smile. "I know what you're thinking. You've heard it before. Special privileges . . ."

Borisov took the key.

"Feel free to borrow any book here and take it to your room."

Yes, indeed. You'll keep a close check on the titles I pick, thought Borisov.

"Aren't you worried what might happen to my soul?" He couldn't resist it.

"Should I be?" said Stephen.

On the stairs, Borisov said "You're not going to convert me, you know."

"I wouldn't even try, my friend."

"I just thought I'd warn you. I don't believe. Not in any of this." Borisov made a sweeping gesture with one hand. "It's too late for me. You have to get at 'em in the cradle."

"Really?" remarked Stephen drily.

In the corridor, they passed two monks, moving silently, their eyes downcast. That was the trouble in this place, Borisov reflected, you never saw their eyes. They were like tonsured waxen ghosts.

"You're restless, aren't you?"

"No," said Borisov. "It's just that this life seems very unreal. It's like being shut in a fish bowl."

"You can get out any time you like, my friend."

Yes, thought Borisov, maybe the time had come. There were things to be done. Things in the real world, the one which really mattered.

But he did not say a word.

He did borrow a book before bedtime, however. It was the *History of the Inquisition*.

Rathbone, when Father Stephen told him, was very interested.

57

Colonel Blau still had his uniform. It hung in the wardrobe of his sixth floor suite in the Park Lane hotel, the beret on the shelf above. They travelled with him wherever he went, and they were, as always, neatly packed in one of the suitcases when he arrived at Heathrow from Dallas.

He was a civilian now, and wore mufti, but having the uniform around made him feel less naked. He sometimes took it out, brushed it, checked the campaign ribbons, polished the silver eagles, then hung it up again, reassured.

It had taken time for him to adjust. Being a civilian had seemed unnatural. Not everyone called him "sir" now. Nobody saluted him, except the doorman when he gave him a good tip. Nobody came to attention when he entered a room. People no longer appeared to be in awe of the big man.

The week in Dallas, though, had done his morale a power of good. He had been heartened by his reception. He had met men of his kind, bluff, hearty men who believed in power. Men of action. They were very rich, most of them. Two oil millionaires. A retired four star admiral. An industrialist with 110,000 people on his payroll. A grey haired veteran Senator. A rancher who owned two million acres of grazing land. They were remarkable men, the Executive council of the Europa League.

They had made Blau very welcome. They told him that they were shocked the Pentagon had got rid of him.

"We need men like you out there," they said. "Men who know what it's all about, and who have the guts to take action. It's people like you, colonel, who know the menace that faces us, and have the know how to tackle it. You know better than anyone that we can't leave it to the chicken hearted fools in Washington and our so-called allies in Europe. We have to do what we can now, and hit back."

It was music to Blau's ears, and he sat, basking with pleasure, as they praised him. He was surprised how much they knew about his methods, and the special unit he had raised in Bavaria.

They asked him about his thoughts for encouraging resistance against Soviet domination in Eastern Europe. They wanted to know if he really believed there could one day be an uprising against the Kremlin.

216

"Yes, sir," replied Blau enthusiastically. "Remember the words of Winston Churchill in 1940. Set Europe ablaze. Hell, if they could do it, we can do it. They sent in agents, didn't they, and organised local underground movements and resistance groups. What they did in Western Europe then, we can do in the East today."

What would you need to set up such an operation, colonel, they asked?

Money, said Blau. And they smiled. That was no problem.

Men, said Blau. Volunteers. That also would be no problem.

"A radio station," said Blau. "To broadcast misinformation. And to send messages to the resistance."

"That we have," they said.

And they told Blau all about it. It was the first time he had heard of Russkaya Volya.

"Who's in charge of it?" he asked.

"Dr Leonard Jury," they told him. "A psychological warfare expert. Does a great job in London. You'll like him. He thinks the right way."

They talked long into the night. Then the Senator said: "That's all very well, colonel, but you need a figure head. The British had de Gaulle. He was a kind of rallying point. A Frenchman appealing to the French. We got to have somebody to rally the Russkies. It's no good you or I telling them to throw out the Communists. There's got to be something that sets them alight, the way Solidarity's done in Poland."

Blau was a very modest drinker, but the convivial atmosphere and the cigar smoke and the heady talk perhaps made him drink a little more than usual. So, eventually, he was rather more forthcoming.

"Gentlemen," he cried, "that's it absolutely. Don't you think I've taken care of that?"

They waited expectantly.

"I've found the man. He doesn't know it yet. I haven't

217

talked to him. It's best we keep him out of it at this point, but I tell you, he's our trump card."

He beamed at them in triumph.

"Well, colonel, who is it?" asked the admiral finally.

"The next Tsar," said Blau.

They sat in silence.

"I beg your pardon?" said one of the oil millionaires. "The who?"

"The next Tsar," repeated Blau. "His Imperial Highness the Grand Duke Vladimir."

"You're not serious!" gasped the rancher.

"Gentlemen, in war anything goes, and we're at war. Let's not kid ourselves. Solzhenitsyn said it right. The day World War Two ended World War Three began. And if we're at war, any weapon is fair game." He warmed to his theme. "We need figure heads. A new tsar is one gimmick. We need to exploit rivalries, jealousies. The Ukrainians hate the Georgians. The Estonians haven't much time for the Russians. The Muslims are unhappy about Afghanistan. We want to stir the mess, and make it boil over. It's been a cold war too long. Let's heat up the temperature a little."

"You're talking about revolution?" The admiral did not conceal his scepticism. "You serious?"

"You bet."

"You got any specific ideas?"

"Yes, sir." And Blau told them. He told them about his plans to sow insurrection. To assassinate, to sabotage, to subvert, to confuse, to undermine. To infiltrate and penetrate. To exploit unguarded weaknesses and disseminate lies, rumours, falsehoods. To spread fear and distrust.

"And, sir," Blau continued, "this man is the hereditary Tsar of All the Russias. His father was cousin of the late Tsar Nicholas. He is the surviving heir. There is nobody else in line. We will proclaim him Tsar. We will raise his banner in Russia."

The industrialist shook his head. "They won't go for it."

"I stake my reputation on it," declared Blau. "We will

218

light the fuse and the explosion will blow the Kremlin and the whole Communist shebang sky high. Then we put the Grand Duke on the throne, and bingo."

"Well," said the Senator after a pause, "it might not work, but it'll give the boys in the Kremlin a hell of a headache."

They asked where the Grand Duke Vladimir lived, and Blau told them he had his residence in Spain. He had been born in 1917, in Finland, when it was Russian territory, and he was hale and hearty.

"I'm sure that if he's offered the crown, he will accept," said Blau.

"The striped pants boys in the State Department would have a heart attack if they could hear you," smiled the Senator, and they all laughed.

"Crazier things have happened," nodded one of the oil tycoons.

They decided they had a lot to discuss and when they met again the following day they asked Colonel Blau if he was interested in coming on the payroll.

"I've got no job," grinned Blau and they shared his amusement. "What's the deal?"

They told him.

"OK," said Blau. "I'll give it a try, gentlemen. I'll do my best."

"Colonel," said the younger oil millionaire, "we're proud to have you aboard."

They shook his hand, and Blau felt, at last, that destiny was playing it his way. The irony was that the Europa League would pay him the salary of a four star general, with all expenses. In a way, it had paid him to lose his job.

The immigration officer at London airport gave him a friendly smile. This man hardly looked like an undesirable alien.

"Welcome to Britain," he said. "What's the purpose of your visit?"

"I'm on vacation," said Colonel Blau.

The immigration officer was quite startled when, purely

219

as routine, he checked the black book and found that there was a special note on Colonel Jerome Blau, and his arrival on UK soil had to be reported immediately to a certain department in London.

In his hotel suite, Blau asked the operator for the phone number he had been given in Dallas.

When it answered, he said:

"Dr Jury? This is Colonel Blau. I believe they've told you about me. Ah, good. Well, I've arrived in your beautiful city. Let's get together, shall we?"

It was a short conversation, and there was very little in the transcription which came to Rathbone's desk. Very little, that is, which told him anything he didn't already know.

58

Later she would understand what they were doing, but the big surprise came when Dupree walked in and handed her the passport.

It was her old Soviet passport, but there was a new stamp in it, square, covering the whole page, inked in two colours with an unintelligible signature.

"What's this?" asked Maya.

"Your visa," smiled Dupree. "For the United States."

For a moment, she stared at him uncomprehending. She was sure she had misheard him. They were playing a game with her.

"Yes," he nodded. "You're free to go to America. It is a special visa. A defector's visa. Your problems are over."

Maya still could not grasp it.

"This is – this is real?" She was beginning to feel elated, yet she dreaded the catch. She was sure there was a catch somewhere. They wouldn't give her the key. Not just like that.

"We don't issue joke visas," said Dupree. "You'll have resident alien status. You'll get your green card."

"Green card?" she repeated dumbly.

"It's a new life for you, Maya," he said. "You can work too. You'll have a labour permit." And he made quite a ceremony of it. He held out his hand. "Welcome to America," he said. She hesitated, then took his hand. He clasped it firmly.

That was when she couldn't help crying. The relief, she was free.

"Thank you," she whispered. "Thank you."

"Don't thank me," said Dupree. "It had to go to Washington. Somebody there makes the decision. But I'm very happy for you. You'll be able to help us a lot now."

"Yes, yes," she nodded eagerly, drying her eyes. Then what he had just said sank in.

"I . . . help you?" There it was. The catch.

He took out a pipe and slowly started filling it. Then he lit it, his eyes watching her. The sweet aroma of American tobacco began to waft across. "You do want to help us, don't you, honey?"

"Of course," she agreed. "But how? What can I do?"

"Oh come on, Maya, you know. There are lots of ways. We scratch your back, you scratch ours, OK?"

She looked genuinely puzzled. "Please?"

He waved the pipe. "I'm sorry. It's a saying we got. What I mean is, we're giving you what you want, so maybe you can give us something."

"Give you what?"

"Plenty of time to talk about that," he smiled.

She thought to herself, what does it matter anyway, I've succeeded. I've managed it. I'm on my way.

"Tell me about him," Dupree said gently.

"Who?"

"Andreyan."

221

She felt a pang. Yes, Andreyan. Poor Andreyan. She owed him everything. If he hadn't left those documents in the flat . . .

"He's not in trouble, is he?" she asked naïvely.

"Why should he be?"

"I stole his . . . papers. The embassy must know by now."

"They do," said Dupree. His eyes never left her face.

Maya's lips trembled. "I'm so worried." She shuddered. "They might hold him responsible. They may not forgive him. I am so afraid what might happen to him."

Dupree went to the window, and looked out at the barbed wire and the guard tower. "He should have been more careful, shouldn't he?" he said, his back to her. "He shouldn't have left it lying around."

She nodded. "Were they very important? A big secret?"

"What do you think?" Dupree swung round and faced her. "Isn't that why you brought them to us? Wasn't that the reason? That you thought they'd be worth a lot to us?"

Maya shook her head. "I looked at the file, I didn't understand any of it. I'm an actress." She gave him a beautifully helpless look.

"And a very good one, I'm sure," said Dupree.

"I just thought they might mean something to you and that . . ."

"And that we'd reward you, right? Like an American visa?"

She lowered her head. "Yes."

"That's honest," said Dupree. "I appreciate that."

Maya smiled wanly.

"But it didn't worry you either, did it?" he went on remorselessly. "You didn't care?"

She sat silent.

"It's called treason, honey. Your people get pretty rough when anybody commits treason. That didn't bother you?"

Maya tossed her head. "I only want to go to America. I want to be a big star. Like Garbo."

His lips curled. "Garbo, huh? You got to get up to date,

Maya." He sucked his pipe. "You still haven't told me about Andreyan."

She was beginning to hate Dupree. "I don't know anything about him."

"Sure," he said. "You shack up in the guy's apartment. You sleep with him. He gets permission to keep you with him in London. But you don't know anything about him. Come on, Maya, you can do better than that."

She swallowed hard. "I know he is a nice man," she said defiantly.

"What about his job?"

Maya shrugged. "He's a diplomat. He works at the embassy. He didn't talk about it."

"And you know he's KGB."

"He may have been."

Dupree reached over and took the passport from her. He tapped it with the stem of his pipe. "You know, honey, we can always cancel it. If you don't want to play ball, there are people who might change their mind about you. Now you wouldn't like that, would you?"

She was starting to feel cold. The dream was beginning to fade.

"Don't you understand?" she cried desperately. "I don't know anything. I came to London with the other actors. I haven't any secrets. Nobody tells me anything. I am not in the special services . . ."

"Special services?" repeated Dupree softly.

She began crying again. "Yes," she sobbed.

"Why do you talk about 'special services'?" he pressed.

"Isn't that what they are? The intelligence service. The secret department."

"Yes," said Dupree. "But the phrase is an interesting one. It is used by the KGB. When they talk about our people. It is professional jargon, so to speak. How is it you use that expression?"

Maya looked confused. "I . . . I must have heard it. Maybe Sergei Mikhailovitch used it. What does it matter?"

"Oh, nothing I suppose," smiled Dupree. He suddenly seemed cheerful. "Here." He put the passport down beside her. "Don't mislay it." He sucked at his pipe. "Damn!" he said, and struck a match. "The darn thing keeps going out on me."

She had a handkerchief out, and was wiping her eyes. "I'm sorry," said Maya, "I must look terrible."

"You look great, honey. Don't worry about that." He came over and patted her on the shoulder. "Just great," he repeated. He looked round. "This *is* a dump. I guess you'll be glad to get out of it."

She sat, looking very insecure. She had picked up the passport, and was holding it again.

"When can I go to America?" Maya asked, and she tensed, waiting for his reply.

"Right now, honey," said Dupree and went to the door. He opened it to let the blonde in.

"Miss Jones will be your escort, all the way. Isn't that right, K.D.?"

The blonde gave Maya an icy smile. "That's right," she said. "All the way. Pack your things and we'll get going."

"A staff car will take you to Mildenhall," added Dupree, "and we'll fly you straight to God's country on a military transport. No civilian airport, no airline. We're not taking any risks with you, Maya."

She didn't feel reassured.

"I'll be right with you, all the way," repeated the blonde. "I'm your body guard." She zipped open her shoulder bag, and showed Maya, for a brief glimpse, a snub nosed pistol. Then she zipped it shut again. "You got nothing to worry about," said Miss Jones.

And Maya shivered slightly.

59

Kleber had been sitting on the bench in the King's Road for five or six minutes before the dark haired girl in the gaberdine raincoat called Lesley joined him.

She had a carrier bag of groceries with her. Before meeting him, she had been shopping in the supermarket further up the road. They sat in silence, and a casual observer would probably have thought, at first, that they didn't know one another.

"Hallo, Eclipse," she finally greeted him, but without turning her head.

"Hallo, Lesley," said Kleber. As always, he had to admire the organisation's staff work. Meeting places, times, locations invariably worked like clockwork. It impressed his orderly mind. He liked things tidy. And he appreciated the logistical backup they gave him.

She came right to the point. "Was it necessary to kill him?" she asked.

"I wanted to cut the chain. He was sticking to me like glue. Following me all over the West End."

"You could have dodged him, couldn't you?"

"He was very good," said Kleber. It was a tribute Alcott would have been pleased to hear. He had always been very proud of his skill.

"It's not what one expects of you," said Lesley.

He bristled. He was not used to having his professionalism questioned. "There's been no fuss," he said. "It hasn't mattered. No headlines in the papers."

"That gives cause for concern." Her tone was disapproving.

"You must leave it to me how I operate," he protested. "I have my reasons for doing something."

"Just so you know how they feel about it," she said coldly.

He ignored that and kept his eyes on three punks with Mohican scalp locks on the other side of the street. What a degenerate city London was, he thought. Winos lying in doorways, skinheaded ruffians pushing people off the pavement, and these freaks parading around.

"Where are you living now?" she asked.

"Behind King's Cross. A cheap hotel."

She frowned. "Not too cheap, I hope. The police check those places far more."

"Well, I didn't think Claridges was quite right," smiled Kleber.

"There was nothing in the flat they shouldn't have found, was there?"

"Of course not."

"Good."

And he knew what she was going to ask next, so he said:

"The photograph of Borisov was in the false bottom of the suitcase."

For the first time she looked pleased. "Excellent. That means they've found it. Well done."

"If that doesn't give them an idea of who's the man in question, nothing will," said Kleber.

She dipped into the carrier bag and brought out a bar of chocolate. She broke off a piece, and started eating it. Then she remembered him, and offered him some. He shook his head.

"When will you make an attempt?" she enquired casually.

"At the right opportunity."

She didn't push it any further. She could detect the undercurrent of his resentment at being questioned. "They're glad it's worked out the way it has," she commented, as a gesture of conciliation. "They feel the operation is proceeding well."

He kept his amusement private. "Operation!" What a

226

pompous way they had. He had an assignment, a contract. She made it sound like the invasion of Normandy.

"It's very useful that they've become aware that you are over here," she went on. "It's an extra bonus."

"Good," said Kleber. "I'm happy they're pleased."

"Perhaps," she added, "we ought to give them an additional hint or two . . ."

Kleber stirred on the bench uneasily. "Look here, don't overdo it. Let them put the pieces together. Don't hand 'em over on a plate."

"Yes." She nodded after a pause. "You're right."

She dipped into the carrier bag again and brought out a folded copy of the *Standard*.

"Have a paper," she said and handed it to him.

"Sure. Save me buying one."

They sat silently for a few moments again. Then she said: "Anything else?"

He shook his head.

"No problems?"

Kleber smiled thinly. "None that I can't cope with."

"All right then." She stood up and took her carrier bag. "Ciao." She walked off, but he remained on the bench for a little while. As far as he could see, everything was all clear. Nobody had detached themselves from the throng as she crossed the King's Road. Nobody was following her.

Inside the folded evening paper was a sealed envelope. It contained spending money, and some instructions. The money was enough for a couple of weeks; they were always generous with running expenses.

The instructions he would burn as soon as he had read them.

Kleber sauntered off, whistling silently. He had never had an assignment quite like this one, but he knew it was important to them.

Otherwise, obviously, they wouldn't pay him so well.

60

She was a 600-ton ex-supply ship, and had seen better days. She flew the Liberian flag, and was positioned just beyond Knock Deep, a quiet shipping channel in international waters, fifteen miles from Frinton-on-Sea. She was, in law, outside anyone's jurisdiction.

The *Ventura* was known to the Essex coastguard. They had marked her down as a pirate radio ship, but beyond that they had no contact with her. As far as they knew, she broadcast gospel music and Country and Western songs, interspersed with commercials for products which are banned for broadcast advertising on shore, like alcohol and tobacco. If the mixture with hymns seemed incongruous, the answer was that she sold air time to anyone who wanted to buy it.

She wasn't the only radio pirate around. A few miles away *Laser 858* rode at anchor, and the old veteran *Caroline* was close by. There were several other vessels with tall radio transmission masts clustered in the area, all outside territorial waters, but the *Ventura* was something different. After dark, she periodically switched wave lengths and started broadcasting in Russian. She beamed out the transmissions of Russkaya Volya.

There was only a crew of four aboard her most of the time. She had no official contact with the United Kingdom. She was supplied, from time to time, by a small tender that came across from Holland. She kept to herself, and others left her alone.

The launch from Frinton that brought Colonel Blau and Dr Jury out to her made a round about trip, first making sure that they were no longer in territorial waters, then swinging back to the *Ventura*. It was like two strangers meeting in no man's land. Their contact was beyond the law.

Blau was not impressed by his first glimpse of her. She looked shabby, and he saw patches of rust on the funnel. The crew fitted her. All of them, except the bearded man who was introduced as the skipper, needed a shave. Their hair was untidy and too long, and one of them chewed gum. Blau would have disciplined all of them immediately. Fourteen days in the stockade might teach them to smarten up.

He and Jury clambered up the rope ladder, and the bearded man came forward.

"Mac's the captain," explained Jury. He looked out of place on the swaying deck in his business suit.

"Glad to have you aboard," drawled Mac, after Jury had introduced Blau. "You could have picked a better day." He looked upwards. "It's going to piss down soon."

"The colonel wants to see the operation," said Jury.

"Colonel is it?" grunted Mac. He indicated the gum chewer. "That's Curly. He's the engineer. And that's Dave."

Dave was smoking, and Blau's eyes narrowed when he saw what it was. The sniff he got only confirmed it. He knew the aroma of marijuana. The last soldier he'd caught smoking a joint got twelve months hard labour and a dishonourable discharge. He looked at Jury to see if he had noticed it too. But behind his gold rimmed glasses he seemed quite unaware of it. Blau set his mouth grimly. This outfit needed shaping up. They looked like a bunch of drop-outs. He had expected sharp, alert people, disciplined and motivated. Not layabouts smoking dope.

"Woody is below, doing the show," said Mac.

"That's all there is?" asked Blau icily. "Just you men?"

Mac seemed puzzled. "Who else do we need? We're not the *Queen Elizabeth*, mister."

Dave and Curly grinned, but Mac saw Blau's scowl.

"Beg your pardon, I mean colonel," he apologised, but rather spoiled it by grinning back at them.

"They spend a week on board, and a week ashore while the

relief crew takes over," Jury was saying. "They play the programmes, and fix any hiccups. They're pretty handy fellows. They keep the transmitter ship shape. Do a good job."

"I'm sure," grunted Blau and his tone was such that Jury blinked nervously.

To the colonel's eye the living cabin, was like a pig sty. Dirty clothes were scattered around, and two empty tins of baked beans lay on the floor. Tacked to one of the walls was a big pin-up of a naked woman.

"Dallas pays for this operation," explained Jury when they were alone. "They bought this vessel, and equipped it with a high power transmitter. It earns its keep with the commercials we do. But the real object you know. The Russian broadcasts."

"Where did you get these men?" demanded Blau. He sounded as he did when he drew up court martial charges.

Jury shrugged. "All over. You can always find men to do things. If you pay the right money."

"That's great motivation."

"It's the sort of motivation you can rely on," pointed out Jury. "They don't have to do much, really. They get the tapes sent out and play them, that's all."

"Everything is on tape?"

"Everything." Jury did not disguise his pleasure at the way it worked out. "We record the Russian broadcasts. Nothing is broadcast live from the ship, except Woody's chatter. And he doesn't say much."

Blau shook his head, frowning.

"Something's bothering you?" enquired Jury.

"Yes, sir. How come the British allow all this under their nose?"

"Ah." Jury took off his glasses and polished them. "If it happened in British waters, it would be illegal. We'd all go to jail. The Marine Offences Act. Two years imprisonment on indictment. Limitless fines." He shook his head sorrowfully. "Very severe."

"But . . ."

"We're on the high seas. Outside the limit. Five miles, 15 or 500, it doesn't matter. Once we're outside the territorial limit. They can't touch us." He looked happy.

The door of the cabin opened and a tall man with short fair hair came in. He looked a different breed from the others Blau had seen. Tidy, smart. He had shaved. His eyes were alert. He was carrying a tray with two mugs.

"Skipper thought you might like some hot grog, gentlemen," he said.

"This is Woody, colonel," Jury explained.

Woody put one of the mugs down in front of Blau.

"Hope you enjoy it, sir," he said.

Blau was impressed. The guy showed respect. Actually called him "sir". He was neat, presentable.

"What's your background?" asked the colonel.

Woody stood very straight. "Army, sir. I was in 'Nam. In the CIC."

Blau's interest increased. "Counter intelligence, were you?"

"Yes, sir."

Blau nodded. That was the way he was used to men answering him. "How do you enjoy the job here, son?"

"It's another way of fighting the reds, sir," replied Woody. "Is that all, gentlemen?"

"Yes, thank you," said Jury. Woody left the cabin.

"Impressive," remarked Blau. "He's worth the whole bunch. It's the Army training, you see."

Jury sipped the drink. "I wouldn't underestimate the others," he said drily.

He showed Blau the rest of the *Ventura*. The radio room with its tape decks and controls, the galley, the bridge. They clambered up narrow ladders, and bent their heads as they passed through narrow passages below deck.

"Just where do you cook up the Russian material?" asked Blau.

For a moment Jury was silent. Then he said: "We have a little studio."

231

"Oh?"

"Ashore. In a country house. Fully equipped. We can record anything there."

"And fake anything?"

Jury blinked. Then he smiled. "Of course, colonel. It *is* black propaganda."

"I'm privileged to get involved," said Blau, and meant it.

Two hours later they were seen off by the skipper. Mac looked as disreputable as ever. But Blau's eyes were on Woody. The ex-GI had come on deck to see them leave, and as the colonel stood in the launch, Woody gave him a salute.

It made Blau feel there was hope yet.

61

Sergei Mikhailovitch Andreyan had a secret persona, that of Mr Ericson, and once in a while, on those rare mornings when he'd said he would be late for work, it was usually so he could temporarily change character. It was easy for Andreyan to become Ericson. It didn't require a disguise. There was no change in his appearance. He just became somebody else. It was that simple.

The embassy did not know about Mr Ericson. Indeed, he did not exist except for those occasional periods when Andreyan assumed his identity. Had he known about him, Colonel Leonov's worst fears would have been confirmed.

Today was one of those mornings he was late for work. As Ericson, Andreyan went to the American Express office in the Haymarket. There he queued patiently at the cashiers' counter, lining up with the tourists and foreign visitors. Then, when his turn came, he bought £5,000 worth of dollar travellers cheques. He produced the money, in cash, from a hold-all, and signed the cheques in the name of Ericson. He did not have to show any proof of identity.

With the cheques safely in his pocket, he crossed the Haymarket, and walked round St James's Square. There were seldom many people in the square, and it was an excellent place to make sure he wasn't being followed. He spotted no one.

Then he hailed a passing taxi and asked to be taken to South Kensington. He had one more thing to do before he turned up at the embassy.

In Gloucester Road he went to the branch of a bank where he had an account also in the name of Ericson, and a safe deposit box. It amused him that no one at the bank had the vaguest idea who he really was. That was so unique about England. People hardly ever demanded documentary proof of anything; not that Andreyan couldn't have supplied whatever was required.

Andreyan unlocked his box, and put in the £5,000 worth of dollar travellers cheques. He already had another £11,000 in neat bundles of travellers cheques in dollars and Swiss francs in the box, as well as two passports, a Swedish one, and a Swiss one. He added to these a beautifully produced British passport in the name of Ericson. All three carried Andreyan's photo, and the personal description fitted him perfectly. He locked the box again, and returned to the vault.

Andreyan had accumulated his secret cache during his stay in London like a squirrel hoarding a store of nuts. It was his fail safe insurance policy. He had decided long ago that there was no harm in having the means to get out. To disappear. But to make the necessary arrangements at short notice was difficult, if not impossible. In an emergency, one had little time, one's mobility might be limited, one's facilities restricted. Much better to prepare when one had limitless opportunity.

If the Directorate but knew it, it was all the result of Andreyan's training. Always be prepared, they had taught him. Leave nothing to chance. He was, in a way, only implementing the Centre's philosophy.

When he gave birth to Mr Ericson, Andreyan had no idea if he would ever need to invoke him. It simply seemed to him good sense to be able to become Mr Ericson under certain circumstances.

No one, of course, knew about it. One night, after he had made love to Maya, he lay beside her toying with the idea of going off with her to far away places, becoming Ericson, basking in the sun, lazing on the beach, but he instantly dismissed it. Maya, he knew, would be the last person he could rely on to keep quiet. Trusting Maya with his life would be very foolish.

He worried about the money a little. The £16,000 had been abstracted from the special fund, the cash that was available day and night for "unofficial" purposes. Quick bribes, instant payments, covert purchases. There were always large sums in the safe to which only Leonov's people had access and he had made use of it, of course. There were always palms to be greased, illicit gratuities to be handed over, certain street activities to be financed. These were transactions for which there were no receipts, and only shadowy accounting. It was easy to abstract a few hundred here and a few hundred there. He had recorded some substantial payments to certain groups which could never be checked, and Mr Ericson had benefited accordingly.

Andreyan didn't like doing it. It was state money, and he was one of those trusted with it. But he rationalised it by saying to himself that the money had not really been abstracted, only put aside. He hadn't spent it on frivolities. Much rather, it was an insurance premium. He would never make use of that money recklessly. He wouldn't gamble it away. It was only there as a life raft.

In less than two hours Andreyan had done his business for that morning. It was time to go to the embassy. They probably hadn't even noticed that he hadn't come to work yet, but there was no point in staying away too long.

234

It was nearly 11 a.m. before Leonov suddenly realised that Andreyan hadn't arrived for work, and it wasn't like him to be late. Andreyan was usually at the embassy by nine, and if he was going somewhere else first he let them know about it.

Leonov went back to the papers he was dealing with, but Andreyan's absence bothered him. His fingers tapped on the desk absent mindedly. Andreyan was a reliable man, methodical in his habits. He was never really late. Ten minutes, quarter of an hour, possibly. Two hours, never.

Leonov picked up the phone and asked for Andreyan's secretary.

"Olga," he said, "could you ask Comrade Andreyan to come and see me."

"I will, when he arrives," she replied. And added: "I'm afraid he's not here yet, comrade colonel." She too sounded puzzled.

"Thank you," said Leonov. He didn't want her to think he was concerned. He hoped he sounded casual.

The grey haired colonel had had a bad night. Too many things were pressing in on him. He had woken up at 3 a.m. and not been able to go back to sleep. There were decisions to be made, and he knew how vital it was not to put a foot wrong. "Igor" had his problems.

He stared for a while across the room with unseeing eyes, deliberating. The new Director at Moscow Centre didn't like him, he was aware of that. Nothing tangible, but he sensed it. The impersonal cypher signals, the curt code messages spoke for themselves. Leonov was experienced at reading the signs. Perhaps the time had now come . . .

But he stopped that line of thought, and once more began tackling the paper work on his desk. He unlocked the steel file containing the material with the highest classification. There was, on top of the bunch, an informative message that the Dutch had seized sixty crates of arms being shipped through Schiphol airport by Omnipol, the security service controlled arms factory in Czechoslovakia, to the Provisional IRA in Ireland. Well, they couldn't blame him for that. But it made him worry about the Cyprus registered trawler on its way to Waterford at this moment, with a cargo of small arms, anti-tank mines and explosives for the IRA, also manufactured in Czechoslovakia. If that got captured, it could be awkward. Some of the arrangements had been made through the London embassy . . .

Which made him think of Andreyan again. Damn it, where was the man?

Leonov opened a drawer and took out the embassy roster. He found the number of Andreyan's flat, and dialled it. He let the phone ring for a minute, almost counting the seconds on his watch, but there was no reply. The colonel put the receiver down and swore softly. Then he left his desk and went down the hall, to the office of Kutuzov, the assistant naval attaché. After all, he was a neighbour of Andreyan's. Didn't he have the ground floor flat under his?

"Dear colleague, how are you?" Kutuzov greeted him. He was a naval captain second grade, and would much have preferred commanding a destroyer in the Baltic to playing at being a desk-bound spy in London. He liked Leonov, but he was also wary of him, because he knew what his job was.

"Your wife, is she well?" asked Leonov. He wanted to play this carefully. No need to let the whole embassy know what was going through his mind. Not at this stage, anyway.

"Frankly, she is bored," said Kutuzov. "She lives for the weekends. She is so fed up looking at the four walls of the flat."

He had got the vodka out, and was pouring it for them. Kutusov used any occasion as an excuse for a drink, even somebody merely dropping by his office.

Leonov took his chance. "Andreyan shares your house, doesn't he?" He hoped it sounded casual.

"One floor up," said Kutuzov. "Quite a lad, your colleague." He winked.

"Really?"

"And good luck to him," said Kutuzov. "She is very pretty. I don't blame him. An actress. Actually, come to think of it, I haven't seen her lately. Has she gone?"

"Why don't you ask him?" said Leonov coldly.

But Kutuzov was not abashed. "That's one thing I envy you people, your freedom to do what you like. If you want to have fun with a lady, you can take her home. Think what they'd do to one of us if we brought a female into an embassy flat. But not you lot. Anything goes."

"Do you see much of Andreyan?"

"You know the saying," replied Kutuzov. " 'Good neighbours go their separate ways.' We keep to ourselves."

"So you haven't talked to him in the last day or two?"

Kutusov put down his glass. The smile faded. "Tell me, why are you asking this?"

Leonov took a deep swig of vodka. Then he said: "No reason. Why should I . . ."

"I thought maybe this might be more official than I realised," said Kutuzov.

"Why, my friend? What makes you say that?"

"Seeing who you are, comrade colonel. If you'll forgive me."

Leonov slapped him on the back and laughed. He did that kind of thing very well when it was necessary.

"Well you couldn't be more wrong, my friend," he said.

"Good," nodded Kutuzov. "I am relieved to hear it."

Leonov declined another drink, and went back to his office. He was beginning to be more than uneasy. Andreyan's absence was ominous.

He sat considering whether he should invoke the emergency procedure. Send a flash signal to the Centre. Inform the ambassador. Start searching Andreyan's office and flat. Circulate each section.

Damn him. This was the last thing Leonov needed. It made his own position very – delicate. It could ruin everything. And he had never really suspected him.

There was a tap on the door, and Andreyan stood in front of him.

"I'm sorry I . . ." he began, but Leonov fumed at him:

"What the hell is going on?"

"I am sorry I'm late," said Andreyan coolly.

"And where the hell have you been?" snarled Leonov. He was slightly flushed.

"I bought a suit," said Andreyan. "A very expensive suit. It's an experience going to a tailor like that. Like getting married, I imagine. He weds you to the suit."

Leonov opened his mouth, and then shut it again. Finally he said: "You could have informed somebody. This is an embassy you know. We keep regular hours. It is not a national holiday today. I cannot recall the Supreme Soviet making a decree giving everybody the day off."

"Be fair," said Andreyan. "I've been working late hours for weeks."

"Yes," snapped Leonov and instantly regretted it. "Don't we know. I'm sure she enjoyed it too."

"Is that all, comrade colonel?" Andreyan had become very formal.

Leonov waved a hand dismissing him. Then he called him back. "Where is the suit?"

Andreyan seemed to him to hesitate. "It'll take a few weeks. They had to make adjustments."

And he shut the door.

The strain was telling on Leonov. He knew that because after Andreyan had gone, the colonel sat gnawing his lip, wondering. Wondering where Andreyan had really been all morning.

And, wondering even more, how much Andreyan knew.

62

That evening Borisov slipped quietly into a rear pew as the brothers celebrated Compline, the service that marks the end of the monastic day. It was dark already and the monks were shadowy figures, their faces hidden deep in their hoods, and their heads bowed.

Borisov shifted uneasily on the hard bench. It was the first time that he had bothered to take a look at one of the monastery's daily services. It's only theatre, he kept telling himself, but he shivered slightly in the gloom. There was only one lamp, for the monk who was intoning the Latin text.

It was curiosity that had brought Borisov. This was the service that warded off the powers of evil, a sort of precautionary exorcism of the terrors of the night, they told him. It protected them against the evil in their midst. This, thought Borisov, I have to see. He came to be amused, but, despite his doubts, he was impressed. The Latin reading came to an end and the light suddenly went out. The chanted hymns that rose up in the darkness were like echoes from mediaeval times. So this was the exorcism of the terrors of the night.

He had the strangest feeling that he was being watched. Not by the brothers, their faces turned away from him. No, by something in the darkness, from the secrecy of the shadows. By the Evil One? Borisov snorted. This was absurd. The mumbo jumbo was getting on top of him. He had been in this place too long.

Quietly, so that he wouldn't be noticed, he made his way outside. He moved carefully, because it was so dark that he could miss a step. They were used to the dark, these monks. Half of their life was spent in it. In a few hours they would be back here, in pitch darkness, for 4 a.m. Matins.

He was back in his room when, half an hour later, there was a soft tap on his door, and Stephen came in. He startled Borisov. The lights in the cells had gone out one by one, and the monks had settled down for the night. Stephen had never visited him so late.

"You're still up, good," said the monk. "May I intrude?"

"I'll be glad to have somebody to talk to . . ."

Stephen sat down. "Feeling a little lonely?" His voice

239

sounded sympathetic. "I can understand it. After all, you're not one of us. You must feel very cut off."

He put a small object on the table. It was a packet of cigarettes. Javas. Russian cigarettes. "A little present for you," he said.

Borisov slowly picked up the packet. He stared at it. "Where do you get these?" he asked.

"I thought you might appreciate a taste of home. You smoke these, don't you?"

"Actually," said Borisov, a little defiantly, "I prefer American ones." He put the Javas down.

"I'm sorry," apologised Stephen humbly. "I am no expert on cigarettes."

"*Pravda*. Javas. You seem to have a very effective source."

Stephen smiled. "The Lord provides, my friend."

They sat in silence. Borisov was conscious of Stephen contemplating him benevolently. It made him feel edgy.

"Did you find tonight helpful?" Stephen asked gently after a pause.

"Helpful?"

"I saw you at the back. During Compline. First time you've been to a service here, isn't it?"

"Why should I find it helpful?" demanded Borisov aggressively.

A wave of the hand with two stumps. "Oh, I can't say. But you must know."

"You're not trying to convert me, are you?" said Borisov and he didn't conceal the sneer.

Stephen wasn't at all upset. "My dear friend, I told you when you came. It's your business. I wouldn't dream of imposing . . ."

"So how could it be helpful?" persisted Borisov.

"The idea is to seek protection. That's what all that Latin was about, my friend. Like an insurance policy."

Borisov looked away. "I don't need protection."

"I'm glad to hear it," said Stephen. "You must be a very lucky man." He smiled. "Anyway, I must go, and you must be tired." He stood up. "You're a remarkable man, my friend," he said.

"Remarkable?"

"I admire your self-discipline. Worthy of a Jesuit."

Borisov was wary. "I don't understand . . ."

"I think you do."

"No," insisted Borisov. "You're speaking in riddles. Tell me."

"Is there nothing you miss? Small things perhaps. A drink. Vodka. Or not such small things. A woman perhaps . . ."

"Are you taking my confession?" asked Borisov sarcastically.

"No. Just admiring your dedication. Forgive me if I presume. I wasn't trying to be too personal."

You're lying, prelate, thought Borisov. But aloud he said: "Don't worry about it. I don't mind." He hesitated. "May I ask you something? If it's not too personal either?"

"Please."

"Why did they do that?" He indicated the left hand. "Why were you a prisoner?"

"I was a spy," replied the monk very quietly.

They stood facing each other. Behind his glasses, Stephen's eyes were rather sad. "It's late, my friend."

Borisov nodded.

"And I will have to get up long before you, I'm afraid," Stephen excused himself.

To his own surprise, Borisov said: "Thank you for coming."

Stephen went to the door and opened it. But before he stepped outside, he turned round.

"Good night, my son," and he shut the door very gently.

Borisov lay awake for a long time, and even when he eventually closed his eyes he didn't sleep well.

He woke up after an hour or two. That was when he opened the pack and smoked a Russian cigarette.

63

"There are reasons," said Cheyne. His eyes avoided Rathbone.
"Such as?"

"Policy reasons. Things which don't concern this department."

"And you accept those?" pressed Rathbone grimly.

Cheyne shifted in his chair. "We all do as we are told. At
least, I hope we do, Colin." And this time he looked
Rathbone straight in the eyes.

"You've got the report. Everything." Rathbone nodded at
the file he had brought in. "It's right there, in front of you."

"I've read it."

"And still you won't do it?"

Cheyne looked pained. "My dear chap, it's not up to me. I
don't deport people. The Home Secretary does it. I have no
power. I can no more deport Mr Blau than I can fly."

Rathbone controlled himself. He was slightly pale. "With
respect. You recommend. One word from you and the
wheels at the Home Office begin to grind. You give the hint,
and they'll kick out Colonel Blau."

"Oh really?" Cheyne was acid. "An American tourist. A
retired Army colonel with a distinguished record. Who has
committed no offence. Just like that?"

"You know what Blau is. You know what he's doing."

Cheyne sniffed with distaste. "I think," he said, "that
you've got it in for the man. The Garner episode rankles.
And that didn't produce any proof really, did it?"

Rathbone kept very calm. "You know what he's doing
over here. It's in the file. If it comes out, it could land us right
in the shit."

Cheyne winced. "Please. Your language."

"This whole Monmouth Street operation . . ." began Rathbone.

"Is outside our jurisdiction."

Rathbone looked out of the window. Then he said very quietly: "Is there an arrangement?"

"Arrangement? What do you mean?"

"That we look the other way. That we don't interfere. Is that it?"

Cheyne pursed his lips. "I don't know what you're talking about."

"I think you know what I mean," said Rathbone thoughtfully.

"Colin, you're beginning to see ghosts. I understand your feelings about this man Blau. We're keeping an eye on him, aren't we? But we really cannot rush into it like a bull in a china shop. I am instructed . . ."

"Ah," interrupted Rathbone.

Cheyne ignored him. "I am instructed that we let things ride. We'll watch Colonel Blau. But keep your hands off him. We don't want any incidents, do we? Any embarrassing questions."

"Those are your instructions, are they?" asked Rathbone. He was trying not to sound sarcastic.

"We are but the servants of our political masters," sighed Cheyne. "You see, that is the price of democracy. It's not easy, Colin, but you know that's the way things have to be."

He got up, went over to the wall and straightened a print of Horse Guards Parade that was crooked. "There. That was beginning to annoy me." He turned back to Rathbone. "Anyway, I don't believe Colonel Blau will be with us that long, do you? I'm sure he's going on to better and bigger things. Then he'll be off our neck, and you'll be happy."

"Ecstatic," muttered Rathbone.

"I shouldn't think our friends in Moscow take him and his kind very seriously anyway," added Cheyne.

"I hope not."

243

"You know your problem. You worry too much, Colin."
He paused. "Is there anything else?"

"Not at the moment," said Rathbone.

"Always nice to see you," smiled Cheyne. "I know you'll
keep in touch."

After Rathbone had left, Cheyne pressed the buzzer. He
gave the dark haired girl who came in the Blau file.

"Put this in the safe," he said. "We don't want it lying
around."

"Right away, Mr Cheyne." She hesitated. "I was wondering . . ."

He looked up. "Yes?"

"I have a bit of a headache. Would you mind terribly sir, if
I went home a little early?"

He smiled sympathetically. "Of course not. Finish what
you're doing and go home. I hope you'll feel better
tomorrow, Lesley."

Half an hour later Lesley put on her gaberdine raincoat
and left the department.

64

Later on he would remember it as the last time that he
walked in the monastery's garden with Father Stephen. The
daily perambulation had become a ritual for the two of them.
They usually walked along the same path, past the fish pond,
and the old tree, then rested briefly on the same bench.
Sometimes Borisov and the monk walked in silence, side
by side, keeping their thoughts to themselves. But today
Stephen suddenly asked him:

"How did you get on with the book?"

Borisov looked blank.

"The book about the Inquisition. The one you borrowed."

"I found it terrible. Frightening."

Stephen glanced at him. "But it intrigues you, doesn't it? I can understand it, you know. They're fascinating, soul hunters. The real soul hunters."

Borisov did not reply, and Stephen went on:

"Ingenious, weren't they? So modern in their methods. 'Do not be too precise in your questions, lest they should suggest answers to the accused.' That could come out of a KGB manual, don't you think?"

"I feel a little tired," said Borisov. "Can we sit down?"

They rested on the bench.

"It is the actual psychology of the Holy Office that was remarkable," continued Stephen. "That was the real secret. Half the time they didn't need to torture anyone. Do you know about the five stages?"

"No," said Borisov curtly.

"First, there was the threat of torture. That in itself had a marked effect. They didn't have to go any further with some people. Then came stage two. They showed you the actual implements of torture. The instruments they were planning to use. That was quite enough for a lot of the accused. Thirdly, they were prepared for the ordeal. By the time they had removed some of their clothes, there was no need to do more. Four, you were tied down." He stopped.

Finally, Borisov said: "And what was the fifth step?"

"Well, that was the actual torture. But half the time it never got that far. The other four stages had been enough."

"Why are you telling me all this?"

"I thought you were interested," said Stephen mildly.

"It is barbaric," shuddered Borisov. "The whole concept."

Stephen leaned forward. "On the contrary, my friend, you will find that Torquemada specifically laid down that the object was to treat penitents mercifully and kindly – as long as they confessed."

Borisov faced him. "Confessed what?"

"Their errors. Their . . . well, what do you think?"

"Can we talk about something else?"

Stephen looked concerned. "Oh, I'm so sorry if the subject worries you. I merely thought that since you were a student of these things, it was a topic that . . . well, never mind. Forgive me. I can be very tactless."

They got up and started walking again.

"Tell me, how long do you intend to stay with us?"

Borisov stopped and looked at Stephen. It was not a question he had expected.

"Oh please, don't misunderstand me," Stephen hastily added, "you are welcome to remain here for as long as you wish to stay. I am simply concerned about your well being. Are you really content here? Do you feel this is where you want to be?"

Borisov hesitated. They continued walking and still he remained silent. Stephen waited patiently. Finally, Borisov said: "You want to be rid of me?"

"My dear friend, I told you, you can stay here, and be welcome. But you are an actor. You crave an audience. You need bright lights. You do not belong here, do you?"

Borisov felt a growing unease. "Where do I belong?" he asked.

"That is something that only you can know," smiled Stephen.

"The voice of Torquemada?"

"Oh come. You know what I mean."

Borisov had a strong urge to look into Stephen's eyes, to read his mind, but he avoided it. At that moment, he did not want to face what might be there.

Stephen's voice came over to him softly, gently.

"Believe me, I understand your problem. And I want you to know that you are not alone. Others have this dilemma. Others have to come to terms with changing sides, abandoning their motherland, sailing, so to speak, under false colours . . ."

246

"What do you mean?" whispered Borisov. He was tense.

"You're not the first one to take this step. You should trust our people. You should trust Rathbone."

Borisov waited.

"He has helped others in equally difficult situations. He's . . ." Stephen hesitated, "he's helping them now."

"*Now?*"

"At this moment. I'm only telling you this to reassure you. So that you know that you are safe over here. That if you leave this place, you will still be well looked after, well protected."

Suddenly Borisov shivered. "What exactly are you trying to tell me?" he croaked.

"That you're not alone, my son," said Stephen and now, for the first time, looked him straight in the eyes.

Borisov's mouth felt dry. He wanted to lick his lips, but he had no saliva. He felt trapped. Trapped by the wall round the garden, the moat round the monastery, by this inquisitor. There was confusion in his mind. Which of the five stages was this? The threat? Or . . .

"Perhaps I shouldn't tell you, but you have to feel trusted in order to trust others," Stephen was saying. "And I trust you."

"Who are you?" whispered Borisov.

"A friend," said Stephen, and put his left hand with its missing fingers on Borisov's shoulder. "If there is anything you need . . . taken care of. At home. In Moscow. A message to your wife. Anything. It . . . can be arranged."

"How?" Borisov's voice was hardly audible.

"A very reliable contact. A man like you. Who helps. A man you've met, my friend. Who, if I may say so, with respect, is as good an actor as you."

Borisov's heart was pounding.

"A man who is working for our side," Stephen said and smiled.

Borisov's eyes were wide.

"Can't you guess?" whispered Stephen.

Borisov just shook his head. His pulse was racing now.

"You can trust him and you can trust me," said Stephen.

"Who?" cried Borisov.

"I thought you knew," said Stephen. "Colonel Leonov. At your embassy. He's Rathbone's man."

65

The debriefing had taken a long time. They had spent hours cross-examining her, about her background, her family. Who she knew, where she had been. Then K.D. Jones had explained the rules to Maya.

"We'll look after you. We'll get you an apartment. We'll help your career. We've opened a bank account for you. All you have to do is say the right things."

"You're very kind," smiled Maya sweetly. "Everybody is being so good to me." And she meant it too. She had never dreamt the promised land would open its doors so invitingly. "How can I ever repay you?"

But actually, she was already giving them a very good return. The Russian actress with the stunning looks who had broken with Moscow was worth acres of space in the media. Not that anybody called her an actress.

The cool blonde who was her shadow hovered around stage managing the transition. It was K.D. Jones who oversaw Maya's grooming and fabulous wardrobe. It was she who arranged lengthy sessions at the beauty parlour and found her the English dialogue coach. And they paid for it all, because Maya was an investment. Then they unveiled her.

Even when she had got used to her, Maya still wasn't sure

whether the blonde was there to guard her or watch her. Not that it mattered, because Maya relished the role in which they had cast her. Nobody had ever heard of her, nobody had ever seen her act, but suddenly Maya Petrova was the famous Soviet star.

She faced the Press Conference at the Plaza in New York, K.D. Jones accompanying her in case she got into difficulties with the language, like the professional she was.

"What are your plans, Miss Petrova?"

"I just want to be an actress."

"Do you have any regrets about defecting?"

"I am so happy to be in a free country. America is so beautiful. The air smells so good."

That was a quote that went down particularly well.

"Did anyone help you to get to America?"

"It is something I must not talk about," replied Maya mysteriously, with just the right hint of cloak and dagger intrigue. "People could be in danger."

They loved that too.

"What do you think about Communism?"

"I know nothing about politics. I am an actress. But it is wonderful to be able to speak one's mind without fear."

"Do you have any ambitions, Miss Petrova?"

"Yes, to make good pictures."

"Do you miss Moscow?"

"New York is much nicer."

"What do you think of Hollywood?"

"I have dreamed of going there all my life."

"What about your relations in Russia?"

"I am sure they will understand."

"Do you intend to become an American citizen?"

"Of course. It will be such an honour and such a privilege."

She smiled dazzlingly for the photographers, and faced the barrage of flashbulbs without blinking. She looked stunning, and they loved her accent.

"You're doing great, honey," said K.D. Jones crisply.

249

Then they flew her to Los Angeles, and explained that wheels were being set in motion for her.

"You're getting an agent," K.D. Jones told her.

Maya frowned. "An agent?" Then her face cleared. "I am sorry, I get mixed up."

"What do you mean?"

"I am so stupid. For a moment, I thought you meant a spy."

"No, honey," explained K.D. Jones patiently. "He's going to look after you. Find you work."

Herman Schneider was a lugubrious fat man whose face lit up when he saw Maya. He had magnificent offices on the twelfth floor of a modern building on Sunset Boulevard, and on his desk was an ornamental sign reading "Thank You For Not Smoking." He, however, had a cigar in his mouth. He rationalised this by keeping it unlit.

"Great to meet you," he told Maya. "My, but you're cute."

He didn't mention to her that he had connections with the Agency at Langley. Nor that he had been a colonel in psychological warfare, and had certain other interesting links.

"I hear you're a great actress," he beamed at her.

Maya did her best to look modest.

"I got a lot of things to set up for you," he announced. "They want to see you at . . ." and he rattled off a string of names and studios.

Maya was delighted.

"Of course, you've gotta be built up," went on Schneider, chomping his unlit cigar. "We want to cash in, right? We need another *Zhivago* for you. I'm already looking. Boy, am I going to package you, honey."

Afterwards, walking along Rodeo Drive, K.D. Jones beside her, she marvelled at the luxurious shops, the sleek cars, the beautiful people. She had achieved it. The key was in her hand.

Naturally, she thought about Andreyan often. She was

grateful to him. Without him she wouldn't have managed it. And there were times when she wondered if they were going to ask more of her. One day, perhaps, they might want something else from her. But that was tomorrow. Today she was here, she was in Hollywood, and the red carpet had been spread out for her.

Suddenly Maya stopped. She had spotted a trouser suit in one of the most expensive shops in Beverly Hills. Even for Rodeo Drive, this place was more than expensive.

"Oh, I love that!" exclaimed Maya. "Don't you?"

"Not bad." K.D. Jones sounded cautious.

"I must have it." Maya had made up her mind. "It is just me. Come on."

As she led the way into the shop, K.D. Jones sighed. No doubt about it, Maya Petrova was going to cost Uncle Sam a lot of money.

66

Gur's arrival was unannounced. He flew in from Moscow and was driven straight to the embassy in Bayswater. He spent half an hour behind closed doors with the ambassador, then Leonov and Andreyan were summoned.

"This is Comrade Gur," explained the ambassador smoothly. "The Directorate has sent him over. You will give him every co-operation, of course."

Yuri Gur was a stocky man who did not smile. His eyes studied Leonov and Andreyan, but he said nothing. He did not even nod to them when he was introduced.

"You will answer all his questions, and make available to him whatever information he requires," went on the ambassador. He spoke in a monotone as if he was reciting a procedural formula. "He has full access to the referentura. Full access. Is that understood?"

Andreyan glanced at the colonel, but Leonov ignored him.

"Any questions?" asked the ambassador.

"What precisely is Comrade Gur's function here?" enquired Leonov.

"I am looking for some answers," replied Gur, speaking for the first time. "Answers to a few questions."

Leonov was unperturbed. "You mentioned full access, comrade ambassador. You realise of course that our section's work is very sensitive. Everything has the highest security classification."

It seemed to Andreyan that the ambassador, usually so aloof and detached, was a little nervous. Without actually looking at him, his eyes kept watching Gur. Now he said, perhaps a little too emphatically, "Comrade Gur has total authority."

"Total?" Leonov's eyebrows were raised.

"Absolute authority," emphasised the ambassador. It was an unusual role for him. He kept himself detached from the murky affairs of his back room spooks. The less he knew, the better. Then he could lie so much more convincingly.

He looked pointedly at the ornamental clock on the mantelpiece. The audience, he signalled, was over. They stood up.

"Let's go to your office, colleagues," Gur suggested.

Andreyan was surprised what a small man he was. His suit was badly cut. The trousers hung too low, the shoulders sloped awkwardly, and his shoes needed polishing. The way he looked, he was either an insignificant functionary – or unassailable. Too important to worry about what people thought of him.

Leonov settled himself behind his desk. It was a rather defiant gesture, thought Andreyan. He wanted to assert that here, he was in charge. He waved Andreyan and Gur into the two armchairs on the other side.

"A nice carpet," commented Gur, looking down. He sounded vaguely disapproving. "Luxurious."

He put his hand over his mouth, and Andreyan saw he had a tooth pick and was digging away at his teeth. Gur had bad teeth, yellow and uneven.

"We have been getting reports," he began, enjoying himself. "Yes, comrades, we get reports you don't know about. From people you don't know." He continued digging at his teeth. "They tell us a lot of interesting things. Very useful, these contacts. Very efficient. Yes, you'd be quite surprised if you knew . . ."

Games, thought Andreyan. Gur is a gamesmaster. It is his technique. He specialises in unsettling people. Making them nervous. Watch your step, colonel.

"So," said Leonov, "the Directorate has sent you. What is it you are looking for? What are these questions you have?"

But Gur was addressing himself to Andreyan. "How do you like London, comrade? Is it a place you enjoy? Do you find your posting here rewarding?"

How thoughtful of the Directorate, Andreyan felt like saying. How considerate of them to send someone all the way to London to find out if I liked the place. How touching of the Committee of State Security to care so much for the welfare and morale of its people overseas.

But all he said aloud was: "Yes. The answer is yes. It's an interesting assignment."

"Good," said Gur.

"But there is a problem, is there not?" broke in Leonov. He was avoiding Andreyan's gaze, and suddenly Andreyan saw the grey-haired colonel in a different light. You bastard, you're trying to offer me up as a sacrifice. "That is why you are here, is it not? To resolve that problem?"

Gur pocketed the tooth-pick. "I have merely been sent to look and to report, comrade Leonov. Any decisions that are required will be made elsewhere . . ."

And for a moment, there was silence in the room.

253

Gur leant back in the armchair and put his fingertips together. "Things haven't been going quite right, have they?" He waited, but nobody said anything. "For example, what has been done to silence the broadcasts? They continue to pour out their lies, their provocations . . ."

"Moscow Centre . . ." the colonel started to say, but Gur savaged him:

"Moscow Centre is fed up, comrade. Fed up, do you understand? This is an illegal radio station on a floating transmitter in the Thames estuary, preaching provocation and sedition, and all you do is send reports to Moscow Centre . . ."

"I'm following my instructions," muttered Leonov.

"Not fast enough." He glowered at them, then turned on Andreyan. "As for your little actress friend, she seems to have found her niche." Gur pursed his mouth. "She is now in the United States, did you know that?"

Andreyan hoped he could appear bland. But inwardly, he was elated. It had worked. She had made it.

"Doubtless selling her body for the almighty dollar," Gur continued. He wanted to be offensive.

Andreyan resisted the urge to grab the seedy little man, to shake him until his bad teeth rattled. He merely commented: "I think we can congratulate ourselves on a very neat piece of misinformation successfully planted . . ."

"If it really misinformed them, my friend." He swung on Leonov. "Then there is the Borisov business. Are you proud of that? Do you expect the Order of the Red Banner for your brilliance?" Gur snorted.

"The British . . ." Leonov began, but Gur wouldn't let him finish. "I know, I know, more misinformation," he spat. "Just who is being misinformed, comrade colonel?"

"What exactly are you complaining about?" asked Leonov. Andreyan admired his dignity. The colonel sat upright, refusing to be browbeaten.

"The London operation is showing signs of slackness," railed Gur. "Perhaps it is the soft life. Perhaps you should experience the hardship of a posting to Kabul. Or Beirut. Perhaps you do not realise how easy life is for you here, and are being seduced by all this . . ." He waved his hand round the room. "Or . . ." He stopped.

"Or what, comrade Gur?" asked Leonov quietly.

"Or perhaps we should dig deeper."

There have always been Gurs around, reflected Andreyan. Plenty of them. In the Cheka. In the Ogpu. And now here.

"Deeper?" repeated Andreyan.

"Yes, comrade. There are curious symptoms. We can't put our finger on them, but they're there. I know it. I can smell it." He stared at Andreyan. "I'm surprised that you can't . . ."

There was a clink of glass, and behind his desk, Leonov was pouring himself a drink of water.

"Of course," the colonel was saying, "if you are wrong, if you don't find a scapegoat, it'll be a black mark for you, will it not, comrade Gur? You come all the way here, and if you return without a scalp, the Directorate will hardly thank you for it."

"That," murmured Gur softly, "is hardly a constructive attitude, colonel. But it helps me."

"Helps you? How . . . ?"

"It shows me what I am up against," said Gur and he seemed pleased. "It confirms the need for some realistic reappraisal."

It was time to call his bluff, decided Andreyan. "So," he challenged, "what do you intend to do?"

Gur spread out his hands. "What can I do?" he asked, almost mildly. "Keep my ears open. Use my eyes. I'll be around. You may not see me much, but don't worry. I'll be around. I promise you that, colleagues."

After he left them, they sat silently for some while. Finally, Andreyan got up.

"I'd better get on with things," he said.

"Yes," nodded Leonov. "You'd better."

When he got back to his office, Andreyan found a message waiting saying Sokolov had called, and wanted a quick chat.

"Did he say what it was about?" Andreyan asked Olga, his secretary.

"You know Sokolov," she said, and he did indeed. "Didn't want to talk on the phone, as always. But he said it was 'quite important'. Couldn't get anything else out of him."

Sokolov was the *Tass* man in London. He lived with his mousey wife and two children in Hampstead, but worked in the Press Association building in Fleet Street. Everyone in the Press Club in Fetter Lane was convinced that he worked for the KGB, an impression which Sokolov relished. He felt it gave him stature. The nearest he came to it, however, was to pass on to the embassy rumours and titbits he picked up during his rounds. And the fact that the British tapped his home phone, and restricted his movements out of London pleased him. He hoped that his colleagues who shared the same building looked on him as a figure of mystery and intrigue.

Andreyan rang him in Fleet Street.

"You have something for me?" he enquired.

There was a pause at the other end. Sokolov rejoiced when he actually had something for the spooks.

"Yes," he confirmed finally.

"Well?"

"I think we should meet."

Andreyan groaned inwardly. He knew it would mean listening to Sokolov complaining about his beggarly cost of living allowance, the need for an increased per diem in London – "You know it is the most expensive city in Europe now, etc" – his wife's migraine, the cough Sasha, his youngest, couldn't shake off, the need for a new office car, the terrible English climate, the lack of central heating in his house, the incompetence of his secretary. Andreyan had heard it all before.

"You sure it's necessary?" he asked warily.

256

"I can't talk about it over the phone," said Sokolov. His tone was reproachful.

"How about next week then?"

"I should have thought it's rather urgent, from your point of view," said Sokolov loftily. "Of course if you are too busy . . ."

"No, of course not," snapped Andreyan. He could see the man running to Leonov, or even the ambassador, whining about the department's lack of interest. He looked at his watch. "In one hour. The Cumberland."

They met in the lobby of the hotel, and Sokolov went through his usual elaborate pantomime of first walking straight past Andreyan and ignoring him, then, after a long and searching look round, going up to him and greeting him while his eyes roamed all round looking for the shadow.

"Let's go and have a coffee," suggested Andreyan irritably.

"Here?"

"Why not?" said Andreyan. He was bored by Sokolov's eternal preoccupation of being British security's No 1 target.

They sat down in the coffee shop next to a table crowded with Arabs jabbering in loud voices, their sickly perfume pungently filling the air.

Sokolov glanced round again, and Andreyan had enough.

"Stop worrying," he said. "It's perfectly all right."

"I am being watched day and night," insisted Sokolov self-importantly. "You should hear the clicks on my phone."

"Sure," said Andreyan. The coffees came, and he pointedly looked at his watch. "Well? What is so important you have to tell me?"

Sokolov lowered his voice. "There is a D-notice," he announced. "They have just issued it."

"Oh yes?"

Tass did not get D-notices. Nor, as Andreyan knew, did the *Morning Star*, the Communist daily. They were kept confidential to other news organisations.

"It is about one of our people," said Sokolov triumphantly. "The actor Borisov. It asks that news media make no

257

reference to or revelations about Borisov or his whereabouts or his activities."

Andreyan was interested, and Sokolov basked in his reaction. "When was this issued?" asked Andreyan.

Sokolov shrugged. "A day or two ago. I have only just found out. From a contact. In Fleet Street."

It sounded so nicely self-important. That would teach them at the embassy not to underrate him.

"Do they give a reason?"

"The usual one, I think. In the interests of national security, is it not?"

Andreyan stirred his coffee thoughtfully. "What do you think?"

To Andreyan's annoyance, Sokolov again peered about. Then he said knowingly: "British intelligence are behind it."

"Yes," said Andreyan drily. "I would imagine so." He regarded Sokolov. He must be somebody's son-in-law, he decided. Or he has an uncle in the Presidium. There could be no other reason why such an idiot would be sent by *Tass* to such a prestigious bureau as London.

"I told you it was important," said Sokolov with self-satisfaction. "That is why I called you at once. I said to myself 'this they must know'. It is these little pieces of the jig-saw that make such an interesting whole, don't they?"

"You were quite right," nodded Andreyan. He'll never shut up, he thought. He'll go on and on.

Sokolov leant forward. "Tell me, comrade, what is it about this Borisov? What do you know about him?"

Andreyan smiled coldly. "I wouldn't worry about it, friend. It is of no concern to you."

Sokolov's eyes narrowed and his face assumed what he fondly imagined to be a cunning look. "Ah, of course, I understand. This is all part of something bigger, is it not? You cannot discuss it, I quite understand."

"You're so perceptive," murmured Andreyan. "We will tell Moscow how helpful you are and how intelligently you carry out your duties over here."

Sokolov sat up. Never had Andreyan paid him a compliment. "You mean it, comrade?"

"I am speaking for Colonel Leonov too," Andreyan assured him. "We are most grateful for this information."

"You have made my day," said Sokolov.

Andreyan picked up the bill, and rose. "I must get back to the embassy," he said.

Sokolov hastily followed him. "Yes, yes, you are right. One has to go back to work, I have to file a special feature to Moscow about the nuclear disarmers. The little matter we discussed will of course remain confidential."

"I am grateful for that," said Andreyan and fled.

He stopped at the news stand, and then he saw Maya. She was looking at him from the front page of an early edition of the evening paper. She was smiling, and the camera had caught her in a flattering pose which showed her lovely legs to advantage.

"Red Star Chooses Freedom," announced the banner headline on the front page.

Andreyan bought the paper. "Maya flees to USA," read the caption under the photograph. The story continued on an inside page of how she had arrived in America, a fugitive from Communism, a refugee from the Iron Curtain.

Andreyan read it in the cab back to the embassy. He had to grin. The CIA had ensured that it would get its money's worth. Whatever they thought of the information Maya had delivered, they were going to get the most value out of her. A beautiful actress defects. A Soviet glamour girl prefers the West. It was custom made.

He looked at her picture, and he could just see her, eyes sparkling, smiling enticingly, looking gorgeous, saying the right things, and enjoying every minute of it. She'd get on famously. She'd say all the right things to the right people.

Andreyan left the paper in the cab when he paid it off in the Bayswater Road. Under the circumstances, it would hardly be politic to display that headline in the embassy corridors.

But as he walked up Kensington Palace Gardens he was very cheerful. Maya had finally made it. She was front page in God's country. It was, thought Andreyan happily, a good investment. What he didn't want to think about was who Maya was sleeping with at night.

67

Kleber went to the Dress Circle coffee shop in Harrods as arranged, picked up a tray and selected a chocolate éclair. He got his coffee, paid, then found an empty table and sat down, as instructed. It wasn't difficult; at eleven in the morning, there wasn't a great rush.

Gur came over and sat down at Kleber's table. He too carried a tray but with a pot of tea. He nodded politely, but said nothing.

Kleber observed him warily. Gur was different from the others. He wasn't a mere courier, a paymaster, a messenger. He made command decisions. He had authority, and he had to be obeyed.

Gur only occasionally operated in the field. The fact that he had come to London himself indicated that something important was going on.

"No lemon," said Gur suddenly. "I hate tea with milk. Excuse me."

He got up and went over to the self-service counter. Soon he was back, with two slices of lemon in a saucer.

"So typical of the English," he went on conversationally, "never any ice in a glass of water, never lemon with tea. They have a lot to learn." He added a slice of lemon to his tea. "It looks as if we are going to have nice weather," he continued. It was the contact phrase.

"The climate can be very deceptive," replied Kleber.

Gur slurped his tea, examining Kleber across the rim of the cup. He put the cup down. "You know who I am," he said finally.

Kleber nodded. "Lesley . . ." he began, but Gur cut him off.

"Never mind," he said sharply. "You know. That is what matters."

Kleber had heard a lot about this man. Yuri Gur was a master of the dark arts. He did not execute. He supervised. He controlled. He had authority which had made itself felt in Beirut and Athens, Brussels and Rome, Berlin and Cyprus. He spoke for the Directorate. Especially those who planned and organised the wet affairs.

"They were sorry to hear about your mistake," said Gur. He left unsaid who "they" were, but Kleber knew.

"Mistake? What mistake?"

"Your rash action in dealing with the British security man. It was unnecessary to be so extreme."

Kleber bristled. "He was following me. He was too close."

Gur terminated the discussion. "I have stated our feeling," he declared with finality.

That's not why you've summoned me, thought Kleber. Just to bring a reprimand. You've got something else up your sleeve. As if on cue, Gur confirmed it.

"I have brought new instructions," he said. "It is felt that immediate action is required. Things over here have been allowed to slip. They can't go on. It is time we showed our teeth."

"My orders are . . ."

"You take your orders from me, now that I am here," snapped Gur.

"And Lesley . . ."

"*I* decide policy," said Gur, "and I expect the organisation to carry them out. Is that clear?"

Kleber shrugged. Why should he bother to argue? He was a contract artist, a freelance. Whoever paid him had his services. Gur represented the people who paid him.

261

"What is it you want me to do?" asked Kleber.

"To kill somebody."

"Of course."

Gur nodded approvingly. This was better. No argument. Straight, business-like reaction. "And of course, you will get a bonus. For any inconvenience."

"Thank you," said Kleber.

Gur passed over to him a folded piece of paper. "That is your target," he said. "It has all the details you need."

Kleber unfolded the paper and read it. Then he looked up. "I don't know him," he said.

It was one of the very few times that Gur displayed something that was akin to a smile. "Well, that makes it easier, doesn't it?" and, without a further word, he got up and left Kleber sitting at the table.

As a businessman, Kleber did not care a damn what assignments he was given, providing the remuneration was satisfactory. But, privately, he sometimes had his own thoughts. So it was as he sat and watched Gur's back disappear among a crowd of shoppers. If somebody gave him a contract to terminate Gur, he reflected, he wouldn't mind doing it for half price. Just to see the look on his face.

68

If Colonel Blau had a religion, it was physical fitness. A man who did not keep his body in trim, who developed a paunch and soft muscles reflected his state of mind and was beneath contempt. Since he prided himself that he never expected from others what he didn't live up to himself, Blau did not spare himself.

Every morning, as soon as he got out of bed, he did thirty

push-ups. He could boast that after each session he was hardly out of breath. He was fit, there was no doubt. He could match himself against men twenty years younger, and come out on top.

Colonel Blau followed his strict personal regime wherever he was. He exercised in his hotel suite as enthusiastically as on field manoeuvres, or in the gym. He watched his diet. He played squash. He drank, but in moderation. Most of his habits were designed to maintain his physical condition. While he still had a command, he made a special point of showing his men how tough he was. He led them on assault courses, climbed over obstacles, took them on in unarmed combat. He was always there to urge them to hit harder, kick harder, and he liked to demonstrate how to do it.

After the push-ups and his shower, he liked to go for his daily run. Jogging was requisite, even in bad weather conditions. He ran five miles each morning, and frequently made his aides accompany him. He liked talking to them as he ran, and if they were short of breath, and found it difficult to reply, he mentally noted that he was dealing with a weakling who should be transferred to another post.

"You're not in good shape, boy, you need training," were words that meant a black mark on the personnel record, and a blight on promotion. Blau, of course, was always in good shape, and his snarl defied argument.

A luxury suite in a Park Lane hotel did not mean that Blau relaxed his life style. He might be a civilian now, but it was necessary to stay fighting fit. After all, he had new responsibilities. The boys in Texas had given him a free hand. Funds were available. They had given him the go ahead to start recruiting. He'd gather together a crack outfit of mercs. Soldiers of fortune, men like the ones he had commanded, volunteers all of them. He'd train them and prepare them and arm them, and who knows, lead them into action one day.

And he'd beef up that radio station. Increase its power. Have it broadcasting continuously. Collect émigrés to do the announcing. Transmit really hard hitting propaganda, that would incite and inflame. Not the kind of namby-pamby stuff Washington poured out through Radio Free Europe.

That was the trouble with Washington. Chicken. Terrified of hitting too hard. Soft pedalling everything. Weak.

Blau rose from his push-ups. He wasn't even perspiring. His breath came nice and regular. He looked at himself in the mirror. You're in fine shape, boy. You've kept yourself fit. He put on his track suit. It was bright red, and embroidered on the left side, right over his heart, was the Special Forces emblem – two crossed arrows and a dagger. De Oppresso Liber. The sons of bitches couldn't take that away from him. The bastards thought that all they owed him was a monthly pension cheque. He'd show them.

Blau took the lift down to the lobby, and crossed over to Hyde Park. He didn't use the pedestrian passageway. That would be cowardly. He ran across Park Lane, dodging among the traffic stream, enjoying it. It was like running the commando battle track, dodging live ammunition.

By the time he reached the park, he had swung into his gait, rhythmic, methodical, effortless. For a man in his fifties, the colonel's legs moved like pistons. He ran, steadily, breathing in the morning air, enjoying the early sunshine. At this time, the park wasn't busy. There were a few other joggers, one or two people walking, but he felt a wonderful freedom. No stupid sons of bitches here to get in his way.

A girl came towards him, also in a track suit, her hair streaming. She was running fast, and she was a beautiful sight to Blau. He had an ideal woman, a tall, shapely Amazon, an athletic girl who would give birth to sturdy, well formed boys, a Diana. And this runner was like that. He gave her an appreciative glance as she sped past him towards Marble Arch. He was slightly disappointed to notice she was panting. What a pity. She should take it in her stride.

Blau knew his exact speed, and the distance he covered each morning. He always timed himself, and since he never flagged, he kept to his private schedule. It was a matter of great satisfaction to him. Since coming to London, he had run this route daily, going in a big circle that took him through a good stretch of Hyde Park. He was beginning to know the stretch well. As he pounded along there were moments when he closed his eyes, and imagined he was conquering new territories, entering unexplored land, a pioneer advancing into the beyond. Then he'd hear a distant police siren, or a plane overhead, he'd open his eyes, and he'd be back in London, jogging.

He came to the old oak tree, and a man stepped out from behind it and stood in his way. Fucking idiot, thought Blau, and swerved to avoid him.

"Colonel Blau?" asked the man.

Blau slowed down. He wasn't going to stop for anyone. It would ruin his routine. He had to jog without break. Who the hell was this idiot?

"Yeah," he called out, turning and running backwards, but at a lesser pace. "What do you want?"

From under the raincoat Kleber was carrying over his arm, he pulled out a pistol. He fired twice, as was his style, and as each of the bullets hit him, Blau reared with the force of their impact. He died before he hit the ground, one bullet through his heart, but the second one was aimed higher, at his left eye. The slug entered his brain and then blew his head apart.

He never had time to think how fitting it was that he should die under fire, killed by enemy bullets, the way he probably would have preferred to go anyway. Colonel Blau had often dreamt of dying a hero's death in action; what he didn't expect was that he would be jogging in Hyde Park.

Nobody saw it, and Kleber walked away from the tree and the body crumpled underneath it, humming. Half an hour later he sat in a café in Queensway having a good breakfast. He had had to get up so early that he hadn't had the chance of eating much before he went to Hyde Park. Now he had quite an appetite.

The lunchtime edition of the evening paper carried the story of Blau's death in the Stop Press, under the heading: "American tourist murdered while jogging in Hyde Park."

"An American tourist staying in Park Lane was found dead in Hyde Park. He had been shot, and police believe he was the victim of a mugger. The dead man was identified by Scotland Yard as Jerome Blau, 54, a retired US Army colonel, who was on holiday in Britain. It is thought he was jogging in the park at the time he was accosted. Police are looking for any possible witness who may have seen Mr Blau, or his assailant."

"They haven't made much of it," commented Cheyne, his voice sounding relieved.

"No," agreed Rathbone tactfully. "Not yet."

"The Yard playing it down, are they?"

"I expect so."

Cheyne nodded, pleased. "He's a good man, Binyon."

Rathbone said nothing, then Cheyne's brow furrowed. "Colin . . . we're not involved? Are we?"

There were times when Cheyne could be very trying.

"I don't quite follow," said Rathbone blandly.

"Oh, never mind." Cheyne looked hard at him. "I suppose you feel it's poetic justice, in a way. I mean, the business with Garner and all that . . ."

Rathbone picked his words. "I don't think Colonel Blau will be missed. Not on this side of the Atlantic."

Cheyne reached for his paper knife and started playing with it. "All right. What do we know about it?"

"It was Kleber," said Rathbone.

Cheyne's hand froze just as he was about to twirl the knife on his desk.

"Ah," he said, then frowned. "How do you know?"

"The bullets," said Rathbone. "Forensic says they came from the same gun that killed Alcott. The bullets all match. And we know who Alcott was following, don't we?"

"Outrageous!" declared Cheyne. "The man must be caught."

"That is a matter for the police. It doesn't concern my section, does it, sir?"

Cheyne raised his head and stared at him. It wasn't often

that Rathbone called him "Sir". But there was more to it than that. He was disturbed.

"Colin, I may have got this wrong, but you sound as if you don't care . . ."

"Care?" repeated Rathbone innocently. He crossed his legs nonchalantly. "I don't get your meaning."

"Don't you?" When Rathbone got obstinate, he could be very difficult. "I got the impression that as far as you were concerned, Kleber could be left to the police." Cheyne waited expectantly. "Well?"

"They've sent Kleber over to do some house cleaning, I think," said Rathbone at last. "In a way, he's done us a service, hasn't he? We are not sorry to see the late lamented colonel bite the dust, and it'll do no harm to our relations with Moscow to have his activities interdicted. That's the phrase in the Cabinet document, isn't it? As long as Kleber does any dirty work we'd rather not do ourselves, well, never look a gift horse in the mouth . . ."

Cheyne gaped at him.

"He'll get his come-uppance," Rathbone went on, "but he may have saved us some embarrassment by what he did in Hyde Park . . ."

"Do you know what you're saying?" gasped Cheyne.

Rathbone shrugged. "Expediency. The name of the game. Yes, he killed Alcott, but he avenged Garner, in a manner of speaking. I don't know if one cancels the other, but it's a useful exercise."

"You sound as if you want to give him a bloody gong . . ."

Rathbone was not amused. "No," he said coldly. "But I have other priorities."

Cheyne put down the paper knife. "I have never liked riddles. What priorities?"

Rathbone irritated him even more by staring over his shoulder at the window. He turned his head to see what he was looking at – it was the potted vegetation on the window sill.

"I see you have a new plant," he observed.

267

It was difficult to keep one's temper with the man at a moment like this. "Yes, yes," growled Cheyne irritably. "You were saying . . ."

"It's very nice, I like it," commented Rathbone blithely. "Where did you get it?"

"Oh I don't know, Lesley bought it somewhere," snapped Cheyne. "Can we get on?"

"What a thoughtful girl your secretary is." Rathbone studied the plant. "The other one died, didn't it?"

Cheyne exploded. "Colin, please. We're not here to discuss my potted plants, for God's sake."

"Sorry," Rathbone apologised humbly. "You're absolutely right." Then he looked at his wrist watch. "Good Lord!"

"What's the matter?"

Rathbone had already got to his feet. "I'm most awfully sorry, I had no idea of the time. I am due at Grosvenor Square ten minutes ago. Will you forgive me?"

He gave an apologetic smile. At the door he said: "I'll be in touch."

"Colin," called Cheyne. On the pad in front of him, noted in his tidy, meticulous handwriting, were all the points he had intended asking Rathbone. There were so many questions . . .

But Rathbone had gone.

69

The important thing was to do it quietly, unobtrusively. Sachsenhausen was asleep at 3 a.m., so the polizei had no problem cordoning off the street that led to the warehouse near the river Main.

They weren't ordinary police, because this wasn't a job for ordinary city cops. They were of the Hesse state Mobile Special Assignment Squad, and with them came a unit from Bonn, soldiers of the crack GSG 9 commandos, who were always on standby for "missions of special significance" and had driven to Frankfurt from their barracks at St Augustin. Accompanying them were the specialists, technicians of the US Army's Special Weapons Inspection Team from Heidelberg.

"I hope your information is right," said Steinhof, of the Office for the Protection of the Constitution. "It would be very unfortunate if . . ." He left the rest unsaid.

They had no warrant. This was too delicate to go through channels. Bureaucracy has its leaks and it had been agreed, at the highest level, that officially this operation did not exist.

But if it went wrong . . .

"Stop worrying, Reinhardt," Rathbone's man reassured him. Creighton had been nursing Steinhof along all evening. For a man who, under Federal Germany's constitution, had secret powers, he had been very edgy.

"How did you find out?" he kept asking. Creighton got quite tired of it.

"I told you," he said again, "we searched the colonel's papers. In his hotel. After he was dead."

"He was very methodical," remarked Steinhof.

"Yes," sighed Creighton patiently. How many times would he have to tell the same story?

"Terrible," said Steinhof. "To think, that he's been keeping these things here. In the middle of town. If they went off . . ."

"Relax," Creighton reassured him. "They're quite safe, I'm informed."

"No atom bomb is safe."

"They're not atom bombs, they're land mines," pointed out Creighton.

He wished Steinhof wasn't so nervous. The significant

thing was that when they had done the job, no one would ever know. That was the agreement between the faceless ones in London and Bonn.

"The fact that ten nuclear land mines went astray must never be revealed," Rathbone had instructed Creighton. "If the media get hold of it, they'll have a Roman carnival. It'll be manna from heaven for the anti-nuclears. Can't you see CND in Trafalgar Square? And the Greens in Berlin? So, we know nothing, we see nothing, we say nothing. Pass that on to our friends."

The warehouse loomed in front of them. It was an old, shabby building, mainly used for the storage of household furniture belonging to American service families. The street in front of it was ill lit, and there was no sign of life.

The Special Weapons major came up to them. "We'll go in as soon as they've effected entry," he said, looking at his clip board. "Our babies are all stored in wooden crates here." He jabbed a finger at a floor plan pinned to the clip board. "Don't let anybody inside except my guys. I don't want anybody else near these things. OK?"

"You are the experts," said Steinhof gratefully. "We leave it all to you."

"Right," nodded the major. "As soon as we have loaded them on to our trucks I want a clearway to Rhein Main airbase. You got the escort all set? Good."

He was a crisp, efficient man, and he turned smartly, and went into a huddle with his technicians.

The vehicles, military and police, lined one side of the street, and there was the subdued chatter of police radios. It was really quite undramatic. A little group of men went to the door of the warehouse, a mobile flood light unit switched on, then soon afterwards they forced the door, and the major's team entered.

"It is incredible," Steinhof was saying. "To think such a thing could happen. It makes me wonder if somebody else maybe, somewhere has purloined a nuclear weapon."

"They're going in," Creighton interrupted him.

An hour later the crates had been removed from the warehouse, and were on their way, by road, across the Main, on to the autobahn to Rhein Main air base, and the waiting Hercules transport plane that would fly them to Nevada.

Steinhof became quite exuberant. "We will have breakfast together, and celebrate a job well done," he declared. "I think we can all congratulate ourselves."

Around them Sachsenhausen was still asleep. It would be another couple of hours before its citizens got out of bed and greeted the new day.

"To think," said Steinhof, "they never even knew what was going on right here, while they were snoring. Come, we will go to the Frankfurter Hof. They do a very good breakfast."

"I'll join you a little later," said Creighton.

Steinhof was put out. "What can you possibly do at this hour?" he asked, plaintively.

But Creighton had already gone to his car, and was driving off. He had to call Rathbone.

On nights like these, Rathbone did not sleep.

70

Borisov hadn't felt it for a long time. Stage fright. The clammy panic as one stepped from the wings on to the stage. It was something that he had conquered long ago. But now the fear was back. He was about to make his entry.

No one had stopped him when he left the monastery. He had simply walked out of his room, gone along the corridor, down the stairs, crossed the court yard, and passed the gate-house over the stone bridge that spanned the moat.

271

He had made for the village bus stop, and taken the bus to the railway station. An hour later he was in London.

It was now that the anxiety had set in. Standing in the street, alone and isolated, perspiration on his forehead, and his palms sweaty. He felt slightly sick. Damn his nerves.

All the days he had spent at the monastery now seemed unreal, like a play that had folded.

He didn't know if he was doing the right thing, but there was no one to turn to for advice. He was on his own, only he could make the decision. It was either a heroic decision, or the biggest mistake of his life.

He knew that he didn't have much time. They would have discovered by now that he was gone, and he could imagine Father Stephen's phone call to the man called Rathbone. They'd be out looking for him.

He needed a drink. The lack of alcohol all the time at the monastery had been an enormous strain. Sometimes, he would have given a lot for a bottle of vodka. Now he needed it more than ever. He walked to a public house, but it was closed. Then he realised it was out of licensing hours. The English and their regulated drinking! God, they took their pleasures sadly. Instead, he went to a hamburger bar in Praed Street, and ordered tea. It was appalling, a tea bag dunked in boiling water, and too much milk. Borisov made a face, but he sipped the liquid. His hand holding the mug was shaking slightly. Steady, he told himself, relax.

A man came in and sat down at the table opposite, reading the paper. For a moment, Borisov felt panic. It was the way the man wasn't looking at him that agitated him. Then common sense took over. Don't be an idiot, he thought. If you start worrying about people because they're not doing anything suspicious, you'll end up in a strait jacket. Take it easy, man.

He finished his awful tea and got up. The man with the paper didn't even look at him, and as Borisov left he continued sitting at the table.

Borisov's ability to memorise his roles was legendary. It

was said that he had never had to be prompted in his entire career. He didn't forget his lines. His memory was something that he had honed and sharpened like a diamond cutter.

That didn't just have its uses as an actor. There were other times when he could rely on his memory without hesitation. The address, for example. The address he had been given in an emergency. Never to be used. Never to be revealed. Only if it became a matter of life and death. Borisov waved down a cab, and gave the driver the address.

He sat back in the cab, breathing heavily. There was still time to pull back. He could tap on the window and ask the driver to drop him. He stared out of the taxi's windows with unseeing eyes, thinking of the monk. The monk who played his little games. Perhaps, reflected Borisov grimly, you said a little too much, my clerical friend.

He had three cigarettes left, and now he lit one in the back of the cab. He felt better after a few puffs, his nerves steadier. He wondered what they would say when he told them the reason he'd been forced to use the address. He had intended to let it remain buried in the deepest recess of his mind. But he was sure he was, after all, making the correct decision. Yes. Now he was sure. They had to know. He had to tell them. It was more important than anything else . . .

The cab passed Camden Town underground station, then turned into a side street.

"Here you are, mister," said the driver. "What number d'you want?"

"It's all right," said Borisov. "I'll walk the rest."

He got out and paid the taxi. He began walking. The basement flat was at the end of the street. No 37. Borisov hesitated a moment. He glanced round. It was a quiet, rather shabby street. A child was playing with a doll's pram further up. But there was no one else about. No car cruising. No idle bystander . . .

Now that the moment had come, he no longer felt unsure. He was in control. It was time to go on stage.

273

Borisov descended the stone steps into the basement. There were two empty milk bottles outside the front door. He pressed the bell, and waited.

The door was opened by a dark haired woman.

"Go away," whispered Lesley urgently. "Quickly."

And he noticed how pale she was, almost ashen faced, like someone who had had a terrible shock.

"Please, you do not understand," began Borisov, as she started shutting the door on him.

"Stay away," she cried, but Borisov put his foot in the doorway.

"I have to see you, something has happened." He pushed his way inside. "I'm sorry, but it is necessary."

He was in the flat now.

"No." Her eyes were beseeching him, pleading.

"You have to send a message," he said tersely. "You have to tell them that Leonov at the embassy is a traitor."

She stood shaking, her face white.

The door to the living room was open, and a man came out.

"Yes, Lesley," said Rathbone. "You must tell them. I'm sure they'll be very interested." He smiled at Borisov. "I'd almost given you up, my friend."

It was not a pleasant smile. Borisov stood in the dingy corridor, numbly trying to come to terms with the situation. But he knew that he had, after all, made a big mistake. He had played the wrong part.

Then he heard, in the street outside, the slamming of car doors, and the door bell rang.

"I think that's for me," said Rathbone. He indicated the living room. "Why don't you go in there and make yourselves comfortable." He spoke as if he was the host, welcoming Borisov and Lesley into his home.

The door bell rang again, longer, more insistently, but Rathbone waited until Borisov and the woman were in the living room. Lesley sat down, stiffly, robot-like.

Rathbone shut the door, and left them alone. He must

274

feel very confident, thought Borisov, leaving us like this, unsupervised.

"You fool," said Lesley in a low, intense voice. "You bloody fool."

"I had to make contact," he replied, then stopped. It was too late for justification.

"You know what you've done," she almost spat at him.

Borisov glared at her. Who was she to lecture him? They were already on to her, the stupid bitch. That's why they were waiting for him. Here, in her home.

Then the door opened, and Rathbone came in, followed by the elegant figure of Binyon. Borisov blinked; Binyon actually had a carnation in his button hole. Binyon gave him a nod, then went over to Lesley. She was staring at him, sitting very stiffly.

"I am a police officer," he said very formally, like a man playing a charade in a party game, "and I am going to detain you for further inquiries. I must warn you that you may face serious charges under the Official Secrets Act."

"What happens now?" she asked quietly.

"That depends," replied Binyon, and to Borisov's surprise he smiled at her. "All sorts of things can happen."

Borisov swallowed hard. They were ignoring him. They were both concentrating on the woman, treating him like a bit player who had no lines.

"I don't know what this is all about," said Lesley, "but I want a solicitor."

"Everything in due course, Lesley," said Binyon with great familiarity.

Rathbone took Borisov's arm. Quite gently.

"Come along," he said pleasantly. "They don't need us here."

They left the basement flat. In the street outside, three cars were parked, all with drivers, and in one of them there were also two men who, with expressionless faces, studied Rathbone and Borisov as they came up the steps.

Rathbone guided Borisov into the first car, nodded to the driver, and it moved off smoothly.

"Am I under arrest?" asked Borisov.

Rathbone appeared astonished. "Arrest? My dear fellow, you *are* melodramatic. I suppose it's your background. No. Not at all. We're going to Soho."

"Soho?" Watch this man, Borisov's alarm system cautioned him. When he's playing games, he's at his most dangerous.

"Yes. I thought we'd have a spot of lunch. Let's enjoy ourselves. On expenses." He sighed. "Not that they give one much of a hospitality allowance these days. Our Treasury is the stingiest bunch of misers you can imagine. We have to justify absolutely everything. Tell me, are they as strict in the Directorate?"

"Please?"

"Never mind. I don't suppose you've enjoyed much haute cuisine lately. Not if I know monastery food."

"You've been there too?" asked Borisov.

"Just to get away. There are times when one needs to be on one's own, don't you agree? Retreat is good for the soul."

They drove in silence, then Borisov said: "All right. What happens to me now?"

"I told you. Lunch."

Bastard, thought Borisov. Supercilious, presumptuous bastard. Dangling me at the end of a hook like some fish you've caught. What did the monk say about the five stages of torture? Which stage was this in Rathbone's world? When did the rack take over? When would he produce the thumbscrews?

They went to a French restaurant where a table was booked in Rathbone's name. "Have you noticed, all the staff are women," pointed out Rathbone. "Only waitresses here. Very French, very pretty. I like the idea of it." He peered over his wine glass at Borisov. "You are thinking, how very sexist. I admit it. But then, my friend, I am a servant of capitalism, a lackey of imperialism." He smiled at Borisov mockingly.

"You are a professional," said Borisov.

"Like you, colleague."

Their eyes met briefly, but Borisov quickly looked away.

"Tell me something I've been wondering about," said Rathbone. "What is your rank?"

"I am an actor."

"Of course. A very good one. A People's Artist and all that. But your other side. The other role you play so well."

Borisov kept his face blank. "I don't understand . . ."

"Quite high, I imagine," Rathbone went on remorselessly. "Top echelon. My compliments. I wonder, actually . . ." He shook his head. "No, I suppose not."

Despite himself, Borisov couldn't resist it. He knew immediately afterwards he shouldn't have risen to the bait. "You wonder what?"

"If you actually outrank me."

He ignored that. Then the waitress brought the starters.

"I hope you like the foie de veau." Rathbone looked at his plate with relish. "They do it with garlic here. Very compromising, but delicious."

He continued making small talk. Borisov kept glancing at the couple sitting at the next table. How absurd this was, sitting in a restaurant, chatting about French cooking, and the wine, when they both knew what they were after.

It was much later, in the flat in St John's Wood, that Rathbone dropped the pretence.

The flat was in a block guarded twenty-four hours a day by porters with a remarkably military bearing, access to which was monitored by closed circuit cameras.

They were on the sixth floor, but they seemed remote from the world outside. Rathbone opened the front door and led Borisov into the sitting room. There was silence in the room, and suddenly Borisov became very conscious of how quiet the flat was. No sound of traffic drifted up. The room was

277

somehow antiseptic. This was nobody's home. It had the neutrality of a dentist's waiting room.

There were big picture windows, leading out to a balcony. Unexpectedly, Borisov had a vision of a figure falling from it on to the pavement thirty feet below. Was this the place where accidents happened? Would they dispose of him here? Borisov looked at him and wondered, could that be what he is planning? A look at the view from the balcony, a sudden shove, and . . .

"All right," said Rathbone, helping himself to a glass of brandy. "Playtime is over."

"Good."

Rathbone smiled. "Tell me, have you ever heard of Skelton?"

"Skelton? Who's he?"

That seemed to amuse the other man. "It's not anybody, it's a small place. In Cumbria. Up north. Very rural. It really isn't much of a place, but your friends in Moscow know it well. That's where all the broadcasts to your country are beamed from. It's our Russian service transmitter."

"So?"

"Bear with me," said Rathbone, sitting down opposite Borisov. "When I say broadcasts, I mean the BBC Russian service. About fourteen million comrades listen to it. Very level headed BBC stuff. The best we can do with such clapped out facilities."

Borisov looked puzzled. "I don't understand."

Rathbone got up, still holding the brandy, and looked down at him. "You must sometimes think this is cloud cuckoo land, my friend. We've been trying for years to set up a radio transmitter that can really be effective. Skelton is forty years old. They've tried to build modern stations all over the place. Somerset. Stratford-upon-Avon. Suffolk. For years they've tried. And you know what's happened? This is a democracy and people object to ugly radio masts and transmitters. They are ugly. They spoil the countryside. They make humming noises. So we're stuck with one

278

pathetic little station." He was lecturing Borisov like a professor.

"What has this to do with me?" demanded Borisov, a little impatiently.

"Everything, my friend. You see, we're gentlemen. Other people are not. They think what we're doing is rather ineffectual. They believe in taking things into their own hands. And they've got the means and the resources. They start their own little radio station. Crude, but effective. Not at all gentlemanly. It sends out rumours and lies and disinformation, quite unofficially. And in its own way it starts to get under the skin of your lords and masters. If I may use such a capitalist phrase to describe the Fifth Directorate. Or at least, Colonel General Zotov. Marshal Pavlov. Comrade Lapin. That's right, isn't it?"

"I don't know what you're talking about," stated Borisov formally. For the record. At least that would be down on the tape. He was sure a microphone was in the standard lamp next to his chair recording him.

"Quite so," smiled Rathbone. He was very smooth. "Anyway, too many people were starting to listen to this little pirate station. Russkaya Volya. The rumours it originated were beginning to spread. It was only a pin prick, a pimple, but you know how painful those things can be on your behind."

Borisov crossed his legs. It was a studied, nonchalant gesture. He thought of yawning politely, but that would have been overdoing it. He was a good actor because he knew when it was more effective to underplay.

"Well, that's it," said Rathbone. He took a final sip of brandy and put the glass down.

"I am still waiting," said Borisov. "To hear about me."

"It's quite simple, isn't it? They decided that they would have to do something about Russkaya Volya. But that meant infiltrating it. So if a well known Soviet actor were to defect, and play his cards right, in the fullness of time he might

279

be asked if he wouldn't like to do some broadcasting to his homeland. The rest is up to him . . ."

"Is that brandy any good?" asked Borisov.

"Five star. Quite palatable."

"May I have one?"

Rathbone was almost apologetic. "Of course. I am so sorry. I should have offered you some. I didn't realise . . ."

He poured a measure. Then doubled it. Borisov sipped it reflectively. Then he said: "It is a lovely story, but it doesn't work. I haven't been near any such radio station. I have made no attempt to become involved. I've been stuck in a monastery. It doesn't work out, does it?"

Rathbone stood by the window.

"Would you like some fresh air?" he enquired. "It's a bit stuffy in here, isn't it?"

Is that the prologue? Opening the window? Borisov watched him.

"No," he said. "I'm fine, thank you." His hands again felt clammy. He hoped he wasn't pale.

Rathbone sat down once more.

"Actually, my friend, you hadn't had a chance yet to do your act. You were working up to it. You were going to make the approach. But then something happened to . . . to upstage it all, if I may use a theatrical term. A piece of careless talk. Our clerical friend. Father Stephen. He let something slip, and it pre-empted everything."

Borisov waited. He knew what was coming.

"He let slip that the Directorate's key man, the controller at the embassy, Colonel Leonov, was our man. And that was something Moscow had to be warned about, wasn't it? Something that took priority, didn't it? If the controller is a double agent, everything is jeopardised. Correct? So what did comrade Borisov do? Being a good professional, he knew this was an emergency. It had to be passed on at once, no matter what the risk. So you did just that, my friend. And here we are." He actually beamed at Borisov. "I'm sorry the game is over."

280

Borisov showed great dignity. It wasn't a performance. It was genuine. It was the bearing of a soldier who had fought and lost, but had nothing to be ashamed about.

"I am just sad about one thing," he said quietly. "That I have failed to get the message through. I tried, I did my best. But you were waiting for me. There was nothing I could do."

It was the moment Rathbone had waited for, had rehearsed, had planned. "The message has been sent," he said quietly. "Moscow has been informed that they have a traitor at the embassy. They have been told about Leonov."

This is insane, thought Borisov. This cannot be. He is the enemy. He would protect Leonov.

"But who . . . who has informed Moscow?" he stuttered.

"The usual source. Lesley. She has sent your message." Rathbone was enjoying every moment of it.

"Lesley?" echoed Borisov. "Lesley is under arrest. Lesley can't send any messages . . ."

A terrible foreboding was growing.

"Lesley is an intelligent woman," said Rathbone. "She knows she could be put away for . . . for all time. We offered her a deal. She has accepted."

"What deal?" whispered Borisov.

"That she passes on the information you brought. That she informs Moscow about Leonov being a traitor."

Borisov almost screamed it. "Why?"

"Because, my friend, he isn't. Colonel Leonov is a very loyal, very dedicated Soviet officer. You snapped up a piece of false bait. How useful of you to misinform your masters in Moscow. We wouldn't dream of stopping the message getting through . . ." He got up and went over to the window. He opened the latch. "We do need some air," he said.

"You know what they're going to do," said Borisov in a low voice.

"I have an idea."

"The Judas. The lying scheming priest . . ."

Rathbone raised a restraining hand. "I'm sure that he's already asking for forgiveness for his sin," he remarked drily.

281

"But really, you do him an injustice. He didn't make you do anything. You jumped at it. And . . ." He paused for a moment. "Your side does owe him, doesn't it?"

He slid open the window. "Come out here," he invited. "The view from the balcony is very impressive. You can see Regent's Park in all its glory."

"No," said Borisov.

"Oh come on," urged Rathbone. "You really should see this."

He came over and, as Borisov slowly got up, took his arm. They stepped out on to the balcony, and Borisov looked not at the view, but down towards the ground.

"What's the matter?" said Rathbone. "Are you worried by heights?"

Borisov held on to the balustrade. Rathbone was looking straight ahead. "Don't worry," he said, without glancing at Borisov. "You're quite safe."

That was the moment, Borisov was thinking, when he would push him over.

"What happens to me?" he asked, and despite himself, his voice croaked.

"Oh, you'll be put on ice," said Rathbone. "For months and months. We're going to take you apart. Debrief you, analyse you, dissect you, you'd be surprised. It's going to be fascinating, unpeeling an actor who is a spy, or is it the other way round? It should be an unusual and rewarding exercise." Then he slapped Borisov on the back. "Don't look so grim. You'll be well looked after. Good food. Good drink. And women. Not to mention other little perks. And think of it . . ."

"What?"

"All the time your pension will be piling up in Moscow." He stepped back into the flat and left Borisov alone on the balcony.

He doesn't seem to care, thought Borisov. He doesn't care if I jump or not. But I'm not going to give him that bloody satisfaction.

He followed Rathbone inside.

"Have another brandy," said Rathbone.

But Borisov was thinking of the man whose death warrant he had sent to Moscow.

71

Gregson had gradually come to terms with solitary existence. He resorted to a device he had read about, long ago, and kept a kind of primitive calendar, making a scratch on the brickwork of the cell wall each day, then drawing a line through every seven scratches. He didn't know the dates, but at least he could count the weeks he was spending in isolation.

There were fewer interrogations now, and he was allowed to sleep through the night without somebody waking him up. The electric light stayed on, of course, and he had a strange longing for darkness. Black, all embracing darkness that shut everything out, so that he could close his eyes, and feel isolated. The bright light that shone down on his face when he tried to sleep was something he still couldn't get used to.

After a while Major Anastas had given up on the unexpected midnight sessions. They had tried waking Gregson up from his fitful sleep, and subjecting him to a barrage of questions and accusations. But the major seemed disappointed with what it yielded.

"You are very foolish, Paul," he complained, sadly. "Help us to help you. Do you think I enjoy these sessions? Don't you imagine that I would rather be in my warm bed than sitting here, repeating the same old questions?"

Sometimes he tried a different approach.

"Do you really think the people who sent you over here are in the slightest concerned about you? Don't fool yourself. They couldn't care less if you're rotting in some stinking cell eating pig's swill. You've served your purpose, Paul."

But Gregson said none of the things they wanted to hear.

Anastas asked him to sign a statement which, neatly typed, was laid before him.

"As you can see," explained the major, "it is just a factual summary of the facts."

"A confession, you mean."

Anastas looked hurt. "Now Paul, you know I wouldn't trick you. What it says here is the truth, isn't it? You posed as a tourist, but you came on a mission for your intelligence service. Correct? You had orders to make contact with traitors in this country, and to smuggle what they gave you back to your masters, right? But you were caught red handed by the alert organs of our state security. Now what's wrong with that?"

"I won't sign," said Gregson.

Major Anastas sighed. "You're putting me in an impossible position, Paul. My superiors expect results from me. They know you're guilty and they look to me to produce your admission in a proper legal fashion. If I fail to obtain a signed statement from you, it will reflect adversely on me."

"Tough," said Gregson.

Anastas changed his tone. "I may not always be your investigating officer," he said. "There are others. And when they take over, they won't be so understanding, I promise you. Take advantage of my good nature. I have colleagues who actually enjoy being unpleasant. They are specialists in their work. It's an experience I wouldn't wish on my worst enemy. You understand?"

"Perfectly."

"And?"

"Sorry, major. It won't work."

After the cell door had been slammed, Gregson was less confident. Maybe he should sign. What did it matter? If they wanted to, they'd manufacture their own confession. And who would be able to tell if his scrawled signature was genuine?

He knew the routine, anyway. He had been briefed in England. If things went wrong, if they caught him, and put him on trial, he would be expected to recant in public. To stand up and confess, like a heretic before the ecclesiastical judges.

"Say whatever you have to to save your neck, as long as you don't tell them the truth. Make up a fairy story. Name names that don't matter. Confess anything you like. Except the real story."

Alone in his cell, he smiled wrily at Anastas and his approach. The last thing he had expected was this KGB interrogator pleading with him not to tarnish his reputation, as he was a man who got results.

Gregson knew what he was doing was dangerous. Now that he had finally defied his case officer, a different persuasion would be used. A more painful one. He tried to anticipate mentally what lay in store. Deprivation of sleep, surely. Keeping him awake so that eventually he would sign away his soul for a few hours' sleep.

Starvation. The food couldn't be much worse, but at least he was still being fed. Maybe now they'd barely keep him alive so that he'd get weaker and hungrier by the day, until for the sake of a bowl of hot soup he'd do whatever they wanted.

Torture? He didn't want to think about that. He knew how sophisticated they could be. They could cause agony in a hundred different refined ways. Such pain that the bravest man began to doubt himself.

The irony of it all was that he didn't know what it was all about. He didn't know what was on the roll of film that had been so important to smuggle back to London. He didn't even know who his contact was supposed to have been. They had told him nothing.

"After all, the less you know, old son, the easier it is for you," they had said.

The easier to refuse to give any information he didn't have anyway.

But it wasn't quite as Gregson expected.

To his surprise, he woke up one morning, and was marched out of his cell to another part of the prison. He thought he was about to get the long expected persuasion. Instead, he had a session with a barber, who shaved him, and cut his hair.

A doctor examined Gregson, and suddenly the food improved. Meat broth. Vegetables. Rye bread. Beef stew. He couldn't believe it.

They brought him books to read. English translations of Russian authors, even a few books by Jack London and Dickens, as well as issues of the *Morning Star*, two days late, flown from London.

It almost unnerved him. Every time the cell door opened he waited for the unexpected. The twist of the knife. The payment that would finally be exacted from him. Because he knew that in this business, nothing was for nothing.

Then Major Anastas came to visit. This time he was smiling.

"Well, Paul, you look great," he greeted him. "Why, I think you may actually put on some weight if this goes on . . ." He picked up one of the books. "Not bad this one," he said. "But if you want a particular author, let me know."

"Thank you," said Gregson, puzzled.

"Is the food all right?" asked Anastas. "I hope the menu is a bit more varied."

"Major," said Gregson, "what's this all about?"

Anastas stared at him surprised. "What do you mean, Paul?"

"The sudden concern for my welfare. The food. The books. The barber. Why?"

"We're not barbarians, you know," said the major. "We care about people."

His face was perfectly straight. Not a glimmer of a smile.

"A bit of a change, isn't it?" remarked Gregson.

286

"We can't have you looking like a skeleton. People will get the wrong idea," said Major Anastas. He slapped Gregson on the back, then he said something very strange. "Good luck, Paul."

Gregson was still thinking about that when the cell door slammed shut again.

72

Perhaps if he had been more alert, Colonel Leonov would have realised something was wrong as soon as he arrived at the embassy. The security guard in the entrance hall did not acknowledge him as he came in, and the man on duty in the restricted corridor looked straight through him.

Leonov made a mental note that he would raise it at the next staff meeting. Discipline should not be allowed to go slack.

The real shock came, however, when he took out his key to open his private office. The door was already unlocked. His section was in forbidden territory. The colonel knew that, as always, he had locked his door the previous evening, and no one outside the department had access – the privacy of his own office was sacrosanct.

He opened the door. Gur was sitting behind his desk, picking his teeth.

"Come in," invited Gur with studied insolence. "I've been waiting for you."

The drawers of Leonov's desk had been pulled open. Files were stacked on the floor, papers lay strewn about, the Gerasimov print on the wall had been taken down, books had been removed from the shelves. Leonov's office had been taken apart. They had searched every inch of it.

Leonov stood very still. "Who has done this?" he asked quietly. He was surprised by his self-control.

"The appropriate authorities," replied Gur smugly.

"I see," Leonov's tone was icy. He went over to the telephone and picked it up.

"Who are you thinking of calling?" drawled Gur. He had speared something on his tooth pick and was examining it with interest.

"Give me the ambassador," said Leonov. Then he became aware that the line was dead.

"You're wasting time." Gur was enjoying himself. "It is cut off. You will be making no more telephone calls in this building."

"Get out," instructed the colonel. "That is an order."

Gur sniggered. It was not a laugh. It was a snigger. "Your days of giving orders are also over."

Leonov stared at him in disbelief. Then he said: "I am going to have you thrown out."

Gur didn't move as the colonel went to the door, and opened it. Leonov didn't recognise the man with the pale blue eyes who stood outside, blocking his way.

"Krylov is taking you into custody," said Gur nodding at the man.

Kleber gave the colonel a thin smile. It was a new role for him. They wanted to get him out of the country, so they had given him a new name, a new identity, a new passport. Now he was Ivan Krylov, he would get through immigration, and off the island.

"Look after our comrade well," Gur instructed him. "He deserves special attention." And he bared his teeth.

Leonov saw the cold eyes of the man, and knew he was looking at death. But he drew himself upright and said coldly: "I'm warning you, Gur. Moscow will know about this in half an hour."

"They know about it already." Gur stopped picking his teeth. "And let me give you some advice, comrade. Your attitude is unrealistic. For a man facing charges of such a

288

serious nature, it suggests foolhardiness or arrogance. You are not a stupid man, so it must be arrogance."

"Charges?" repeated Leonov. "You are raving."

Gur stood up, rather like a judge pronouncing sentence. "I have to inform you that, on the instructions of the Central Committee, you are suspended from your duties forthwith," he intoned. "I and Krylov will escort you back to Moscow on the next flight."

"This is madness!" exclaimed Leonov. He turned, but Krylov stood in his way.

"I warn you," called out Gur, "Krylov is armed. I would hate to think that you were attempting to escape . . ."

"All right," agreed Leonov. He was trying hard to organise his thinking. He prided himself that in an emergency he was always cool, practical. "What am I supposed to be guilty of?" he asked, in an effort to gain time. Time to wake up from this nightmare.

"I think you know," said Gur.

"How could I know?" His voice was firm. "This is all nonsense. I demand to be able to communicate with Moscow."

"It is Moscow that has ordered your arrest," insisted Gur.

"For what?"

"These games are pathetic," sneered Gur. "Treason, of course. Violation of Article 64."

Suddenly the clock stood still for Leonov. It was like the old days when he had been a young man, and the party arrested you at the whim of a commissar. But that was long ago, decades ago. In Stalin's day. Now it was different. Surely it was different.

"What is your evidence?" demanded Leonov. "These lies, for which somebody will pay, I promise you."

"Don't make threats, comrade," hissed Gur. "It does not help your case." He held out his hand. "Give me your keys. We will send people to your apartment who will look after everything."

For a moment, the colonel hesitated. Then he shrugged and passed his keys over.

"It is always sad for me when I see a servant of the state who has been corrupted by our enemies," said Gur piously. "This gives me no pleasure, I assure you. The only satisfaction one has is that a traitor has been brought to book. How very sad for your family though."

"Go to the devil!" snarled Leonov.

Gur smiled. He didn't often do so, but he always relished it when they began to crack.

"Let me know when you are ready to sign a full confession comrade," he purred.

It was, after all, only a matter of time.

But Leonov was thinking of Article 64. The one that said that those that were found guilty faced punishment of death.

73

"This is all rather unfortunate," said Cheyne.

Actually, you mean "embarrassing", thought Rathbone, but he kept that to himself.

"You know how they hate this kind of thing," went on Cheyne. He always adopted code when he was on delicate ground. "They" were "them". The ones upstairs. The ones who made the final decisions. "We really didn't need it. Not in our own department."

There was the code again. Rathbone recognised it from long experience. It was "we". "Our" department. It said don't think you're immune, Colin. If there's any flak flying about, you're in the firing line too.

"I had of course no idea she was anything but utterly loyal and trustworthy." Cheyne was laying the groundwork. If there should be an inquiry, Rathbone would be called as a witness, and it was for his benefit that he said it. It could do no harm when he came to repeat it. "I might tell you that I regard it almost as a personal affront. The woman has betrayed me."

She's also betrayed the country, old boy, but that's an aside. Rathbone looked suitably understanding.

"I hate to think what it is going to do to our image," Cheyne rambled on. "The headlines. The scandal. We've had so many knocks in the media. So much disloyalty in Whitehall. The Ponting creature. That typist. All the rest of them. It's very unfair on the rest of us. And the Americans!"

"What about the Americans?" asked Rathbone.

"They'll gloat. Our friends are so smug when this kind of thing happens."

"They've got their moles too."

But Cheyne was in full flight. "That's almost the worst part of it, the damage it does to our reputation. You and I work loyally for years, quietly, discreetly, and a few head-lines bring us all into disrepute." Then a thought seemed to strike him. "There *do* have to be headlines, I suppose, Colin?" It was a desperate clutching at straws.

"Of course," said Rathbone.

Cheyne swallowed.

"In the normal way of things," Rathbone went on.

Cheyne stared at him.

"In the normal way of things she gets charged, she gets sent for trial, she gets sentenced. All very good front page stuff. But you see . . . ." Rathbone paused. "She hasn't been charged."

"What?"

Rathbone took the plunge. "I've made a deal with her. She does what I want her to do. She goes on working for them, but what she sends them is what I give her. And in return, no charges."

Cheyne was opening and shutting his mouth like a goldfish having difficulty breathing. Finally he spluttered: "You can't. I mean, damn it, you have no authority, if we

291

drop charges, I . . . good God, it has to go to the top, the Attorney General, the cabinet, you can't simply . . ."

"I have," said Rathbone coldly. "I already have."

"You didn't even ask my permission!"

"No," said Rathbone.

"Good God!" gasped Cheyne again. "You stand there and . . ."

"No headlines," pointed out Rathbone. "You did say something about no headlines."

"If they find out . . ."

"Who's going to tell them?"

Cheyne reached for the dagger on his desk. He began playing with it.

"You're going to use her as a double agent? To send misinformation?"

"I've turned her," nodded Rathbone. "She had no choice, did she?"

"Will it work?"

"It already has."

Cheyne sat up. "Leonov?"

"Exactly. She passed on that he was betraying them. That he was working for me."

Cheyne spun the paper knife. "You've sent him to his death," he said finally.

Rathbone shrugged.

It was then that Cheyne decided that, eventually, he would get rid of Rathbone. When the time came, he could take over some other section, be transferred to a different directorate, perhaps even be assigned overseas. It would make him feel more secure, more comfortable not to have Rathbone around. He was too ruthless, too independent. He was his own man, and that was something Cheyne didn't like. Rathbone did things on his own, and, what was worse, kept them to himself.

"You know who's taken over from Leonov?"

"No," said Cheyne.

"Andreyan."

292

"Ah."

"Andreyan is acting head of the section as from today."

"Big promotion," said Cheyne.

"Gur is a surprising man. I think he would have frightened Himmler. He's destroyed Leonov but he seems to have taken to Andreyan. He made the decision. So Andreyan is now privy to it all. Top man in London."

"You seem pleased," said Cheyne.

"I am." He started to say more, but stopped.

"How do you know about all this?" asked Cheyne.

"Andreyan told me," said Rathbone, and smiled.

74

As the maritime forecast had warned, the mist reduced visibility soon after midnight, and vessels that passed in the dark were like shadowy outlines. From the nearby shipping lanes came the occasional echo of a distant siren or the faint, rhythmic throb of an engine, but the ships themselves remained ghostlike, unseen.

The *Ventura* was showing her navigation lights, but there was other illumination. It came from her portholes, some deck lights, and the glow in the wheel house. When somebody opened the door of the cabin, the light inside silhouetted him. There was no reason to be blacked out. Like other radio pirates at anchor off Knock Deep, she had no need to conceal herself.

Despite the mist, her position was clearly visible on the radar of the Soviet trawler *N.I. Komsomol*. She was a curious trawler, flying a civil ensign, outwardly a fishing vessel, but festooned with special electronic equipment which enabled her, when required, to be the eyes, and to some extent the ears, of any naval strike force.

Her crew too were hardly fishermen. They didn't wear naval uniform, but that was the only concession. Their discipline, the speed with which they obeyed orders, their alertness was that of crack service personnel. Which is precisely what they were.

On its way across, the *Komsomol* had played a little game. There was no point in keeping radio silence, that would be unduly suspicious behaviour for a "fishing" boat. So wireless traffic was maintained. But it was innocuous stuff, to which NATO radio monitors could listen to their hearts' content. Just the kind of messages a fishing boat would send.

The captain had not opened his sealed orders until the *Komsomol* cleared the Baltic. After he had read them, he'd burnt them. It would never do if, by mischance, they fell into the other side's hands. The orders had delighted the *Komsomol*'s captain. As a navy man, he had commanded several covert missions in this boat, but they had mostly been surveillance operations. Dogging NATO ships, hanging around the fringes of naval exercises, eavesdropping on their radio transmissions and studying their tactics. It was important work, but he found these spying cruises rather monotonous. Once, it was true, jets from a US aircraft carrier had angrily buzzed him, but usually they treated the presence of the *Komsomol* with lofty disdain. Now at last he could have a little action. He could show them his teeth. As long as he didn't get caught. That was why he blessed this mist. The intelligence people couldn't take any credit for it, of course, but if they had arranged it, it couldn't have come at a more opportune moment.

When he told his first officer what the mission was, the man whistled. "It could be risky, only twenty miles from the English coast," he said.

"Seventeen miles," corrected the captain. "Pick the men."

"I shall ask for volunteers," said the first officer.

"No," insisted the captain. "You will select the men who are most capable to do this. I don't just want enthusiasm. I want the best suited."

The four men who were chosen were told to remove their name tags, and anything personal that could identify them. It was, they were told, simply a precaution.

As the captain had pointed out to the first officer, if anything went wrong, and their bodies were washed up, the British wouldn't be fooled. They'd know they were Russians, but they damn well wouldn't be able to prove it.

When the four were given their detailed orders, their faces remained impassive, but they exchanged looks. They had been seconded aboard the trawler from a naval Spetsnaz brigade, each one a crack Marine commando. But this was the first time they had been given such instructions.

On the *Ventura* the first nightly transmission from Russkaya Volya had already been pumped into the ether. The ship was sending out two broadcasts a night now, and before long, Dr Jury had indicated, there might be one an hour.

Woody was manning the radio room. The other three were in their bunks. At this time of night, it only needed one man to keep operations ticking over. Woody could turn all the knobs and push all the buttons that were needed. He knew the equipment so well, he could operate it while half asleep.

Everything was set for the next broadcast. The tape was ready. Forty-five minutes to go before transmission time. Woody yawned, and leafed through *Playboy*. He had already gone through it twice, and even the centrefold was no longer an attraction. He got up, and stretched his arms. He opened the door of the radio cabin, and stepped on deck. The fresh air would wake him up.

He didn't see the two rubber dinghies that were being paddled towards the *Ventura*. Nor the four men in them, in balaclava helmets and black track suits. All Woody felt was the cold, and the mist blanketed everything. He went back into the radio cabin, shut the door and poured himself some coffee from the thermos flask. It tasted lousy. He looked at the electric clock. Time was passing slowly tonight. He wondered if the stuff they were broadcasting was doing any good. Was it really effective? Did anyone listen to it over there?

Woody never heard the four men climb aboard the *Ventura*. They moved silently, not saying a word. He heard the door of the radio cabin open.

"What's the matter?" he called out, not even bothering to turn his head. "Can't sleep?"

One of the men fired. He had a Makarov 9 mm pistol, but it looked longer than is usual, because a silencer had been screwed into the barrel. He fired three times. Plop, plop, plop, and Woody's brains splattered across the control console of the cabin.

The man gestured, and the other three, also armed, made their way below decks. Only Mac woke up in time to see his killer, but that was only a couple of seconds before his skull was blown apart. Dave and Curly were shot in their bunks and never knew what happened.

The four men did not say a word, but they knew exactly what they had to do. Two of them were carrying waterproof satchels, and now they went to different parts of the vessel, and planted the black boxes they had brought with them. They co-ordinated the time with their watches, and switched on the boxes. A little red bulb glowed on each, beside the time switch.

Then they gathered on deck, and the leader gave a signal. Quickly, without a word being said, they clambered down to the two rubber dinghies they had tied to the boat, and they rowed away into the mist.

The raiding party was back on the *Komsomol* in half an hour, and the captain congratulated them on the efficiency with which they had carried out their mission. The trawler was already underway, eastwards. No radio signal was sent to signify that the mission had been accomplished. The report would be made verbally.

296

An hour later the *Ventura*, a ghost ship with four dead men aboard, exploded. It was a blinding, ear-shattering explosion. Four bombs, accurately timed for simultaneous detonation, planted in strategic parts of the ship, calculated to rip her apart, and blow her to eternity.

Russkaya Volya had gone off the air once and for all.

75

"Horseshit!" swore Dupree.

Cheyne winced. The Americans could be very crude.

"I don't believe a word of it, and neither do you," continued Dupree. "Don't insult my intelligence."

It was difficult, at times like these, to be polite to them, thought Cheyne. One tried very hard to be diplomatic, but when they were in a mood like this, they brought it all down to basics.

"Accidents will happen," he remarked mildly. "She was an old tub, in a bad state of repair, and she didn't exactly have the most professional crew, did she?"

"And she blew up," Dupree snapped his fingers, "just like that, huh?"

"Perhaps the galley . . . or her fuel tank . . ." suggested Cheyne. This was getting tiresome.

"Oh, come on," sneered Dupree. "Do me a favour."

"Well," said Cheyne rather stiffly. "That is our belief, and those are the findings of our report to the Joint Committee. There was an accidental explosion, and the vessel broke up and sank. Regretfully, there were no survivors. A lifeboat went out, and a helicopter was sent, but they didn't recover anything."

"Damn convenient."

Cheyne blinked. "What do you mean?"

"You talked to Northwood?"

Cheyne sat very still. "Northwood?"

"Sure. The Navy. NATO control. They were keeping tabs on a Soviet spy trawler. Just off the coast."

"Oh." Cheyne's face betrayed nothing.

"You didn't know that, of course," said Dupree sarcastically. He didn't spare Cheyne. "Visibility was bad, but they had her fixed on radar. Couldn't make out what she was doing so close to that channel. There was nothing for her to spy on. No warships. No exercises."

Cheyne could be adept at stonewalling. "I'm afraid I don't quite see . . ."

Dupree's chair creaked as he leant back, contemplating Cheyne. "A real coincidence, wouldn't you say? This Russki suddenly appears from nowhere, just outside territorial limits, right on top of the radio ship, which, suddenlly, without explanation, explodes." He smiled coldly. "You mean, Northwood hadn't told you? The Navy never informed you about the trawler. Jesus, old friend, you ought to shake up your pals at MOD."

Now he's becoming impertinent, thought Cheyne. But he controlled himself and merely asked: "There is a connection, you think?" It sounded good, as if the thought had only just struck him.

"Well, it just could be, wouldn't you say?" Sardonic as hell. That's how Dupree wanted it to come out.

"What an interesting idea," mused Cheyne, as if it opened new possibilities. The Navy report lay in his safe. Northwood had even identified the trawler. The *N.I. Komsomol*. Radar had been shadowing her continuously, and as the Navy investigators had reported, the explosion was so violent that it left nothing. No wreckage. No flotsam. It didn't suggest an accident. It was man made.

"You know what I think?" said Dupree.

Cheyne waited.

"I think you're pleased it worked out this way. You

298

wanted it to happen. Get rid of the fucking thing. You didn't want it on your own doorstep in the first place. They've done you people a favour. Check?"

God, thought Cheyne, the Americans are undiplomatic. Does he have to say it all? Couldn't he take it as read? Doesn't he realise there are things that are better unsaid? The idiot surely doesn't believe I'll ever admit he's right. Why make it embarrassing for all of us?

"Of course not," said Cheyne smoothly. "Far from it. Never crossed my mind."

They faced each other for a moment in the third floor office at the American embassy like two players waiting for the next cue.

Then Dupree smiled. "How about lunch?" he suggested. "Would you like to try the commissary downstairs. They do a mean hamburger."

That was better. Now, thought Cheyne, he's behaving like a diplomat.

"Actually," he said, "why don't you come to my club? I'm sure you'd like it. I think today . . ." he glanced at the calendar on the wall, next to the portrait of President Reagan, "ah yes, today it's roast beef."

They left Grosvenor Square together in a cab.

"Did you ever listen to the damn station?" asked Dupree.

"Good Lord no," said Cheyne. "I sleep at night."

76

Andreyan rang the third bell of the red brick house in Harley Street and a white-coated receptionist opened the door. She was fair haired, but her make-up was restrained. She looked efficient.

"The eleven o'clock appointment," said Andreyan and she nodded.

"The second floor," she said, directing him to the lift.

He pressed the second button, and the old-fashioned lift began its laborious ascent. On the second floor, Andreyan got out. There was only one door on the landing, and he opened it. He was in a book-lined room with a desk, a sofa, and two armchairs. Rathbone was behind the desk.

He stood up as Andreyan entered, both hands held out.

"My dear friend," he said, "it's been a long time." He held Andreyan's hand firmly, tightly, in both of his, then he guided him over to one of the armchairs. Rathbone settled himself on the sofa.

"You knew I'd be coming eventually, didn't you?" said Andreyan.

Rathbone nodded. "Of course. We both knew it." He looked round. "What do you think?"

"I'm impressed," said Andreyan. "It is a good set up."

"No set up," Rathbone corrected him. "This actually is the consulting room of an eminent psychiatrist. He sometimes, er, does things for us. I've borrowed it, just for today. Downstairs is an excellent dentist, on the ground floor a gynaecologist known to all the debutantes in London, and above us is a dermatologist. You take your choice." He paused. "So, you can always tell your people you've been to a dentist in Harley Street. Just in case anybody is curious."

"Why should they be?"

"Ah," said Rathbone, "I'm sorry. I've probably got the wrong idea. I imagined that now you've been promoted to such a senior position at the embassy, your absences are liable to be noted . . ."

"You've been reading too many books by defectors," smiled Andreyan. But it was a taut smile.

"Good. Then we can relax." He glanced at the desk at a vase of flowers. "This is not being recorded, Serge. But it can be, if you want to."

300

Andreyan shrugged.

"Well?" said Rathbone.

Now that the moment had come, Andreyan felt curiously nervous. He had rehearsed it in his mind, he knew exactly what he was going to say, but it still didn't come easy.

"You know what I want," he said.

"No," said Rathbone. "You must tell me."

Then Andreyan knew that Rathbone had been lying. It was all being recorded. Not that it mattered. He had gone too far to draw back. They had probably photographed him as well. Perhaps in the lift.

"I want to come over," he said.

"To our side?" Rathbone was crossing the T's and dotting the I's. "You wish to join us."

"Yes," said Andreyan.

"Are you sure?"

Andreyan smiled wanly. "Would I be here otherwise?"

Rathbone studied him thoughtfully. "I'm a little surprised, Serge."

"Why?"

"Coming on top of your promotion. I would have thought you'd enjoy your new status. After all, it is an important job."

Andreyan looked away. "You know what's happened to Leonov?"

"I've heard . . . rumours."

"So much for the job," said Andreyan. "It is hardly a sinecure."

"Oh come," said Rathbone, "you're exaggerating. These are not the days of Beria. Times have changed. The Stalin purges are over. People get fired, yes. They get demoted. They don't get shot."

"They don't?"

There was a pause. Then Rathbone nodded. He leant forward and pulled a notepad towards him. He wrote something on it with a silver pencil. "You don't mind if I make the odd notes?"

301

"Please," said Andreyan, "be my guest." And Rathbone grinned. Then he said suddenly: "Why?"

Andreyan frowned. "Why . . . what? I do not quite understand . . ."

"Why do you want to defect?"

"I wish to . . . join somebody. On this side."

"Maya?" said Rathbone quietly.

"You know?"

"Of course."

"I would like to be with her," said Andreyan simply.

Rathbone nodded like a man who had fitted all the pieces into the jigsaw he was completing. "She is in America," he said.

"I know," replied Andreyan. "I want to join her there."

"So you want to defect to America?"

"No," said Andreyan. "I want to be with her. If that means going to America, yes I will. I would just as soon be in England. I rather like it here."

Rathbone smiled thinly.

"But," went on Andreyan, "if necessary I will go over there."

"Tell me. If she returned to the Soviet Union, what would you do?"

"Let us keep this in the realm of reality," said Andreyan coolly.

He waited, but for a while Rathbone just stared at him. Finally he said: "All right." He put the pad aside. He clipped the silver pencil into an inside pocket. "It's a deal."

Andreyan suddenly felt empty. There was no elation. No triumph. He had succeeded, but it was hollow. Could it be this simple? "You mean, you agree?"

"Yes," nodded Rathbone. "Welcome aboard."

He stood up, went to the desk, bent down and opened a cupboard door. He brought out a bottle of Scotch and two glasses. "No vodka, I'm afraid," he said. "He doesn't stock any. But this calls for a drink. Anyway, Scotch seems

302

appropriate wouldn't you say?" He poured them each a drink and gave a glass to Andreyan. "Here's to the future," he said, and clinked his glass with Andreyan's.

"It was mineral water last time," Andreyan reminded him.

"What a good memory you have," said Rathbone with his thin smile.

They drank in silence. Then Rathbone said: "One little point. We don't want you to come across yet."

Andreyan froze. He clutched the glass, but the warmth that had flooded him after he drank was fading.

"What we'd like you to do is to carry on, stay at your post at the embassy, do your job, and just keep us informed from time to time about things that might interest us."

"Spy for you," said Andreyan hoarsely.

Rathbone pulled a face. "Oh come. We don't use words like that, you and I. No, you merely bring us up to date. Tell us what's going on. Who's doing what. Perhaps what Centre wants. That sort of thing. Quite simple, really." He took a drink of Scotch. "You won't do anything silly of course. Don't steal things. Don't copy things in the referentura. They watch you through that cubby hole. No, use that excellent memory of yours."

"No," said Andreyan.

"I thought," mused Rathbone almost reflectively, "that you wanted to defect."

"Yes, but . . ."

"Well, before you do you can do us a little service. Buy your passage, so to speak."

Andreyan knew what the game was. He could draw the blueprint. He knew how it was played, and he knew he had no option.

"How long?" he asked in a low voice. "How long do I have to do this before I can come over?"

Rathbone shrugged. "Not long. But who can say? A year? Two years?" His eyes were hard.

"A . . . year," repeated Andreyan. "Two years . . ."

"While it is safe," said Rathbone reassuringly. "Of course, if we get the slightest hint that they're on to you, we'd pull you out and you can start making sweet music with the lovely Miss Petrova. By the way, she's in California now. Getting the most gorgeous suntan I hear."

But Andreyan was clutching the arms of his chair like an accused man on the stand.

"But now," he cried, "I want to defect now."

"Too soon, too early, Serge. A waste of a golden opportunity. They've given you the key to the goodies. We must really have a few samples. We can't just pass up such an opportunity."

"That is not the deal," said Andreyan.

Rathbone purred. "On the contrary, that *is* the deal."

A grandfather clock was ticking somewhere, and now it struck the half hour.

"And if I don't . . ."

"Then there is no deal," shrugged Rathbone. Then he glanced at the vase of flowers on the desk, and Andreyan knew what was in his mind.

"All right," he said, his voice was croaky, his tongue thick, his mouth dry. "All right."

"Excellent. Delighted to have you join us," said Rathbone. He stood up and Andreyan rose too. He felt shattered, like a man who had taken a final plunge into a waterless swimming pool.

Rathbone put his arm round his shoulders. "You've made the right choice, old friend, you really have, and I'll see you get your reward." He was beaming. "Well," he added, leading him to the door, "you'll be hearing from us, don't worry. You'll get your contact. We'll take care of everything. Just leave it to us. Carry on normally. Oh, and one thing . . ." He stopped and suddenly he was a different man. No smile. No bonhomie. A set face. His expression grim. "It hardly needs saying, Serge, and I know you won't take it amiss. But don't lose your nerve. Don't for instance play a double game. Don't sell us out. Because if you were so foolish, I'm afraid we'd have to let your people know about your extra mural activities. From now on, you belong to us. I'm sure you understand."

Andreyan realised then that it made no difference for whom he worked. Them or them. They were all the same. They played by the same rules. They shared the same philosophy. They were of a kind. "I understand," he whispered.

"Of course you do," said Rathbone. His face was human again. He was smiling. "Would you like another one for the road?"

Andreyan shook his head.

"It won't seem all that long, you know," Rathbone was saying. "And think of it, you'll be with her. It's something to look forward to, isn't it?" He took out a book of matches and pressed them into Andreyan's hand. "Here. You'll find a phone number there. Use it only in emergencies. In case something goes really wrong. Memorise it. Never forget it. Then throw the matches away."

They were at the door. "You're starting a new life, Serge, a new beginning. Good luck." He held open the door. "Take the lift down. Just press the button."

He made it all sound so easy. He shut the door and Andreyan felt very alone.

He took the lift down, and in the entrance hall the receptionist in the white coat was waiting.

"Have you made another appointment?" she asked.

"Yes," said Andreyan. "I have made another appointment."

The minute he got back to the embassy, Andreyan went straight to his office where he worked alone for the next thirty minutes. Then he took the elevator to the basement.

The cypher room had barred windows and there were always two men in it, so that no one was ever left on his own. The door was kept locked, and when the buzzer sounded one of the men peered through the peep hole. No pass or badge admitted anyone. Recognition was the only ticket; the face had to be known. It was a room most people in the embassy never entered, but Andreyan was one of the select few. Andreyan pressed the buzzer and an eye appeared behind the peep hole. Then the door opened and they let him in.

The room was air conditioned, but oppressive. In it, one had the feeling of being confined, cut off. It was difficult to visualise that outside its walls, not far away, was Kensington Gardens, children playing, and model boats sailing on the Round Pond. This was another world.

Strip lighting shone down from the ceiling, and much of the space was taken up by coding machines and electronic gear. There were also a couple of filing cabinets with special locks, and a safe. Despite the filtered air, it had a slightly stale atmosphere. Perhaps it was due to the room always being occupied.

The duty clerk was a tall, thin man with cropped hair. He wore a roll neck sweater, and corduroy trousers. He was a military man, seconded to London, like his colleague. The cypher room personnel lived a life apart, keeping to themselves, never going out on their own, knowing that they, more than anyone else, were under constant scrutiny. It was a tiresome job, twelve hours on, twelve hours off, six days a week, round the clock, sitting in the room, isolated, cut off, decyphering, encoding, checking and double checking, often not understanding what the hell the message meant anyway.

They could smoke. They could play chess. They drank tea. But they were not allowed to sleep. They could not make an outside phone call. Their only contact was with the radio room next door, where the messages they handled were received or transmitted. There the operators had the same strict routine. They too were military men, hand picked.

"Encode this," ordered Andreyan. He gave the duty clerk a folded piece of paper.

The man took it, looked at the electric clock on the wall, and logged the time.

"Priority," said Andreyan. "Use the special cypher. It's for the Director himself."

The special cypher. For the Director. This must be something very important, thought the clerk. His colleague looked up, interested.

The cypher clerk unfolded the paper and read the message. Then the clerk read it again.

"You want to send *this*, comrade?" he asked in disbelief.

"Exactly as it is," nodded Andreyan.

The cypher clerk hesitated. It was not for him to question the content of messages to the Centre, least of all messages sent by the section. The spooks operated in mysterious ways. But this message . . .

"They will probably demand a double check," said the clerk. He could see the message being queried. Moscow wanting to make sure this was really meant seriously.

"They won't query it," said Andreyan firmly. "When will they have it?"

The clerk glanced at the clock again.

"If it is transmitted as soon as we have processed it, Moscow will have it in half an hour . . ."

"See to it," said Andreyan.

The clerk pushed forward the ledger in which he had recorded the time.

"Will you please sign . . . here, comrade, next to this entry." He pointed at the line.

Andreyan frowned. "Why? That is not routine."

"The nature of the message," explained the clerk apologetically. "In case there are any questions. About the origin."

Andreyan signed his name.

"We will deal with it right away," said the cypher clerk. He had handled many curious signals and messages in this job, but never something quite like this.

"Good," said Andreyan. "Rush it."

He left the cypher room, and the door was locked behind him.

Andreyan couldn't blame the man for his reaction. After all, it was not every day that a member of the embassy informed Moscow that he had gone over to the other side.

77

The taxi dropped him outside Fortnum's, and after he paid it off, Andreyan stood for a moment remembering the day he had walked along here with Maya.

He could see her now, auburn haired, the eyes that held so much promise, the kissable mouth smiling at him. He desired her very much, and their separation had not made her more distant. She was very much in his mind, the things she had whispered to him in the dark, the warmth of her embrace, her scent . . .

But now he had to think of other things. He waited until the traffic lights changed, then crossed to the other side of Piccadilly. Despite himself, he kept being reminded of her. Burlington Arcade. The shop windows. Her delight with what she saw.

Andreyan walked towards Dover Street, trying to shut her out of his mind, for the moment. It was important that he had a clear head.

He entered the Aeroflot office and went up to the ticket counter. What was more normal than a Soviet embassy official calling on his national airline to see about a Moscow flight?

The girl at the computer terminal smiled up at him.

"Can I help you?" she asked in English.

"I have an appointment," replied Andreyan in Russian.

Like the other girls, she was a Soviet dependant who

308

worked at Aeroflot. Her husband was a member of the Russian Trade Delegation at Highgate. She glanced at a clip-board, then nodded.

"Yes, comrade Andreyan," she said, "will you please come this way."

She led the way to the back of the ticket office, and knocked on a door.

The man who asked Andreyan to enter had only arrived in London that morning and would be back in Moscow within twenty-four hours. He had travelled on a specially prepared passport which identified him as an Aeroflot Operations Manager. Purpose of trip: a routine visit to Aeroflot's London office. There was nothing to indicate that he held the rank of major general, and had come over as a result of the coded message Andreyan had sent to the Director.

He was an important man, with great power, and Andreyan came into his presence wearing a dark suit, as a token of respect. The general was not a man you trifled with.

The office had been tactfully made available to the visitor from Moscow. On the walls were tourist posters advertising vacation spots in Russia.

"Sit down, Sergei Mikhailovitch," said the general. That was a good sign.

Andreyan sat down beside a glass table that had a model of an Ilyushin airliner on it. He sat very stiffly, on the edge of the chair. It was protocol. Andreyan searched the general's face without trying to make it too obvious. But the dark eyes above the high cheek bones betrayed nothing.

"You're playing a dangerous game, you know that," said the general, without further preliminaries.

"I'm aware of it, comrade general," replied Andreyan.

"If things go wrong, nobody will be able to help you. Naturally, we would try, you know that, but there's no guarantee."

"Of course not," agreed Andreyan.

"What you are doing is above and beyond the requirement of duty."

"Well," shrugged Andreyan, allowing himself a wry smile, "it's too late to change my mind."

That was a mistake, he knew at once. The general did not smile back. His face remained impassive.

"A double agent runs double risks." The general sniffed. "I would not like to be in your shoes, my friend." He stared into Andreyan's eyes, as if he wanted to bore deep into his mind. "You can fool some of the people some of the time, but not all the people all the time, isn't that what they say?"

"Yes, comrade general."

The general flicked an invisible speck of dust from his well cut suit.

"I have come over specially to reassure myself. I wanted to have a look at you. I wanted to see what kind of man it is who is prepared to do this."

Andreyan shifted uneasily.

"Look at me, Sergei Mikhailovitch."

Andreyan's eyes fixed on his.

"You think you can get away with it?" asked the general.

"I hope so. I would not try it otherwise."

The dark eyes were still watching him. "They believe you? They think they can trust you to betray your motherland?"

Andreyan nodded.

"Why?"

"Because . . ." Andreyan swallowed. "Because of the Petrova woman."

The general's eyes flickered. "I see. That is the prize they offer?"

"If I want to see her again. That is their condition. I work for them."

The general sat forward. "And she is worth that? She means that much to you?"

"She is good in bed," replied Andreyan brutally.

"So are other women, comrade."

"I know that. But they think I'm infatuated with this one."

"And are you?"

310

"I like to fuck her," said Andreyan. "But I wouldn't sell out my country for her."

"Good," nodded the general. "That is what I wanted to hear. I believe you. When a man is really in love with a woman, he does not speak of her like that. You are a realist. Excellent."

Andreyan remained silent. His thoughts were not for the general.

"Before I left Moscow I had another look at this man Rathbone's dossier," said the general. "Do not underestimate him. He is cunning, unscrupulous, shrewd. You must have done some brilliant acting to convince him. But don't be fooled. He will watch your every step."

"I know," murmured Andreyan. He thought for a moment. Then he said: "How do you wish me to operate? How can I be of most use?"

"Quite simple," said the general, ticking off each point on the five fingers of his left hand. "One, you will continue in your post at the embassy. Acting as Section Head. This will make you of great value to them. Two, you will supply them at intervals with material and information which we will prepare for you. Three, you will keep us informed of what they want to know and you will try to identify their other sources of information. Four, you will let no one else at the embassy know what you are doing. No one, you understand. Five, you trust no one except us. You're dealing direct with us. You will use a special code. Is that all clear?"

"And for how long will I do all this?" asked Andreyan quietly.

"Until we say enough." The general reconsidered. That sounded a little callous. He could see Andreyan's expression. "As long as it works, my friend. A year. Maybe two." He shrugged. "Who can say? But be assured, we will have your interests at heart. If we think you are in danger, we will warn you, and get you out."

Andreyan nearly laughed. It was so ridiculous. The general sounded just like Rathbone. He was saying the same thing. Stay at your job. Spy for us. Just a year or two. But, don't worry, we'll look after you. If things go wrong.

"One other thing," continued the general. "I hardly need say it, but this is no game. Don't get any ideas."

"Ideas?" repeated Andreyan. He wanted to sound naïve, but he knew so well what was coming and, inwardly, he couldn't help feeling cold.

"Be quite clear whose side you are on," the general was saying. "Don't think we will not be aware of everything you do, everything you say. You will be playing with very dangerous fire, comrade, and I'm warning you not to get burnt. Never forget your duty. Never forget your obligation. After all, you don't want to let your family down, do you? Think of our relations in the motherland."

There it was. The threat. The warning.

"I think of them all the time, my general."

"Good. Then you won't make any mistakes."

Then, just as Rathbone had done, he produced a bottle and two glasses from a cupboard. But it was vodka, not scotch. He poured them a measure each. The Gorbachev edict against alcohol was ignored. The general gave Andreyan a glass.

"Your health, Sergei Mikhailovitch," he toasted and they clinked glasses. It was as near cordiality, as the general would get with a subordinate. He tossed back the slug of vodka, and refilled the glass immediately.

Funny how they like to seal arrangements with alcohol, thought Andreyan. He and Rathbone.

"As for the technical arrangements, we will be sending you detailed instructions," said the general. "Secrecy is essential, naturally, and no one is to know. No one, remember. Your role is only privy to us. Not even the ambassador must be aware."

"I understand."

"You will keep us informed of course about how you make contact with them?"

Andreyan thought of the book of matches. "Of course."

The general nodded approvingly. "Your motherland will show its appreciation. This will not be forgotten, I promise you. Your family will be proud of you one day."

Again, the reminder . . .

The general put down his glass. "Good luck."

Andreyan stiffened to attention.

"Thank you, comrade general."

The general held out his hand.

"We will be thinking about you."

His grip was firm, confident and reassuring. Just like Rathbone's.

In fact, did it matter any more whose hand it was? Or which one he finally betrayed?

Andreyan took a deep breath in the street outside. Whatever happened from now, whatever he had to do, the only one to whom he would be loyal would be himself.

And Maya.

She could never betray him because he had no illusions about her. But he wanted her, he needed her, and he was going to have her. No matter how long it took, or how twisted the road that led to her.

As for all the others, the ones who would call him traitor when they found out the truth, well, they deserved one another.

The surveillance report on Andreyan made a special point of noting how cheerful he looked when he left the Aeroflot office in Piccadilly.

78

Rathbone had only flown into Berlin the previous evening and, if all went well, he'd be on a plane back to London before lunch. By tea time, hopefully, he'd be in his office in Great Peter Street once more. If all went well.

They arrived at the Glienicker Bridge at 6.45, quarter of an hour before the deadline. They parked the car near the guard hut. Rathbone and the liaison man got out. The others stayed in the car.

His watch said 6.51, and zero hour was set for exactly 7 a.m. The border guard gave them both a mug of coffee, and in the raw morning air Rathbone was grateful for it. The enamel mug was chipped, but the coffee was hot.

"They'll be there already," said the liaison man peering across the bridge. Rathbone could see a couple of uniformed men on the other side, but that was all. "Behind the guardhouse probably," he went on.

"Damn cold," said Rathbone, clutching the mug.

"Is it?" The liaison man didn't seem in the slightest interested. He kept staring across the bridge.

"They'll come half over, and we start walking towards them. There will be a mutual recognition, and then each side stops half way, the exchange takes place, then we all go back to our respective territory."

"I know," said Rathbone irritably. "We've been over it."

The liaison man deigned to turn his head. "It doesn't do any harm to go over it again," he said coldly. "After all, we don't want any hiccups, do we?"

Just because you're in the front line here, you don't have to be so bloody patronising, thought Rathbone.

"Funny thing," said the liaison man conversationally, "it's always this bloody bridge. They were exchanging people here when I was still at Cambridge."

"Really?"

"Yes," said the liaison man, his eyes fixed on the Eastern side. He pulled out a pack of cigarettes and offered it to Rathbone who shook his head. "I remember eating crumpets in my room when Abel was exchanged here. I had the radio on. Little did I think . . . '61, wasn't it?"

"February 1962," said Rathbone.

"Shows how time flies." He lit his cigarette. Rathbone was unimpressed by the liaison man, and wondered who had recruited him. He was too young, too cocky. Then Rathbone thought, God, perhaps I've been in this business too long. Now all the policemen are starting to look young.

"Ah," said the liaison man suddenly. "Things are happening."

A man appeared on the other side, and stared at them through field glasses. Rathbone looked at his watch.

"I'll get him," he said, handing his mug back to the guard.

The liaison man nodded, and Rathbone went back to the car and opened the door. "Out you get," he said.

Borisov emerged and stood, glancing around. Behind him the security man got out. He stood behind Borisov, and Rathbone wondered where he had his gun. In a shoulder holster? Or in his belt? Or, perhaps, in his pocket? Unlikely that. It would be awkward to draw.

"It won't be long now, Evgeny Alekseivitch," grunted Rathbone. He didn't hide his lack of enthusiasm. Cheyne was making a mistake. They shouldn't let him go. He hadn't even managed to unpeel the top layers. They should hold on to him. But Cheyne would have made a good Pilate. He wanted to wash his hands. The Foreign Office wanted to be rid of the whole business.

"So, this is how you treat people who ask for sanctuary," said Borisov.

"Oh, come on, we've been over all that," replied Rathbone. "We've played the game."

"But you will never be sure, will you?"

"Of what?"

"Who knows?" smiled Borisov. "Maybe you've made a big mistake." There was malice in his smile.

"Let's get on with it," said Rathbone. They started walking towards the bridge. "Incidentally," he remarked, as if a casual thought had just come to him. "You've heard about Colonel Leonov . . ."

Borisov stopped.

"It was a *Tass* item. Just a short announcement. Apparently he was executed this week. For anti-state activities. I thought you might have seen it."

Borisov was pale. But he said nothing.

"They didn't go into details, but he was apparently tried by a military tribunal in secret. Creates rather an interesting situation, doesn't it? What are you going to tell them once you're back home? That you made a terrible mistake, and passed a piece of misinformation which led to a faithful servant of the motherland being wrongly executed? Or will you keep quiet about it, and bask in the reflected glory of having uncovered a 'traitor'?" Then Rathbone shrugged. "It's up to you of course, but you know what I'd do in your position? Keep quiet. Save your skin. You might even get a medal." And he smiled benignly at Borisov. That was when he hated Rathbone.

They came to the guard hut.

"Right," said the liaison man. "Off you go."

Rathbone and Borisov walked slowly on to the bridge and began to cross, staying in the middle. Towards them, from the other side, two figures approached. At the centre of the bridge, they all stopped face to face.

Rathbone recognised Gregson. His appearance had changed. They had cropped his shock of hair, and his head

316

was covered by stubble, but he was the same man whose photographs they had shown him. The man who looked so nondescript, the erstwhile research assistant, arrested in Leningrad while on a package tour. A nobody who the Foreign Office was, however, curiously anxious to get back into its hands.

As exchanges went, it would be a minor affair, getting little publicity. They weren't nuclear scientists, or diplomats, or big time spies. They weren't stars. Only supporting cast.

They had fattened up Gregson, but beside the KGB man at his side he looked gaunt, hollow eyed. His imprisonment had left its mark on him. But he was smiling.

The KGB man held out his hand, and Borisov moved forward and grasped it. Nothing was said, but they too were smiling. Only Rathbone's expression stayed frozen.

Gregson stood at Rathbone's side, and Borisov turned his back on them. He never said a word. He never looked round. He and the KGB escort started the return walk to the other side of the bridge.

"Welcome home," said the liaison man warmly to Gregson. He shook his hand, and Rathbone was surprised at the enthusiasm he suddenly displayed. "It's been a long time, Paul, but it's good to have you back."

Gregson shivered a little in the morning cold. "It feels good." He gulped. "You know, there were times when I thought I might not make it."

"Don't worry," said the liaison man, "we were going to get you back no matter what."

"You know what happened?" Gregson seemed worried. "You know how they caught me?"

"Not now. Plenty of time for that."

They ignored Rathbone, then, almost as an after thought, the liaison man seemed to remember his presence. "If you come with us, we'll drop you off at Tempelhof," he offered.

"That's very kind," murmured Rathbone.

"No bother at all," said the liaison man, "you don't want to miss your flight."

317

In the car, Gregson sat between them. At times he still trembled. The security guard rode in front with the driver.

Rathbone kept thinking of Borisov. Why did the politicians always interfere? Why didn't they let him do things his way? There was so much he still had wanted to squeeze out of the man. So much he wanted to know . . . But suddenly both sides wanted a small gesture, a token, and two pawns were swapped . . .

"Will you be debriefing me?" Gregson asked Rathbone suddenly. He was aware of him at last.

"No," said the liaison man, before Rathbone could reply. "He is not one of us."

He thought about that for a long time. It really was becoming an interesting question, just who was on which side.

79

Maya was being interviewed in the Pink Turtle. She liked the ambience of the Beverly Wilshire Hotel, and all it stood for, and when the lady gossip columnist asked to meet her for a little chat, she suggested the hotel's coffee house.

Maya was enjoying life. The CIA had kept its promise. A labour permit. An apartment in Westwood. A screen test, a contract to make a TV mini series, and lots and lots of publicity about the Soviet actress who fled to freedom.

She had taken to Beverly Hills, and Beverly Hills opened its arms to her. She was a catch for any hostess, and she looked gorgeous at poolside parties.

"But don't you miss Russia just a little?" asked the lady columnist.

Maya shook her head emphatically.

"No, no, no, I have a new country, America. That is now my home."

"Don't you miss your friends?"

"My friends?" She smiled. "I have new friends now."

"How about a boy friend?" asked the columnist hopefully. She was determined to get good copy out of this.

"It is early days," said Maya diplomatically.

"But you must have had one," pressed the columnist. "Did you leave one behind?"

Maya hesitated.

"Well . . ."

"Yes?"

"There is an old Russian saying," said Maya. "'A dog barks, the wind blows, and the caravan moves'."

The columnist frowned.

"I'm not sure I understand."

"It means," said Maya, "that things change."